ANYONE'S GAME

Anyone's Game

LESLEY CHAMBERLAIN

Dear Cath,

thank you for all those lifts to Middlesbrough and happy riding.

Lesley March 2014

HarBOUR

First published in paperback original by Harbour in 2012
Harbour Books (East) Ltd, PO Box 10594
Chelmsford, Essex CM1 9PB
publicity@harbourbooks.co.uk
www.harbourbooks.co.uk

A catalogue record for this book is
available from the British Library.

ISBN   978 1 905128 198

Typeset by Antony Gray
Printed and bound in Great Britain by
TJ International Ltd, Padstow, Cornwall

for Pavel
Díky

PRELUDE

Some of us are intensely conscious of standing alone, and to me Leksy McFadden had that look about him. In the foyer of the Albert Hall, in the glass enclosure built during the last refurbishment, he was on his feet, reflecting on who knows what human vice, while occasionally studying his nails.

We were a small audience of people gathered to listen to exacting music in the heart of London. It was a warm, dry night in August.

The weather should be warm in August, but perhaps because it was exceptionally so, and already pitch-black outside, where the headlights passed in a shadowy sea of moving metal, it created a sense of adventure. I kept looking at him.

He was in his seventies, tall, impressively and amply white-haired, but rather untidily dressed in a corduroy jacket and a shirt without a tie. We spoke, eventually, not because of the glass box which marked us out as lovers of late Stravinsky, but because the book I held in my hands was 'Bely's masterpiece', as he observed over my shoulder. His move, not mine.

'Alas,' I said, 'it's hardly known in this country.'

With a slight, perhaps defensive, smile, he asked: 'Is there a reason for that?'

'Experiments in art mostly pass us by.'

I supposed he was a teacher of Russian.

'My mother was Russian.'

'Aaah!'

And there this story began, though I could hardly hear it through, let alone write it down, that evening. Even as we exchanged these preliminaries, the five-minute and three-minute bells rang. We sought our seats in different parts of the stalls. Moreover, as soon as the lights moved from the audience to the stage, we were lost in what we had come for. Stravinsky was an old man and this was his last creation, when he tamed his *Rite of Spring* into a requiem mass.

Realising what was happening, I was full of horror and only his art made me listen. He seemed to view human beings as puppets. The ground cracked and parted beneath our feet under a firework canopy of sound. I knew no more severe rejection of *jouissance* in the history of music. Stravinsky was back in his native Russia, and Slavonic voices were whispering in the onion-domed church.

I scrolled my programme and reached for my jacket. I couldn't lose Leksy McFadden and waved my baton at him across the emptying red-plush rows.

'You should have written your mother's story down,' I said, as if that might counteract what we had heard.

'I'm not a woman. I'm not a writer. I'm too lazy. Also, she had her faults, look – '

But I already doubted he could get shot of me. I had detected an uncertainty, so I had a hold on him and would make him speak.

His second wife had died recently and he was at a loose end, he conceded. And so we settled on the Polish café in South Kensington and began meeting there on Tuesday afternoons.

'Tell me about your mother,' I begged Leksy McFadden, and, over our first coffee and *mazurki*, he took me back to a morning in May 1919 when a weathered Russian boat docked at Constantinople.

1

The young woman who came ashore looked too well dressed to disembark from that battered craft. The port sergeant looked at her documents, indicated his colleague and said: 'Please! This way!' This one, so thin he seemed to peer down at his own body from the top of a ladder, led her to an office about a hundred metres away.

The immigration office was a shack. But the way she stood there, glowing, her fine skin, on her hands and her flushed face, filled it with distinction. The officer at the desk thought of a peach and blushed.

I have of course to imagine her story, from what her son told me, and those notebooks and diaries that survived: hers and those of her friends. But I have stayed as close as possible to what happened, out of sympathy for her, and sympathy for all of us, passing as we do, most of us, in and out of this world, unknown and quickly forgotten.

Wordlessly the official stamped her passport. When erotic interest passed into fatherly concern he wanted to ask – he looked a final time at her papers – this Sophie Asmus: Where are your parents, young lady? What is your social class, that you should be allowed to run about like this? But he only nodded and said something to the thin official who, like a straight cane to support her gorgeous flowering, accompanied her back to beside the boat.

'She was a pioneer,' my companion said. 'Only for what?'
    'That will be for you to tell me.'

Behind her sour-sweet Russian voices clashed with Turkish gutterals. Some Russian shouted a God-defying, 'So what?' A gob of spit like raw egg-white round a chewed husk landed on the cobbles.

Other passengers were clamouring to get off. 'No chance! *Nel'zya!*' the fat policeman at the shore end of the gangplank yelled the most useful Russian word he had learnt. 'A few hours on shore is what you want? Don't make me laugh!' The passengers on this little boat, apart from her, were peasants, just seeing what advantage they could get out of the local shortage of goods and the shifting borders round the Sea.

The Turks treated Sophie Asmus differently because she had an educated, middle-class air and papers.

She retied her headscarf and stood for a moment. North, south, east or west?

A man spoke.

'Do you need help, miss?'

This very polite, very correct man in a peaked cap and leather gloves, and carrying a leather-upholstered cane, addressed her. He was much smarter than the seedy port police, and he spoke English, not just a few words.

'It depends what you mean by help.'

'I wondered what a woman like you was doing in a place like this.'

'I'm running away.'

He blew a little air out of his nose and tapped his cane on his palm. Had he not been in uniform he would have smiled at the childishness of her answer.

'Are you Russian? Can you read the name of the ferry?' The boat, which had ceased to belch slate-coloured smoke into the azure, had a Cyrillic name on its flaking white bow. He stared at its crazy, bobbing, between-worlds motion.

'*Chaika*. It means seagull.' He looked to her so distinguished and so orderly beside the crude Russian sailors and the robed Turkish fishermen from the Asian shore.

In fact they stood, two young white Europeans, quite out of place on that Constantinople foreshore, not a year after the end of the Great War, and with Russia divided against itself, Red against White. His task was to search any boat going back to Russia. Gold, weapons, explosives: all manner of stuff was getting through to the Bolsheviks. He had to suspect her of being a carrier but dismissed the suspicions as foolish.

'How do you come to know English so well?'

'I had a nanny who came from England.'

'What was your nanny's name?' Then he remembered what an idiot he was, to hearken so readily to the sound of his own country. He took off his glove and held out a hand. 'Lieutenant Duncan McFadden, British Army, Miss – '

'Asmus. Sophie Asmus.'

'Where did you board the ferry?'

'Sochi.' The way she said it the 'o' was long and un-English, more like 'oa', and the 'i' disappeared, which is why he didn't recognise it at first.

'Sochi's pretty damn far for a boat like that.' He glanced back at the resting *Chaika* which had made the journey from the eastern end of the Sea.

'They don't care. They do it all the time. Must you ask me so many questions?'

He believed her. Times were difficult. Perhaps she really was running away. She was carrying a cloth shoulder-bag of sorts, but it seemed almost empty.

'There's a café where we can get some refreshment. May I invite you, Miss Asmus?'

As they walked alongside each other, over the harbourside cobbles, he almost offered her his arm and she almost took it.

'I'm not a smuggler, you know,' she smiled.

The name Wiener Bankverein had been painted high on the stuccoed façade of the newish building that dominated the wharf. It broadcast its foreign name out over the Golden Horn, just where that graceful cul-de-sac meets the Bosphorus.

She asked Lieutenant McFadden what the Austrians were doing in Turkey.

'The Austrians came here before the war to get rich.'

'And do you approve of that?'

'You use other countries to make money, you make them extensions of your own country and then you drain off all their wealth to use at home. Of course not.'

She nodded, as if what he said was self-evident, and looked around.

*

I asked Leksy whether she was ever a Communist. He shook his head. 'But stubborn as they come; determined to do things her own way.'

'It's Veener, by the way. It means Viennese.' She corrected him. And then, 'Is that what my father calls the colonial mentality?'

'Pretty much.' He took a step back in the conversation. 'What did I say?'

'Weener.'

Ahead of them a heavy white sunblind, like a scallop-edged bed-sheet, created a dark, soothing interior hidden from the sun, and there they entered.

She glanced in the mirror as they sat down, as the proud young do.

'I can understand why you wanted to leave Russia. We only get bad reports of what's happening there. But wasn't it dangerous to travel alone?'

'Not more dangerous than staying. In my country if you don't get shot you die of something, there's so much hunger and sickness. People die every day, even if they're not fighting.'

The waiter poured their coffees from a steaming long-handled brass pot and set down two glasses of water alongside. She was nineteen, he a few years older.

'And now?'

'I'm on my way to Paris.'

'Paris!' No place in the world seemed more appropriately glamorous for the woman he'd just met. He'd never been there himself. But he'd heard tell.

He offered her another coffee and called for pastries. And then he said the most impossible thing.

'We must see about getting you back.'

She slammed the small white china cup into its saucer. 'Who's we? You've got no right.'

'Miss Asmus, it's too difficult to be a woman alone in a country like this. If I think of how one of my sisters would manage . . . '

'Help me move on is what I'm asking. I've not come *here*, to Constantinople. I want to go to Paris. Or London. Or Rome.' She

12

looked at him directly.' The coffee flushed her cheeks. 'If you can't help me I should go now.'

'Don't go.' He looked at his watch. '*I* have to go. But later – '

'Later?'

'Trust me. I'll do what I can for you.'

They walked a little again. 'We call it Conny. Beautiful, isn't it?' A fresh mid-morning breeze ruffled the water. A scant twenty miles northeast of where they were standing the Bosphorus flowed into the Black Sea.

'Perfect conditions for civilisation. Once at least. What does your father do?'

'He's a doctor. We used to come to the Black Sea for holidays.'

'Miss Asmus, may I call you Sophie? He'll worry about you if you don't go back. I could try to send a telegram.'

'No!' She grabbed his arm. 'I'll get in touch with him when I'm settled.'

I said to Leksy I supposed there was always a battle of wills between them.

'Just man and woman,' he replied.

I liked that.

Standing on the cobbled quay, he could still feel where her hand had gripped his sleeve. 'Look,' he opened his wallet. 'Here's enough for a meal and a hotel, at least for tonight. Croker's would be best. I need to discuss things with my commander. I'll be back here at six this evening, if . . . if you would care to meet me.'

She didn't know what a commander was but she nodded.

He showed her which way to walk up to the old citadel. 'How will you spend the day? I really can't make it back before this evening.'

She fished in the shoulder-bag. 'I've got a book, and a sketchbook. My time won't be wasted.'

He watched her make her way up towards the Galata Tower as if she had belonged there all her life.

2

Close to Karakoy Square an Armenian businessman kept a tall thin modest hotel. There, since February – and it was now May – a small British military team had been at work. They came ahead of the Expeditionary Force and established themselves on Mr Haroutiounian's third floor.

'We often talked history when I was a boy. My father was nostalgic for a time when he was "with world events" and remembered the details of that short interlude in his life.

'How, for instance, Mr Haroutiounian welcomed those men in uniform! He was glad of the income from the British Government, but it was nothing compared with the Ottoman undoing they were assisting. "Five hundred years!" Mr Haroutiounian exclaimed, whenever he met a British officer on the staircase, as if freshly astonished that the defeat had taken so long. He greeted the British Intelligence men that spring as if they had been sent two thousand miles expressly to do his bidding.

'It was the end of the Ottoman Empire, and what a headache that caused in Whitehall. My father was part of that.'

'Good God, man, we were about to send out a search party.'

'Corporal,' said Duncan, who was an hour late. He grinned at the young man in charge of signals. Duncan McFadden had a quiet, indeed mostly silent humour. Nor, under present circumstances, did he insist on his rank.

Through the enfilade of gilded guest rooms Captain Gillard was reading at his desk.

'So what is it, lieutenant? I can see you have something to tell me.'

'A few Russian arrivals down at the port, sir. They all seemed to be local traffic. Refugees in ones and twos. I plan to check the ferry before it leaves.'

But the elation must have shown in his eyes.

'That's not what you wanted to tell me.'

'Sir, I'd like to help one of the refugees, a young lady.'

'Oh, goddam it.' Gillard waved away his own smoke.

'On the contrary, sir, it would seem to me a privilege to help a young lady like that.' Glancing at Rory Weight, Duncan raised an eyebrow. 'Later then.'

When the span of time labelled 'later' seemed to have expired, Weight began: 'You can dance to Morse Code, did you know that, sir? Long, short, short. Long, short, short. The man begins on the first beat, and then there's this nice little skip, after which they begin to warm up and smile at each other.'

He took off the headphones that wired him to his desk and demonstrated, one elbow crooked so he could hold her by the tips of his fingers, the other arm boldly extended. Long, short, short. Long, short, short.

Gillard retorted: 'When I dance, corporal, it will be with a woman, not an armful of air.'

Duncan asked: 'Isn't it, "Slow, slow, quick quick slow"? I seem to remember my sister . . . '

'Different step, lieutenant.'

Gillard added sarcastically: 'Gentlemen, I'd like to think we have more important things to do than practise our dance steps and rescue damsels in distress.'

'Sir.'

'The best would be to make sure your young lady gets back across the water safely, lieutenant. We could pay her fare. Strictly unofficially.'

'In that case I'll need a few days' leave to escort her, sir. She can't go alone.'

'She came without a man,' Gillard puffed. 'How did she get here, anyway, I mean money-wise?'

Duncan hadn't asked that question. 'Presumably she bought a ticket. In any case she couldn't have had the slightest idea of the risk she was running, travelling alone. To Paris, or Rome, or London, she said she was going.'

'What *risk*, lieutenant? Would *you* look at a woman in that situation with a view to taking advantage of her?' demanded Gillard.

'Of course not.'

'And yet that's what you're afraid of?'

'In others, yes.'

'You see that's just what I was getting at the other day.' For Gillard was in the middle of a long dialogue with himself about how the world was changing. About how, with the big empires gone, the world was suddenly peopled by individuals, men and women equally, who deserved the same moral chance. For which, not to speak of the government in London, men like him and McFadden would have to make a huge effort to free their minds of prejudice.

'Pride, McFadden! Weren't you and I talking about the rise of general humanity just yesterday?'

'Sir, we were.'

'Then you must believe that the Turk is no different from the Englishman, because that is the new future of the world. We are all humanity and we will gather together in small nations. Those nations will cooperate in the name of peace. And not abduct our women. Women may also look after themselves, in future. London won't like it, of course.'

Duncan insisted quietly. 'I would still like to accompany her, sir. Wherever she goes.'

'We'll talk about it later.'

'Sir! She doesn't deny she took a chance. But then she did meet *me*.'

'Oh, look at that, she met *you*!' Gillard thought, but didn't say it.

'Now look at the time! Lieutenant, I want your opinion. London will want every possible interpretation of Kemal's speech to choose from. Sweet, sour, salty, acid – everything we can dish up for them to misuse. By 1600 hours our time.' Mustafa Kemal was the nationalist leader who worried London. London had so many worries.

'I'll tell London Kemal's had a meeting with Lenin,' Gillard threatened, whenever he got angry with his masters.

Duncan took the proferred typescript and once more retired to his desk.

3

The young woman the lieutenant wanted to rescue wasn't at the café when he arrived at six. She'd gone straight to the Croker Hotel and stayed there through the day. She bathed and afterwards spent ten, perhaps twenty, minutes in vague reflection, in the embrace of thick white towels. Then she'd read and slept the hours away.

He got the receptionist to call up and ask Miss Asmus to come down to the lobby, and when she did his heart played havoc with his smile and his ability to talk straight.

'Gillard – my CO – thinks you should return to your parents but I can come with you.' When he saw she wasn't listening he finished off. 'But we can talk about it.'

In fact Gillard had been brutally honest. 'I recommend you for the intelligence service, Lieutenant McFadden, as one of the more intelligent casualties of the war, and what do you do but fall for the first man-eater who steps off a Russian ferry into your path. Send her back across the water and if she wants to find you again she will.' But Duncan pushed Gillard's advice out of his mind. Arthur Gillard had reason to be bitter, he thought.

'I won't go back whatever you say,' she insisted, her beautiful hands splayed on her thighs.

'But your parents . . . '

'They'll understand. I'll write to them. Duncan, you don't realise . . . besides we met, didn't we?'

'We did meet and I'm glad.'

'I am too.'

He took her arm and they relaxed, strolling along the road for a short distance until they reached the restaurant in the *rouelles* of the old city.

He told her about his work, to which she replied she admired all bids for independence.

'Was your father naïve?' I asked Leksy.

'Innocent, certainly. But equally she didn't set out to betray him.

She wasn't evil. Just – '

'Go on.'

In 'the best French restaurant in town' the tables were elaborately laid and most of the food imported.

To start the waiter recommended asparagus. 'That's for me,' she said. He took the cream soup. Afterwards the house speciality was fish straight from the sea. He ordered poached turbot.

It was a supremely comfortable place for Europeans to dine. Fans cooled the air and the way the dark wood contrasted with the crisp white linen gave the impression of cleanliness and precision.

'I have to have it poached. But I suppose a little digestive trouble is better than being dead.'

'I guessed you fought in the war.'

'Not much actual fighting. I spent four hundred and sixty-three days in hospital and then the fighting was over. You could say it actually spared me. Only mustard gas does things to your insides so it's difficult to eat normally,' he added, as the fans whirred overhead. 'So I have to watch what I put down.'

'And did you count all those four hundred and sixty-three days when you were lying there?'

'Certainly I wanted to live.'

The waiter took their plates with an obsequious bow.

'I used to imagine time marching on my side. A whole army on my side. A boy's fantasy, not a soldier's. I pictured my victorious campaign while I was just sitting there resting and waiting. '

'I would have read a lot. And kept a diary. I wouldn't have wanted to sleep at all, in case someone thought I was giving in. Wasting the life I had.'

'Did you keep a secret book, as a child?'

'I did.'

And, with that, he got her to talk about the country she was fleeing.

She began: 'I was at school when the February Revolution happened. We filed into assembly and for a moment everything seemed normal but then our headmistress appeared on the stage. "Girls, most of you will have heard of the Revolution that has taken place in our country.

There will be no more singing of the National Anthem after services."
She was disturbed. We didn't know her like that. Suddenly she was a
real person and we felt sorry for her.

'In the next few weeks everyone got excited. We made a play for
Easter. There was Old Mother Russia, dressed as a witch. No one
wanted to play that part, so we drew lots and the one who drew the
shortest straw was a boy called Dima. He got dressed up in black
robes and he had to come on stage and then fall through a trap-
door. He didn't know how to pretend to fall so we put some steps
for him to walk down. Well, then everyone said it was just a play
and we were grateful to him for his really awful acting. Then, in his
place, a beautiful slim girl dressed all in red, and with a red flag, and
dark hair and creamy-white skin, rose up out of the trap-door.'

Duncan asked: 'Was it you? It could have been you.' It was how he
had already placed her in his imagination, stepping forward on to a
wondrous scene, in which she played a great role.

She sipped from her glass.

'It was the last fairy tale I believed in. Masha Sokolova played the
Revolution. She was the one who held the red flag aloft and I cheered
her on. The name can't mean anything to you.'

'Was she as beautiful as you? She couldn't have been.'

'She was brilliant in our play. She waved the flag and we stamped
our feet and sang the Marseillaise in Russian. You see we did feel
so positive about it, singing about our new Ross–i–ya. But then
life became so hard and so many people were dying. Lenin's own
mistress died of typhoid. It was not in our newspapers. But everyone knew.'

'I didn't know Lenin had a mistress.'

'Why should you?'

'Our Intelligence . . . ' he shrugged. 'So, go on, after the Revolution
– '

'After the Revolution my father took us south and there I used
to go out on a ferry to the markets along the coast to find food for us.'

'That's how you got the idea of the ferry here.'

'I got talking to the sailors, and I met Pyotr Nikolaevich, the
captain.'

Duncan had spotted that brown-toothed salt and viewed him with suspicion.

'I had money from Moscow. We weren't short of money. There was never anything to buy. I realised I had to get away. I didn't want to die like Lenin's mistress.'

Duncan asked: 'Is your father a Bolshevik?'

'Duncan! What's a Bolshevik? My father wants to see our suffering country haul itself out of the nineteenth century and lead a rational and decent life. But I couldn't wait. I – I wanted something for me.'

Tears welled in her eyes.

'Let's get you back now, Sophie. Gillard's actually agreed to help us.'

'O–oah. *Bozhe*. I'm happy.'

'Dear God' it meant, and expressed both horror and relief. He took her hands across the table.

As they walked back to her hotel arm in arm, ahead of them they could see the lights of the bridge and the other side of Constantinople across the water.

When she'd gone up to her room he went back and stood by the water alone.

Leksy said: 'Personally I think the Revolution unbalanced my mother, for she became obsessed with preserving her freedom ever after.'

4

When she had finished school in the summer of 1917 her mother had urged her to learn basic nursing, which she had done, grudgingly. She had no intention of following her parents into medicine. As a volunteer through the summer she had made bandages. Her fellow volunteers were all women and there they sat, at long trestle tables, in clinics and spare premises across the city, sewing gauze to wool, while, somewhere out there, the men Sophie's generation ought to marry were dying. She and her friends might not have men at all. So the question arose, could a woman be *all* she was without a man?

Would marriage even be necessary, if a woman was to be, above all, herself?

'When my mother left Russia the first time she was reading a novel called *The Keys to Happiness*. It was by a popular writer called Anna Verbitskaya. I've still got her copy on my shelves. Miss Verbitskaya equated happiness with the achievement of romantic love so perhaps Sophie did believe in love when she met my father, if not in marriage.'

'That's a rather cool way to talk about your mother's attitude to love.'

'I'm trying to tell you the truth about her.'

After Duncan left she wasn't tired. She'd slept half the day. So she dressed again and went downstairs. The porter, whose desk was lit, stirred and snorted but didn't lift his head as she crept out. In the farther darkness the single moving light of a motor ship was visible. The small native ships passed through this narrow channel and sailed out towards the open sea.

Soft footsteps startled her.

'Sorry, miss. No offence intended.' The voice had a British accent and a youngish man smoked ecstatically as he walked. 'What a night!' he called, from inside his dream. 'What a joy to be alive!'

'It is.' She stretched out her arms and lifted her face and felt a faint night breeze on her skin. The dark water was hatched with rods of light.

The hotel slept. She had to pull the brass bell beside the entrance, and listen to it ring three times before the door opened. The sleepy old minder frowned and shook his head.

A German *Federbett* topped the huge high bed like whipped cream on a cake. She lay upon it, in her slip, her shoulders propped against the headboard, and looked around, still alert. In the corner stood a black upright chair in a startlingly modern style. It was like a three-dimensional playing card. The four of diamonds was cut out of the armless back and meeting it a right angles was a seat pad in red velvet, just like the ace of hearts.

She swung her legs down, found her sketchbook in the cloth bag

21

and drew the chair, which trumped the whole scene around her with its untraditional, detached, modernity. Then carelessly she opened her book, to help her pass the night. Finally she slept a few hours, but with the curtains open so that the light would wake her.

At dawn, her dawn, she set off once more and watched the sun steal up behind the sleeping mosque on the far hill and set it on fire.

5

The next day, as the wooden boat cast off with only a handful of passengers, it was a momentous journey that lay ahead of Duncan McFadden, one by which he hoped to win Sophie Asmus's hand.

As the *tsish* of the prow cut through the water, he kept his head covered and wound a drab cotton scarf around his neck. The ghosts of ancient sentrymen watching from crumbling castle towers nodded them past. By the time they entered the Black Sea, on the shores of which she had holidayed with her family, the sun was already high in the sky. There was no shade except below deck, but in this exotic place which had suddenly delivered him such a gift he wasn't about to hide.

The Russian boatmen were silent and the Scottish officer had no language to tempt them out of it. The sun was merciless. He moved a bag containing provisions for the Asmuses under a bench.

In the mirror of the water he replayed his parting from Sophie.

'I suppose you believe in love?' He must have tried to sound worldly.

'Not in the "love" that is used to keep women under control,' she noted in her diary.

The skipper came down from the wheelhouse. 'Heh, Mr British Officer, stealing away our Russian beauty!' He pointed to him and laughingly put his hand on his heart. '*Khoroshenka! Belle femme! Borzhuazka!*' The captain told him the new love of his life was a bourgeoise with film-star quality.

'I'm a lucky man,' Duncan replied, guessing at the meaning.

He had the feeling that only now, as of a few days ago, had he become truly part of the human race. He had loved his mother and sisters, but that was dedication and tenderness, whereas the emotion he felt now was all those things and desire too. Thank you, God, for letting me into the best human secret. Well, if not to God, to whom do you talk about such things as happiness?

He returned to his not-reading. He found it hard to decide whether Arthur Hugh Clough, a man of his great-grandfather's generation, wrote poems that were daringly modern or tediously old-fashioned. When the arid comparison of the passing of the ages within his own family was no help to him, he closed the book without regret and just sat and gazed around.

On his second morning, when he seemed to have dreamt himself out, he was more sanguine. The Black Sea was an ancient site of civilisation. One day he might have time to study it. He figured a map in his mind. His work came back as he gazed into the green-black depths. Just next door to Conny, just a few ports on across the water, the Bolsheviks were trying to transform Russia. Thirty bodies had been washed ashore with rocks tied to their feet, the bodies of White prisoners, which seemed evil, even in war.

How far now, he gestured to the captain, who held up ten fingers. As once again he closed his eyes under the stars, the sweet smell of hashish wafted over the deck.

In Batumi he caught another smaller ferry to Sochi.

In Sochi he hitched a lift on a horse-drawn cart going southeast and it carried him closer to the mountains. The long straight road, green and flat as a marsh on either side, seemed endless. Ahead, like a lodestone, stood a vast rugged pyramid still bearing gashes of snow. As if some Pythagoras had set him a puzzle he could only solve by completing this journey he squared up to the mountain and asked what it wanted of him. There was something mythical about under-taking a task like this for a woman he had only met a few days ago. The grand undertaking connected him to all good things. He liked himself for it.

As the driver sounded the name of the small town in the foothills and pointed, Duncan consulted the map Sophie had drawn for him. 'That's fine. I'll get down here.' He pressed some coins, also Sophie's provision, into the man's hand. Now, to the receding sounds of a horse's hooves, he began walking.

Few people were in the dirt streets. From the barely distinguishable central square – today was certainly not market day – a path led up to the wooden bungalows that made up the village. The ground was hard and smooth and bare underfoot where so many feet routinely walked. He found a turquoise-painted wooden house with lace curtains. When he knocked no one answered, so he sat outside and observed the dust on his boots.

Her father, a tall, greying man with a full moustache and beard, appeared first, looking to the visitor like Tolstoy, the only Russian a twenty-four-year-old Scottish officer knew the look of, besides the late Tsar and the dancer Nijinsky.

Not expecting to be understood in English, Duncan began by announcing Sophie's name and miming a boat on water. Her father, not wanting the neighbours to see the show, ushered Duncan inside.

'She sent me. Your daughter is safe in Constantinople, Dr Asmus. I'm with the British Army there.' When it occurred to him that a doctor might know Latin he plunged into the heart of the matter. '*Ego amo filiam vostram. Habeo letteram pro vobis . . .* '

'Welcome, sir!' There was Pa, smiling, shaking Duncan's hand, explaining that he did in fact know some English. 'We had an English nanny. Well, Scottish, actually.'

'Of course.' Duncan handed over the letter Sophie had reluctantly written.

The house rented from a grateful former patient was cool and the few rooms spacious. The unpleasant smell of poor sanitation mingled with strenuous efforts to keep it at bay.

Setting the letter aside, her father declared: 'My daughter is crazy, no? *Sumashedshaya*. Ha, ha, ha.' He patted a chair. 'Sit down, *Herr Leutnant*. You must be our guest.'

They talked about the state of the world – poetry and miracles are for when a man is alone. Duncan spoke English and Pa a mixture of languages. As they approached the subject of Russia Pa grasped the visitor's forearm. '*Herr Leutnant*, now the Bolsheviks have taken

Odessa it seems to me the Whites can't recover. The Bolsheviks will take power unopposed!'

'And will that be good for your country, Dr Asmus?' They looked each other in the eye, whereupon Pa whispered loudly, with bluster even, as if the tea and conversation had suddenly tipped him over into drunkenness. 'Oh certainly. A new world will be made in my country. Though, of course, one shouldn't expect too much, *Herr Leutnant*.'

Duncan had resigned himself to being addressed in German, and even to a Bolshevik victory, which he was persuaded to want, quite out of line with the official policy of his country, when a tall woman with a soft face, no longer young, interrupted them. Mariya Asmus wore a printed blouse and plain skirt and when Duncan stood up to greet her he shook a fine-boned woman's hand just like Sophie's. She made herself tea to join them.

'I intend, Mr and Mrs Asmus, to ask Sophie to marry me. I have made this journey at once to reassure you that she is well and to ask for your blessing.'

'So we are to welcome a son-in-law!'

'Getting married! Why only yesterday she was going to school. But that's wonderful. Welcome, Mr Doon–can!'

Pa produced brandy to toast the forthcoming wedding.

'Is it vodka?'

'Not down this way. A different firewater.'

'In Scotland we drink whisky. Another time I will bring you malt whisky.'

Pa ran his nose appreciatively over the surface of the brandy and said he looked forward to 'a wee dram'.

'Of course. Of course.' Their Scottish nanny had liked a tipple.

'So now, Mr Doon–can, I will find you a towel and make you up a bed for the night.'

Alone Duncan gratefully rinsed away the sweat that had caked his body for the last two days. Gillard had told him the Garden of Eden was down this way and he might just be right. He sighed with happiness.

At dinner, Sophie's mother insisted: '*Vy znaete*, Doon–can, my daughter is a very special creature. '

'I love her very much.'

'But you hardly know her,' said Mariya.

Duncan shrugged. 'How long did Adam and Eve take getting to know each other,' he asked.

'God had a plan for them,' said Pa.

'Exactly,' said Mariya.

'I brought you a few supplies.' Duncan overrode the faint objection. From his pack he unloaded three tins of corned beef, some flat bread and some apples and dates. 'No, no, not now. Enjoy them when I've gone, and think of us.'

The three of them ate rice with nuts and dried apricots and some nutty oil, and drank more firewater with it.

'Do you plan to have children?'

'Mrs Asmus, it's my dearest wish to have children. I came close to dying a few years ago and since then I've dreamed of a son.'

Then the visitor excused himself and went to bed.

Next morning, they had breakfast and then Pa shook Duncan's hand.

'I'll take good care of Sophie. You can be sure of that.'

'Don't forget now, keep in touch! We're far away, but not in spirit.' This was Mariya, who, not afraid of banality, used it to cover things she sometimes did not quite feel.

'We will, my friends.'

'We waited five years to get married.'

'Too long! I had so much desire for you I couldn't bear it. A man could become quite corrupted . . . '

'We managed.'

Duncan reversed his path along the straight road. He walked and then thumbed a ride to the water in the thickening light and heat of the morning.

Gillard had recently asked him: 'Are we to feel optimistic about the new world order? The German empire undone, the Turkish and the Austrian no more, and the Russian in chaos, and only us and the French left with any clout here in the East.'

He'd answered equivocally then, but about his own new world order he had a much better idea now.

26

'It's going to be wonderful, sir, although I know it can never be that for you, having lost your son.'

He did feel most heartily sorry for Gillard, who had made a bad marriage, and then lost his only child in the war. Gillard had secured him this posting, and he admired and looked up to him.

Almost two days later at nightfall, which was late in the evening, Sophie was sitting on an iron bollard, on the Constantinople quayside, watching the ferry's approach. She had been thinking about their future life together. That her fiancé had been as good as dead, and had stamped each of four hundred and sixty-three successive days with his will to live, only strengthened her own resolve to live a *modern* life in her future partnership with him. Their world would be rational, which meant to her that there would be space and tolerance for everyone to be free. Although what that might mean for man and woman together she didn't know.

'I thought something might have happened to you in that crazy country of mine.'

They hugged.

'I had the happiest of times meeting your parents. Here,' he reached inside his jacket, 'they answered your letter.'

She opened it reluctantly and she flushed as she read it. It was short. They wished her sincerely well and reminded her where her home was if ever she needed it.

Duncan took her hand and kissed it and as he did so she laid her other hand on top of his bristling dark hair.

She buried her face in his shoulder, and he stroked her hair.

'Will you marry me?'

'Of course, my darling.'

6

They were walking hand in hand by the water.

'You didn't want to get married in church, did you?'

'Absolutely not. I told you, I'm not a believer. And nor are you. Of course that makes it harder to believe in the body *and* the spirit,' she debated with her future husband. 'Because if there's no God what does "the spirit" mean?' The question had been set by one of her teachers a year or so back.

As they stood in their favourite spot by the water, on the far side of the square, beyond the fish market, rather than engage with the question, Duncan asked: 'How did a man with such deep theological preoccupations come to be teaching in a girls' high school?'

'I've no idea.'

Sophie let go of her fiancé's hand, walked ahead of him and then turned back.

'For the spirit to show itself in fact there has to be willing renunciation, our teacher said.'

'Clough believed that too,' Duncan said, 'and rejected it as unmodern.'

'I agree. We make our happiness. We need courage and determination, not resignation.'

'It's only not very poetic,' Duncan said finally, 'a world without self-sacrifice.' That was why he had such trouble with the poems.

They went and ate an ice cream in the elegant café beside the Wiener Bankverein, to avoid the temptation of going to her room.

She told Duncan Arthur Gillard had taken her out in the office Austin while he was away. Duncan didn't know whether he was surprised or not.

'Like to have a go at the wheel?' Gillard had said.

'He let you drive? My word, you must have impressed him.'

'He said there was a first time for everything.'

'Well yes, but – '

'But nothing. I enjoyed it.'

*

'Here,' said Lesky, 'There was a photograph,' and he produced, from an envelope, one of those tiny scallop-edged snapshots from the time. It showed a solid vehicle, its body not much modified from a barrel, but made glamorous by its gleaming cockpit-like controls, presumably in brass, with flickering dials and a heavy steering-wheel, and over the whole a canopied roof.

Gillard told Sophie he called the office motor 'The Mistress'. She wrote the fact down in her diary with a question mark beside it.

'I didn't know it had a name,' said Duncan, suppressing his irritation.

The engine ignited and began turning over energetically.

'We're off! No we're not.'

The Austin rocked forward and stopped.

'Try again now, easy, easy with the clutch, a tad on the accelerator, that's it, atta girl!'

'There was dust everywhere. I couldn't see and my heart was pounding.'

'But you enjoyed it.'

'Yes, really.'

Arthur had said she was a quick learner. She had giggled girlishly. She didn't really know what Arthur Gillard was about.

'Honk the horn!' Arthur had leaned over and squeezed the black rubber balloon which sent a ball of air down the brass bugle. Fifty years ago it would have taken the breath of a young soldier to clear a path for an officer like Gillard. Now it was a mechanical device. Honk! Honk! 'Have you no fear, you curs?' He shouted gleefully as the dogs that occupied the Conny streets retreated as slowly as they dared, with lowered tails and turned heads signalling deep personal offence. They caused many accidents.

Gillard spoke to the front windscreen, shouting to make himself heard over the roar of the engine. He said driving gave him the same sensation as he felt when riding a horse. Together horse and man could achieve the heights of speed and pleasure, if only they knew how best to cooperate with each other. Sophie, who didn't understand the force of that remark, replied that she had only ever ridden side-saddle in the park in Moscow, which was a *comme il faut* affair.

But then there was a silence and she blushed. She felt trapped, with all her attention engaged in manipulating pedals and watching dials. 'You drive. That's enough for me.' She brought the car jerkily to a halt and he came round to the driver's side and she slid across the bench seat.

They rode for a while in one of the silences that kept recurring.

'I feel terribly old beside you.'

'That's because you are.' She broke the tension with that and they laughed. 'Out with it then! When were you born, Captain Gillard?'

'1880. Back in the nineteenth century.'

'I know *when* it was, for heaven's sake.' (She instantly grew up several years talking to Arthur.) 'I just don't know what it feels like.'

'I'm damned if I'm going to tell you anything so intimate.' Then he asked: 'So what do you want to be then, Sophie?'

'True to myself.'

He hesitated. 'I don't want to be rude, my dear, but isn't that absolute nonsense?'

'We'll see,' she replied gaily.

Then on the way down they ran out of petrol.

'That's not like Arthur.'

'I think he did it deliberately. For his amusement.'

'But that – '

'He wanted to spoil our happy trip.'

'Surely not.'

Leksy shook his head and said he didn't understand. Arthur had always been a family friend. And now what he read in her diary . . .

'I said, "You mean we've run out of petrol? What do we do now?" There were no houses, no cars, nothing. He helped me down and we stood together leaning on the side of the car waiting for another vehicle to pass.

' "It's hot," I said. "I can't stand out here like this."

' "Come, there's some shade on the other side."

'He took my hand and guided me away from the road. I went and sat on the step beside the open passenger door.

'He watched me for a moment, then I had the impression he suddenly needed to be alone. He waited on the hot roadside. It must have been twenty minutes before a boy on a donkey passed.'

Duncan said: 'Gillard is a man of such power and insight. But ever since the death of his son – '

'Is that it? I didn't know he'd lost a son. Poor Arthur.'

She went on: 'He called the boy over and sent him off with a jerrycan and the promise of a reward. More if he came back within the hour. It all felt a bit peculiar.'

'But you said everything turned out well in the end.'

'Except that he cut his finger. I said: "Your finger's bleeding." He said he'd cut it on some rough metalwork, but I thought it was deliberate.

' "It's nothing."

' "You might get tetanus. Let me – "

' "I'll do it." He got out his handkerchief.

'The boy was back within the hour, with his father in a horse and cart. The poor horse was covered in sweat.'

Duncan almost shouted: 'But Gillard's been good to me. God knows where I'd be without his support.'

Then he added: 'It gets lonely out here. Your arrival has affected us all.'

7

Duncan had to buy a ring and had no idea where to go in Conny. The office translator advised him to try the pawnbroker's shop in Avoglu Street.

'Isn't that too cheap?'

'Nonsense! Where do you think the Russian grand duchesses go with their treasures when they arrive here? They have to sell their superb jewellery for a pittance. You'll get a bargain, thanks to Bully. Just make sure you mention my name.'

As Duncan left, Bully called out: 'Tell Stavros your bride is Russian. He'll give you a double discount. That bloody Greek likes Russians.'

'You English, I Greek,' said the bloody Greek.

Duncan who had been expecting a swarthy man, wondered at his flat face and golden-brown hair.

The bridegroom in uniform examined the gleaming stones set in bands of gold.

'Come off it, man!'

'Old boy, I cannot go lower. Why you not value your bride?'

'But I do. I do. Most highly. Look here, Stavros, Bully said we could work something out.'

'Old boy, so now you creep in your English way, eh? Give my Turkish friend some funny English nickname so he sounds like one of you? I send greeting to Bulat but you simply make fool of me. And him.'

'Look, Stavros, I'm marrying an apparition. I want her to have the best. I'll go as high as I can.'

It was all an absurd waste of time and energy, but half an hour later they struck a deal.

'Ts–ts–ts.' The pawnbroker made himself sound like a dying insect, while Duncan came away with an impressive silver ring with an emerald stone the colour of Sophie's eyes.

Sophie had no advisers so she improvised. She walked one morning down to the pebble-grey Crimea Memorial Church close to the water.

An unmistakable Englishwoman was arranging flowers in the cool body of the empty church, with the relentless eastern light reduced to a stripe of angelic revelation across the wooden pews and jutting out into the nave.

She was in her late thirties perhaps. She looked intelligent with a high brow and wide-open eyes; kindly too, and made only a touch unusual by her straight, wiry, already grey hair.

'Are you English? This is going to sound ridiculous but I just had to find someone to ask.'

As they sat and chatted on a shaded bench in the garden, Elspeth Sparrow and Sophie grew quickly fond of one another. Perhaps it was the unspoken feeling that they could have changed places. Each

32

could have managed to be the other and enjoyed it, looking and talking like that.

'Is this what England looks like?' Sophie asked, viewing the dark leaves of a holly tree, and letting her eye travel up the spire.

'Why, I suppose it does! But once you've been here for a while you know the difference. Not only the heat and the light, and the sky, but the birds, my dear, they don't sing the same song as under an English sky. As our men who fought in the Crimea found to their cost. That's why this church is here. The politicians and the generals create a fiasco and then we build a very pretty church in which future generations enjoy a sanctuary created by guilt over the past. Sorry, Sophie, that turned into a speech.'

Sophie wished she knew more. More history. More politics. More life. 'So you'll help me prepare for my wedding, Elspeth? I'd be ever so grateful.'

Elspeth Sparrow had the sense of a human being still unfinished – and, of course, how else could it be, with a girl of nineteen.

'Try this one on. It's about your size. If it doesn't fit we can alter it.' They too found themselves in Stavros's pawnshop on Avoglu Street.

'I love it! I love it! You'd take a hundred less, wouldn't you, sir?'

'Dear lady,' replied the owner, with his sad insectile clicking, 'Ts–ts–ts. I cannot let it go for so little! I have a wife and her children to feed.'

'But it suits me very well, don't you think?' Sophie having slipped into a back room with Elspeth to try the dress on had emerged and was parading a little up and down in a way that was making the Greek faint.

'Indeed, indeed,' he clicked.

'Take it, Sophie, you couldn't do better.'

She turned dressed as a bride to the pawnbroker. 'You'll take three hundred then?'

'Dear lady, you are in possession of the greatest of God's gifts to a woman, and still you wish to bankrupt me.'

Now she laughed openly, and her beauty radiated from her in what Stavros felt to be intoxicating waves. She went off with a bargain, to the unmistakable sound of ts–ts–ts.

'Elspeth, I'm so excited.'

'As you should be, my dear.'

'Dearly beloved, we are gathered together here in the sight of God, and in the face of this congregation, to join together this man and this woman in holy matrimony . . . ' Gillard's leather-bound Army Service Prayer Book, which set down the words he was required by law to speak, gave authority to the ceremony; and hearing himself, he couldn't think what had come over him the previous week, and was utterly repentant. He had a good speaking voice, resonant with his class and education.

'Wilt thou have this woman to thy wedded wife, to live together after God's ordinance in the holy estate of matrimony? Wilt thou love her, comfort her, honour and keep her in sickness and in health; and forsaking all other, keep thee only unto her, so long as ye both shall live?'

Sophie's tall slender figure was sheathed in stiff cream brocade, with matching gloves to her elbow.

At Croker's Gillard ordered French champagne, from which, light-headed and garrulous, they moved on to a grand lunch laid out on a starched white tablecloth in a glorious and mostly empty dining-room.

During the toasts Gillard turned publicly to Duncan. 'What's the best we can hope for your wife's country, McFadden?' And then answered before the other man had a chance. 'That Bolshevism stops killing people and starts to build a civilised country.'

'I'll drink to that,' said Sophie.

'Did Gillard approve of the marriage, in the end?' I asked.

'He knew my father's romantic adventure was dangerous and might not turn out well. But he acquiesced. "We must all of us put to sea at some time, trusting that we will arrive. There's truth somewhere ahead." '

'Gillard features in your mother's story as someone important to her without her realising.'

'They were a bit like each other. And, at the same time, he was a good friend to my father. There was only that one occasion on which he could be faulted. When they were still abroad and his fate weighed upon him.'

'I would like us to drink to my new country,' ventured the translator.

'Over my dead English body, Bully. What do you think we British are doing here?'

'But, sir, Bully's right. Here's to Kemal and Turkey! What are we doing here in Conny? Getting in honest people's way, for utterly selfish reasons.'

It was a difficult moment. The signals corporal could have been court-martialled for insubordination and mockery. But Gillard waved a dismissive hand and everyone was relieved. 'You're a bloody young defeatist!' he said. 'What is that stuff you smoke?'

And so the festivities ended, as a Scottish officer took a Russian bride in Constantinople, envied by all the men around. Duncan and Sophie told Bully they privately looked forward to his country's independent future and then after a posed kiss Elspeth whispered in her ear and Sophie took Duncan to stroll around the shaded garden of the Crimea Memorial Church, where at last they could be alone.

Later, in her room in Croker's Hotel, with the sumptuous bed-clothes and the playing-card chair, they undressed a little and lay beside each other. They held hands, they brushed cheeks.

He wondered if she had a sexual past, and whether it mattered to him.

'Not much,' she said, which was true. Mostly her experience had been a matter of curiosity.

Afterwards Sophie looked directly into the small, dark, button-bright eyes of her husband, flickering on the white pillow: 'Which is to say, I nearly had a lover.'

Duncan was vaguely curious but no longer anxious.

'He was German, well, half. *Germ–hun*, as Gillard says. What we called the imperialist war had just ended and we were still in Moscow. We were supposed to hate Germans, because so many of our soldiers had died, but Pa always said nationalist feeling was just an excuse to behave badly. We took in Johann Kohlhaas. Pa said Johann could teach me German to earn his keep. And so he did. We probably saved his life.

'I remember how it happened. I wasn't a bad student. We always spoke several languages in our house.'

'That's how you knew how to pronounce the name of that bank. Thanks to Johann.'

'Wiener Bankverein! I can tell you it gets harder than that. The day I mastered the last of the modal verbs Johann made a big thing of it and said we should celebrate with a glass of schnapps. He said he was so pleased with me, I can remember it now, he came up so close to me and I could smell the sausage on his breath and then we were lying on the sofa in his room, kissing. "*Was wir wollen, das sollen wir, wir können es und wir dürfen es.*" That was a joke, putting all those awful verbs together in one sentence that said, basically, we can do what we want if we want it enough.'

'Sofka, please let me. I promise it won't hurt.'

'It makes babies, Johann. *Kinder, verstehst du?* We can't do that.'

'He kept trying. He was just a normal man. But then he made me angry. I shook myself loose of him and got up and felt ill. He wasn't nice. He was cross. "Now we'll both get a headache," he said. He took my hand to make things easier for him. I felt terribly clumsy but somehow he made me feel I owed it to him.'

Duncan nodded. So far not so terrible.

'And you, darling?'

'Oh, here and there, no one who mattered.'

He stroked her from head to toe. What bounty nature had bestowed on them, as a couple.

In fact, as Duncan knew and kept to himself, there had been no previous woman at all in his life. He had never developed as a sexual creature. That night he experienced something like growing pains. His new body hurt. The war and getting wounded had frozen him and he had to thaw out and begin to live again. He kissed her and they slept.

Honk! Honk! The bugle of Arthur Gillard's office Austin sounded in the square. Captain Gillard, with plenty of petrol in the tank this time, drove the newly-weds in ceremony, manoeuvring around the canine hazards, with the white blinds flapping like so many bedsheets pinned out on washing-day, and the pretty wooden casements of the old houses casting thin strips of shade into the street below. Passers-by stared at an unreal sight, as the British vehicle crossed the bridge and made its way to the European railway station.

'Goodbye, Arthur, and thank you!' Gillard turned his head to get a touch of Sophie's lips, which had been aimed at his cheek. 'I especially won't forget our trip.' She clapped the Austin on its flank.

'Have a good journey!'

'Oh yes and thank you for the tickets,' called Sophie.

At the station the smell of the coke engine powering up to take them home was intoxicating. 'I love trains and places!' She named Paris and Rome and London, none of which she had ever visited.

'You'll love Scotland,' he said.

'I can't wait.'

She revelled in the journey north and west. When the train followed a curve in the track she stuck her head out of the window, against all the rules, to see the whole flexing iron beast in motion.

Music came into her head.

'Did you study music?'

'The usual piano lessons.'

'Me too.'

Duncan in his shirtsleeves gave a sudden vigorous tug on the hard bench so it extended with a judder into the aisle. They hauled down the fresh bedclothes from where they had tossed them on the top bunk. Gillard had treated them to a whole compartment in the over-night Pullman as a wedding present. Now Duncan locked the door and pulled down the blinds.

Technically they had made love the night before, but they both knew this was the time that counted because they had lost their fear and were adequate to the task.

'What?' He half-woke from the stupor into which he had abandoned his soul.

'It won't come off that way. It's cut to fit the body. See?' She pushed the delicate straps back into place and ran her hands down either side of the silk casing that still kept part of her flesh from view.

'I could tear it off you. I would do that.'

'Here, look, give it a little tug for me. Gently.'

Duncan sat back on the opened bench, and pulled his bride on top of him, now finally concentrating on pushing up the slip, so that when she came the first time it was still masking her face. Her head slid into the corner where the bench met the wall and he lay on top of her. 'Is it all right?'

'Yes,' she whispered. 'It's fine. Don't stop.' The empty bunk above towered over her, with the yellow light by which no one was reading, and footsteps passed in the corridor.

8

She peered at herself in the mirror with faint puzzlement then scrutinised the empty compartment. Her husband was pleased with her and she smiled back at him. From Aberdeen, with photographs of Loch Lomond and the Isle of Mull behind their heads, and a mirror, a new world held them fast.

'Arthur Gillard said, "All the world's most valuable advances are achieved in the crucible of conflict." What do you think he meant?'

'Did he sound off so pompously? He must be trying to persuade himself the war got us somewhere.'

'Could one say the century started disastrously for England?'

'If only they'd admit it. '

'How strange that the disaster here is quite invisible.' As if to come closer to the green and settled landscape outside she got up and stood at the window. 'The countryside *looks* wonderful.'

'It is. No doubt about that.'

They had spent four days on trains now, albeit with a London interruption, and England and Scotland provided the best views in the world, he said.

'The world waits to see what will happen in Russia, I suppose.'

'Your father told me a Bolshevik victory was cut and dried.'

'Really? Did he really say that?' Still oversupplied with energy, she took two steps in every direction of the small carriage and so delighted him that had it not been a public space he would have pulled her on his knee.

'When people meet you in Knockie they'll be astonished.'

'Dun–caaan!'

The countryside in the evening light was cool and fresh, heavenly and ravishing, despite, she thought, being somehow like a game for children, all divided up into neat fields bounded by hedges. Everyone from Conny was still in her mind, jostling there with the Russia she had left and what she had taken from London just yesterday. It had reminded her of St Petersburg. Without the canals, of course, but with the grand imperial buildings.

But she could see London was also much larger and wealthier. She observed the lordly neo-classical buildings, representative of wealth and power; gaped at the militaristic open spaces; wondered about the joys of so many different restaurants; asked Duncan about the other famous men's clubs. London had a certain dedication to pleasure. The dell with the little lake in St James's Park was a perfect place to roll in the grass and swim on a summer's day. Did the King walk and swim there? Duncan guessed not. He had his own gardens and ponds.

'Naked is the best way to swim.'

'Have you ever done it?'

'Once.'

She was, he reflected, always slightly ahead of him in physical things.

She said: 'Next time we're in London I'd like to go to Speakers' Corner.'

'Why on earth?'

'It's a place where people say what they think.'

'I still don't think *you* need to *go* there.'

'I should like to hear *all* the different views people hold.'

'But *why*?'

'To work out what *I* think. It's important everyone does that.'

'Scotland is actually quite far from London,' he said, finally.

'Nonsense! We're used to huge distances in Russia. This is a tiny island in comparison.' She glued her nose to the closed window. 'I'd just like to go to London from time to time.'

'We'll see.'

'I can go alone.'

'Why should you go alone? We'll go together.'

'I'd love that. Just us.'

A smut, which had settled on Duncan's white collar in those wilder minutes when she had hauled the window down and a gale blew in, had left a grey streak on it like a tiny comet.

'A souvenir of our trip,' she said.

When they finally got out of the train, reduced to three carriages for the last stage of its long haul to the far north, the cold air stung her cheek, and she smelt fish. The air was clear and pure, with a distinct chill.

In the silence an unfamiliar sound, like a muffled cymbal coming to meet them over the footbridge, made her look up. A tall, sturdy young man appeared to carry their luggage back up the clanging iron stairs for them. 'Sophie, this is Mr Dewar. He was at school with my younger sister Alison.'

She nodded, without the general knowledge of her new home into which such small details fitted. As they descended to the station-master's house on the near side, closest to the little town, she watched 'Mr Dewar' load their suitcases, and the bound-up rug that was their parting gift from Conny, on to a trolley. Calling him Micky, Duncan asked about his work as a porter and heard back from Micky Dewar that these were hard times for the fishermen.

As Micky wheeled their load down to the house, the new Mrs McFadden walked ahead. She was looking forward to unfurling the rug. He pushed the trolley faster to keep up with her; suddenly they were all three of them running, and young – just separated by class – husband, wife and servant.

'Whoa there!' cried Duncan. 'We'll get there soon enough.'

'But I want to see where we're going to live! It's so exciting.'

Duncan took his wife's arm. 'Here we are.'

'Oh, my!'

In the distance she glimpsed the sea, and would have lingered.

But two women who had been standing in the lit front window appeared at the open door, in the space between two mock-classical pillars, and beckoned.

'Darling, this is Fanny. And Alison.'

The women scrutinised each other. Sophie, the avowed atheist, noticed they both wore crucifixes.

'Welcome, Sophie,' said Fanny, observing her long graceful figure and lively expression. 'You must be tired, my dear.'

Behind Duncan she made her way upstairs.

'Here we are, round the corner and through that door.'

Duncan sniffed the air and set the suitcases down. 'Smells a bit musty, but we'll soon put that right.'

She looked around. The room was tiny.

Moscow rooms were much bigger, and she said so, to which he replied: 'I read that the Bolsheviks were dividing them up and stuffing ten people into one flat.'

'That just tells you how big they were in the first place. Still,' she turned to her husband, holding him at the waist, leaning back to a get a clearer view of him, 'what I like is that this little room is just for us.' The trail of the minute comet was still visible on his collar.

'It is.'

'Where's my tiny glimpse of the sea from indoors then?'

The name of the house was Seaview and he had told her of the view from the bedroom window. She was determined to hold him to it, as if they had struck a deal. She had seen the sea out there in the bay, slate silver in the May evening light, as they approached from the station.

'Lift me up. I still can't see it.'

'You have to pay a forfeit for no sea view.' She meant it too. 'Kiss me. Again. Shall we just go to bed? I'd like to lie with you and watch the sky.'

His refusal shocked her.

'Why ever not?'

He bent over her as she sat at the dressing-table mirror. 'I don't have to tell you, do I?'

'I'd like to hear it. Really I would.'

An extraordinary sound, half bell, half earthquake rumble, interrupted them.

'Lord, what's that? It's like the young man running over the bridge.'

41

Her relieved husband cried: 'There, you see, Fanny's banging the gong. Supper's ready.'

Downstairs the great suspended disc of bronze on the hall table, with the velvet-covered striker hooked in beneath it, was still quivering. It was like a single cymbal, detached from an orchestra. Or a giant footfall, from the clanging bridge. Or like . . . But she turned to the company.

Fanny poured them a sweet sherry in the front room. That room was also a little musty, and cold, since it was the first room to lose the sun in the day. Alison slipped away to check the table which had been laid for hours.

'Mmm, food. Thank you, Fanny. That's just what we need.' They all sat down together, although the sisters didn't eat. They exchanged platitudes about the journey, and the horrors of London, over which Sophie demurred, for she saw nothing wrong with crowds. Duncan caught up with life in Knockie. They were collecting for the planned war memorial, said Fanny. 'It's to stand outside St Peter's,' added Alison.

'Ali, how you've grown up!' He was her brother, but Alison was pleased that as a man he noticed her womanly progress, for she had never known her father.

'So, how do you find your brother after so long?' asked the new sister-in-law, as they sat over a bowl of soup followed by rice pudding for him, and ham and salad for her.

'It's wonderful to see him.' Fanny McFadden's answer was totally opaque.

Leksy remembered: 'She had a slight accent on the 'o' sounds. "Alisoane", my Aunt Fanny said. "What a lovely hoame you have," and so on. I'm sorry to say they treated her as a foreigner. She was a stranger, their brother's mysterious new wife, brought back from abroad.'

Duncan said later that if Fanny was stiff it was because looking after him had been her job since she was a girl.

'I can help you wash up,' Sophie had offered.

42

'Oh no, dear, not tonight. You get some rest.' Fanny spoke, her hands full of stacked used dishes, while Alison ran hot water in the porcelain sink in the scullery.

So the new couple retired early and though Duncan had not responded enthusiastically when Sophie had found his hand under the table, during the family meal, the night, when it came, was, as it is to all loving couples, the always miraculous gift.

'This must be the best kept secret in the world.'

'The best of the secrets. I love this with you.'

They quickly fell asleep under a heap of wool blankets and a slippery green-satin eiderdown.

9

The Army, courtesy of Gillard's not very accurate counting, had been generous with his leave, but now the ethereal cloud he had floated on since a beautiful Russian woman stepped ashore at Constantinople finally came down to earth, and he reported to Regimental Head-quarters in Cowie, ten miles away.

In the morning, waking to her absent lieutenant's still warm imprint in the high wooden bed and moving into it for a while, Sophie lay and listened to the high-pitched birdsong outside, with a bass line of shoebrush on leather. Women's voices blurred into the clang of an enamel pail.

Down in the parlour, breakfast had been laid out for her, along with a note in a very neat, joined-up hand. She helped herself to marmalade, a taste familiar to, if not beloved of, Westernised Moscow families like her own.

When she went out to explore, the sunshine softened the harsh outline of Duncan's small home town, dominated by its fishing. Even so, Sophie was unused to even the humblest buildings being made of stone.

A fishwife down on the quay noticed the newcomer had an energetic way of walking.

'Good-morning to you!' Sophie waved.

The old port was a large rectangle of water half-enclosed by a stone wall, a calm anchorage keeping out the great sea beyond. She walked beyond it all the way to the east beach, where she took off her shoes and stockings and walked across the pebbles and sand.

Why shouldn't the King swim naked in the lake in St James's Park?

Long flat waves flowed over her feet like necklaces trying themselves on the collar of the beach. She lifted each foot high in turn and plunged it back, splashing her skirt. Children too were paddling in the sea. Little groups of families were camped on the sand, for, said Fanny, who was a teacher, it was the half-term holiday. Fanny still had to go in and prepare. No! She went in because she liked her job.

The little town had two faces, one turned to the train line and the other to the sea.

From the harbour Sophie looked back up the low cliff where either side of the valley the better houses stood. The arrival of the railway had encouraged pompous houses like Seaview, on the western side, to be built among the remnants of the old stone cottages. There it stood, an artless double-fronted villa, mainly painted cream, with a little decorative brickwork above the windows which gazed obliquely across the bay.

The granite house Duncan had inherited from his mother was ugly, except when light streamed in through the front bay windows and forced the unyielding building to smile. The classical pillars either side of the front door were absurd. Inside Sophie crept from room to room where the crochet stitch she personally had never mastered seemed to cast giant thick-threaded spiders' webs over every surface.

In the bedroom she unrolled the rug from Conny and tried to imagine it in a transformed sitting-room downstairs, where they would sit and talk and read in the evenings. When Duncan came back, at six, she was pleased to see him, and resolved to make the effort it would take to adjust to her new life.

He cycled to Cowie and back. She walked beside the sea.

After the satisfaction of his return his first days back at Headquarters disappointed him. He was going to be doing a lot of paper-pushing, sifting and coordinating, so that some superior could finally send a telegram, top-secret, to a man on the ground like Arthur and tell him the Prime Minister declined his advice. Yet the advantage of the Intelligence job was that he still spent much of his day reading newspapers and other reports from around the world. He liked to feel he was 'with world events' and his work gave him that impression.

'How was your day?'

'Everything old and new at the same time. I can't complain.'

'I went exploring. I think I'm going to like Knockie.'

Soon after he walked in, they sat down to a high tea of something easily digested: scrambled eggs or fish in white sauce. And so the days took shape, regulated by work for those who had it, and the shared table.

Alison was quiet, and only came into herself when they were alone in the morning.

'Alison darling, how do you like the new short skirts? I saw a woman in London who looked superb in one.'

'Not much call for wearing them round here.'

'Nonsense. They must be easy to sew, with no waist and just a few pleats. I'll pop by the shop later.'

Alison, who worked in Knockie's draper's shop, looked surprised and pleased. 'In that case it's at the far end of the High Street. You can't miss it.'

'I'm sure I can.' Sophie actually liked getting lost. 'Won't you show me round the garden?' she asked Alison.

'I'd better leave that to Fanny. She does the garden.'

But on a sunny morning early in June Sophie was already out of the door.

The garden, which sloped steeply, had the same pretentions as the house but despite them was much more likeable. It was like a pinprick Versailles, with its urns containing the last of the tulips, and steps and a little balustrade, dividing the top formal third, where there was a bench, from the lower meadow of grass. In the wilder garden the broom was in full swing, its tiny flowers creating a mist and exuding a charming fragrance. Pink rhododendrons created a chilly opulence at the bottom end under the wall. You couldn't see the sea from the walled garden, but overhead small clouds were speeding across the bright blue sky thanks to a brisk wind.

In the early evenings, and at the weekends if Fanny was not weeding, Sophie urged Duncan out into the garden so they could be alone.

'Put me on your shoulders and see if I can see the sea.'

He knelt in front of the bench under the window and she took off her shoes and climbed up, her stockinged knees pressing against his ears.

'Put your hands under my feet. I'll have to stand up.'

'See it now?'

'Not quite.'

'Now?'

'Y–es. Yes.' He staggered towards the grass where they toppled over. He wanted to lie on top of her, but he remembered himself.

That first morning in the garden, she asked, 'Shall we pick something for a vase, Ali?' Colour was needed to supplement the stringy tradescantia on the bedroom mantelpiece and the parlour palm in the front room.

'On your head be it, Sophie!'

'I'll take the risk.'

Alison looked at her watch. 'Heh, I'll be in trouble if I don't get a move on!'

She smiled a lot on her ten-minute walk to the draper's. No one was ever late in Knockie unless they were ill or there was a family disaster, but now here was Sophie who was quite different.

'What ages are the children you teach, Fanny?'

'Boys and girls up to the age of eleven.'

'Both together? I'm glad to hear it.' She told Fanny about her father's progressive views and Fanny invited her to the granite building with a yard like a cattle pen,

'Children, we have a visitor. This is Mrs McFadden, who comes from Russia.'

Large eyes peered at her. There were angelic faces, and some less beautiful, and some already encumbered by spectacles. She liked young children's company, for they were honest in what they saw and uninhibited in what they said, and drew; and how easily they laughed.

'I'm so glad you love children,' said Duncan, when she told him.

46

At break she stood with Fanny 'on duty', and the children having fun sounded like the seagulls that brought Duncan's boat safely back to Conny. Fanny wore leather gloves that held the tongue of the brass bell until the little hand of her watch reached ten forty-five exactly. Then she let it loose and the sound of the law of the land rang out. Back inside the children filed into their classrooms, which all opened off a central assembly room with a stage and a piano at one end. 'Girls, you will have heard that a Revolution has taken place in our country. There will be no more singing of the National Anthem.'

'During the war Fanny trained as a teacher in Inverness.'

'Is that so?'

'Alison worked in the munitions factory in Crombietown.'

'Is Crombietown a big place?'

'Quite,' said Alison. 'You must go there.'

'Sophie sewed bandages for the Russian soldiers who got blasted to pieces by Austrian munitions.'

'I did.'

'What an unfortunate thing war is,' said Fanny.

'There I agree.'

'I liked our factory,' said Alison. 'The other girls were always good for a laugh. In fact, I think that during the war life was more fun than it is now. At least it drew us all together.'

'Ali, really! It was a time of the most terrible sacrifice. Fortunately we live in a new age now,' said their brother.

He meant, among other things, the League of Nations. She knew that from her newspaper-reading. Sophie felt, however, that for all the talk not much that was 'new' was happening of its own accord in the circumstances she called her own.

'You were saying, about the new age, darling,' she said to her husband.

'We're the new generation. We have different attitudes. And we'll keep studying.'

Fanny of course agreed but Alison pulled a face. School had done nothing but teach her to read and write, and she was quite lazy.

Duncan took that moment to announce that he had applied to do a degree by correspondence with London University.

'I should do the same,' Sophie said. 'I *should* study economics like you, Duncan, since it's the modern science, although my inclination – '

He put down his knife and fork. 'Will there be time for that, Sophie?'

'What do you mean? I've got loads of time on my hands.'

The sisters stopped eating and watched.

She restated her position more calmly. 'Of course there will be time. If there's time to breathe there's time to study, that's what Pa used to say. We can all study together. We can form a commune for self-improvement.'

'A commune! What kind of an idea is that?' demanded Fanny.

'A modern idea!' shouted Sophie.

'Then there would be no one for the washing-up,' giggled Alison.

'We share the jobs out so everyone can develop equally. I can actually take on more jobs. I don't have enough to do.'

A certain awkwardness hung in the air from that night.

10

In Constantinople a Turkish woman pushed Gillard off the pavement. He wasn't complaining personally, but his superiors should take in what a gesture like that meant.

'Quite right! They don't want someone else's empire stuffed up their backside.'

'Steady on, old girl!'

'But isn't that the truth of it?'

London accused Gillard of being too close to events to understand them and Sophie felt angry for their dear friend.

She could see Karakoy Square, with white crescents on red cloth everywhere, and hundreds of milling, excited men, drawn together by pride. Everyone in Cowie, and London, not to mention abroad, knew General Milne's intervention in Conny had been a dire mistake. The Royal Navy battleships would have to retreat from the Bosphorus now and Britain was humiliated.

Gillard (who sent news in a private letter) told Duncan he was considering resigning. He summoned Rory Weight to his desk and told him to lay off the hashish if he didn't want a court martial. 'Poor young bugger, I really went for him. The place went quiet all afternoon. Then we had a coffee with brandy and I apologised. It's been a help to have the Sparrows agree with me.'

Sophie commented, as the letter was read out to her: 'Perhaps you'll have to have a revolution here and become a different country too. There must be other people who feel Britain hasn't properly begun the twentieth century, in truth.'

'It won't happen. What would we change into?'

In the midst of such conversations Sophie was all the more determined to find time at least to read the newspaper.

Duncan ended his letter, which he also read to Sophie: ' "On the other hand, as you say, Arthur, why not bow out and let the Turk get on with his own life? The future belongs to small nations, not big beasts. Yours ever." '

'That's right,' she said.

In his office, Duncan, with one of his assistants, pondered the map.

'This is the route the Greeks took, sir.'

After the Greeks landed troops in the port of Izmir, with British encouragement, that summer, no wonder a Turkish woman pushed Captain Gillard off the pavement.

'I can think of a single Greek pawnbroker by the name of Stavros who will be pleased with today's news. Otherwise a Greek invasion is the worst possible thing. And now the Turks and Greeks will fight and more people will get killed. In confidence, nothing Britain does seems right these days. Meddling in other people's affairs. Setting old enemies against each other. Seeing ourselves as philhellenes.'

Back home he found Sophie and Fanny arguing about just such consequences.

'We've all seen bad things. Our job now is to put life back together again,' his sister said.

'*Back* to what? You can't put the clock *back*, Fanny.' Sophie laughed to excuse herself the triteness of her words.

'I don't see why not. If you built a house and someone knocked it down, wouldn't you build it up again?'

'Agreed, but there would be things that I had always disliked. I wouldn't build those up again.'

'I think we mean the same thing.'

'I doubt we do.'

'There you see, you enjoy picking quarrels with me. Duncan's right.'

'Not at all. We're just different.'

Sophie turned to her husband to avoid quarrelling with Fanny any further. 'Alison and I chose some dressmaking material today. Green for her, blue for me.'

'Oh yes.'

'And you must come and choose, Fanny. I've bought a pattern. It doesn't look too difficult.'

I've enough dresses, dear, thank you.'

'Nonsense, no woman ever has enough dresses, isn't that so, Duncan? By the way we'll need to get the man to overhaul the sewing machine. There's something wrong with the tension.'

He nodded, his mind finally dislodged from the inappropriate philhellenism of his country's ruling class, which seemed inevitable unless more men like himself could make it through the ranks. 'Alison, you can see to that for Sophie, can't you? Ask Mr Rogers to pop by, if he would be so kind.'

'We haven't seen Mr Rogers for a long time.'

'That's his choice,' said Fanny.

Sophie drew a breath, gave Fanny a look, and then the married couple withdrew to the front room where it was still light outside.

'I've had some ideas about refurnishing the house.' She stared at the antimacassars which sucked the grease from heads that settled against the chairbacks. *Bozhe, quel horreur*. How she longed for those missing heads of interesting greasy-haired strangers with whom to discuss the world.

'Oh yes?'

'Our rug from Conny, for instance, couldn't it go in this room?' She was hoping, with his permission, to remove every trace of crocheting, and green velvet, and every tassel and fringe. She dreamt at night of stealing down with a pair of dressmaking scissors and snipping and unravelling the lot.

50

'Perhaps we could have it in our bedroom.'

'But why? No one will ever see it there!'

'Sophie,' and he had in that moment a warm feeling of being back in his home town, whose alleys he had walked as a boy, 'I know that you are technically – ' he hesitated, 'the mistress of the house – but you have to understand that people – my sisters – draw strength from what they have known. It would be cruel to take that away from them. We're not alone in the house, Sophie. It's my duty to look after my sisters.'

'Don't go on.'

'I must. What would you have me do? Put my own kith and kin out of the door?'

'It's just . . . A wife needs to be free in her own home. You might give some thought to that.'

He put down the economics textbook he was struggling with and kissed her on the forehead. 'I'm sorry, darling, I've got a lot on my plate. Arthur's considering resigning and if he does where does that leave me? I ought to resign too, in solidarity.'

'But you can't! What would you do?'

'Exactly. We have our family life to consider above all.'

In fact, when the lamps were switched on in the evening it was a cosy room and even a delight for the eye, its surfaces softened by many fabrics. Sophie got up and drew the curtains herself as they discussed Arthur. She sat at her husband's feet and he stroked her hair.

'Will our first child be a boy or a girl?'

'I've been meaning to talk to you about that.'

'My dear Sophie! Any child of ours will be my heart's delight.'

11

The following Saturday was a warm late-June day and they took the afternoon to explore the more rugged parts of the coast where she had not yet walked alone. They left Knockie hand in hand and followed the path which began beside the beach and slowly climbed.

The sand-coloured soil was hard and dry. People passed, wishing them good-afternoon. Dogs ran ahead, turned and looked back, waiting for their owners to catch up.

'We might get a dog. What about a collie? They're so intelligent.'

'Peter Bruce breeds dogs. Not collies though. I think it's King Charles spaniels.'

'I'd prefer a collie.'

He was glad to be out, but he felt easily tired. He had to point out that taking on a dog just as they were starting a family might not be the best timing.

'I – ' And she was going to say what she had to say. But then her attention was caught elsewhere, for they'd reached the castle.

'Knockie's one famous site.'

'It's fantastic. It looks so ancient and primitive.'

However old it actually was, now it was almost submerged in grassed-over rock.

It made a great impact on her.

'It's better from here. You can't see it for what it is up close.' A row of arched windows which must once have looked out from high above the ground were now just stone patterns in the hillside.

It was a place where many local people, over the years, came to be alone with their thoughts, Duncan said. 'There's an engraving of it in the Buchan Arms, of what some eighteenth-century artist decided it used to look like.'

But the antiquarian record didn't interest her, only what she could experience now. They were sitting in a slight hollow, where the grass was short and soft like moss. The sea was invisible from where they sat but they could hear it pounding at the rock, drawing away the loosened fragments of stone, then flooding it again. And here were these once-lived lives, almost totally submerged in the rock.

She'd brought milk for her husband to drink. He looked to her rather thin. Together they put that down to the long cycle journey to Cowie and back every weekday. Shouldn't he take the bus?

'You know what, Sophie? I need a son. When I have a son I will feel that the world has prospects again. Because he will be our son.'

'Duncan – ' she took his hand.

She was not yet twenty. They had their whole married life before them. And still she didn't say.

The bone handles of the knives and forks which emerged clean from the enamel bowl in the sink looked as if they had been permanently discoloured by nicotine, like the teeth of the skipper who had brought her from Sochi.

'Do you hope to get married, Alison?' She looked up at her younger sister-in-law who was drying.

'Sophie, I would get married if I could find the right man. The problem is there aren't many to choose from. Especially not in Knockie.'

'Go to Crombietown then, go to Edinburgh, go to London!'

'How am I supposed to do that?'

'You earn money, don't you?'

'We pool most of our earnings, to pay for the running of the house.'

'So it is a commune then! Keep a bit back for yourself! I'm sure no one would notice. I won't tell.'

'I think she was trying to convince herself she'd made the right decision, getting married.'

'That it would all turn out well.'

As Leksy and I talked on – it was already our third meeting – I was pleased to feel in him some sympathy for his mother as a human being who, quite legitimately, wanted to be free.

'We can liberate ourselves, you know. I read this book, well, it's a pity I can't give it to you because it's in Russian but there's this man and he says to the heroine, you know, you women, you kiss your chains, but you should free yourselves. It's called psychology. If you can understand yourself then you can be free.'

Alison gave Sophie a look which irritated her.

'I'm sure you could free yourself, Ali.'

'But do I want to?' the younger sister asked, and that was irritating, for it made her seem stupid.

'That's for you to decide. I want to. For me.'

'For you, yes. That's about it.'

53

Alison concluded that Fanny was right and Sophie was rather crazy and rather selfish.

Walking alone it hung over Sophie that she had to say something important to her husband.

'Come on, let's go out. It's a beautiful evening.'

'But Sophie – '

'Duncan, it's summer. Besides, I love the lanes. They're like a maze.'

That persuaded him. He too loved the lanes that fleshed out the heart of the old port.

'There's something I want to say – '

The statement surprised him. She was always talking.

'It's about . . . the risk we're taking . . . about my getting pregnant.'

For a moment he thought it was already good news. There was enough time for her period to be late.

'To be honest I am hoping for a son.'

'I'm only just twenty – '

'The perfect age, according to medical science.'

'Not medical science, this is about me. I –'

But still she didn't manage to tell him that she had been to see Dr O'Neill, who had supplied her with a Dutch cap.

'Why was it so hard for her?'

'She must have guessed he wouldn't approve. It was that that really set a wedge between them. It effectively destroyed their marriage.'

In their first days they had taken risks but not long after her arrival in Knockie Sophie had taken herself to John O'Neill's surgery. For a place of barely two thousand inhabitants, Knockie had three churches, all Protestant, and the surgery was positioned between the draper's and the second of them.

'The Presbyterian mentality must have oppressed her.'

'It's true her upbringing was free of all religious pressure, so when she sensed it she hated it.'

*

Something masculine and even military, with an orderliness which reminded her of Gillard's HQ in Conny, made O'Neill's surgery, in Sophie's estimation, a frightening place for the female body to enter. The public waiting-room was nondescript, but once you got inside the consulting room, then the smell of antiseptic, and the polished, dust-free surfaces and the sleekness and heaviness of the medical instruments all seemed to be gendered masculine, and they were like swords, as against the embarrassment of anything floppy and bladder-shaped, which seemed to come straight out of a woman.

'Come in, do sit down, Mrs McFadden. What can I do for you?'

Oh, that was nice for a young woman to hear! He didn't sound like his surgery at all.

Dr O'Neill was in his forties, she guessed from his straight, crew-cut grey hair, and he had the clearest, whitest skin she had ever seen on a man. He surely did not drink alcohol or smoke. But there was a kind light in his eyes, that offset the severity of personal discipline, which inspired her trust.

'I'm not ready to have children, doctor. I want to delay my family a little.'

The device she needed was concealed in a small unlabelled black box.

'It's a little inconvenient, my dear, and you will need to practise. Make sure the cap covers the cervix.' He screened her with a green curtain, as, perched on the metal bed, she drew up her knees and took a scientific approach to her own insides. The cap was fashioned of thick rubber and the round spring that held it in place at the top of the vagina was so powerful it was hard to compress the whole device, between thumb and forefinger, as she was bidden, in order to introduce this barrier against conception into the depths of her womanhood. She immediately knew she would not perform this operation in front of Duncan, but would need to be prepared in advance.

He anticipated her fears. 'Men in Scotland, Mrs McFadden . . . '

She smiled. 'I'm sure I can learn to be discreet.'

As Dr O'Neill packed up her new equipment she gazed, sitting across from him, at two small paintings on the wall, and finding she couldn't see them clearly, she got up to take a closer look. They were not like the illustrations to *The Pilgrim's Progress* that decorated the walls at Seaview, but highly coloured, angular portraits, one of a rumbustious fat man, perhaps the artist's self-portrait, and one of a woman in a hat, with her head cocked at an angle.

'What were they?'

'They were both by Fergusson, after he'd studied in Paris.'

'She must have felt they reflected some awareness of the new psychology.'

'They exuded the pleasure, and the colour, of the good life she always dreamt of finding in Paris or Rome or London . . . my dear Mama!' Leksy had tears in his eyes.

His emotion reminded me of old Stravinsky's savage rejection of *jouissance*; a composer who in his old age positively wanted to whip his listeners into obedience. My own sympathies will always be with the expansive, delirious Wagner, as the greatest modern poet of human aspiration, as opposed to Stravinsky, with his young paganism and old man's humility.

'What one needs from great art is guidance on how to shape pleasure,' I said. 'Religion can't do that any more.'

'What good company these portraits must keep you, Dr O'Neill.'

'Do you like them, Mrs McFadden? I bought them in Edinburgh to cheer up the place a little.'

She repeated how much she did.

She didn't manage to tell Duncan any of this, however, as they untangled from the embrace she had sought to cover her embarrassment.

12

She went to explore Crombietown. She put on a pale muslin skirt and a loose grey-blue silk blouse with fine broderie anglaise stitching and loose sleeves to the elbow. Her lower arms, and her neck and throat, where she wore a string of pearls, were tanned from the sun.

Opposite the church, where the ground had been cleared for the war memorial, she stuck her hand out. The unmistakable sound of the combustion engine turning over as it waited at the Knockie junction to make its first stop outside the church, and then the driver's horn, as he arrived, marked the start of an afternoon excursion.

Peter Bruce, the one who bred King Charles spaniels in his free time, took her fare and watched in his mirror as she settled in her seat for the half-hour journey.

She was certainly a looker.

Out of the window, along the road that followed the coast although the sea was mostly out of sight, fields with and without sheep and occasional farm cottages passed. Scotland in sunshine was quite bearable, although never in any of its moods like the paintings in O'Neill's surgery.

'A big town, you said, Alison!' She shook her head and vowed to tell her sister-in-law she was completely wrong when she got home.

Nevertheless there was a busy central High Street where both sides were lined with shops and the shops all had their green canopies out on this warm day. Beyond them lay whole roads of granite houses like Seaview. Sophie strolled aimlessly but happily, eyeing the unwearable clothes behind the yellow cellophane curtain that obscured their colours but stopped them fading in the sun. At the west end of the High Street was a Municipal Hall and a Library and the well-tended 'Pleasure Gardens', with statues of mermaids and angelic boys supposedly representing the collective dream. A dream of her own skirted the idea that, though resistance was great, women's lives would prosper when the secretiveness of middle-class society softened into gentle discretion. Then one could begin to talk about civilisation. Women would prosper psychologically when men laid down their defences. She sat for a while, and then made her way back to where she had seen the words engraved in stone: Public Library.

When she got home she found Alison and they had another cup of tea. Alison objected to Sophie's mocking tone. 'So what's a big town if it's not Crombietown?'

'All right so it's a big town. Tell me about Mr Rogers. Why does Fanny go funny whenever Mr Rogers is mentioned? Surely not because you work in his shop?'

'He proposed to her and she turned him down.'

'How can that be?'

'She said he wasn't good enough for her.'

'That's telling him. By the way what do you think of Dr O'Neill? I find him a good sort.'

'He gave me some pills for period pains. I didn't think anything.'

'He's on our side, as women.'

'On our *side*, Sophie? Really!'

'I'm telling you, Ali, it will be a struggle. We need a revolution of our own.' Something about hearing herself actually speak those words made her smile. 'You know what I said about the new psychology. Dr O'Neill knows about it. He thinks it will make the world a better place for you and me.'

'It's not bad as it is.'

'In intimate things, I mean.'

'Oh, those,' replied her younger sister-in-law darkly.

'On top of which I decided today I'm going to do a secretarial course.'

'Oh yes?'

The declaration seemed to require a coda. 'Because I want to be able to earn my own living. It's to do with that.'

They waited for the kettle to boil with Alison silent.

'Revolutions are not what you read in the papers, Ali. Or at least they're not only about men waving flags. They're about liberating ourselves from the irrationality of the past.'

The younger sister replied at length: 'As you said, Sophie, your parents are intellectuals in a different way from how we understand the word.'

Sophie started. Those words couldn't be Alison's own. She didn't talk like that. She didn't think like that. 'Is that what Fanny said? About my parents being intellectuals?'

'Duncan actually.'

Sophie felt a little hiccup inside, imagining her husband explaining to his sisters that his wife was a little strange, and arming them with appropriate responses.

She cast a glance around the scullery, with its slimy green paint, and thoroughly disliked it.

Then it happened. Returning from the bathroom, Sophie fluffed up her pillow before turning back the bedclothes. She cast off her thick wool dressing-gown and got into bed.

Her husband turned to her, kissed her and began to tug off her nightdress.

'Oh, Duncan, wait! Wait, darling, please, I'm not ready.'

'That's not what the rest of you is telling me.'

'Really, I must stop for a minute.' She pushed his chest away from her with some effort.

He waited.

Switching the bedside light back on, in the muted glow beneath the silken tassles she opened the drawer and showed him the contraceptive device, washed and powdered in its box. It was an ugly contraption. But medical science had invented it to prevent conception. 'You see, we're terribly lucky, I think, to live in the times we do. We're free. We can enjoy each other without worrying. And we can plan.'

He sat bolt-upright, talking to the middle of the room. 'Take that thing away from me, Sophie! What on earth are you doing with it? This . . . this obscene bit of rubber. Surely we should have discussed it? Whether to have a child or not.'

'Don't shout.'

But she felt like shouting at the thing herself. It was ugly and the smell of the spermicide clung to her hands. 'It's difficult to talk to you about intimate things, Duncan, I couldn't find the moment. I did try, believe me, we were out walking, twice in fact, but then I couldn't just leave it. It was urgent. '

He disliked her in that moment. She had kept her deceitful strategy from him.

She disliked him. He was unfair. Her body was her own, she protested.

'And as for John O'Neill . . . ' he muttered.

'You may think you own John O'Neill as your friend. But as a doctor John O'Neill is a free man. And a good man. A woman must be able to receive impartial advice from a doctor, surely.'

'His job is to advise you as my wife.'

'Rubbish! I am my own person. I – '

'Goddam it, will you shut up?'

'Duncan, no–o, please! You're hurting me.'

But she was like a rag doll clutched to him.

'Don't, oh, no, please.'

A bewildered and fascinated Alison listened to the row from the next room.

13

'She was his equal, and both were determined people.'

'And so she developed a life of her own.'

'Je m'appelle Sophie McFadden et j'adore la littérature française.'

'Parfait, mademoiselle!'

'Madame!'

'O là là, je vous demande pardon, Madame Sophie. Prenez place! Installez-vous! Where does your French come from, my dear?' Sophie was younger than the rest and she had an accent the teacher at the Crombietown French Circle couldn't place.

'Je viens de Moscou.'

'Tiens, et moi de Limoges.'

There were between ten and twelve of them, all women, who gathered round the conference table every Tuesday morning at eleven. Maître Claude Garon had founded the group some years ago, coinciding with his retirement to the seaside town.

Peggy Ferguson, a well-dressed, well-spoken woman extended a hand. 'Welcome to the French Circle, Mrs McFadden.'

'Likewise,' said Maud Arrowsmith, who ran the local bookshop and had enjoyed measuring her talents beside those of the newcomer.

Peggy whisked Sophie off to lunch at the Eagle.

They were joined by Louise Southam, wife of the town's chief architect and a spasmodic, social, attendee of Claude Garon's class. Both wanted to hear more of what brought Sophie McFadden 'to this part of the world'.

'Well, obviously, getting married.' They sat at Peggy's favourite table, in the bay window, beside the fireplace, and ordered schooners of dry sherry all round and a hot lunch.

'What we want to ask you, Sophie, is what it was like out there? How did you survive? Are you perhaps a revolutionary yourself?'

Sophie laughed, keen to diminish the differences that made her a stranger. 'How is it in Russia? You ask me. Well, some people lead easier, freer lives than others, like here, and that's most of the trouble. What to do about it.'

Since no solutions presented themselves to that general dilemma of inequality leading to misery for some and joy for others they moved on to talk about Louise's sister who had just got divorced.

'Did I hear, Sophie, that in Russia they've introduced "free love"?'

'That's true.'

'But that's extraordinary. How will society hold together without marriage?'

Sophie shrugged, as any intelligent person might.

But after Sophie had left, Louise said she was certain Sophie believed in free love.

Lunch with Peggy, preferably without Louise, became a weekly habit.

'Look, I've got something to say.'

'I knew it. I could see it in your face,' said Peggy.

'Yes.'

'Sophie, dear, congratulations!'

As Sophie made her announcement she told herself she would still be who she was, even though she was to have a child she hadn't wanted so soon in her life.

They smoked again over milky coffees. The Eagle was always busy on a weekday lunchtime.

'Have you got a date?'

'The second week in June.'

'My eldest was a summer baby.'

'When they're old in their class at school it gives them a better chance.'

'School! That's a long way ahead.'

Sophie and Peggy, for they were the two who took to each other, came out of the warm stewed air of the tavern into the cool and windy high street, and parted.

In fact Sophie was in a state of extreme confusion. On the journey back to Knockie, Peter Bruce watching in his rear-view mirror thought he saw Mrs McFadden in tears, though perhaps it was just peakiness from you know what. As they said goodbye on the steps down from the bus, and he beamed at her, she asked after his dogs.

'Little beauties,' he proclaimed, dismissing what he had heard, that Mrs McFadden was an advocate of free love. She seemed so nice.

Whatever she was an advocate of, she couldn't bear to go straight home so early and when Peter Bruce left her beside the church she took a turn past Alison's shop, stared in and waved. Then she made a large loop which took in the old harbour. *Prima gravida*, the seagulls screamed. John O'Neill had confirmed it.

'Oh but, Sophie darling, that's wonderful.'

And there were tears in his eyes equal to but quite different from the tears she had wept the night it happened.

But Duncan was becoming ever more strange to her. He appeared in a suit on a Sunday. 'Some occasion I should know about?' she asked sarcastically. 'Some tea with the entire Bruce clan?' She felt wildly hostile.

'I'm going to church.'

'I seem to remember marrying a progressive man.'

'Sophie,' he lowered his voice, 'in Knockie, as you may have noticed, it's important to fit in. No one demands to know what you actually have in your heart.'

'I know. It's called hypocrisy and feebleness.'

'She was extreme,' said Leksy, 'as a matter of temperament. It's a human condition often confused with being passionate about certain causes.'

I replied that she cared for self-knowledge, which surely she grew towards.

'If it was self-knowledge, in the end it came at a very high price,' he avowed.

14

Arthur Gillard declared that Sophie's pregnancy was worth coming home for rather more than the mess of his professional career. That autumn the White Army recovered in the north and east. The chances were the Bolshevik uprising would now be crushed and Russia could return to a more moderate path, which in turn calmed Foreign Office fears of the Turk. Compensating him for having ignored his advice hitherto, his masters now promoted Gillard to major and invited him to begin his new duties at home by addressing senior colleagues in Edinburgh. The offer was generous, and instead of resigning he acquiesced, which left him cursing the average human moral fate, above which his own failed to rise.

'Our political masters really are a rum lot.'

He and Duncan drank to that in the bar of his hotel.

'Sophie have any feelings about what's happening back there?'

'I don't think she's bothered either way, so long as her father is safe.'

'You liked him.'

'Oh yes, quite a character.'

Arthur slumped into his preoccupations. 'I tell them the Reds should take over Russia and Kemal take over in Turkey, which they ignore and disagree with, and then they promote me to make me shut up. Ha!'

'You should be a newspaper correspondent. You'd have more freedom.'

'Never! That would be far too disorderly an existence for me. You see I need the Army. That's why I hate them.'

Duncan, as he sped on two wheels down the long hill towards Cowie, was nevertheless happy that Arthur was back, and not second to that, that he had a child on the way. Whizzing down Cowie hill he relived his boyhood, and the pleasure was only clouded these days by the prospect of the return journey.

The few motor vehicles that passed him – people round here don't have the money to buy themselves private motor cars, he heard himself address the chamber of concerned local councillors whose number he had recently joined – well, even the most powerful of those motor vehicles had to crawl in low gear up this damned mountainside. What a slog! He couldn't even make it halfway. Immediately at the bottom he got off and pushed. And still he had to stop every few minutes to find more room in his lungs. A bus passed, and a motor, and another cyclist who was even now standing on his pedals and pumping with each side of his body to get more leverage. Duncan pushed his machine in a dignified fashion up the hill as the red light of the dynamo trailed by the energetic pumper flickered in the distance and vanished. What an absurd display! Why do young men show off so?

That he had to work so hard to make the top of a hill he had raced up as a boy he needed to tell to someone, however, for he was only twenty-five. I know that You don't exist, God, but who else speaks the language of existence but You? I just have to ask You. Is my life to be good and long, despite everything, or my premature end long drawn out? Why do you offer me a full life and then every day threaten to end it?

At O'Neill's surgery two people were ahead of him. Mr Rogers, Alison's employer, and Mrs Forbes, the widowed owner of the Buchan Arms, occupying herself with her knitting. Duncan acknowledged them but refused to be drawn into conversation.

Mrs Forbes nodded back at him. To ask after his health where they were sitting would have seemed foolish.

Mr Rogers, Fanny's rejected beau, seemed to have matured in the flesh to no purpose. His masculine gender, his creased dark suit, his paunch, served what end in nature, exactly? Duncan was in a frightful mood. Then he remembered Fanny had reproached him with getting more like his acerbic wife every day, and that he had promised to try to curb this trend.

He associated Mrs Forbes entirely with the Buchan Arms, with, incidentally, its engraving of McClintock Castle. He was glad Sophie found something to like. As for the Buchan Arms, which became an issue because the Church despised the sale of alcohol, Duncan didn't know who to side with. Why shouldn't Knockie have a social centrepiece? As his wife said, one or two drinks were not going to ruin a man, although, it was true, he personally never went to the Buchan Arms unless he attended a function there. Drink didn't exactly recommend itself, having destroyed his parents' marriage. Still surely Mrs Forbes was the good woman she seemed. The way Knockie divided itself along the lines of the damned and the saved, and how he was now forced to take sides to be accepted as a Knockie local councillor, depressed him.

Mr Rogers was in and out. Nothing much the trouble there, unless it was terminal. The frightful mood had not abated.

'Lieutenant McFadden,' the nurse looked up.

Dr O'Neill, whom he had known from his schooldays, stood up and extended an arm as Duncan went in and closed the door.

'Sit down, sit down! What can I do for you?'

Still Duncan bristled. The cold stethoscope on his white chest intruded into his private being. The need to defend himself also against the advice O'Neill had given his wife, and that damned gadget, made it difficult to get the words out that expressed his fear.

To which incoherent jumble came the calm answer: 'You've a while yet, man. What's the panic?'

'Be more specific, John,' he cried, seeing the red light of the other man's dynamo receding from him, leaving him plunged in darkness.

'Ten, twenty years, how am I supposed to know? You could see your grandchildren.'

Duncan subsided.

'My money is on a boy, by the way. That suit you?'

His confidence grew again. Greedily he imagined not only a son but a grandson. That would take the McFaddens into the twenty-first century, provided the world stayed peaceful.

'Stupid but I'd rather the McFaddens didn't die out.'

'You are crazy, man. To have these thoughts at your age.'

But the panic had to do with once again letting little Knockie set the terms of his existence. In the Army he had escaped that confinement. Probably it was the debt to his mother which led to his insistence on having a child. Something of her he wanted to carry on, in case, well, he couldn't really hope Fanny would have children, and Alison seemed to have no energy in that direction.

He ran his eye round the surgery and then walked across it. 'Your patients must enjoy coming here, John.'

'So long as I haven't got bad news for them.'

The window of the consulting room looked on to a well-kept garden, punctuated by familiar shrubs at routine intervals. The doctor and his family lived in the rest of the house.

'I mean you've made it pleasant. Sophie must like it. She says Seaview is dreary and old-fashioned.'

John O'Neill wanted to say he couldn't start writing prescriptions for interior decoration. On the other hand environments did seem to affect what people called their souls. Nowadays when a doctor qualified he was urged to study some psychology, to understand the souls in which people buried their needs. Maybe in fifty years' time doctors would be writing prescriptions for furnishings.

Duncan turned from looking at the two colourful modern paintings on the wall. 'I wanted a son.' As if having those two modern works of art in his own home would have blocked that ambition.

'As I say, you stand a good chance of having a son, my friend.'

'That bloody gadget' came to mind as a cause for renewed anger. A married man could feel wholly justified, protesting. But the impulse receded.

Duncan tipped his cap to Mrs Forbes, just as she was counting the stitches she had to cast on. She was the little port's social centrepiece. People needed a place to meet and commiserate. He would never again cast aspersions on the Buchan Arms.

The ailing man wheeled his bicycle home through the high-walled lanes.

*

'Fanny, we must talk.'

'Sophie,' Fanny took the recently confirmed *prima gravida* by the shoulders and looked upon her even kindly, 'you can't come here and expect us to change to be more like you.'

Fanny had a large, square face, and when as always in public she scraped her hair back into a bun, her high brow and cheekbones stood out.

'You won't make me the same as you, Fanny. I have my own ambitions which are quite, quite different.'

'And we have ours.'

The difficulty lay with who should determine the cast of Duncan's life, but it couldn't be said.

15

Sophie had told Duncan she wanted their child to open his – or her – eyes to rooms full of colour and light. The scullery, with its dark shiny yellowy-green paint, was particularly abhorrent.

'It makes me vomit.'

Her husband replied: 'I'm sure it will pass. What did Dr O'Neill say?'

'Why should I ask him about how to decorate my house? If you won't do anything I'll tackle Fanny myself.'

When around four-thirty in the afternoon Fanny distilled herself some health-giving brew with which to wash down a slice of toast and butter, Sophie joined her and set out her plans.

'We've no spare money for decorating. Especially not with the bairn on the way.'

'So my baby is now the reason why change won't happen instead of the reason why it should.'

Quite forgetting Fanny for a moment, she looked away from the green-slime paint of the scullery, over the cold faintly sticky linoleum which led into the hall, and out into a more beautiful life. She summoned to mind the colours in the little paintings in John O'Neill's surgery. One day the vision of that artist would translate into how she would furnish her house in some other life.

'That's nonsense about the cost. I'll paint the walls myself if I have to. I'd like my child to come into a world that's a joy to look at.'

Fanny strained her brew and set out her tea on a tray.

Sophie leaned against the lintel as she waited for the kettle to boil again, She examined her own consciousness and tried to understand how it worked. 'You know, Fanny – you know, one has to relax a little bit to be happy. Live for the moment.'

'I'd rather you didn't practise your new-fangled ideas on me, Sophie. Heaven forbid that they should reach baby.'

'You think he'll overhear? That's a laugh.' But the matter was serious. Sophie blocked Fanny's path. 'Fanny, the new century is not going away. And nor is what I believe in. We're not going to live half our lives in secret any more. Especially not us women. It's taken the twentieth century a while to start properly. As long as I've been alive. But we can get it right, with honesty, and confidence. My idea of how we women should live is not going to change just because I'm carrying a child. There must be reason and equality. Then there can be hope.'

When Fanny shook her head Sophie felt sorry for her. But it was false to think she was in the superior position, and Fanny began to think Sophie was a real troublemaker, as she followed her into the dining-room where the exercise books in need of correction were stacked and a meagre coal fire flickered in the small grate.

Christmas came and they all went to church, even Sophie. There was a four-together walk after lunch, round the village and down to the sea, then tea with the Bruces.

Then it snowed again and the snow lay on the ground for three days.

New Year was a town feast marked by Scottish dancing and singing in the Buchan Arms. Sophie for the first time saw Duncan wear a kilt and wondered at how little she knew him. Since autumn he had also grown a beard. On the morning of 1 January 1920 they all put on overcoats and hats and gloves and scarves and went down to the crumbling quay no one would pay to repair. Not the government. Not the council. Not the owners of the fishing boats. Louise

Southam's ex-brother-in-law, Angus Nove, had written a letter to the local press encapsulating the popular view: that it was the Germans who should pay, for having destroyed world markets with their war. The whole of this country it was easier for Sophie to call England was so distressed at the innocence it had lost, and yet it wouldn't admit it.

As the wind scoured away the clouds, the local brass band played. Mr Rogers stood at the far end of the second row, blowing like a baroque putto into his mouthpiece and sliding the arm of his instrument with mechanical efficiency. All that effortful sound rising into the air and dissipating back into nothingness. Sophie noted down that she liked to feel human energy could be harnessed to some real end, and not just evaporate with the passing of a life.

Then it was Russian New Year, as only she called it, but the date on the calendar was useful to many people that post-Hogmanay of 1920, because it marked the occasion when the Whites, despite all prediction, failed to take Petrograd. The shocked analysts in London and their colleagues in Aberdeen and Cowie once more went into conclave. She pictured her father shrugging, with a faint smile on his face, having conceded he was wrong, but now able to retract his concession. 'Things happen the way they happen. Pushkin said that. It's probably for the best.'

Sophie trailed after her sister-in-law. 'In any case I'd be grateful if you could move that compost bin outside. It's that which makes me retch.'

'The sickness will pass.' Fanny held fast. This was her home too.

In January in the Knockie inner town, that tight weave of a few small criss-crossed streets that Sophie loved, along with the sea and McClintock Point, Fanny was back at school every weekday, while a quarter of a mile away, along the more open East High Street where the bus passed, Alison expertly unfolded her reams of cloth and held them taut against the brass tape-measure on the edge of the counter. Customers gave her tasks to match the unmatchable and left swatches for comparison with the books of samples. She probably enjoyed that exercise best, because it involved some imagination, and she could see how much it pleased her customers if she could solve their dilemma. Knockie women, most of whom had at some time attended the same school that Alison had, bought dress material and suiting and rummaged through the remnants basket at the far end of the counter for bright pieces to make cushions and scarves and patchwork. They needed trimmings to cover upholstery seams, and metal buttons to cover with fabric and set in place to form attractive gathers on a chair back. Mr Rogers sat in the back room with the door open in case his expertise or authority were needed. In the meantime, he busied himself with orders and receipts and tax matters, and the racing results. In quiet moments Alison rocked on her feet and stared out of the window.

Sophie left alone tried on her husband's clothes. His shirts and jackets nicely covered her bump. With a tailed white shirt of soft cotton she pulled on a pair of his calf-high boots, nothing in between, and examined herself in the mirror. She wore his ties around her neck, with nothing beneath, so that the long tail of silk plunged down between her breasts from the loose knot she tied around her neck. It was fun to dress up as a man and have secrets, in a village where, every time she went into the post office to write again to her father the postwoman, June Bruce, had the stamps and the airmail sticker for Russia ready.

In Crombietown she was freer. She walked about as far from the Library and the Pleasure Gardens as it was possible to go through the town without getting into the country and then back again; retraced her steps; pursued her course; changed her library books and enjoyed her friends.

Still for real, introspective, excursions she needed the castle and the sea.

The cliff path was rising now, with green fields to the left, and with it her own determination. When Sophie turned to take in the view Knockie had shrunk to a cluster of stone houses in the valley, around the rivermouth, with only the great spire of the Free Church of St Peter to distinguish it.

Back home she kept the bedroom very warm with a little two-bar electric fire confiscated from the sitting-room.

He couldn't bear it. 'It's terribly hot in here.'

She also didn't want him around. 'I need it. This is such an uncomfortable house.'

'I'll see if Fanny needs a hand,' he said.

She called after him: 'Duncan, I'm going to get the decorators in. There'll be white in the scullery for a start and something friendly in the bairn's own room.'

He came back. 'Would she have liked to go to dinner with Arthur and his wife? He had decided for her that she would not.

When boredom hit her, the frustration of her freedom, she always did *something* with it. She did the clothes thing over and over because it was exciting. She opened the grim, heavy, brown wardrobe which took up a disproportionate amount of space in their bedroom and took out in turn his shirts, his jackets and his trousers, and those seductive cavalry boots. Over her naked body she buttoned the long-tailed white shirt and slipped her bare feet into the boots, and paraded. Her slender thighs were shamelessly displayed in the space in between. To the shirt further unbuttoned she added a tie at half-hitch. Then she changed them both for a tweedy sports jacket over her own enormously stretched camisole. In another age she might have disguised herself permanently as a man and run away to sea.

Otherwise she took Dr O'Neill's advice to get out. She would walk to beyond the horizon, to where no one here imagined a woman alone could go. She chose the gorse-strewn headland where the path emerged into the open opposite the submerged hilltop castle. She would have walked out to sea if only that were possible, a feeling she had the very night they arrived from London: that she didn't want the train to stop even if it ran out of rails. To travel on was the thing.

It was a time of self-enquiry and rebellion. The sea was a pathetic living being because it could never affect what was happening on its human shore. Yet as she walked along the cliff path, watching the waves rise like lions rampant and crash like human folly and trickle away, she felt another consciousness alongside hers, a friend in the joy and struggle to live.

At the war memorial site she watched as the stone cross was manoeuvred into place to stand outside St Peter's. June Bruce caught a glimpse of her, holding her head high. Sophie, whose name and pregnancy evoked the suspicion of 'free love' among the people of Knockie, or perhaps they were just mystified by the McFadden marriage, walked on.

On the headland every stone and every crevice and every dead insect, every stray feather and bone, and perhaps every bird wheeling overhead, was the same as last time. She liked the familiarity of that.

The castle itself was one of those sublime vantage points, such as Arthur Gillard had shown her in Conny, that was both beautiful and bewildering. You just looked at it, and the rocks all around, and listened to the sea, knowing you couldn't learn how to live from gazing at nature and yet that somewhere in nature you too belonged.

One day she bought a bottle of whisky in the Buchan Arms. People would notice, and talk, but what of it, she jeered in her anger. 'A present for Jim Bruce on his retirement from the railway,' she said.

'That's very thoughtful of you, Mrs McFadden.'

Mrs Forbes behind the bar reflected how upset the Temperance people would be to know the users of alcohol had a new recruit.

'Fanny and Alison well?'

Sophie nodded.

'You must miss your country.'

'Now and again.'

Mrs Forbes, turning to draw a pint for June Bruce's elderly father, wondered whether the McFadden baby would come out speaking Russian. As she did so Sophie stood prettily reflected in the mirror behind the bar, amid the forest of bottles.

She slipped the heavy glass bottle, with its square shoulders, still wrapped in the tissue paper that made it suitable for presentation to an esteemed member of the community, into the pocket of her long mackintosh, and made her way down, away from the station and past the Free Church, seawards. It was a rare gorgeous early-spring day, with a light, teasing wind and almost unbroken sunshine. The salt air filled with the smell of freshly turned soil in the neatly kept gardens along Crombie Street. She passed the green, recently mown recreation ground, where the boys and the men played football, and the public baths. A track between a tall-chimneyed granite-faced house and a modest whitewashed cottage showed how many people

72

before Sophie McFadden had wanted to escape Knockie and conjoin with the sea.

This was not life as she had planned it, and the Scotch, like her dressing up as a man, underscored her disappointment.

16

The baby grew huge. When it turned in its unseen pouch it touched a nerve that sent shooting pains down her right leg and would have flung her to the ground if she hadn't tottered and reached for support, which made people in the port of Knockie and the town of Crombietown even sympathise with Mrs McFadden, for it couldn't be long now, and perhaps she could be forgiven for buying herself a bottle of Scotch.

He might kick her while she was standing on the edge of the cliff. But surely he needed his mother and would be gentle. She swigged the whisky from the bottleneck and let it run its fiery course. She never drank so much as to enter a tunnel from which there was no exit. A real Russian *zapoi* lasted weeks and went through stages that only a doctor or a poet of darkness could imagine. But she drank now, a little, to feel free and make time pass.

Then it occurred to her who could do the decorating.

Knockie was a small place and all she had to do was keep her eyes open. 'Mr Dewar! Mr Dewar!' She spotted him leaving the Buchan Arms.

Alison at least had agreed to move farther upstairs so they could have the baby close by.

Micky Dewar spread his large right hand over the surface of the wall.

In the bedroom beside their own there was a patch of damp in the angle between wall and ceiling, above the window which looked east over the lanes. The existing paint was brown, with a floral paper on the wall.

'I'd like the paper stripped off and the walls plain.'

'I could start on Monday.'

'Monday, then?'

'Monday next week.'

'But what about the damp, Mr Dewar?'

'Nothing, Mrs McFadden. Only an old stain.'

In the evening she told the family over high tea. 'Micky Dewar is coming on Monday to do the baby's room.'

Even Fanny acquiesced. Everyone felt sentimental about the approaching birth.

'Poor Mr Dewar. Everyone must give him some work. I'm sure he's a good decorator.'

'And Mr Dewar's friends? And their friends? It's the government needs to step in where unemployment's concerned.'

'It's all very well to generalise, Duncan, but I'm thinking of one person.'

'But politics is a matter for generalisation. If we can't paint a general picture we'll never get the government to help this area.'

'Yes, yes, of course you're right.' In Crombietown she found a lovely blue-grey distemper and paid to have it delivered. She waved to Louise Southam but didn't cross the road. Friday passed, and it became the weekend.

Stripping the layers of old paper took Micky a full day. He smelt of tobacco and the house felt quite different when he was there. She took him a cup of tea at regular intervals. There were two layers, one for Duncan's mother's generation and one for her mother's. Bit by bit Micky washed away the choices made by Duncan's mother and grandmother as if they had never lived. He wetted the layers of paper with warm water and a sponge and then clawed at them with a scraper. Make way for the new! New life is queuing up for a space! It was a brutal process, but it was in her and her child's favour.

'Mrs McFadden, I ought to line these walls if you just want them painted. We need three rolls of lining paper ideally.'

'I'll order them in Crombietown tomorrow.'

'I'm sorry to put you to extra trouble.'

'No, no, I usually go into Crombietown on a Tuesday. They could deliver them on Wednesday I'm sure.'

Micky ended up pasting the lining paper to the wall on Friday, and taking advantage of the weekend to let it dry.

'Does it always need two days to dry?' Instead of which she asked: 'Do you believe in free love?'

He couldn't believe she'd said that. He didn't even know what free love was.

'Exciting place, is it, Moscow?'

'Very exciting.'

'Not like here then.'

'No. Not like here.' She was standing in the doorway and he dared look her in the eye.

On the second Monday, for this was now quite a drawn-out job, he had two coats of distemper on the walls by lunchtime. He said he couldn't come on Tuesday, which quite suited her, so the gloss was only finished on Wednesday morning.

'If you'd like to inspect – '

'I would. Oh!' The empty space made her twirl about in the unfurnished room. 'It's lovely. Truly lovely.' He threw open the window to get rid of the unpleasant smell of oil and lead and watched her dance.

'So we'll meet again? I often walk out to McClintock Point.'

No, no, he hadn't heard. 'Give my regards to Mr McFadden. If there's anything he's not happy with . . . '

'Oh, yes, oh, yes.' She saw him down the path.

They met opposite the submerged castle. She knew every rock and bush. He startled her nevertheless.

'Don't be frightened, Mrs McFadden.'

'Micky! I'm so glad you've come.'

'The baby's huge.' He studied her. 'It's a long walk in your condition.'

'Touch it.' She took his hand and made him blush.

She stroked his face and brushed his lips with hers. Finally she stepped back as if he were a picture she were painting.

His upper lip was trembling. 'I remember the day you arrived. You walked so fast I had to run to catch up with you. And I said to myself: one day, I'll have a woman like that, who walks fast.'

'You don't mind?' She indicated the baby that lay invisible between them.

Not speaking, he put his hand on the bump again and she covered his hand with hers.

They sat down, leaning against the prickly bank. She stroked his soft, damp, mousy hair.

'I asked you if you believed in free love.'

'What's that?'

'I suppose it's this.'

'Doesn't have to have a name, does it?'

'No, no, you're right.'

They were kissing. His kisses were enquiring; not timid.

'No,' she said. 'Not here.'

They met, who knows? the next day, the day after? He knew a bothy where he and his pals had gone to smoke cigarettes, when they were boys, and to feel they were the exciting new generation; ten years ago now.

There were a few planks resting on a couple of rocks, and more planks to sit on. He helped her to sit down on the planks, where he laid his coat, though she was perfectly able. What he was about to do did not come naturally to him, he had to admit.

'It's all right, you know. Love is love. Everybody feels it, everyone wants it.'

'But Mrs McFadden you're married and – '

The extent of his shame for what he ought not to do made him giddy.

'Come and sit beside me then. Or don't you want to?'

He should have hated her in that moment. But then she said: 'I need you, you see? I'm the kind of woman who doesn't want to be married . . . like this.' She gestured through the stone walls of the little hideout vaguely back towards the town. 'If I could design human relationships and society everything would be different.'

'You might make people unhappy.'

'I might. I'd make others happy.'

'Like you.'

'Like us. Look, Micky, the thing is to be free. You're not free. Look at you, so full of fear.' She stroked his head and leaned towards him. 'Relax. You make both of us feel clumsy.'

So he did relax, and then the fire spread, and there was no turning back.

'Sure, Mrs McFadden? Sophie?'

'Sweet friend, this is what we're made for, you and me.'

'Oh goddammit!' It was like hurling himself over a cliff. 'I'll squash the littl'un.'

John O'Neill told Leksy years later that his father was a traditional man who probably neglected Sophie while she was pregnant. But I believe she was also a woman who, for all her intelligence, sometimes forgot the difference between fact and fantasy. She wanted her baby made anew, freely.

'So that's how I came to have the second of my three fathers.'

'Indeed.'

We had to smile.

In the bothy they fell over each other. They manoeuvred. They reached out. They became quickly so familiar with each other that they began to joke at the baby's expense, that the poor creature might need to take cover; wear a hood; but surely he would understand.

They walked back to the castle one fine day in the first week of May. 'What do you think? Did the woman at the window have a lover?'

'It was you and me. We only don't remember.'

The earth was dry, the grey roots forcing themselves up through cracks. The deep pink blossoms were bursting out. An ant ran over her hand.

On the golf course, John O'Neill asked: 'How's Sophie?'

'I think she's fine but that doesn't mean I understand her moods.' Duncan left that remark to sink in. 'Look, John, to tell the truth I was furious about that gadget you gave her.'

The doctor stopped in his tracks. 'You've a child on the way, man, doesn't that please you?'

'Damn it, man, it created a difficulty between us.'

'I'm sorry to hear that. Your wife came to me as her doctor. I presumed you'd discussed the planning of your family.'

Duncan practised his drive with a vigorous swipe at the air. 'So far as I was concerned there was nothing to discuss.'

O'Neill held up his hands.

Duncan was lost for a moment as to what he actually wanted to say but then what emerged as he set his ball on the tee was, 'She's well out of Bolshevik Russia.'

'You mean you rescued her.'

'In a manner of speaking.'

'I hope you never let her feel that.'

Neither of them played well. They had walked over to a bunker of sand, where O'Neill was trying to chop his ball back on to the course. 'It's extraordinary how you two met.'

'You can say that again.'

'Is she in touch with home?'

'She writes to her father. She follows what's going on there in the papers.'

O'Neill achieved his shot and they walked on.

Duncan drove off anew, with one of those rare cracks of the whip which makes golf seem suddenly like a man's game, rather than genteel time-wasting.

'She calls herself "a Bolshevik of the heart".'

O'Neill suppressed his amusement.

'It makes it difficult for us all to live together.'

'Duncan, man, she has a fiery nature. That's why we love her.'

They played on, more or less evenly.

'Perhaps Sophie should do a degree.'

'Perhaps after the baby.'

'Duncan, having a baby does not disable a woman.'

The next party waited impatiently as they wandered off into the distance.

17

Duncan waltzed about the room, stroking his son's dark and hairy head. He stared in disarmed astonishment at the child who nestled in his shoulder. Alison entered the bedroom with a broad smile and a giggle concealing the fact that she had no idea what to feel, or what she should say.

'Our new mother should rest now.'

Fanny went to take him.

'Leave him with me,' Sophie insisted and was allowed to have her way.

She loved the tightly wrapped white bundle in her arms, with his waxy pink skin and questing blue eyes. Leksy, she said, follows shapes around the room. Leksy always knows when a new shape enters.'

Her husband was more practical. 'The vicar asked about a date for Alex's christening.' They had officially agreed to call him Alex but privately she favoured 'Leksy', which surely sounded somewhat like 'Micky'.

'Is a christening necessary? Neither of us believes in God.'

Duncan moved to the window. 'I'd prefer to avoid a scandal, Sophie.'

The congregation dressed up. Alison wore a cloche hat and the fashionable black dress to mid-calf they had sewn together. She took a shawl to keep herself warm in the church and Sophie said she should try not to wear it, because it made her outfit less glamorous. 'But I'll be cold, Sophie!' Fanny made herself almost elegant with a new dark green dress she had taken the train to Aberdeen to buy. A choker of small black rings in some fine material showed off how young her throat was and a mustard-coloured wide-brimmed hat which half-hid her eyes drew attention to a mouth grown almost soft with the enchantment and kindness that the birth of a new child spreads. Sophie herself eased over her head a blue crêpe de Chine dress she had bought with Duncan when they first passed through London. She smoothed it over her slim hips and once again flat belly and felt well. Her body was her own again.

As the family gathered beside the font made of the same stone as the sunken castle, and the men and women of Knockie filled the benches, among them Mrs Forbes and Mr Rogers and John O'Neill and Major Arthur Gillard, the new arrival rolled his eyes around God's interminable spaces.

The priest, new to Knockie, was pale, clean-shaven and reserved.

Until the shock of the water the baby was silent. But back in his mother's arms he shrieked, fixing his eyes on the blue crêpe and searching for her breast. 'Poor little thing,' said Fanny, watching the tiny mouth open and close like a fish's.

All the minutes her Leksy was in the priest's hands Sophie wanted to snatch him back.

Gillard was among a few who noticed her de-christen him with the tip of her tongue and her own saliva. 'Be your own man, Leksy!'

'Congratulations, Mrs McFadden.'

'Why thank you, Major Gillard!' She acknowledged his promotion.

'Sophie,' he took her aside. 'You look simply marvellous.'

They were similar, in the ambiguities they fell into and the daring freedoms they extracted from them, at least in their minds. He'd known that already in Conny, when she was barely matured as a woman.

'Thank you, Arthur.' He handed her a glass of champagne and kept one for himself. He toasted her over the lip of the glass. Champagne was a rare treat in Knockie which Gillard had afforded the young family.

Fanny, spellbound and rejoicing, was named and blessed as Alex's godmother, and had been allowed to carry the baby , wrapped in an embroidered christening shawl Alison had sewn for the occasion, across the village as the party trooped into the Buchan Arms for refreshments. There were crustless cucumber sandwiches, and tinned-salmon sandwiches, and vol-au-vent pastry cases with chicken in white sauce, and the plates soon emptied.

'So you're more worried about Russia than Turkey these days, in your Foreign Office. '

'Your Russian friends are dangerous liars and quite uncivilised.'

'That's unfair.'

'Ah, Mrs McFadden, you're a Bolshevik at heart your husband tells me.'

'Of the heart is how I've tried to describe it. Obviously not very successfully.'

He indulged her. Whatever she was he liked.

18

'*Je suis née à Moscou et longtemps j'habitais cette ville. Je me souviens . . .*'

The room was at the back of the Crombietown Library and a pretty light fell on them through a series of panelled, particoloured windows that looked out on the side of the Pleasure Gardens. It added to the magic.

She did impress them, Leksy repeated. The way she spoke French gave them the impression she had just walked out of *War and Peace*.

'I read the notebooks,' I said. 'The French Circle was a time of revelation.'

'It was like her reaction to those paintings in John O'Neill's surgery. She immersed herself in the differing spirits of men. The books she loved gave her the space to understand herself.'

After the second meeting of the French Circle, Miss Arrowsmith had caught up with Mrs McFadden in the High Street and urged her to visit her bookshop. She was a small, neat, efficient-looking woman, with premature grey hair, who in her swift independent stride resembled Sophie.

On the threshold, as if from beneath the doormat, a bell sounded. It put Sophie in mind of clanging bridges and crashing cymbals and Fanny's gong. 'Beware, all ye who enter here!'

A middle-aged man looked round from where he was filing new stock.

'And this is Stephen.'

Sophie shook hands with a thin, reticent man, actually about Duncan's age, in shirtsleeves and heavy brown-framed glasses.

'I guess you ladies are good at the parley-vous,' Stephen said, and immediately regretted it.

'We're not bad at all,' replied Maud, and that was the relationship between them.

Maud was a passionate independent scholar who held out in her superior way against such gossip you wouldn't believe! That study made the womb barren and denatured a woman was typical of popular opinion.

'*Voilà les tomes dont tu as besoin*, Sophie. Charles Baudelaire's *Poésie*, introduced by Paul Valéry. Most of us buy an English crib too, for which I can recommend Charles Baudelaire, *Selected Poems*, with an introduction by J. Middleton Murry, London, 1915. Mr Murry, no 'a', is quite a *savant*. *Madame Bovary* you know. Stephen will make you a nice parcel.'

And he did. She watched him. He made a wonderful job, like a nurse, of the corners.

Sophie tore open the parcel and began reading as soon as Peter Bruce let her on board the 3 p.m. bus.

She let that novel ravish her – but then hurled it away. What woman could share in that denigration of another?

The poems by Baudelaire, by contrast, were true and kind.

Claude Garon presided over those Tuesday-morning meetings with the authority of a schoolmaster and the heart of a friend.

'It is Baudelaire's deliberate rejection of a happy and comfortable existence we must *celebrate* . . . and that Christ-like compassion which left him so vulnerable that his only defence was high fashion. You know that the only way he could keep hold of himself, among the poor and the sick and the destitute, was to dress up to the nines!' Claude told the circle, which provoked an agreeable murmur, shifting into uneasy laughter.

'Ladies, I don't know how it is for you, but for my part I am amazed at how people incline to talk about failure – and the human failures Baudelaire went among. People speak of failure in life when they have no real inkling of what the opposite might be. The one positive state they contrast with failure is material comfort. But material comfort can be no *real* person's ambition. I am not preaching poverty and resignation. But perhaps it is the case that the real, satisfied spirit of a person can't begin to grow until there is some adversity. Certainly that is the place from which Baudelaire's poetry springs.'

'*Je l'ai beaucoup aimé,*' Sophie declared.

Still from Sophie they wanted not philosophy but the disclosure of secrets. 'Sophie, what is it like *en Russie*? We hear so much in the way of political upheaval. Seriously, will you tell us one day?'

'Ah, Peggy! I'm not the one to tell you. I've been away now for more than two years.'

But Peggy insisted she talk to them about revolutionary Russia, as if forcing her to take sides. Crombietown, where the rumour of her free love had spread, demanded to know Madame Sophie better.

In the Crombietown library she became a well-known figure. Had smoking been permitted in that silent, disciplined reading room her pleasure would have been complete. The town speculated upon her as a connoisseur of the cigarette, smoked in a long holder. And finally experienced her as a public speaker.

At that public meeting in Crombietown urged upon her by Peggy Ferguson, Madame Sophie made her oratorical debut. 'You may understand the Revolution as having a primarily political programme, ladies and gentlemen, but no great vision can be realised without a change in human behaviour. We must have more honesty in society about real needs. And not just material needs. I can tell you first-hand that the Bolsheviks have not "scrapped the soul" but have freed the physical life from religious constraint.'

Free love, they knew it!

'Equality for men and women, ladies and gentlemen! Equality means the same education, the same responsibilities and the same rights.'

A heckler insisted the Bolsheviks were the enemies of mankind.

'In that case so am I.' She returned his gaze.

There seemed to be a number of Communists in the audience, who asked Sophie about the theorists of the Revolution. She couldn't answer, so those who could did. Angus Nove, well-known in the town as an agitator, leapt to his feet and stayed there, reeling off names.

Jim Bruce's youngest son said he understood the class war but rejected the violence with which it was being carried out. 'They say priests are being shot.'

Nove told the young Donald Bruce that was absolutely a Western lie.

'I beg to disagree,' insisted Peggy's husband, who as a solicitor was a prominent figure in Crombietown. 'The Communist regime is criminal.'

The meeting had long since run away from Sophie when Maud, in the chair, turned to her. 'One last message for us, Mrs McFadden?'

Sophie got to her feet. 'Why yes! Down with the landowners and the capitalists! And long live equality and free love!'

Duncan stared at her.

'Can you make sense of what she was doing?'

'She was gathering strength, building on the expectations others had of her. Without "being Russian" she was nothing to them, and so she used their expectations to feel her way in life.'

19

'Would that be via Aberdeen, Mrs McFadden, or via Inverness?' Malcolm Bruce had replaced his Uncle Jim as the stationmaster. He was a conscientious, always busy man, thin and nervous. He liked people, he said. But when you met him he was 'like a man fond of cricket but who only ever played in the nets, not the open field'.

She could now make trenchant judgements of other human beings, based on her year in Knockie.

'Inverness,' she said, on a whim. She carried a vanity case which had been a present from Duncan for her birthday.

The metal footbridge had been given a new coat of white paint.

Flaubert, that bitter patrician content to make sport out of a woman's downfall, what sense of beauty and goodness did he have compared with Baudelaire, who after a long journey at sea told the story of the bored sailors, so out of touch with decency on their equatorial crossing that they shot down an albatross for diversion. Who were the great mockers of life? She hated these destroyers.

After so many barely stirring villages she was pleased when they halted at the occasional town. The convoy of carriages, which had increased since Knockie from three to ten, finally drew parallel with tall yellow-brick London terraces coated with soot.

The shops of Oxford Street grew ever more imposing as she walked towards Marble Arch. The irregular ways of trade overlaid the regal regularity and breadth of that long straight road. Everywhere, on the pavements and inside the stores, goods were for sale. Mannequins modelled the latest daring fashions. How fashion quickened the blood! Skirts were a good four inches shorter down here, where the weather was milder and all the world brought its influence to bear. Crossing the broad street to the fanfare of a bobby's whistle, she finally spied the name North Audley Street and found where, by telephone, Peggy had booked her a room.

The room, soft-furnished in chintz, with a hand-basin, and a view from the fourth floor down into the street, was so pleasant she instantly imagined a lifetime there. She watched the passers-by for a while, then she had a bath in the tub along the corridor, changed into pyjamas and ate the sandwiches she had brought from home. Because she couldn't roam the streets alone in the evening, she sat in that hotel room and reflected upon her marriage.

'Remember that mistress of Lenin's I told you about? Her life was wasted. What no woman must do is waste her life. We're going to have such an interesting life together, Duncan. I'll learn about history and politics . . . and England . . . I really only know England from story books. Let's drink to England.' She had raised her glass in the restaurant where they dined on that brief London stopover on their return from abroad.

To an England so desperately grieving for its lost Eden she had drunk a toast, but now that that moment was past, either England's loss had to be denied, as Fanny tried to deny it, or everything had to change.

'Isn't it somehow worse when a beautiful person dies young? Really dies or even just dies in spirit? I think so. That's not going to happen to me.'

'Your mother and father both worried about not living enough.'

'As she told him even in Constantinople, she did not accept the doctrine of self-sacrifice.'

In Conny, Sophie had pictured her future husband as only what she saw, a man with no attachments, no background, no past. He had done the same, because he imagined only settling her in a new country; re-creating her, as husbands immemorial have wanted to do. She would be a new person there and he would be too.

But he regressed, whereas she, four floors up in North Audley Street, was only beginning to see the possibilities.

20

'How's Leksy?'

'Running about. Talking. Wearing Mrs Grant out with his energy. Peggy, I must tell you. I want to leave my husband. I made the most terrible mistake marrying Duncan.'

Peggy had a nurse's calm and practical intelligence. As if Sophie were claiming to have lost something, Peggy wondered whether she had spent long enough looking for it. 'Everyone has the occasional doubt.'

'I bet you never considered leaving Alan.' She paused to hear an answer, but none came.

'Everyone in Knockie knows me. I need you to post a letter to Russia from where it won't be noticed. And then to receive the reply. And give it to me.'

Sophie leaned forward over the brown sea in her soup bowl. 'Will you help me, Peggy? I can't do more than tell you what I've told you.' She handed her an envelope addressed to her father.

Peggy stowed the letter in her large ivory-coloured leather handbag, smiled, and patted the bag. Then they ate what they could of their haddock and peas and drank their tea.

Alan Ferguson had reservations.

He flattened his lips against his teeth and drew his whole mouth out into a grimace. 'I'm a lawyer. We lawyers are a suspicious lot. If I forward a letter in a language I can't understand it feels like I'm running the risk of receiving stolen goods. '

'Get someone to read it for you then.'

He looked surprised. 'You don't object to that, Pegs?'

'I want to help her.'

Alan asked around. Someone knew an émigré Russian who taught at the School of Slavonic Studies in London. 'Some Eye–van Dombrovsky.'

'Are you sure he's a Russian? He may be a Pole.'

'Goddammit.'

Dombrovsky, a mild-mannered literary critic who stayed abroad when the Revolution happened, replied by return of post.

He had tiny neat handwriting. ' "Dear Mr Ferguson, thank you for your enquiry. I will help you if I can but I must confess it is very difficult for me to follow Russian émigré politics and I can't be a hundred per cent sure about any conclusions I reach." You can say that again, Mr Dombrovsky. That's why I'm asking you.' Alan read the letter aloud over breakfast. 'Look here, even he says that to enter Russian politics is to enter a maze. God forbid!'

'I don't think Sophie has anything to do with politics.' Peggy pulled her toast into pieces and spread one of them thickly with butter and marmalade from the portions she had loaded on to her plate. 'I rather pushed her into that.'

'You could have fooled me from the way she spoke at that meeting.'

'As I say, that was my doing. I wanted to see her appreciated. There had to be some reason to invite an audience. But, Alan, you can't just send Sophie's letter to Mr Dombrovsky. You might not get it back. You must make a copy.'

'Of the Russian? It seems to me, my dear, that we're going round in circles.'

'In that case you'd better take it to London yourself.'

'I'll have to swear him to secrecy.'

'And so you will. And we'd better take the pledge ourselves.'

In fact Alan Ferguson steamed open Sophie's letter over the kettle just to make certain that a man of his education really couldn't understand it. Then he dried and refolded it and took it in the inside pocket of his suit jacket to London.

In his warm and well-proportioned office, courtesy of the University of London, where he sat surrounded by his books, Ivan Dombrovsky scanned the letter written in a bold hand so unlike his own. 'It's from a woman who wants to leave her husband. It's from a woman who is very fond of her father and wants his approval. And money. Mr Ferguson, I feel that you and I are prying.'

'Can't be helped.'

'That's all then.'

'In that case,' the lawyer got to his feet, 'thank you so much for your trouble. Here's my card. Do, Mr Dombrovsky, send me your invoice. I am, to repeat, most grateful.'

Alone again Dombrovsky sat with his hands behind his head in the rotating wooden chair the university had so thoughtfully provided for moments of reflection. He had whirled himself dizzy when he first moved into that room. What a web of untruths and half-truths and distrust we live in! God help us!

'Her father will notice that the envelope's been steamed open in transit, of course.'

'He needn't jump to the conclusion it happened our end.'

'I didn't know you had so much conspiracy in you, Alan.' Having resealed the letter carefully, Peggy Ferguson posted it when she went to Edinburgh, registered, with stamps guaranteed to carry it to Russia.

Sophie McFadden, Madame Sophie of Knockie and Crombietown, soon to become Sophie Asmus again, now began to dream intently of leaving Knockie and when Leksy was three she finally did, taking him with her to the place she called home before she was married.

21

A chicken poked its head out of a half-closed bag.

'How's life?'

'I could start to tell you, dear, but we'd both miss our stop.'

The woman took the boy's hesitant forefinger and brushed it against the chestnut feathers. The beast was jabbing its neck forward in mid-air.

'The drivers are all drunk these days.'

'That's a scandal.'

'They're drunk because they don't get paid. They don't pay them because they're drunk on home brew. God knows what goes into their hooch but it takes them far, far away, my dear, from where you and I are standing.'

Sophie felt amused and happy to be coming home. 'Perhaps they'll find what they want one day.'

'They're nothing but parasites and idlers behind steering wheels. That's what's wrong with our country.'

'It's going to get better now, I'm sure of that.'

The tram doors folded back in a series of jerks. Sophie glanced out of the window and grabbed her son. 'Come on!'

Outside the dusty street smelt of kerosene.

'Preobrazhensky Street?' she enquired.

The blond passer-by had the body of a lumberjack. 'Don't ask me, lady. I'm not from here.'

'Who can help us?' She turned, Leksy all the while holding her hand. 'Excuse me . . . '

A second man, with high cheekbones and dead eyes, grinned facetiously. 'You're not going anywhere, mother. Your kind don't live here any more.'

Which made her tell him off severely.

'Fuck you,' he cursed, leaving her to wonder whether to spit at her would have been worse.

Finally they found the way and she rang the bell of a newish, well-kept building in the heart of the city.

Her kindly father stooped down and took Lesky's hand. 'A pleasure to meet you, sir. *Ochen' pryatno.*'

With Ma Sophie hugged wordlessly, spying the new flat over her shoulder.

'You're back!' her father breathed.

'You'll have to do for yourself, Sofka!'

And with that, apologetically, both parents were gone to work.

When she and her son got up it was mid-afternoon. 'Mmm,' she exclaimed, 'fancy finding ourselves here! Did you sleep well, my Russian *mal'chik*?' He was silent and clung to her.

They ate *kasha* in the kitchen before dressing to go out. When the lift clanked and a weight went down as the pulley hauled up the car she felt the same childlike excitement as showed in his eyes, though he was still apprehensive. She took his hand as, downstairs, three floors beneath where they now lived, the huge door beyond the marble walls and the chandelier opened on to an unfamiliar street.

Central Moscow, spacious where official prestige mattered, nicely jumbled and hidden where it didn't, was still elegant and outwardly calm. Balletic and faintly greening birch trees reached skywards from pavements where muddy compacted snow had shrunk to traces staining shady patches. The outgoing winter was all used up. Whatever had changed, and in every direction some small change met her eyes, she imagined the city still rich with talk and pleasure behind its closed doors. People would be laughing and drinking and plotting round their tables. There was no comparison between life here and life in that cramped little port between the railway and the sea. For one thing we're not so inhibited here, we let our emotions run free. She gave money to a legless concertina-player. The other beggars noticed and began to hobble and shuffle, not towards her, but towards him.

'Comrade, you have to share the lady's charity with us. We're all equal now,' one shouted at the concertina player.

'You could pull your weight if you learnt some tunes,' retorted the musician, bent over himself, counting. Resignedly he let the coins leave his hands as fast as they had arrived.

She laughed even as she inspected her laughter. Russian humour was crazy. 'Good-day to you, gentlemen.'

The city looked as if it were undergoing a spring-clean, only instead of carpets hung out of the windows there were red placards proclaiming HOPE.

'Amazing, isn't it, Leks?'

'What do you remember?'
'Not a thing.'

She did their shopping with a glad heart, and only as she fumbled with her new keys on their return did a stranger whisper into her ear: 'Heh, *Burzhui*! This is a workers' state. There's no place for you here any more.'

'What did the man say?'

90

'He said I was lucky to have a nice little boy like you.'

Inwardly she cursed her detractors, in a language she had never used before.

The very next evening they reorganised the flat so that mother and son had a large room of their own. Pa had been using it as a study but, since he had no time to study, he said, how could it mean anything to him to give it up.

Pa made everything into a Russian joke.

They toasted the new room with a glass of champagne and urged it to welcome its new inmates.

'In the street people see me as a lady.'

After the nasty whisperings, she had looked at herself in the mirror and seen an elegant figure in a suit of muted green wool, the jacket with a pretty scalloped neck that allowed a high-necked blouse to peep through.

'*Burzhuazka*, eh? That's not good,' Pa said.

'Look at us,' said Ma, who still looked bourgeois, but in a studiedly modest way, as if she could have passed in any age and place in her crimson suit and thick stockings and flat shoes. Pa wore a grey suit but left his white shirt open at the neck.

'I can find a job,' said Sophie. 'I'm trained as an English secretary. Forty words of typing a minute plus shorthand. I can translate from English.'

'Great, you can spy on their embassy. Our government will pay you for that.'

'Don't joke all the time, Pa. This is serious.' She felt a touch uncertain. 'I really want to go to the university.'

'That's right. That's what you must do.' Pa raised his glass. 'Here's to a better life all round.'

They clinked glasses.

'So, Sofka, it wasn't easy for you over there.' If Ma thought her daughter ought not to have made such a hasty decision in the first place, she didn't say.

'Scotland was too grey and wet and depressing.'

'The Russian soul belongs to the steppes, not the cold sea, Pushkin said.'

'Maybe that was it.' Although she knew Pa could make Pushkin say anything.

'By the way, daughter, why is Russia like soup?'

'I don't know. Why is Russia like soup?'

'Because it gets stirred every now and again, and all the bits on the top sink to the bottom.'

'And vice versa,' added Ma.

'Our crazy country. Good job I didn't write to you at the old flat.'

'Commissar Malakhov decided we belonged here. You couldn't know that.'

Pa struck an attitude. 'Your mother told them our old flat would do nicely.'

'I can imagine.' Ma was so forceful it was hard to think how Comrade Malakhov had dared defy her.

'But they said three families were now living there and surely we did not want it back in that condition.'

'I had to agree,' said Ma.

'Such are the problems with being top brass.'

'Is that what we are?'

'Because of the way they stirred the soup.'

'Nonsense, Grisha, it's because we're doctors that now we're near the top.'

'That doesn't sound a bad thing,' said Sophie. 'Doctors can help people. I had a doctor in Scotland – '

' "Comrade, I said," ' Ma continued to reminisce, ' "I'd like to take the books and the pictures with me." '

' "You can buy all that again, mother. Folks like you will be well-paid." '

'My dear wife, fancy calling you mother! The young folk these days are not polite.'

'Another consequence of stirring the soup.'

'It happened to me on the street. The men were so rude.'

To which her father suddenly objected and drew a line under their criticisms. 'What can you expect, Sofka?' And to his wife: 'That's enough! They were deprived of an education. Sometimes the soup must be stirred. It's only fair.'

'But, Ma, what did they *do* with all our stuff?'

She remembered some books of her own; toys even. She'd hardly finished school when they left the flat.

'Burnt it for firewood mostly,' Pa said.

'The cold was terrible that year. You remember Dmitry Pavlovich – ' and Ma named an elderly neighbour who had died of cold.

In her mind Sophie revisited the vermilion banners decorating the streets with the message of HOPE, and pictured them as the exact opposite of the black cloak of death. 'Ma, how does it happen for someone to die like that?'

'You just nod off to sleep. It's not so bad.'

'All the same death is to be avoided,' declared Pa. 'Pushkin said.'

22

She took the tram to the old flat off the Garden Ring. The bell made no sound because there was no bell. She waited half an hour till the big rusty iron door to the courtyard opened and someone emerged whom she knew.

'Andryusha, it is you, isn't it?'

Her schoolmate and neighbour had the same spectacles as when he was a youth but behind them he had grown into a lean, gangly young man with the faint outline of a moustache on his upper lip. He greeted her cautiously.

She laughed off her almost four years away. 'How's everyone from No. 103 doing?' The schools had acquired numbers in place of names.

'Sasha Meidan is dead.'

'Oh, he should have avoided that.'

Andryusha shot her a funny look. 'He got into some fight in the street. What else. That nun Masha Sokolova married Misha Radzinsky. You remember him?'

'Always a joker.'

Andryusha nodded. 'And Dima Forsh entered a seminary. The rest of us are still studying.'

'Dima's a priest? A priest?' she repeated incredulously, of the boy who had played old Russia, opposite Masha's new, in their end-of-term production. Dima who had a crush on her in the fifth class.

'Yep, Dima has taken God to heart.' Andryusha stopped, took off his spectacles and peered at the smeared lenses before replacing them. He seemed to want to say more but stopped himself. 'So you, Sofka, are you coming back to the university?' Her former neighbour and schoolmate thought her important father could doubtless smooth a path for her.

'I will if I can. I hear it's not easy.'

'They keep changing the rules. You can study this, you can't study that. Some of the subjects have been abolished. Some of the teachers have been abolished.' He almost smiled.

'Dear block 103!' She patted the cracked stucco wall. 'Same old rat family round the dustbins?'

'Now into its 150,000th generation.'

'See you around then.'

'*Poka*, Sofka.'

He went off towards the tram stop, relieved not to have been asked any more questions.

Leksy was a quick learner. Soon he could say 'It's raining' and 'I'm hungry' in two languages. Everyone praised him. 'Our little Russian boy!'

' "Red",' Pa said, holding up a tomato with a chuckle. ' "*Krasny*".'

'Did you remember any of that language later?' I asked Leksy.

'I was sixty when I went back to it. Some.'

'So Sofka, your studies . . . ' her father enquired.

'With that professor of literature, I thought . . . what was his name? Aikhenbaum?'

'Aikhenvald. He's gone.'

'Abroad?'

'Let's hope so, for his sake.'

'Pa!'

'Sofka, what is the one message we in Russia have to offer the world? Not to take life too seriously. You must learn to joke more. Preferably before you enrol with whoever.'

Ma added: 'It's true, Sofka, it's mostly new names in the universities now. I don't know where they found them all.'

Pa banged the table as if he were drunk. 'My dear, you know perfectly well. In Russia we're never short of people because we don't care whether they're dead or alive. If we're short of manpower we resurrect the dead. Everyone's heard of dead souls who count just as well as the living kind. That's our philosophy. Our politics. I always forget which came first.'

'Doesn't really matter, does it?' Sophie loved her father infinitely.

'Thank you, my daughter. No, it doesn't matter a damn.' He was bright-eyed with tears.

Ma concluded: 'We'll find a kindergarten for Leksy and Sofka will study.'

'I will.' And education was still a magical idea for her, as fondly she remembered Claude Garon's unintended Crombietown Ladies' Academy, beside the North Sea, where her grown-up existence had begun.

'Things *are* settling down. They're even starting to publish books again. Those devils of private publishers all ran away to Germany and had to be replaced.'

'We never heard what happened to Johann,' said Ma, her memory triggered by the mention of Germans.

'Johann! *Was wir wollen, das dürfen wir.* Don't mention him, please!'

Sofka laughed away the trivialities of the past.

'Mama, where have you been? We've been waiting ages. Nikita said we'd have to go off without you. I'm hungry.' The boy poured out a stream of insulted Russian and English. She put down her shopping-bag and picked him up and held him till he calmed down.

The kindergarten was staffed by former peasant girls and a couple of young men whose job seemed to be to hang about. One, while chewing sunflower seeds, watched Sophie and her son with such muddled sentiment in his eyes it took her imagination straight back to the dirty patches of snow prolonging their lives in the shade.

She went over and introduced herself and shook Nikita's hand.

Burzhuazka, she could see in his eyes, and wished him good-afternoon, to which he didn't reply but finally spat out his chewed seed husk.

'What did you learn today, sweetheart?'

Her son whispered something into his mother's delicious ear.

'Leksy, that's terribly rude!' And she caught the eye of the youth, watching them with a crooked smile as they went home.

She needed a new set of clothes: something that felt right for the place and time. Good that Ma had rescued the Singer from eviction at the old address, for there was nothing suitable to wear in the so-called shops. Nor any fabric with which to make a new outfit.

So she bought the largest possible size of second-hand man's suit in a Commission shop in a street just off Tverskaya. The Commission shops were a new version of pawnbroker's shops. They were places where objects were never redeemed by those who had given them up for cash in hand, for instantly they got the cash their lives moved on. They paid for some necessity and wondered what next to give up. But if the cast-off objects could prompt a poetic vision they might just find new owners. Ergo a fat man's suit from the old overstuffed days could clothe two young women now, or be made into a stunning costume for one tall, elegant and innovative woman, with plenty of cloth left over for school clothes for her son.

Pa got the suit cleaned for her at the hospital. Chemical dry-cleaners had disappeared from the streets. The hospital staff accepted a tip and were quite willing. They amused themselves imagining the passing of some great fatty of the old days, whose station in life allowed him lethal quantities of pancakes and cream. At least he left a useful legacy.

She sketched her vision for the suit. It was to be a grey sleeveless trouser suit inspired by two triangles whose points would meet at her trim waist. She cut the pattern from newspaper. Plain paper was short but a piece of broadsheet did the trick, with joins.

As she laid the newspaper templates against the cloth to cut out her material, it struck her what an uninvestigated object the human being was. The quasi-geometric shapes of her body, reduced to a pattern, were floating disconnected in the air. At the same time each shape was covered with writing from edge to edge, as if the author of her being, having made her bodily, would still not let up. Every part of her was written over with would-be explanations and instructions. Sophie Asmus never had her own beginning. Line after line of close commentary on how to be came as if printed in Cyrillic on her skin, down her arms and up her inside leg, across her breasts and her back: a physical life with instructions for use. She shook off the unwelcome impression.

Surely one could cut a pattern to *change* the shape of one's life. As tailor to her self, she was suddenly full of wonder at what human creatures might be meant for. To philosophise, to politick, to make things and to experience joy.

23

The air was hot and dry and dusty, with the trees too skimpy to give shade. Russia seemed to have forgotten to plan for summer.

'Excuse me, do you speak English? Can I have a word?'

Sophie's loose angular top showed off her smooth, faintly sun-tanned neck. The dark-haired woman who spoke to her was pretty too, with her hair cut in a bob and her slim body encased in a striking red and black tunic, over a long skirt. She spoke an English that didn't sound like her mother tongue.

'Of course. How can I help?'

'I've been ringing the bell for ages,' complained the foreigner, indicating the rather grand building behind her. 'No one wanted to let me in.'

Sophie tossed back her head and raised her eyebrows in mockery of the heavens. 'My dear, no one *ever* answers the door at an Institute here. But don't you go blaming *that* on the new government. It's an old old tradition. At home we answer, but not in public buildings.'

'But why on earth? I thought I'd go crazy.' She gave a last tug on the brass bell for good measure, and they both giggled like schoolgirls.

Sophie put an arm round the stranger's shoulder. 'A first tip: if you really want something in this country you must be prepared to be devious to get it. It's . . . ' She threw her head back, a rather theatrical new gesture she had adopted. 'It's a kind of game we play with each other. A way of not getting bored. A way of keeping our souls in training for hard times.'

'That's very philosophical!'

'Oh yes, everything we do has a reason.'

The brunette smiled broadly. 'I knew you looked nice. You're funny too.'

Sophie returned the compliment. She so liked the look of the stranger that she instantly wanted to design a suit for her.

'So, spill the beans, why do you want to get into the Institute?'

'I wanted to photograph it as an old building with a new use. And the people who come and go: I'll snap them too. The worker-students. The Red worker-teachers we've heard so much about.' There was a camera hanging round the visitor's neck. 'And people like you, who look wonderful – '

Sophie rallied. 'So you've come to take pictures of our experimental land, Girl-from-Abroad?'

Shyly the other replied: 'I wanted to see how things were coming along.'

Sophie held out her hand. 'Sophie Asmus. Only don't expect too much. We haven't had long.'

'Beate Wischnitz.'

'*Also aus Deutschland!* Beate, pleased to meet you.'

'You speak German too!'

'*Stimmt's.* Have you got time for a coffee?'

'I'd love a coffee. I haven't had a good coffee since I left Paris.'

'It won't be a good coffee.' Sophie leaned far back, happy and in command of her world. It was a new gesture that overtook her in Moscow, an expression of exultation at sheer human possibility, and transcendent joy in that. A tram thundered past. 'This way!' The very trams thundering past, real instances of those dynamic lines in the paintings she loved, seemed enough to make the ambitious new city cohere. It would find its course. The two women walked abreast of each other, along a pavement which consisted of raised flattened earth bordered by a huge iron waste pipe, and turned into a side street.

In crepuscular surroundings they found an empty table. Sophie took a piece of newspaper from her bag and wiped the top, while her new friend watched.

'I'm from Germany originally. But I moved to Paris.'

'Paris! I've always dreamed of going to Paris. No one's life is complete before they've been to Paris and Rome and London. By the way I love your tunic. To get any kind of coloured fabric here at the moment is just impossible.'

'Not even red?'

They laughed. Sophie thrust her head back. 'Not even that. It all goes to make flags.'

By the way, I took a few pictures of you coming out of the Institute. I hope you don't mind.'

'No–o.' She dismissed a slight anxiety. 'Seriously, Beate, we want people to give us a chance. So many people hate us over there for daring to start again.'

'But you have admirers across the world.'

'That's a nice thought.'

'So she did identify with her country after all?' he asked me, to which I replied, on the basis that I had read her notebooks, and evidently he had not,

'Yes. The first time she really tried to make something of it. Besides, it was a little like her.'

The German visitor fished in her bag for a notebook.

'Better not.'

Without demur Beate took to repeating what Sophie told her, to fix it in her mind. It was a technique she could rely on, since invariably she could remember the sound of her own voice. 'So, after the war everyone had to start again. It was only in Russia – '

'Exactly. We had the courage. In England all they wanted was to go back to the previous century and pretend it hadn't happened. You

99

lose millions of men, you put up war memorials everywhere, and then *ça y est*. You can forget.'

'I agree, here you can see the change.'

'Bye-bye nineteenth century. St Petersburg still looks a bit like London, but we'll change all that.'

Beate would file a spectacular report filling half a page of the *New York Times*. The headline was: NEW WOMAN TRANSFORMS MAN'S SUIT. TAKES ON NEW SOCIAL ROLE.

'That suit makes you look really modern.'

'Well, thank you! I made it myself.'

'As you say, she really made something of it.'

'She had her own take on what the Revolution was about. She became more important to herself as a carrier of the times when she went back to Russia. Like the poets she met and the painters, she made herself into something for people to think about.'

The pub, the local, the *traktir* Sophie favoured was not much more than a cubby-hole where ageless, befuddled, florid men dulled what reflexes they had left. The tables were dirty with slops and the floor was a place where it was better no one looked. Sophie caught sight of a gnawed chicken bone.

'As you see, it's a bit grubby.'

'Ladies, you must be disinfecting yourselves with foreign smoke even to sit here for five minutes with scum like us. This is no place for souls used to bourgeois comforts.' The speaker could have been a priest who had taken to the bottle, or a relatively clean and articulate tramp, with blood-filled cheeks and a stringy pale beard.

'Mind your own business, comrade!' Sophie carried her head high.

'Ekh, a lady eh? You've taken the wrong path and no mistake.' He gesticulated with the cigarette he was smoking, which had a thick paper mouthpiece.

'To put it politely, comrade, get lost! We're here for a drink, just like you.'

'The day you'll be like me heaven will be born on earth.'

'Now that's enough.' Fetching two coffees from the counter she

100

ignored the tramp or priest or whatever he was. She liked this working-men's bar because no one would expect to find her there and she could decide who to be.

She took her new friend's hand and squeezed it. 'Beate, welcome to Moscow! My father says you can tell we're making progress here because when a man falls over he's more likely to be drunk than dying.'

Beate, not at all sure she understood, surveyed the bleary unwashed figures in whose company they sat.

'They must have looked magnificently out of place, two young women in dazzling modern clothes.'

'She once claimed she inspired a line in the poet Khlebovsky about two butterflies in a coal-hole. She met him in Beate's company.'

'Don't!' Sophie pushed their 'coffees' aside. 'God knows what's in them or on the cup. Interesting to be here though, isn't it?'

The light was black-blue, transfixed by a shaft of white light from a couple of high windows cut into the thick walls of this old part of Moscow. Beate consulted her light meter. She shook her head. 'On the way out maybe.'

'Everything is still in a transitional state here.'

'Of course!' They took another of Beate's Gitanes each and continued to smoke the superior 'disinfectant' foreign brand ostentatiously. Sophie produced her cigarette-holder which her new friend admired. 'Such fun!'

'So elegant, my dear.'

'When were you born?'

'1901.'

'We're sisters in time! You know what I think, Beate Wischnitz? You've come to Moscow to have fun. You like adventure. Like me.' Her head was way back behind her now, so full she was of every kind of physical and mental excitement.

'It was a gesture of hers. I remember it now you describe it.'

'It's thrilling. Our government is looking for the true foundation of human life.'

'Not the lies we're fobbed off with in the West then.'

'Tssss. Patriotism. Doing your duty. Dying for your country. Believing in God. That's all lies. I had an earful of that over there. The future is here.' She paused. 'With no more wasted lives. Did you ever read Baudelaire?

'He said every evening when they light the lamps in the big cities thousands of people will die that night, never having lived. It plagues me. Every time I enter a second-hand shop I worry who used this lamp, this book, these trousers before. Did they live enough? Must I live for them?'

'I adore Baudelaire. Creator of beauty and lover of women. A prophet.'

'Sister!' Sophie laid a hand on Beate's. 'Look, I can't stay long. I have to pick up my son. But when we meet again I promise I'll do what I can for you. There are loads of people you can talk to. We can take some trips together.'

'*Mon dieu*, you've got a child too! Sophie, fancy being a mother on top of all this!'

'It is – well, my parents help me.' Sophie wrote down her telephone number. 'If it doesn't work look for me at the Institute. It should work but you never know.' She tossed her head back, wide-eyed with joy. 'So we'll be in touch.'

24

She was an hour late to collect Leksy. She justified it to herself on the grounds that to make a new friend was the most important thing of all, but Leksy wasn't impressed.

'Ma–aaaa!' The boy ran round her a few times, droning her name before clasping the loose trousers that encased her slender legs, not some fat man's from a bygone age. 'Nikita says he'll take me away and lose me if you don't come on time.'

'Stuff and nonsense.' She called out down the corridor. 'Comrade, I'm sorry I was delayed. It won't happen again.'

The boy pointed, but the kindergarten assistant wasn't visible anywhere. Sophie looked into the headmistress's office. 'Comrade Bitova' said the title on the door. But she too was gone.

"Mama, let's go home. Let's go home to grandpa's house.'

'Exactly where we're going. To the flat. Now, did you learn anything today? *Rasskazhi!*'

He stopped, put his bag down and showed her a salute.

'So they're training you to be a soldier! Anything else?'

' "May there always be sunshine, may there always be sky, may there always be Mama, may there always be me!" ' He stood on the pavement, singing.

'Why, what a song! Although do you need to be a soldier? We're all going to live in peace.'

The boy ran ahead, positively looking forward to the red marble and the chandeliers at the entrance to his new home, and the big room full of light and dust and books, where he could draw on the floor, and soft chairs where he could fall asleep. 'I like it. It's a good song. A good song!' He shouted and his voice trailed away.

He ate a good tea, but afterwards he was quiet.

'You're tired, Leksy.'

'I don't like Nikita. He calls me Our Little Lord from England.'

Sophie sat sewing. 'Don't trouble yourself, Leks. I'll have a word with Comrade Bitova. Sleep now.'

'How's Leksy?' Pa asked.

'They single him out a bit at the nursery. But he's strong. He'll cope.'

The boy, who would soon have a nice pair of knickerbockers to wear in the same grey suiting as his mother's costume, was lucky to have Pa as well as his mother to watch over his development. Pa was even writing a book on child development. The problem was he had no time to pick up his pen.

Sophie did pick up hers, but only to write her diary.

The Department of Anglistics, which accepted her, used as its seminar room the former boardroom of a Viennese bank. The staircase was grand, and on the walls the bank's old paintings still hung, looking out on the students who sat at the grand table where the moneymakers of a quarter of a century ago had clinched their deals. Sophie recognised the pale, passive face of Masha Sokolova, now twinned with her own reflection in the mirror-calm sea of mahogany. She turned to look at the object herself. Masha's too-long, over-abundant dark hair was held back by a clip at one side, giving the impression that since school she had declined as a woman. Meanwhile her expression was one of deliberately manifested 'sealed lips', as if she were playing a party game.

'Masha! Long time no see. How are you?'

'You're back from abroad Sofia Grigorievna – ' Sophie was surprised by the reluctance with which Masha spoke to her at all.

'At last I am – '

But Masha seemed to struggle to find an attitude towards Sophie that freed her voice. Eventually she found it.

'It must have been a torture living in London.'

'It was an experience. One needs experience.'

'The injustice of capitalist society! The obscenity! The contamination!'

'I wouldn't go that far. England is full of people eating too much and going about with no particular purpose.' Sophie had a particular vision of Piccadilly Circus where the motors went round and round, and from which she generalised quite unfairly.

But rather than listen to Sophie's response Masha looked knowingly at a young man with strawlike hair whose crimson sweater was frayed at the cuffs. His turn now.

'Pay attention, wife!' he responded. 'This one's from Over There. Treat her carefully!'

Was he joking? Sophie wondered. Is this what Pushkin would have said? Surely he didn't mean it? The blond hair that sat high on the crown of his head made Masha's husband seem ridiculously girlish, while he was pretending to be a savage. Sophie held on to that contemptuous thought to steady her.

'What's all this nonsense? I was married in England for three years. I had many experiences there for which I'm grateful as a grown-up person.'

'Exactly,' said this Misha Radzinsky, who, also as if he were playing a children's game, could make his high-cheekboned face darken at will. 'You learnt to see things their way. Which means, once you're back here you're a spy for them.'

'You're dangerous whatever you are,' said his wife.

'But that's ridiculous!' But, as she took an empty seat a few places to the left of the still empty professor's chair, she was aware of the other students observing her. As much as she wanted a good look at them, too, to see who was to her taste, she felt a faint need to shelter.

None of the women in the class was as beautiful as Beate. But then an androgynous creature entered. She was a tall woman with very short dark hair like a helmet, cut straight across her high forehead, and wearing a man's shirt with the sleeves rolled up, and brown corduroy trousers. She sat down opposite Sophie, her face a blank to all around her.

The professor arrived and took the register.

'Ah, so her name's Vera.'

As for Professor Davydov, who was outlining the method his class would adopt, he seemed only a few years older than his students.

'Are you suggesting, professor – ' a young man conspicuously small in stature, wearing a suit far too big for him and little round steel glasses, interrupted.

'I'm not suggesting anything, Pavel Abramovich, I'm telling you, and everyone make a note of it, please, everything that we study here requires a concrete approach. Now we apply our studies in a direction useful for everyone.'

'He wants to be useful like a doctor,' Sophie thought, 'even though his subject is not medicine.'

Davydov was very tall and thin and looked as if he might snap in a high wind. Nature also disfavoured him with a bad skin.

'No more high-class tosh for us then. That's a relief. I could never understand what those old bourgeois authors were talking about. So boring! ' smirked the girlish Misha Radzinsky, who, Sophie decided, was an exhibitionist desperate to assert himself as a man.

'That's a rather sweeping statement,' said the scholar in the over-large suit. 'Or rather, a series of them.'

Sophie caught Vera's eye and they smiled.

Misha, isolated for a moment, scowled.

'The scholar' had one of those ugly serious faces which burst into attractive life when he spoke, and Sophie admired this Pavel Abramovich and wanted to know him better.

Vera Nikolaevna had a rather deep voice and spoke slowly, so no one could avoid hearing what she said. She said: 'This is a foolish attitude. Our century has everything to learn from art, if we are all to be artists of Life.'

'Can we get on?' asked a boy with rubbery lips. 'It seems to me these remnants of the bourgeoisie are deliberately holding up the class.'

'Thank you for that observation, comrade. I have made it clear, have I not, that anti-social behaviour won't be tolerated.'

'What's anti-social . . . ' began Sophie, but stopped.

After the class Pavel Abramovich whispered: 'Welcome, all the same.'

'He hates me because I've been to England but why does he hate you?'

'My wealthy family.'

'That's ridiculous. Our generation is here to make things anew. All of us.'

'You have to agree with him if you want to get on.'

'Not on my life! But you and I, we can be friends?' She said it too warmly for him not to feel shy and she noticed him shrink a little.

Meanwhile, she wanted a word with Vera Nikolaevna too, but the tall woman with the cap-like haircut had already disappeared.

25

'What job are you after when we graduate?'

'I'm already there, Sofka.' As friends they had dropped the polite patronymics. 'I'm a critic. You start a job like that when you're ready. It just happens.'

'That's why our prof regards you as a rival.'

'We're both new kinds of men in our field. I'm an avant-gardist

106

and he's, well, a new kind of cultural policeman. It takes our country to invent something like that. When they threw out all the old university staff they had to replace them in a hurry. So they had these intensive training courses for worker-teachers. Made them learn a lot of stuff off by heart. They even relayed knowledge over a loudspeaker while the new teachers-to-be were asleep. *Nota bene*, one: no one can accuse us of being parasites if we're signed on with a real worker-teacher; and two: they teach us by rote with the intention of creating a civil army.'

She remembered the salute Leksy had been practising and frowned. She thrust her head back. 'I'll seduce Davydov into giving me straight As. Then I can choose to do anything I like. I'll take what I can from all this and make my own way in life.'

'Sofka, I'm a bit of a pessimist when it comes down to it. Please be careful.'

She laughed. 'Be careful? What will they do to me?'

He shook his head.

Vera Nikolaevna said she would give the new academic regime a try because she really did wish wholeheartedly for a society 'in which each of us can freely become what we are'.

Which made Sophie happy to be in her company, whereas, to be honest, Pavel Abramovich Berman *was* a pessimist.

Vera worked in the new library for the humanities, with its big plain desks for sharing and political pamphlets and newspapers piled high. You could read older books there but there was a sense that the age required something more topical and practical than all but a few nineteenth-century authors offered.

To that end cultural workers guarded the lift that brought books from the stacks. They wore white overalls, as if they were pharmacists or doctors and had the task of testing a formula or promoting a certain understanding of good health.

She subdued herself and offered to try to fit in, but for every book Sophie consulted they demanded proof of matriculation. To get a novel by Virginia Woolf she had to get a letter from Professor Davydov counterstamped by the Faculty Office and present it to the Director of the Library.

They hindered her in subtle ways too. 'You can't bring that coat in here.' It was her best wool cape from Scotland and she feared having it stolen.

She even reproached herself. So, read something else! So, don't fuss so much about material things.

Her consolation was Vera.

'Verochka!' They walked up the stairs together to the open-plan workroom where, evidently, Sophie sat and worked to be near to Vera. 'Verochka, *kak dela*?'

'So-so. I'm switching to linguistics in the autumn. I can't see any point in Davydov.'

'What's linguistics?'

'It's a science, Sofka dear, by which we dismantle language just like we dismantled bourgeois life. We might reassemble it in a better order. Or maybe we'll leave it loose.'

'Leave it loose.'

'That has its limitations. It's difficult for society to pull together. Well – '

Vera was like a new kind of warrior, Sophie thought. Tall and lean and fit, leading an opposition all of her own. They were all three of them like that, she herself and Pavel Berman and Vera.

'As you know, Sofka, they like anything that can pass itself off as a science. I intend to use the new science of words to keep an eye on their own tricks. Passing philosophy off as politics. Passing politics off as philosophy. I'll examine their "philosophy" with a rigour they've never seen before.'

'There's always a kind of officialdom, isn't there, in anything one does. Anything one thinks, anything one enjoys. And it seems to exist to reduce the pleasure, and keep the thinking in order.'

'That sort of thing.'

Sophie shook her head. 'The officials want us all to become cadres and we need someone like you . . . '

'Don't use that word cadre, Sophie. That's their god-awful word for their obedient puppets.'

'I won't become that.' She thought of her husband, and his friend Arthur, who at least had each other for support.

'Don't leave the Institute, Vera. I need you there.'

Vera leaned over Sophie and kissed her on the lips. 'I'm here for you. You can even come with me if you like.'

'Over the whole of her Russian experience hung the burden of conformity, freer but more lethal than it had been in Scotland.'

'She could have ended up in prison.'

'In the end she felt that everywhere she went. Round every corner lurked a policeman ready to accuse her of not playing the right game.'

The sun was shining a few weeks later and Sophie and Vera walked and sat down on a bench that looked down over the river. The sun fell on their faces and when it didn't they held their faces up to where it might be.

In the afternoons they lay in bed in the tiny room Vera had found for herself, on the top floor of an old building that was being used as communal apartments. It was more of a cupboard than a room. The facilities were on the next landing down and she had to bring up water in a bucket to wash. But it was warm, as the central heating that warmed the whole building reached the peak of its force under the roof; and, the greatest of blessings, it was private.

What Sophie didn't get from her friendship with Pavel she found in her passion for Vera. Vera's lovemaking was so much more imaginative than Duncan's had been, and Sophie responded to her with an intensity that was new to her. They had to gag each other not to alert the neighbours below. Sophie had never before thought about going to bed with a woman, but when the moment came her enthusiasm and admiration for Vera left no question about it.

They lay with their legs intertwined, their thighs moist and their nipples still erect, intoxicated by their mingled scents. In that tiny yellow-ochre room, with barely space to put their feet down on the floor for all the books and boxes of possessions and the little corner where Vera kept dry food and a spirit stove, the way they lay together was a painting that waited for another age to paint it.

'Pavel was terribly brave. He told Davydov: "I am no bourgeois, comrade! I only think if art spreads some message, as Misha says, like furthering the interests of the working-class, that's still not *why* it exists. For why art exists you need a quite different notion of truth linked to the sheer joy of the human encounter." '

'The human encounter,' said Vera, running her hand over Sophie's flat white belly. 'Without this no art, no love and no truth.' Sophie held Vera's head. Her fingers lost themselves in the bristles of her short hair.

They excited each other then rested a while again.

' "But that's metaphysics and we don't believe in metaphysics!" You know how our spotty prof talks. "I must inform you, Pavel Abramovich, that the correct name for the philosophy of our times is – "

' "Don't tell me, Comrade Professor! I'll remember in a minute." Pavel's got such a dry manner. He always makes me smile.'

'Dry is the only way one can be with the new worker-teachers. Either that or drop out altogether.' With her tongue Vera painted hieroglyphs on Sophie's belly.

'You drive me crazy.' She dug her hands into Vera's head. 'Drop out?'

'The time will come when we'll all have to disappear. Or turn into people like them.'

Sophie sat up. 'You think that too? So does Pavel – '

'I'm sure. We have to enjoy our freedom while we can.'

'Hell.'

'You exhaust me, darling, in the best of ways.'

Sophie sighed so deeply, as if she'd never sighed before. Not even with Micky.

'Pavel Abramovich was looking at Davydov. He wanted to make him feel a fool. "But are you sure, Comrade Professor, that our times have got it right?"

'Davydov flushed so that his whole face was burning. "Of course I'm sure."

' "In that case we must agree to differ."

'Then the Radzinskys started up. "Can you two just shut up? Some of us are trying to work." '

'Poor cow wants to pass her exams and be of service. Take care, though, Sofka, it's women like her will be the death of us. Both sexes can sign death warrants.'

'Darling, I have to go.'

Sophie dressed, watched by her admiring lover. 'I want to introduce you to Beate, my German friend.'

'I'll be jealous.'

'You will. She's gorgeous. But then what about me? You might fall in love with her. How about Friday?'

26

Dr Asmus knew full well what was happening, with the children being schooled as soldiers and the university teachers functioning like policemen. But he believed that like a well-constructed boat properly sailed the new society would right itself in time. He ruffled Leksy's hair. The boy must know he was loved, even if there weren't explanations for why his sandwiches were stolen every day.

'Our Leksy seems fine to me. How's your counting, Leks? And now backwards, 10, 9, 8 – excellent.' He held his hand in place as a bridge for the train to run over while advising his daughter to pack three sandwiches instead of two.

'I do already. I'm not hopeful about whose belly they end up in.'

'By the way, Sofka, you look wonderful.'

She looked in the mirror to confirm her father's compliment. She did have a certain physical bloom about her.

He presumed she was having an affair which she would tell them about in due course. Or not.

'Our Moscow obviously suits you. Nice people on your course?'

'Some. Some less so. But Pa, if you don't agree with what they're teaching, what do you do? There's a risk you'll come out without a degree, and then what?'

'Keep it to yourself. Don't annoy them just for the sake of it.'

'It's about friends, Pa, more than me. They need supporting.'

'You'll know the moment, Sofka.' He patted her shoulder. 'Your mother not home yet?' He wandered off to the kitchen to make a sandwich.

Beate snapped queues in the streets, with, above them, the propaganda bunting strung from every building. She showed the photographs to Sofka and Vera as they sat together in the workers' café, not drinking a thing.

Vera singled out from among Beate's photos a full-length portrait of a pretty blonde village woman aged about thirty, in thick peasant stockings, a knee-length full skirt and a quilted jacket. The woman was carrying a shopping-bag in one hand and a literacy primer in the other.

'That's how I found her. I didn't ask her to pose.'

Sophie said. 'I can imagine in years to come people will look at these photographs and marvel at how it was and not know whether Beate's compositions are history or art.'

'I'm just a witness,' said Beate.

'Whatever you are look after your negatives,' said Vera. 'Have you got them somewhere in a *very* safe place?'

'On me.'

'Not on you. That's no good. The body's not sacred here, when it comes to it.'

'I'll find somewhere. Can we talk about something else?'

Beate went back to her room in the National Hotel where the fees from the *New York Times* more than paid her bill. She hid her rolls of film in different places. Some she stitched into the bottom of her suitcase. Some under the crown of her hat. Others she stuffed in the toes of a pair of extra-large rubber boots she had bought for the purpose, covered with a crumpled nylon stocking so she could pretend that was the remedy for the overlarge boots. She also left out one or two rolls on which she deliberately took uninteresting shots, to avoid arousing the suspicion she was hiding anything. What did it mean that the body wasn't sacred?

'There's a lot in her notebooks about Beate.'

'A version of her own story, I suppose. She could have been

112

the photographer coming from abroad, instead of the prodigal daughter . . . and all of them were caught between the innocence of their dreams and the reality that awaited. Yet she had a different temperament from Beate. Her fascination with extremes took her where Beate did not dream of going.'

'We must be together as much as we can be, now. It's worth everything to know what happiness can be.'

Vera was strangely silent but Sophie dismissed it as deep satisfaction at their being together.

She went on: 'I never know whether to be sorry for Pavel or to congratulate him on his courage on managing to survive quite alone. "No man is an island", but he seems to manage it.'

'When I think of artists and critics I think of loneliness. In a good sense or whatever. They're training us to deal with it.'

'That's not what Davydov thinks.'

'Bugger Davydov. Everyone knows he hasn't got a clue.'

And after that Vera stopped attending the English classes, just as she had forewarned, although she said nothing more about her linguistics course in their place.

Now Sophie only pretended to take notes.

'I would say that you are the class enemy, Pavel Abramovich, and that you have no place here. You too, Sofia Grigorievna, a woman who has such an idiosyncratic idea of what it is to be modern' – there was a suppressed giggle at that – 'if you support Our Critic as you seem to.'

'I support him.'

'They're saboteurs, that's what they are,' cried Masha Sokolova. 'They keep wrecking the professor's classes for the rest of us.'

'Do shut up, Masha. You're a brainless idiot. And a coward too.'

'Shut up! Shut up, you foreign slut!' she screamed, while her husband reminded the class: 'Everyone here knows you're an imperialist spy, Sofia Grigorievna.'

Pavel Abramovich shook his head at such nonsense.

'I haven't done anything wrong,' Sophie protested.

'Nothing wrong? How can you say that, you foreign slut? You left us for a bourgeois country.'

'So what? I'm back now.'

'As we are only too aware. Cherry-picking what is on offer without the slightest concern for the working people of this country.'

Round the beautiful mahogany table, implicated through no fault of its own, the Anglistics class of '23/'24 agreed in chorus that Sophie Asmus was the enemy.

'Behold a woman who took no part in the Revolution but who's had the cheek to come back to profit from it. Sofia Grigorievna, you really have no right to speak your mind round this table.' That was Rubber-Lips.

Misha Radzinsky, whose sweater filled the whole room with the smell of stale cigarette smoke, added: 'Comrades, if I can sum up, we have in our midst two reactionary individuals who are selfish elitists.'

Pavel Abramovich wasn't capable of raising his voice. He spoke slowly instead. 'You're a fucking philistine, Misha Radzinsky, married to a nasty and dangerous dimwit peasant. No one in their right mind would want to be equal with you two.'

At which point Sophie threw herself back into the fray, telling Masha Sokolovna this was her country too.

'Oh, just listen to Mr and Mrs Arty Farty! Pavel Abramovich, Sofia Grigorievna, you'll regret speaking your minds and disrupting our class. And as for that half-man, half-woman you're in love with – '

Sophie reeled. 'Something else you don't understand, eh? You can't even do *that* with any imagination, is that it?'

It was an ugly occasion but finally Professor Davydov was grateful to the young married couple who supported him, however they did it, for it gave him time to recover. Finally he got his voice and thoughts back together again. 'Exactly. *Tak tochno.*'

Meanwhile Rubber-Lips took verbatim notes on what had happened, which resulted in Sofka's expulsion, and Pavel Abramovich's too, from the university.

27

'Hi, Olya, I wondered . . . '

'Sofka, heavens, I thought you ran away to Scotland.'

'I spent some time in London. It's a great city. Now I'm back. I wanted to see Kolya.'

'You're interested in Kolya? That's a joke. You must be hard-up for a man to want Kolya.'

'Never that, darling. I'm not even sure men are the better choice. But Kolya's a painter, isn't he?'

'He's an artist, my dear. He does all sorts. That's what he calls himself. Father says he's a parasite.'

'Is your father normally an unkind person?'

'None of your bloody business.'

Sofka was lucky her old classmate Olya didn't hang up. She'd always been tiresome. 'Look, you can understand. I'd like to get back into the old scene.'

'Good luck to you then, Sofka, you'll find him at the Checkmate Café. But don't get him into trouble.'

'I told you, it's not because I fancy him – '

'And I'm telling you he's an imbecile. Weak in the head. And you've been abroad. Sounds like a right messy partnership to me.'

'Trust me, Olya. And thanks.' Sophie hung up.

'In her diary she drew a picture of herself, in the grey triangle suit, and wrote above it: "Me as a Futurist!" '

'Enlighten me.'

'A Futurist plays games with words. To remind people we always need new language if we are to have fresh ambitions. Language can't rest . . . not for a minute. The printed page is always moribund and stale.'

'My mother the Futurist!' Leksy whistled.

'Once an education at the university had become impossible.'

*

At school Kolya Lukyanov had been a nervous boy with a bush of dark curly hair. Hoping she would recognise him, Sophie set off for the Checkmate Café.

The moment she entered it was more her kind of place than the university. For a start the women wore trousers and bright lipstick. She spotted Kolya because of what he was wearing too.

He was still nervous, and now he was thin to the point of being angular, but then everyone was.

'That's a gorgeous shirt, Kolya!' It was emerald green silk, full in the cut and belted at the waist.

'Sofia Grigorievna, isn't it? Well, hello, what are you doing here? No, don't answer. Much the same as me, I suppose. Do you really like my shirt? Honestly? I got it from a Commission shop. Her Highness won't be back to redeem it in a hurry. She was much fatter than me, as you can see.' The young writer–artist–parasite plucked at the reams of spare cloth gathered into his body. There was a promising act shaping up there as a circus clown.

'It's great to see you. Tell me what you're up to.'

'I'll say it without embarrassment and with the total conviction I feel. I've devoted my life to art. Art's the only way we can bring about a true revolution.'

'But that's great.'

'If only, Sofka.'

'You must know Pavel Abramovich.'

'A critic, isn't he?'

'The best. Like you.'

Kolya looked doubtful.

'I'm a performance artist. You could come to one of our performances, Sofka.'

'I thought you were a painter.'

'God, Sofka, that's so old-fashioned! You sound like my father. These days an artist is a performer. Painters, actors, dancers, singers: we're all in the world of revolutionary art together.'

' "*Getsamtkoonst*",' a passer-by in a pink shirt volunteered helpfully, albeit in tortured German.

'Who's that?'

'Khlebovsky.'

'The great Khlebovsky at last! And what does he mean?'

'That it will all come together one day.'

'The poet she gave the image to, of two butterflies in a coal-hole?'

'Exactly. She met Khlebovsky at the Checkmate Café.'

'You want to meet Khleb?'

'I'd like to hear him even more. But go on, tell me what *you* perform.' She risked sounding condescending to any other artist in the presence of the great Khlebovsky.

'It's like this . . . to render the stream of experience so anyone can tap into it.'

'But there are things I want to call mine.'

He shook his head. 'They've corrupted you over there, Sofia Grigorievna. Made you far too bourgeois. Well, I suppose that was inevitable.' He took a breath. 'We're really trying to get away from what "I" think and feel. It's about being in the world alongside each other. You really should come to one of our performances, Sofka. Then you might get it.'

'Definitely I'll come.' She liked Kolya. She thought his father must be a real villain, his sister too, to condemn him so.

'Dima, what are you doing here?' Another face from the past appeared. 'Kolya, you know Dima Forsh?' Evidently the artist did, but he didn't want anything to do with him, and disappeared.

The darkly robed seminarist, odd among the silk-shirted poets, came over to her and kissed her hand.

'It's good to see you again, Dima.'

'You too, Sofia Grigorievna. You've been somewhere, if I'm not mistaken.'

'England.'

'England!'

Dima Forsh was the last old classmate on her list. Since their schooldays his face had been transformed by the prolific black beard and moustache fringing his small pink mouth.

'I heard you'd joined the priesthood.'

'I've commended my soul to God's use, that's true, Sofia Grigor-ievna,' he smiled with an air of genuine modesty.

Though she had not known him well, he had always been such a sensitive and kindly boy. 'Call me Sofka. We're old friends, aren't we? Where are you living?'

'In the monastery on the south side.'

'May I come . . . ' She was thinking of herself, but also of Beate.

'No women, I'm afraid.'

'That's a pity.'

The priest managed to sound sad in a special way. Not grief, not ennui, not misery, just pure Russian *grust*. He'd made his decision and certain deprivations followed from it.

'Dima, is it true that people spit at priests now? We've been hearing all this propaganda at the university, and I've seen stuff written up on trains and posters . . . '

He waved a pink hand dismissively. 'Christ has prepared us well for such trials.'

She leaned over and kissed him on the forehead. He blushed.

'Still you risk coming here.'

Dima sat opposite her, with a glass of water. 'Old friends of mine come here,' he said. 'We're all looking for truth in our different ways.'

Kolya, who was lolling against a door frame, waiting for Sophie to be free, suddenly shrieked at the priest: 'That's not true! This priest has no place here. He should get out while he can.'

'Kolya, leave him! What are you playing at? Dima?' she called after her old schoolfriend.

'Don't be afraid for me, Sofka. Trust in God.'

'Dima – '

'Good riddance to that *pop*,' said Khlebovsky, joining them. 'You really shouldn't bother with him, Girl-from-Abroad.'

'I don't care what you say.'

'You must. All priests are counter-revolutionary swine,' the poet with his huge head and firm, muscular body bellowed.

Kolya introduced them belatedly: 'Khlebovsky, this is Sofia Grigor-ievna and she really gets what we're trying to do.'

Khlebovsky poured her a glass of sweet Crimean wine and raised his own.

'As I was saying, we're all caught in the net of our physical individuality. Consciousness is just the brain signalling from where it's caught in the net.'

'Kolya – ' she cursed herself for drinking the wine. She surely knew better than to touch *anything* when she was out and about. And then the way Kolya had driven out Dima was scandalous. But Khlebovsky was about to perform so she hung on. She had to hang on to some passing ship.

Kolya introduced him with a drum-roll on the table. 'Comrades, we invite you to listen to the birth of language out of the spirit of darkness. The Poet of Revolution invites you to hear with new ears. He proposes to you a new transnatural language. Please welcome . . . Khlebovsky!'

' . . . melt all forms of human speech
into one unified conversation of mortal men!
. . . refashion that star-cluster.
And you dawdlers, deceivers, you pitiful madmen, you drunkards,
scatter across the winds, part of the past
like chopping blocks and the wedding rings of the last kings . . . '

She drank in the message. These were the years of self-discovery, of a new world growing up as yet without a name, a world to which she belonged.

She got her hair cropped short and started tucking her loose trousers into a pair of half-laced peasant boots. She wound a long orange scarf round her neck.

'I only wish I could understand. It sounds fantastic,' said Beate.

The smoke made their eyes smart.

'It's all there definitely. But who on earth could translate it?'

They were drinking the same thick, sweet red wine out of tumblers as gave her a headache when she first drank with Kolya and Khleb. At first she'd had a permanent headache but now she'd got used to it.

The dense crowd of bodies and the warm evening made their clothes stick to them.

They smoked Beate's Gitanes.

'Were you shocked that I was in love with Vera Nikolaevna?'

'Not at all.'

'I'm glad I got married once. One has to give everything a try, even bourgeois marriage.'

'I suppose I will give it a try, when I get back to Paris.'

'Is there someone?'

'Serge is his name.'

'I'd rather just have affairs.'

'How *is* Vera?'

'I haven't seen her for a while.' In fact she hadn't seen her for two weeks. 'But I'm not worried.'

'Free love is all very well, Sophie, but children need parents.'

'Any two good people can be parents. For Leksy it's me and my father.'

'Maybe.'

'No, you have to believe me.'

But in any case Beate struggled to hear and see and breathe in the stifling and crowded atmosphere.

Now it was Kolya delivering a series of sounds.

'*Beeeeesh . . . to . . . noz . . . ukbannn . . . . . . woq.*'

' "Melt all human speech . . . " That's what the man said.'

They clinked glasses.

'I don't quite understand what he's up to but it's an extraordinary place here. One can be entirely oneself.'

'Do you understand?' Leksy asked me.

' "Melt all human speech," as the poet said. They were releasing the unconscious. It was a way out of the Russian prison. No official-dom could follow them there. All done with Russian humour, of course.'

Truly, from the midst of the impromptu gallery upstairs, through a haze of blue smoke criss-crossed by people carrying glasses of liquor, Sophie looked down on something unnameable. Moscow on nights like that overflowed with young people looking for some new truth to live by, a truth never to be named but in whose arms one could expire in delight, even in the mysterious absence of one's lover. The whole city seemed to be one continuous gallery, or was it a theatre, with everyone dressed in costumes.

I said to Leksy: 'Call it Moscow 1924 or 1925 if you like. But you know how it is, names and dates are loose and baggy holdalls and people stuff them with this and that, and only if you were there, carried along on the atmosphere, could you know what was true.'

28

Vera came back and they had an evening at the Café.

'Darling.'

Then she disappeared again.

Dima came and went.

Sophie arranged for Beate to take photographs at Leksy's kindergarten. Over the months she had got to know the headmistress a little. Comrade Bitova seemed to be a kind woman who taught the children about flowers and insects and birds and kept a rabbit in a cage so they could have a pet. She explained to Beate *off* the record that she did what she did out of a mixture of tenderness and duty towards the coming generation who would have all *this* to deal with and would need to hang on to some slender contact with nature to cope.

It turned out to be the kind of occasion out of which Pa would readily have made a joke.

Yelena Ivanovna Bitova was her full name, and with only the likes of Nikita on her staff, it turned out that she needed to talk. She wasn't well educated. Indeed, she was full of gossip. But Sophie with all the pressures in her life quite warmed to that.

'They say they dissect the brains of the dead these days. If you dissect the brain of a woman murderer you can find out why she turned out that way. They've got an institute for it.'

'A special institute for the dissection of brains?'

Bitova nodded. 'The Virtuous Institute for the Transformation of All Values. VITAL for short. They dissect the brains of priests too, so they can do away with those with similar brains before they grow.

121

Criminals, priests and anyone funny in the head.'

Yelena Ivanovna Bitova sat there in her lab assistant's white coat.

The teacher's office was another high-ceilinged room with handsome cornices.

'Why are we drinking out of these fine tea-glasses and not you?'

'Someone stole the others.'

'That's just mean.'

'Do go on about the murderess, Comrade Bitova.'

'Well, I've only got this third-hand, mind. She killed a young woman. She said she wanted to taste what it was like to inflict death with her own hand, before she killed herself.'

'A psychopath.'

'An unfortunate, certainly. But the thing is, if we can understand this woman's brain, we can eradicate from our future world what caused her destruction of another person, and, in the end, also of herself. It will certainly lighten the teacher's burden if they can stop, hmmm, what shall we say, the negative forms of life growing.'

'Life's not a sum that adds up, Comrade Bitova.' Sophie found herself dealing with another incarnation of her spotty Anglistics professor. 'It doesn't seem right to look at it like that. Besides, some people do evil things and there will always be evil.'

'Sofia Grigorievna! I have to disagree. With all the negative forms of consciousness that do exist here we have to try *something*.'

'Do you punish the children?' asked Beate.

'What I say is the experts who say no to punishment don't have to do the teacher's job.'

'One of your assistants, Nikita, is rough with my boy.'

At which Comrade Bitova reeled. Criticism of her school was inadmissible. 'But life's not a sum that adds up, Sofia Grigorievna, you said that yourself. Surely you don't want to complain. I mean, I'm taking quite a risk for your friend here, to be honest with you. In my view it's still all a wonderful experiment to see what positive things human beings are capable of.'

Sophie who had been staring at some wild flowers in a milk bottle on the windowsill, smiled, and Beate imitated her, and then, with relief, they left.

The problem was . . . the problem was . . . that a revolution always fell into the hands of types just made to be officials.

Only Khlebovsky could manage the Revolution.

He was dancing barefoot with his arms round an invisible partner when he invited Sophie to join him. She was missing Vera, she wished Vera were there to share the ultimate experience of the Checkmate Café with her.

'Heh, Girl-from-Abroad!'

She didn't resist because he was the very spirit of the Revolution.

'So tonight we will make a poem together.'

'Oh yes, I so much want – '

'We meet at midnight. You will be there too, Kolya.'

Kolya was trying to balance a wooden brick on a glass marble on the seat of a wooden chair. ' "Ladies and gentlemen, our new politics. We must free ourselves from that too." All right, Khleb, so long as I've finished here.'

'Crazy!'

'You said it. But what can you expect of the twentieth century in its juvenile years, so driven by hope?'

The painter and the poet took Sophie by each arm. Otherwise she might stumble on the pavement where the pipes ran over the surface. Where the streets were paved, the cracks between the slabs were chasms and there too they might lose her. But she was light and they liked taking her in their arms and giving her a nice ride. She helped to buoy them up too.

Khlebovsky stopped and put her down to salute a street light. 'Oh new-made nest of light!' he crooned, 'circle where red storks gather;' and Sophie waited for all the stray dogs of Moscow to join in.

They danced in a chain. They formed a train to bring the news to each house in the street. Heh, citizen, the future is here! You haven't noticed? It's name is joy. Today is the day you transcend the humdrum!

Khleb and Kolya and Sophie shouted in turn, and together: 'People, when you wake up tomorrow, everything will be different. We will make a future happen for you in which you too will be free to find life a delight.'

In the quiet of the night, with no one watching them, they set to work with pens to rewrite the city. On house doors 3 became 8, 1 became 7, numbers grew by ten, twenty, thirty. Addresses touched infinity.

'To the Centre', read a signpost. 'Rubbish! That's not the right direction. Wherever you want to go, first go in the opposite direction, citizen – '

'That's it. You must go wrong before you go right.'

Khlebovsky had this naked strength which allowed him to bend not only words into fabulous new configurations but metal signs at will. 'Whoever thought you could make a journey to the centre just like that? Without a detour! How brainless folks are!'

'Oi, boys, I'm out of breath!'

'No time to stop, Sofka. Our task is to ensure that the man of the future awakens for the first time to where he is going.'

With Kolya and Khlebovsky, Sophie wandered along a path that zigzagged across the tramlines.

'And the city itself? The city too needs to be released from the deadening grip of all that is OLD.'

Khlebovsky raised his arms out into the night from the middle of a bridge: 'People, behold your world and now change places with it! Give the city its freedom!'

'Be the tram!' Kolya began, indefatigable. 'Be the lamp post and the dog and the bridge!'

'People, live again through new roles and new speech!'

Sophie held on to Kolya round the waist as they zigzagged across the road repeating the sounds of his poem. *Ha–ma–oo! Wah! Wah! Hah–gan!* They called themselves the defenders of free experience and scattered syllables across the city . . . *ba* . . . *pi* . . . *tu* . . . *ka* . . . *po* . . . *dyn* . . . *fee* . . . *lod* . . . *und* . . . Like the sea brings in a new tide every day so the man of the future would re-form his language.

As two trams whined past in opposite directions that seemed

enough to make the city cohere. Only a minimum was needed. A few straight lines in motion and a stream of liberated syllables powered to seek new meanings.

To be in that Moscow was to be drunk on freedom and the good news that things fall apart.

29

Then the power cuts began. You couldn't read. You couldn't heat water, you dared not go out into the street, although people still did. Beate was refused official cooperation and moved from snapping bright white classrooms to capturing stinking latrines in weed-strewn courtyards. She photographed flats chock-full of people who claimed they lived there, and overcrowded trams. She shot the city in the evening when the electricity failed and windows went dark and trolley-buses ran out of juice.

In the hotel they stole her decoy film, and when she complained the *dezhurnaya – femme de jour – de jour – naya* – she worked it out for herself – looked at her with all the condescension of a servant who no longer feared her mistress and had never liked her.

MATERIALISM IS THEIR PHILOSOPHY AND IT'S NOT WORKING! was the headline on one of Beate's reports in the *New York Times*.

'Father Forsh, you could go abroad. I could help you.'

'My place is here.'

'But they'll kill you. You're a private person. They're greatest aim is to destroy people like you.'

'Am I so private? I talk very loudly to God and anyone can listen. Besides, they need me really. Thank you for your kindness, but I'm not going anywhere.'

Shadows suddenly surrounded them. Dima felt a blow to the side of his head. 'Run, *mademoiselle*, run! It's me they want.'

Beate told herself the priest's robes would protect him. She hid behind the entrance to a courtyard and snapped the horrible scene.

'Foreign bitch, after her!'

'Run, Beate, run!' She wondered why she hadn't heard those words before. By the time she got to her hotel she was shaking violently and vomited in the washbasin.

But now they knew which hotel she was staying in. The next day Nikita and friends surrounded her in a back street. While two of them held her the kindergarten assistant took the camera from round her neck and smashed it. 'We'll have you next time, bitch.'

She telephoned Sophie, who came over. Two days later Beate left for Paris, just as soon as she could get a train ticket.

Sophie looked in the mirror and found that her skin had thickened, that her complexion was marked by redness on her cheeks where fine blood vessels had burst. Her voice was sharper and when she went out in the street she knew how to get on to the tram ahead of others and keep her place in a queue and defy any official who blocked her way.

Vera's room had a government seal on it.

She went to see Pavel Abramovich who with no way to earn his living couldn't afford to go out. He had a charming room, thick with carpets and paintings, rescued from his parents' looted villa. It didn't seem right to suggest he took them one by one to the Commission shop, but they might mean he could survive a little longer.

He made tea. 'Now, Sofka, have I got a story for you!' It was an unexpectedly jolly meeting, in view of all the other miserable goings-on. 'I have to tell you of the demise of one Sergei Ivanovich Davydov.'

'But, Pavel, dear, his job is to persecute *us*. Seriously, is he dead? That wouldn't be fair. I came to like him really.'

'Not dead. But listen. Once upon a time, actually one morning when he wasn't teaching, he picked up the heavy bakelite receiver in his office. "*Yes!*" he rapped.'

Davydov had a peculiar accent which Pavel imitated. Sophie almost choked on her tea.

' " . . . *Ba . . . pi . . . tu . . . ka . . . po . . . dyn . . . fee . . . lod . . . und . . .* " came the voice down the phone.'

' "I'm sorry, sir . . . "

' "I'm sorry too. Can you hear what I'm saying to you, Comrade Professor? Can you make any sense of it? How do you account for your students prancing around in fancy dress talking about the word-in-liberty, Comrade Professor? What nonsense have you been allowing them to spout? What the hell has that got to do with us?"

'Well! He cringed. That mean creature cringed like a cornered beast. He pleaded that he had followed his instructions to the letter, where-upon the chairman of the Committee for Overseeing the Institutional Transformation and Advancement of Learning told him only a dolt would do that.

'They punished him by, you'll never guess, by taking all the nice furniture and pictures out of the Institute. Apparently he loved them! He thought they created a really chic environment. They took those Matisses away to galleries, so they said. I don't believe that. They're on some new fat cat's walls. The Institute now displays new work by peasant-artists.'

'Poor Davydov.'

'Yep. They really managed to hurt Davydov. He said he couldn't do his teaching without a source of inspiration on the walls. So they sacked him. The last anyone heard of him he was on a drinking binge. Sailing God knows where.'

'That's a Russian fate if ever there was one.'

'Only not for us, eh?' Pavel Ambramovich remembered he was teetotal and Sophie remembered she was a woman.

'You're very thin, Sofka. Do take care of yourself.'

'You too.'

They embraced loosely and she left.

Khlebovsky shot himself that autumn. Sophie had to doubt the rumour because, bull though he was, she so wished him to live. But his death was in the newspapers.

Kolya Lukyanov performed verses from Khleb which sounded out over the tears of the mourners at his funeral.

> 'Your textbook twitter bores us, stories of black swans,
> how once a black swan dwelt far to the south –
> but now a swan with scarlet wings
> flies on the waves in a blizzard of bullets.
> It's time for you tsars to keep your appointment:

your time is up, your scaffold is erected.
And the secret every army keeps is this:
when the bride arrives her dress is crimson red.'

The verses were hard to understand so that the officials couldn't immediately get hold of them and turn them into something else.

Because Khlebovsky had liked the childlike tall white flowers with red stars at their hearts that people carried in procession when the city was in carnival mood his bier was covered in miniature versions of those flowers, while the mourners carried the originals like pikestaffs.

Pavel Abramovich came along and was so weak people had to support him as they would an old man.

Dima was still limping from having been kicked in the kneecaps. He had two black eyes and a bandage on his head.

'Good food, eh.' At the wake he sliced some coarse horsemeat salami heavy with garlic and put some pickled cucumbers on a white saucer to share with Sophie.

'Remember my friend Vera . . . if ever you hear where she is let me know.'

'God will watch over her.'

'Don't talk nonsense, Dima.'

The speeches over, the friends of Khlebovsky began to drink. Even Pavel Abramovich was drunk. Sophie couldn't get up next morning nor the morning after.

'As if her time in Moscow was one big trip.'

'She needed to journey far out of herself to discover what she was in search of.'

'The times encouraged her.'

'As they would do for your generation in the sixties.'

'Not me. I was too old. My daughter enjoyed the sixties. She's a professor now.'

I didn't know what to say to that. It was that woman's grand-mother's story I was telling. When that grandmother was still so young, and had so much promise.

*

128

'Sofka . . . '

'Leave me Pa, I'm tired.'

Dressed only in her night things, Sophie lay about the flat. Leksy, undelivered to the school he hated, played on the floor.

The big light sitting-room was full of dust, but none of the Asmuses minded about the dust. Dust was a delight. As Pushkin said, it showed how light the room was.

'Oh, Pa . . . '

'You'll have to leave,' he said.

When they came to arrest her she was already gone.

30

I laughed at Leksy. 'Are you saying your mother wasn't civilised?'

'She was immature. The things she responded to over there . . . '

That conversation took place about four on a winter afternoon, when no one would willingly have stayed out on the street. London's dry pavements were pale with cold and swept by a raw wind. People came in with red cheeks in search of coffee and those special little Polish cakes called *mazurki* I had learned to covet for the way the pastry dissolved in my mouth. The windows to the street were steamed up with talk. People alone were reading.

Leksy went on: 'You've got this fixation that she was about grand things to do with Art and Truth whereas what was she other than a crazy dreamer?'

'Leksy! Let her live! Don't stick labels on her!' I must have raised my voice, because a few people broke off chatting, or reading, and looked round.

But he insisted on being practical. 'She needed to marry again, wherever she was. Unlike Maud Arrowsmith she hadn't inherited a bookshop from her father. What could her father give her to take with her? He had no gold and roubles were useless. She had nowhere to live.'

'And who would you have had her marry?'

'There must have been loads of candidates.'

129

'Did you find marriage so easy yourself?'

'Of course not.'

'So wish her well on her return to England!'

At Victoria the cabbies queued beside a new hotel where an elegant woman in a Scottish woollen coat and an astrakhan hat, holding a pensive boy by the hand, entered. It was a damp morning, grey but not cold, and the November warmth made her anxious to change her clothes. The air smelt of coal and a tobacco that was not Russian. The colour red was evident though, and it made her smile through her tiredness. Doubledecker buses blazoned unfamiliar destinations.

'Are we going to live in this castle?'

The hotel had corner turrets for lookouts to target the enemy, and flew the Union Jack.

'England has a rather grand idea of itself,' she muttered, stepping inside anyway.

Which left a tall boy of five briefly puzzled, until the soft carpet under his feet diverted him. He stamped with all his might, and was puzzled to find only the dullest drumming came out of the staircase that led up from the reception desk.

She turned the key in the lock of a far too expensive room.

'Which bed would you like?'

'This one by the door, Mama. I'll be the first downstairs to explore. So are we going to live here in this castle?' He was trampolining on the bed.

'Leksy, take your shoes off at least.'

She eased off her hat and loosened her hair from where it had been pinned high.

'How am I doing?' she asked the mirror. It answered that it wasn't sure. She took off her coat and splashed her face with water at the washbasin.

The high ceiling overrode the functionality of the cream-painted room. It would do for a couple of nights.

On the second bed she lay down and closed her eyes. As two years contracted into two hours, and her life-clock ran backwards, she wondered about Vera; how she would send news, and how she, Sofka, now Sophie again, might get it. The name of Micky Dewar also crossed her mind. That winter she had received two letters from Scotland. In one Duncan wrote, care of her father at the hospital, that as soon as possible Mrs Sophie McFadden would become his ex-wife. He commented, in a way that let him down, that with parents like hers who could protect her, to return to Russia had not required much courage. Idiot! she thought now, without sympathy. What's that job you do? Is it Intelligence they call it? She didn't regret him one bit. The other letter was from John O'Neill, which she had read and folded away.

Her son was now asleep, flat on his back. She took his shoes off, planted a kiss on his forehead and covered him up.

Then she too slept.

Next day her contempt for her estranged husband seeped into her general view of life around her. Everything here was too dainty to be true. In that extreme life that had opened up to her over there she had known joyful, expansive, childlike freedom; only for it to collide now with the tidy-mindedness of evil.

'She was a child.'

'In her senses, but that's surely right.'

Mother and child took a long slow walk down to the Thames hand in hand, stopping to sit on an iron-and-wood bench overlooking the river.

'You can smell London! Mmm, it is a gorgeous city, I must concede.' Coal, and damp air, and the sourness of the river filled her nostrils. 'See who can hold their breath longer!' When her lungs burst she clapped his thigh. 'You win.'

Pedestrians and red buses passed overhead, across the bridge, and barges ploughed the grey river.

'Do they have kindergartens in England?'

'Not the same.'

'Good.'

'Oah, Lesky.' Suddenly she was crying, and he had all the weight of her grief to bear.

She shook herself out of her unhappiness.

'I spy something beginning with B.'

'A bus. A red bus. Mama, you always do buses or trains.' The traffic flowed over the bridge. 'I'll be hungry again soon.'

'So we'll eat something again soon. Come, now! We'll take a bus to the centre.'

They clambered up to the top deck, her boy with his long straight legs, and bright eyes, and lovely inquisitiveness.

Her anxiety had been tiredness.

In the Oxford Street Letting Agency, which had a solid wooden door with a bell, but nothing like the thickness of a street entrance in Moscow, Sophie saw herself reflected in the glass of a print on the opposite wall. It was a pen-and-ink sketch of the White Cliffs of Dover, the lines of which stood out from the deep crimson mount. The walls of the office were also a dark red. Sophie was a match for the elegant surroundings, but that did not make the place congenial.

The letting agent would have been a waitress had fate placed her in a lower class. While she waited for the poet to love her – Sophie did her a mental kindness and entrusted her to Baudelaire – she went through her standard repertoire in a snobbish, strangulated voice. That she had to work at all, owing to a divorce, made her resentful, and she took out her resentment on her card index and on her foreign-sounding client whose answers were not promising.

What area? What *kind* of area? *Roughly* what price? To all of which Sophie could truthfully say she had no idea. She flicked her eyes round the room and tried to discern addresses by reading the index headings sideways.

'Victoria is a possibility,' she said finally.

'Pimlico then. Let me see.' Some distantly detected affinity with Sophie, perhaps no more than her quality of speech, softened her. Once shaken out of her self-pity, the woman was not a bully. 'Where are you from, if you don't mind my asking?'

'Russia.'

'Russia!' She wanted to say that everyone knew about Russia now because the Labour Party so admired it. A working-class revolution was just around the corner for Britain too, if the Labour Party had its way.

'Would the boy like paper and pencil to draw with?'

'That's very kind.' Leksy looked up at the word 'boy'. He then settled himself on an upright chair by the window. As the freshly sharpened black lead cut through the paper's white snow, he thought of skis and sleighs and of himself as Russian.

His mother was suffering, for reasons that escaped him.

'Maybe something on a weekly basis? We're not staying long.'

The agent stacked her tokens of information like a deck of playing-cards. She tapped them this way and that. 'Your Russian ballet is wonderful. That man who jumps so high in the air!'

'Nijinsky.'

'That's the one. Such a difficult language to pronounce, I always think.'

Sophie knew nothing of ballet. Her parents had always been too busy to take her, then as a teenager she became an avid reader and lover of paintings. Now she loved whatever she had found at the Checkmate Café, which meant dancing with Khleb and Kolya through a sleeping city that longed to wake up to a life less banal.

The agent nodded before summing up: 'So, Mrs McFadden, I'm afraid there's just nothing on our books that fits what you're looking for. In Central London these days there's not enough quality accommodation to go round, even for those who can afford it. Best to keep looking in the newspaper. Or you could try a "board" in the street, for that kind of let.'

'I see. Well, thank you.'

Leksy, abandoning his pencilled house with scribbled tree and expressive sun and quiet moon, felt the tension streaming out of his mother as they rejoined the street.

'Something wrong?'

She shook her head. 'We'll try somewhere else.' But it seemed there was nowhere she could house herself or say what had happened to her. Words she could share with others would not deliver the message.

Her son felt gloomy but when they walked there was so much new to see that the gloom dispersed. She too was relieved that the moist air which had promised rain all day had still not delivered, and they could enjoy being outside.

In Marylebone, where they next found themselves, there was, indeed, a board with handwritten advertisements for rooms to let. She drew a pencil and a notebook from her bag and ran her eyes over the backs of envelopes on which the various notices were neatly written by hand, in ink. To all offers of rooms a coded condition attached: NCOP.

'Show me.'

She lifted him up. 'Eey–s–o–r,' he read as if it were in Cyrillic, for the letters were almost interchangeable.

He made her laugh. It sounded like Russian for 'rubbish'. But she said: 'Let's give it a try.'

A grey-haired red-faced old man with a shining pate opened a glass-panelled door up a short flight of steps. He was breathing heavily and resting on a stick, while his wife half behind his shoulder stared at the two figures on her doorstep. 'I'm afraid you've come in vain if you're looking for a house that takes children,' the man said, politely enough.

'But that's absurd, he's my son,' Sophie protested.

'I'm afraid you really will have to look elsewhere. As we said on the notice . . . ' With Sophie still on the doorstep they closed the door.

Back at the board one advertiser spelt out the prohibition: NO CHILDREN OR PETS. Each word underscored three times. Eyesore, eyesore, eyesore. Rubbish, rubbish, rubbish. 'That's just what it is. LABNHBNA. What would you make of that, Khleb? Lodgings Available But No Human Beings Need Apply.'

That evening they ate roast chestnuts from a street brazier. The bulk was satisfying. But the sweet-savoury stuff inside the charcoal-dark shells was so dry and powdery it stuck to the roof of your mouth and left you fishing around with your tongue to clear it. It wasn't an ideal meal. Meagre too.

Then it was back to their castle of a hotel, up to the second floor and along a maze of thickly carpeted corridors, and into bed early.

'Oah,' remembered Leksy, staring at the moulded ceiling before she put the light out. 'Oah and not oh.'

'As in?'

'As in "hoame".'

134

'The other way round now, Leks. Home. Boat. Road. Sleep well.'
She switched out the light and dreamt of Vera.

'I always thought that affair happened because there couldn't be anything with Pavel Berman. Because he wasn't made that way.'

'Oh no, it wasn't second-best. How like a man to imagine it must have been. Whether it would have lasted as a love affair, and as a marriage, is another question.'

Grigory Asmus had once met, at a pre-war conference in Helsinki, a London-based colleague in paediatric medicine. It was ten years ago but he had written down the professor's name and the address of the hospital, just in case. Like the Just-in-Case string shopping-bag you carried with you in Moscow, in the hope that there might be something good to eat on some stall or other, by chance, Pa kept a list of Just-in-Case names and they were of people who nearly all lived abroad.

As they approached that red-brick cathedral of medicine Sophie rejected the very idea of being ill. She positively detested hospitals. Some juvenile complex with regard to her parents' profession took hold of her and she was bristling with negative feeling as she set in motion the revolving door.

'I'd like to see Professor Huntley, please.' At the curved oak reception desk, busy with the winking lights and bells of an internal telephone exchange, a pleasant face looked up at her. Leksy yearned to help the Englishwoman put the plugs into the holes and say brightly, 'Good-morning, St Bartholemew's Hospital.'

'I don't have an appointment, no.'

'In which case, madam – '

'Please announce the daughter of Professor Asmus from Moscow.'

'Just one moment.'

As they climbed four flights of stairs, Leksy was nimble and his mother in her victory hardly less.

The English specialist in children's medicine wore a dark suit with a red bow tie and a matching silk waistcoat. In Moscow he would have been a Futurist poet. He gestured vaguely at Lesky.

'Mrs – '

'Mrs McFadden. Sophie Asmus was my maiden name. And this is my son Leksy.'

As the two males shook hands, the older one cast a professional glance over the younger. 'What seems to be the trouble?'

'I haven't come about Leksy.'

'I see. Do sit down, Mrs McFadden.'

'It's a practical, not a medical matter. I believe you are a colleague of my father. Perhaps you can help us. The situation in Russia is such that, although my father is an eminent man, I can no longer live there. I find myself here and – '

The specialist tilted his head, as if he had not quite heard Sophie's diagnosis of what ailed her. 'And Mr McFadden?'

'We're separated.'

'I'm sorry to hear that. To live with only one parent is never good for the child.'

She almost raised her voice. 'Things are as they are. It will be much better for both of us if I can find us somewhere to live. I'm not sure how one goes about it, however, when English landladies refuse to take children. They seem to regard children as being in the same category as animals. And, you see, my father is too far away to ask and I'm sure he would think I was doing the right thing by seeking out the advice of one of his esteemed colleagues.'

The specialist's small, neatly shod foot tapped under the desk. Only a naïve outsider would have interpreted his gesture as a predisposition to sympathy. He rang a bell, 'Mrs Davenport, would you come in, please?'

'I'm going to pass you over to my secretary, my dear. I'm sure she'll think of something.' His attention had already turned back to his agenda for the morning.

Mrs Davenport shook her head once the door was closed. 'He's always brusque. Don't take it personally.' She sat them down and produced a boiled sweet for Leksy. Sophie who did take it personally nevertheless felt an ease sweep over her for the first time in a week. They chatted easily and Valerie was as candid in her answer as Sophie was with her entreaty.

'It's not going to be easy, Sophie, do you mind if I call you Sophie?

A woman alone with a child must be a widow and, if you don't mind my saying, you don't exactly present yourself as a widow.'

Leksy writhed, unsure of various meanings, but strongly intuiting them.

Sophie gave a mild kind of snort. The two women exchanged silent sentiments on all manner of unspoken things to do with being themselves in a world of men.

'Digswise the best thing is to try "farther out". Perhaps Crystal Palace.'

'Crystal Palace? That sounds exciting.' Sophie knew the name from the famous glass pleasure house.

'Good luck then! Goodbye, Leksy!'

They parted with mutual reluctance, mother and son once more passing through the revolving doors.

On a map of London supplied by the hotel, Sophie noted the general direction and they took a train and walked, south and then north and then east, where they eventually came not to Crystal Palace but to Penge.

'Pyenzh, ' he said, for he could read the name of the station.

'Penge!' Sophie pointed urgently and repeatedly to her hard palate. 'Ehhhhh!'

'Ehhhhhh!' he bawled back at her.

The room they viewed, with a bay window and on the first floor, was in a house not unlike Seaview, but built of brick rather than granite. It smelt a bit musty. Perhaps all English houses did. The landlady left them alone to make up their minds. Sophie got side-tracked into thinking the boy just had to learn English if they were going to live in Penge and reverted to pointing to her hard palate. He pointed to his own and they collapsed laughing on the bed.

A moment later she bristled.

'Is there something wrong?'

'Eyesore. Rubbish. But what can we do? We'll just have to put up with it.' The double bed, high off the ground, with a heavy brown wooden headboard, smelt unfresh. Gracelessly it occupied too much of the cramped space.

As they sat there, perched on one side of the eiderdown, they saw the pale, faded floral wallpaper as having absorbed the dirt and ennui of every previous occupant. Dark-brown paint surrounded the sash window frame and covered the skirting-board, and the dado rail and the towel-stand were the same colour: all of which seemed to be a sad misunderstanding of the colour of wood in nature. Not only that. The room in Kingswood Road SE 21 was in a part of London which immediately struck Sophie as poor. People were ill-dressed and looked unhealthy. On the High Street as many horses and carts as motor vehicles went about their business, apart from the omnibuses. Also this was Penge and not Crystal Palace and they couldn't even see the giant greenhouse built to house tropical gardens and replica cultural treasures and draw visitors from all corners of the globe. Only Sophie imagined telling others they could, if they stood on tiptoe and were satisfied with a ten-per-cent view. The modest rent included breakfast and an evening meal at 6 p.m.

'She was ricocheting between her two worlds.'
  'I think that's right.'
  'And all for what?'
  'What happens when you rub two stones?'
  'A spark.'
  'She was that spark. She felt herself to be a spark.'

'We'll take it.'
When she had paid a week in advance, they went and fetched their luggage from Victoria. Returning with it directly this time, they climbed the iron steps of the railway bridge over the track and felt the whole structure resound to their footsteps. Like bells welcoming them, it sounded, and if you knew the savage, unmellow clang of Russian churchbells you might just imagine that London bells had a gentler tone.

Leksy stamped his feet and made the metal sing. 'Wo–heh, magic bells when you walk over the bridge!'

Again, but now in a new room, she switched out the light.

31

In the mornings Sophie read newspapers and magazines in the oak-furnished Penge Municipal Library. Leksy drew houses and suns and moons and sleigh tracks beside her in what became an agreeable routine. The trick was to imagine where you might fit, and whether you could bear it. Not among exiled dukes and duchesses, nor hitching a ride on the rag-and-bone cart that passed the house on Tuesdays with a possible Russian name painted on the side, Peters, Scrap Merchants. Mr Pay–terrss might be Russian but she couldn't imagine working for him. On the other hand, see here, a Mr Ilinsky who ran a caviare import business from an address north of the river needed a secretary.

The premises were shabby, confined in a tall narrow house with small rooms and dominated by the staircase. A secretary appraised Sophie silently. No woman could fail to notice Sophie's agreeable height and slender calves and ankles. Also, in fashion nothing like the suit she was wearing would arrive on London streets for years. The grey suit made her chic, while giving her freedom of movement to stride out, to run, to climb stairs two at a time, as she needed.

Mr Ilinsky sat at a wooden desk and she on an upright chair placed for the purpose of interrogation in the middle of the low-ceilinged, entirely functional room with a single sash window. The place needed some decoration if she were to work there: more than just a calendar on the nicotine-coloured wall. The light from a blustery blue-grey day strained to get in past the debris of city life impastoed on the glass.

She looked around as if she found it agreeable.

Would it not be useful to employ someone with Russian, she began. She could do all Mr Ilinsky's correspondence in both languages for him, for she had good typing and shorthand. French too, and even German, if necessary.

He didn't speak. He was middle-aged with receding hair that gave him an enormous brow and an air of intelligence, but that impression might be deceptive. He seemed not to have the practised English politeness to deal with the situation. He flushed red in his silence.

He took his glasses off and mopped his brow. He stared at her as if her audacity in coming into his office to ask him for work eclipsed all other qualities. 'Russian, are you? My father was Russian.'

'Russians are citizens of the world.'

'Alas, my dear, alas!' He got to his feet slamming the desk. 'Russians are stinking people and they live in a stinking country that can go to hell.' He threw out his arm. 'You can clear off now. Go on, clear off! I don't know what got into Geraldine letting scum like you in here. You're all the same, Red or White, arrogant Imperialist bullies the lot of you. You think you've got the God-given right to march in where you're not wanted.' He was shaking, as if this was the last effort he would ever make to return aggression that had been unfairly meted out to him. 'Geraldine, will you see the young lady out?'

Sophie could see he was in some way maimed. 'But, Mr Ilinsky, I don't see what you take me for or why I should put up with your abuse.'

'Murderers of my country. Anarchists. Chaotic people with no principles. Stay away from me.' He slumped back down into his chair. She thought he'd suffered a heart attack but the secretary, who must know him better, only stayed in the doorway. He pulled himself together and found a more suitable public voice. 'My apologies, madam, but it would not be suitable for you to work here. Please leave.'

She left him and emerged, into a street of insurance offices, desperate to recover but with no park bench in sight. Finding herself on Ludgate Hill, she finally went for a cup of tea in a café near St Paul's Cathedral.

'She had difficulty slotting herself back into public life over here.'

'Because everything now depended on her national origin, and she didn't understand herself at all like that.'

'In her notebook she described her national identity as, "alas, my only calling card".'

'That's what happens. Let's not pretend much has changed.'

Mrs Foster, who couldn't help making herself a servant, even in her own house, showed Valerie Davenport upstairs one Saturday lunch-time not long after.

'My goodness! Well, come in! What a pleasure, Val, how on earth did you find us?' As they embraced, Sophie was embarrassed at the cheap room, with the piles of envelopes on the table beside teacups and a barrel of biscuits, and the smell of mutton fat and tobacco that wafted up from the ground floor.

Val waved at the boy, who was playing on the floor. 'Hello, Leksy, I remember you.'

He wasn't forthcoming.

'I have to confess it's the third weekend I've scoured the boards around Crystal Palace. I happened to see you coming back just now.'

'I just popped out to the market.' Sophie took Val's fine-wool coat and hooked it on the back of the door, on top of her own.

'It's really was a fantastic coincidence we met as we did, and you know it set me thinking. We've had these Russian neighbours for a couple of years and I always felt ashamed we hadn't spoken to them. They keep very much to themselves, but you know, neighbours are neighbours. In short, we've got to know them a bit now and my husband and I thought you'd like to meet them.'

'Russians?' Sophie reflected warily. For some reason she remembered the revolving door that she and Leksy had passed through entering and leaving the hospital where they had met Val. The image calmed her. Those were the doors she had to pass through, and evidently more than once.

'Well yes, I would. Certainly.'

'Mrs Berman, the mother, is quiet as a mouse . . . '

'Berman did you say?'

'Barman? I think it's Berman. Now that her daughters have arrived they play the gramophone and dance in the garden. We certainly know they're there. But won't you come over and judge for yourself? Teddy and I would love to see you and we ought to get to know them better. We'll arrange a little party.' She paused. 'Maybe our neighbours can help you, Sophie.' Valerie was not quite sure what she felt, but there was about Sophie a sense of a fledgling tipped out of the nest. She needed to be put back.

*

'Was Val's impression of her right?'

'No. She was beyond that. Had she been "put back" her life would have been over.'

Valerie wrote down her exact address, so Sophie would find her way and so they could properly keep in touch.

'I liked you from the start.'

'Same here.'

Sophie was left praying that the Bermans wouldn't turn out to be angry Poles. But then she thought she knew them from a distance already.

The three women renting the villa next door to the Davenports all had the same bold and penetrating dark eyes. More like headlights than almonds.

Yulia Andreevna, the mother, with a wild mop of grey hair and a string of beads to her waist, offered her hand. The forthright daughter, who introduced herself as Lili, wore a bundle of garments loosely belted. She gave the impression that, whatever she might cover herself with, she would have worn her nakedness most happily. 'Does the King swim naked in St James's Pond? It's very pleasurable to swim naked, I'm told,' Sophie reminded herself.

The younger sister was more suspicious and greeted Sophie with an edge of sarcastic aggression.

'I didn't catch the name.'

'Elsa.'

'I know your brother. Isn't he Pavel Abramovich Berman?'

'The one and only.'

Thereupon Russian engulfed them. All of them happily swam in their own language, overjoyed to share it.

Lili knew the Checkmate Café well.

> 'And there will be more weeping than in a week of meatless
>   days.
> There will be beautiful colours, an eyebrow will scratch a
>   grackle's wing.'

'Bravo, Khleb! *Molodets!*'

142

'I was the only physician left in this madhouse, and I brought you my medicinal poems.'

'And they turned around and killed you with them.'

'It was too much for one man to bear. He died for all of us.'

'I can see that.'

'How do you know Pavel?'

'We were on the same course together at the university.'

Mrs Berman shook her head. 'He should have gone into business.'

'Ma works for our Russian trading company here. She can't imagine anyone would ever want to do anything different.'

'You work for the Soviet Government, Mrs Berman?'

'I do.'

'I've told Ma a hundred times. Pavel couldn't do that. He lives for art.'

'But, Mrs Berman, have you been in touch with him in the last few months? You should maybe – '

'Pavel hasn't got any money and he doesn't want to travel,' tittered Elsa. 'So we've left him to his fate.'

'I was worried about him when I left,' said Sophie, picturing that severely weakened figure, among the rugs and paintings he refused to sell to the Commission shop. But she changed the subject. 'And do you know Kolya Lukyanov the performance poet?'

'They all perform,' retorted Lili.

'Not many poets can climb a lamp post like he can. You should have seen him.'

'Performing like a monkey?' enquired Elsa. 'Climbing a lamp post and calling it art?'

'Don't take any notice of Elsa, Sofia Grigorievna. She always dismisses what she doesn't understand.'

They had to remind themselves that Moscow was far away from where they were sitting now, in soft chairs sipping milky tea from cups with saucers; saucers out of which no one ever *drank*.

Teddy, because he had no idea what to say to these four strange females, felt awkward in his own house. Valerie was of no help to him in the kitchen, so he invited Leksy to come upstairs and inspect the train set he had kept since his boyhood. The boy ran ahead willingly.

Which only allowed Sophie and the Bermans to become all the more absorbed in the life they shared.

Elsa said: 'I've been here a bit longer than Lili, for personal reasons.' Her eyes shot up to indicate some contemptible other who was responsible for her plight.

'Oh yes?'

'I'm divorced and I've got a job in an architect's studio.'

'Sounds perfect.'

Elsa sent those huge eyes skywards again and shrugged.

'Have you seen English houses, my dear?' She burst into tinkling laughter. 'They know how to build doll's houses no human being could possibly enjoy living in and they construct ugly overblown palaces for the rest. Wealth here goes hand in hand with ugliness and showing-off, except for a tiny handful of people with taste.'

'Speaking of palaces, although not overblown, I would say, timid rather, more . . . ' Sophie had been disappointed by the conventional shape of the Crystal Palace when she actually saw it.

'Besides which I don't earn enough to buy myself a tube of toothpaste. Really, ask Mama. I have to live off Mama.'

'As do I,' said her sister, as if that was a fair defence of the awkward situation both Berman girls found themselves in, in exile.

'You might write something about living abroad and try to publish it.' Which sounded even as she said it like Sophie talking to herself.

'I'm too lazy for that. Why can't I have a husband like Lili? Lili's got this rich Russian husband in Germany whereas what am I to do in London? It's all for show here. Nice job, nice people and incredible meanness holding it all together.'

'We should all go to Paris. Now that's a nice free-minded place,' said Lili.

'I've always wanted to go to Paris. I know this wonderful photographer who lives there – '

'Who, Sophie? Do tell!'

'The *family* hasn't of course *left* Russia, we merely travel a lot,' Mrs Berman was explaining. 'We're *used* to spending *part* of the year abroad,' she insisted.

And it seemed in that moment that the element in which the Bermans lived was air, a nice free feeling from within but subject to all sorts of interpretations from without; and Sophie learnt something from that.

'Have you found, Sofia Grigorievna, that in London you are simply not *allowed* to be a Bolshevik because it would be bad form?' asked Elsa.

'Elsa thinks no rich man will marry her if she confesses to being a Red.'

'But *you* married here, my dear,' said Mrs Berman. 'Mrs Davenport tells us you married a Scot. You surely can call yourself at home in this country.'

'Ma! Marriage solves nothing in our generation. It's so easily undone it doesn't mean anything. You're insulting Sophie if you're saying she needs a husband to define where she belongs in the world.'

'I'm not insulted, Lili. It's just a divorced woman in a bourgeois society is . . . not free . . . or at least not as free as she thinks. And then it's difficult to know how to present herself.'

Sophie had weathered two unwelcome overtures on London Bridge.

'What, in her diary?'

'You can read them for yourself. Men whispering in her ear.'

'Isn't that so, Elsa, about a divorced woman in a bourgeois society . . . '

'Absolutely true. Where is one supposed to go? One gets so lonely!' squealed the youngest Berman.

Teddy and Leksy returned down the stairs. '*Mama, posmotri!*' The boy entered the room engrossed in a toy engine he had been given to keep.

'Does he know English?'

'Perfectly well. But you know how it is.'

'Will you show me?' asked Elsa in stiff English, but suddenly with a good heart.

Valerie felt when she re-entered the room, ostensibly offering more tea, that the best she could do had been done. The room reverberated with whatever these intense people had been discussing. They were intense, weren't they, Russians?

'More cake, Elsa?'

'I'd love a little piece, Val.'

'Shouldn't you watch your figure?' teased Lili.

'There have to be some pleasures at a time like this. Don't you think, Sophie? But you look as if you starve yourself.'

'There isn't the occasion to eat. You know how it is.'

'Heavens!' said Mrs Berman.

Valerie and Teddy laughed awkwardly.

Then the Bermans got up to leave, as was the polite thing after taking up almost two hours of their neighbours' day. Sophie and her son left straight after and the door closed a final time.

32

Another name from her notebook for another day was Sir Peter Salomé, on whose final letter she put an acute accent, with a question mark. She walked three times past his High Holborn office, in one of those mock-Tudor buildings where the road opened out, planning what to wear and what to say. Finally one morning, courtesy of Mrs Foster who was prepared to babysit Leksy, she returned to Holborn alone.

Sir Peter's moustache was in the English style of the day and didn't droop. He didn't look Russian to her, but anyway, what did it mean, 'to look Russian'? What was visible was the still boyish face of a man well over fifty.

From behind the vast leather-topped desk where he read his papers in a soft light Peter Salomé glanced at his visitor. He wondered at himself, admitting a complete stranger, 'opening himself to the public', as it were. But the euphoria of recently receiving a knighthood from the King of England made him long to bestow kindness and recognition on others. He felt rejuvenated. For the first time since the death of his son the previous year his life seemed to have a shape

146

which confirmed benign forces at work. He had faith again, and that allowed him to cope with accident and error. All men needed faith in humanity and Jesus Christ to carry on in difficult times and they especially needed it if they had anything to do with Russia. Peter Salomé was well-received in the highest English circles when he said that. The generals and the politicians liked their version of Jesus.

'What can I do for you?'

She could hear the unconcealed accent.

'Good-morning, Sir Peter –'

In that huge, pleasant room, all hung with velvets and leathers, and oil paintings of ducal ancestors actually belonging to no one, Sophie relied on her pleasant appearance to make a good first impression. She wore her other suit, the one in which she had arrived in Moscow, which was an olive green skirt to the mid-calf, and a broderie anglaise white blouse, frilled and high at the neck and cuffs; and long beads, which were the fashion, with a matching green jacket, fitted at the waist.

'It's very good of you to see me.'

He too knew a Russian accent when he heard it, slight as it was.

The Tsar had committed fateful errors. Pyotr Karlovich Salomé had warned him personally. 'Don't, sire! Don't leave your wife to run the country! She's a vulnerable woman, she's seen as a German, and, worst of all, she has flatterers on whom she has come to rely.'

When out of a domestic tragedy a national catastrophe loomed, Pyotr Karlovich offered his resignation. The Tsar angrily rejected it. 'Stuff and nonsense. You hold a post in my government and I will decide when you resign.'

'What can I do for you, Miss Asmus?' After her first naïve attempt with Mr Ilinsky, though they were hardly the cause of the disaster, she left off her wedding ring and used her maiden name.

'Tell me how I can live in this city, Sir Peter! How does one find work at the right level? How is it possible to allay English suspicions?' Her voice got louder as she spoke, but she did her best to address him as an equal.

'Dear lady!' He felt her distress. He pondered it as if it were his own. 'Let me think how I can help you.'

'Of course I was obliged to let His Majesty's will prevail, but by the end of 1917 there was no country left for me to hold a post in. That's when I came here.'

'To all our benefit, Sir Peter,' had been what the King himself said, after the sword touched his shoulder. 'Arise, Sir Peter!'

He rang a bell and asked his assistant to serve them coffee. A tray was brought with a tall china jug, an open smaller jug of hot milk and a bowl of brown sugar. Sir Peter served it himself. 'How do you take it? White?'

'One sugar. Please.' Sir Peter's cups were bone china, almost too delicate to hold, and had a gold rim.

He knew it was his knowledge of finance had made him welcome. It was after all as a banker that the British sovereign had noticed him, after he wrote articles in the newspapers. But it had helped that he was also a gentleman.

And was she a lady, or what?

'Tell me about yourself. How is it you find yourself here alone, Miss Asmus?'

When she confessed her situation straight out he agonised with her, which his gentlemanly training made it possible to do. And then politely, not to make her feel the least inequality between them, he told her about that part of himself which preceded the catastrophe. How he had studied banking in Berlin. How people always thought he was a Jew, though – for all the difference it made – his ancestry was actually French Huguenot and Baltic German, into which his mother had added the Russian element.

He spoke an elegant, rounded nineteenth-century Russian. *Gozpozha* Asmus, he called her. Not 'Comrade' as they did in Russia now; unless they suspected you of being a spy.

'From what you tell me it's become impossible over there.'

'I feared for my son's well-being and for my life.'

He knew it and every day seemed to confirm it. Because now politics was everything in that country, no Russian was free anywhere on earth. Every Russian had to declare himself, herself, Red or White, for fear of being defenceless. Or leave. And even then. Better to have an alias. Best of all the protection of a king.

He looked at her kindly. He had interests of his own he had to protect. But they did not rule his entire conduct.

'You say you have typing and some shorthand? It seems to me you are excellently qualified, *Gozpozha* Asmus.'

She saw him write something like a doctor's prescription. He called for his secretary and handed it to her. She in turn came back with a sealed envelope.

'From the ashes of pre-revolutionary Russia I rise up,' the beneficiary had thought to himself as he was knighted.

Sovereign and subject had the standard chat after the ceremony. 'Poor Nicky. Such a tragedy! And the whole family! Surely they could have spared the girls.'

Poor Nicky indeed, stuffed down a well with his throat cut, or was it a bullet through the heart, somewhere in Siberia.

'The Tsar should have left sooner, Your Majesty, but where could he go? No one would have him and his dear family.'

Sir Peter had said as much to the King as he dared, in reproach. He had to accept that England's friendship with Russia was always troubled, one way or another, though it had given a deracinated banker a home.

He came round to the front of his desk and briefly bowed to Miss Sophie Asmus in the German fashion, though without clicking his heels. He handed her the envelope and saw her to the door. 'I hope this will be helpful to you.'

In the tube, slicing through the top of the envelope with an impatient thumb, she was astonished to find the envelope contained only some money, no written note at all. It was enough to pay her rent for two weeks, but nothing on which she could build. She longed to run back and protest, but you don't understand, I need to work, but the impulse was useless, and she suppressed it and just the hurt remained. She returned to her long watch for signs in the street and opportunities that might crop up.

33

It was May now, the weather was bright and the wind brisk and almost warm. The globe that crowned London as the world capital of entertainment rose above the more prosaic roofs of St Martin's Lane, while Sophie below, entering through nicely worked oak doors into a silent and empty foyer, enquired after the stage door. The house of the handsome and curvaceous new theatre was currently packed night after night.

Back outside she crossed the road to stare up at the electrically lit globe once more. Then she made her way to a back street behind the theatre, where once the horses had been stabled. Fetchingly dressed in the geometric grey suit with a long bright scarf at the neck, under an open coat, she waited outside for curtain down.

As the dancers finally emerged, the prima ballerina was still clutching her bouquet. She and members of the company talked of a strain overcome in the form of an uneven floor, and of an appreciative house. The evening had been magical, the manager said. His appreciation of the power of his dancers never waned.

Sophie stepped forward. 'Tamara Nikolaevna, allow me to introduce myself. I saw the headlines. *The Times* was ecstatic.' Indeed, the Ballets Russes seemed to have arrived in London from another planet.

The dancers smelt of strong perfume and a hint of sweat, odours which began to disperse in the outside air.

Tamara Nikolaevna stopped and looked on her kindly, like an aunt on a niece she couldn't quite remember. '*Zdrastvuyi, milaya, kak tebe pomoch?*'

No one had addressed Sophie in the familiar way since she left.

'I just wanted to hear Russian spoken again.'

'Of course.'

Tamara's manager was a short, balding man fancily dressed in a grey suit with a mustard-coloured shirt. He had the jovial manner, and the unintended suit creases, of his profession.

'Well, what have we here? A beautiful and genuine Russian lady? My dear, can it be that you are alone?'

The dancers around him joked and tutted. 'Here he goes again! Don't touch him with a barge pole!'

'Do not mock, ladies! Tamarochka, be so kind, introduce me – '

'Sophie, have I got that right? Sophie, this is my manager Vanya.' As she acknowledged him Sophie relished the jostle of the crowd. Autograph books were passed from hand to hand over the sea of bobbing heads and flash-bulbs popped as cameras snapped. It seemed a long time since she had been in adult society.

'Beautiful stranger, shall we pretend to fall in love?'

'Why pretend?' tittered one of the dancers.

The manager raised Sophie's hand close to his lips but didn't kiss it. He had shiny skin and tiny feet in black patent pumps.

'What a night this is!' exclaimed Tamara.

'Your triumph, my dear, as much as Sergei Pavlovich's.'

Tamara was dancing Odile in Diaghilev's *Swan Lake*.

'Tchaikovsky. Now there's a melancholy Russian composer!'

'Have you seen Tamara dance?' asked one of the troupe.

'Alas no. I've only been here a short time – ' Sophie lied.

'Really, you've only just come from there? Do tell.'

They climbed into their cars and swept her in with them.

Tamara whispered: 'How is it over there?'

Sophie fell into her part as a messenger from Moscow. 'Just as it always was.'

'But worse. I know. I know exactly.'

Sophie answered Vanya, over his shoulder, that yes, she had heard Russians did well in Paris.

'The Maestro lives in Paris,' said the dancer.

Tamara recalled: 'When I first arrived in London, I didn't know a soul and I couldn't even ask for a cup of tea.'

'Only three words are necessary in any language,' said Vanya, turning. 'Man, woman, love.'

'Vanya, don't talk nonsense.' Tamara resumed her story. 'I had to trust people to be kind to me.'

'Sergei Pavlovich – '

'The Maestro – '

'The selfsame. He put me in a hotel in Leicester Square where there

151

was a barrel-organ outside. It made a terrible racket. I lay there on that soft bed staring at the windows, wondering what would become of me, and all I could take in was that noise and the fact that the windows were filthy.'

'Tell Sophie the story about your toes bleeding because the floor was so bad.'

'But that often happens. No, that time, my dear, I cried because the food in England was so awful.'

The car halted and men in fancy dress opened the doors. People started to get out. Tamara took a good look at Sophie standing there on the pavement under the awning of the great hotel. She must have liked what she saw because then she hugged her. 'What do you do? Dance? Sing? Play?'

'I'm too tall to dance, Tamara Nikolaevna, too lazy to practise and frankly tone-deaf.' But no one cared about the answer. They had brought her along for the fun of it, and now one by one they passed through the revolving door. The party was on the top floor of the Savoy, where Tamara and her retinue occupied a suite of rooms. There were flowers everywhere and an icon had been placed in a corner.

'Mmm, herring!' said the dancer, sniffing the air. The bread was soft and English, but the little open sandwiches looked scrumptious. They were jewelled with real black sturgeon caviare, or concrete-carpeted with a fat slice of rollmop herring, or canopied in yellow cheese sprinkled with paprika. At intervals stood open pots of dill pickles which the dancers loved.

'Salt and no calories,' said Vanya, who then amused himself by sending a champagne cork up to the ceiling. He filled glasses which the guests passed from one to another.

'Is that for me?' An interestingly dressed woman about Sophie's age approached.

'So you're a stage designer! That explains it. What's your name?'

'Nadya.'

Their fascination was mutual.

'Sophie, I love your suit.'

Something about what was happening on the ballet stage enhanced the impression Sophie made on her second visit to London. The

Ballets Russes gave their audiences a preview of an as yet unknown freedom of body and soul. Sophie appeared to have been nurtured in the same spirit, one that the stage designer recognised.

In fact Nadya had only recently arrived in London with her husband, who was 'in the film business'.

'Is your husband Russian?'

'He's a bit of everything, *das bist du, ne pravda li, mon cher*. A real mongrel.'

They laughed over that. Looking across the room at the short, sturdily built man with a powerful head made Sophie think of what Pavel Abramovich might have become had he chosen a different life. He could have been living with his Russian wife in a Bayswater bedsit and calling himself a businessman.

'Leave it, darling, people really don't want to know,' said the husband, who came over reluctantly when summoned, and drifted off again.

The wife confided in Sophie. 'He thinks we'll be rich again soon. Once rich always rich, he says. I'd like to know how.'

The stage designer was considerably taller than her husband, pregnant and radiant, and Sophie was attracted to her and wanted to prise her away from him.

'When's the baby due?'

'August.'

'Nadya, to have a child is such a blessing.' Sophie became maudlin with champagne and company.

'Lady Perron,' murmured Vanya, over her shoulder. Lady Perron had a fine-boned face reminiscent of one of Sir Peter's expensive tea-cups. Everyone attended to her.

'Of course the ballet is a spiritual matter. But try telling some critics that. We have to overcome so much Victorian prejudice against, how shall I put it – ' here she managed to look entranced ' – the freedom of the body.'

Sophie remembered a morning in Scotland when she had dipped her feet in the sea. She remembered the hieroglyphs Vera painted on her belly, with her tongue. She saw Kolya Lukyanov shinning up a lamp post.

Tamara Nikolaevna reappeared. 'You're quite right about the prejudice, Lady Perron. My first dressing-room in London I had acrobats on one side and a freak show on the other. That was what management thought of me.'

'Some people really are slow to change.'

Sophie addressed Lady Perron: 'But the ballet is only on the stage. When will the real revolution happen in London?'

'Well said, my dear.'

'No, but really. Art needs to take the whole of society with it.'

'Exactly, darling,' said Tamara Nikolaevna. 'Sergei Pavlovich says it will take a third revolution of love before the world finally opens its eyes to Art.'

Lady Perron said all that was most interesting, and turned away to talk to faces she knew, on themes she recognised.

For a moment Sophie stood alone. Then Tamara Nikolaevna came back. The two of them moved into a quiet corner.

'You should find an English husband, my dear. English men can be very kind. Much more considerate than Russian. It's one of the *avantages* of the culture.' She used the French pronunciation and then she winked. 'All you need is a decent sort.'

'But he was decent . . . '

'I've got an English husband myself.'

'She married him *avant la déluge*,' said Vanya. 'He's a great sweetie.'

'As everyone here knows.'

Someone turned the lights out for a prank.

'Oooh, Alfred, don't do that!'

'Aaah! Ladies, the witching hour!'

'How about a swim in the Serpentine? We'll get the cars to take us to Hyde Park.'

Alas the proposal fell flat.

Instead Vanya was trying to keep a champagne glass balanced on his forehead while leaning backwards.

Sophie joined the chorus of people who counted to ten while he held that difficult pose. 'Eight . . . nine . . . ten!' She clapped her hands in delight. For a moment Vanya reminded her of Kolya.

'I'll not move until Sophie drinks the champagne.'

She lifted the glass and drained it with a wink at him and a round of applause.

Her head felt light. There seemed to be an unlimited supply of Moët and people were eating chocolates with it.

But then Vanya clapped his hands and called time, and all the dancers got to their feet and made for the door as if it were the midnight scene in *Cinderella*.

'Lovely to meet you, Nadya.'

'You too, Sophie, good luck.'

'Will I see you again?' Sophie whispered to Tamara Nikolaevna.

'Look in your coat pocket, darling. It was lovely to meet you, truly.' In the doorway Vanya waited to sweep Tamara under his midnight wing. 'Ladies, come along please, time for your beauty sleep!'

Someone collected the icon that had blessed the gathering and wrapped it in a towel.

Her head felt like lead and her heart wept.

It was almost midnight, and the railway was not a place for a woman alone to linger. She ran all the way back to Kingswood Road and the sound of the clanging bridge in her head was overlaid with the clack of her heels on the pavement. Indoors, still in her coat, she slid paper notes silkenly between her fingers.

Bozhe. It was enough for a year's rent.

34

A man in a bowler hat was resting his forearms on a pulpit and addressing the crowd. She hadn't seen a pulpit since Leksy's christening.

'There are forces of good and evil . . . The Lords of the Dark Face . . . A great battle for the kingdom of goodness awaits us . . . '

'I can't see.'

'Poor lad. Put him on my shoulders. He'll get crushed here.'

Tall Sophie stood just above the sea of hats, beside the kind stranger. When she tugged at her son's bare leg he smiled down at his dear Mama.

'Are we going to allow our inner forces of light or the powers of darkness to win?' the man cried. A blackboard leaned against the hem of the pulpit, and it was a strange sight, for with its hectic display of symbols, equations and numbers it suggested that one side could be balanced against the other.

'Does he do magic tricks?'

'That's exactly what he's proposing, young lad. Comes up here of a Sunday afternoon and shouts his nonsense.'

'I suppose you're a rationalist,' Sophie said to the man who had her son on his shoulders.

'I'm an honest man, madam. This is the rant of a charlatan.'

The speaker hammered on his pulpit. Perhaps somewhere in the world they buried people upright in oval containers just like this, and then rammed on the lid. She scoffed, and yet she listened. 'How easy not to fight and find reasons to withdraw from the battle . . . '

There was evidently a great battle in constant session in the universe between those who knew what was right and those who didn't and she wondered where –

'If I had my way that policeman would take this lunatic away and stop him poisoning people's ears with his cosmic struggles . . . '

'Why is he drumming the box?' asked Leksy.

'He's . . . cross.'

'*Serdytsya?*'

'Da.'

So now their neighbour in the Speakers' Corner crowd knew they were Russian, though he didn't seem to mind. Huge old Victorian oaks in full leaf clustered around them. A great green shaggy backdrop obscured the noise and the buildings at the top end of Oxford Street.

'Dear Lord, we pray to be free from all evils. Give us intelligence, spiritual vision, victory over delusion . . . '

'He could do with a bit of all that.'

'Patience and forgiveness, truth, self-harmony, peace – '

An appreciative hum passed through the crowd.

'Freedom from fear, harmlessness and non-violence, ever-quietness, satisfaction, simple austerity, generosity, honour not dishonour . . . '

'Calls himself an orator? Sounds like a bloody shopping list to me.

156

Just don't believe a word of it, madam. The man's a danger to the public. An imposter.'

When Leksy got down the man stood for a while then, tipping his hat, vanished through the crowd.

She stood for a moment nonplussed. Then she sat, with her son, on a bench, and smoked the one cigarette a day she had decided to afford, consequent upon the ballerina's gift.

On the bench she could still hear the speaker preaching but no longer see him. A plump policeman watched the whole scene from a distance, legs akimbo, chinstrap dangling, while Leksy ran his train along the slats of the seat.

'A first function of our faith is to create an effective type of personality to listen to the Lord and resist evil . . . To those who are ever in harmony, the Lord gives the Yoga of vision and dispels their ignorance of the true path.'

Perhaps that's my trouble, she thought. I don't know what to think. I ought to be able to stand up there and say clearly what's right and wrong.

I'm lowered in the world . . . because I don't belong anywhere.

They ate their lunch, wrapped in greaseproof paper and then in a brown paper bag. Marmite sandwiches, cut into quarters, and an apple each.

'Heh wait, Leks!'

But she had promised him they would visit the boating lake and he set off impatient for his sight of water.

It lay in a slight dell, like the spot across the city where she would have loved the King to abandon protocol and dive in. On its calm surface lovely model ships made of prettily painted wood, with wire rigging and canvas sails, floated along. But not everyone had a boat, and those without were throwing stones into the water. By the time she arrived to take up a vantage point without spoiling his game Leksy had joined two stone-throwers, smaller and larger than he was. The smallest boy with glasses was the best throw. Leksy held his own but his curiosity about how the stones hit the water distracted him. The big boy gave Leksy a shove and Leksy shoved him back.

Leksy came over to report. 'His name is Alan. He asked me my name. I said it was Alex.'

'Why did you say it was Alex? Only Daddy calls you that.'

'He said Leksy's a funny name.' The boy turned his head in the direction of the heftier, less reflective of his two companions.

'Alan. Aah–aah–aah – lan! Did you tell him anyone would think he was going to sneeze?'

Her son shook his head. 'Leksy's the funny name.'

'Who does he think he is, telling people what they can be called?'

She couldn't persuade Leksy to agree. Eventually they went for tea. Back at the spot where the orators were trying to goad the crowd into a new life with new values, she couldn't resist. Now it was a woman addressing the crowd. A woman! Just imagine!

'Wait, Leks. Just a minute!' The woman wore a hat and a cloak and looked conventional. But when she spoke that impression was entirely dispelled.

'Incessant pregnancy reduces marriage to a form of female illness.'

The crowd jeered. 'God help your husband, you old crow.'

Sophie shouted: 'Not at all. A modern husband should be proud of an enlightened wife.'

'Don't speak, Mama!' Leksy tugged at her. The surprised young couple beside her moved away.

The speaker had a high forehead and a long face. She was rather attractive, and spoke with the voice of a true leader, rather than wheedling like a demon newly-hatched from a diabolical egg. 'Thank you for your support, young lady.'

While Sophie recovered from embarrassment at her own boldness, nimbly the speaker turned the tables against her detractor. 'What does the young gentleman think married love is, if not consideration for the health and well-being of his wife? Is it by the number of his children that we should assess his moral and economic contribution to life? I say to you, sir, what you say to me, "Where is love in your life?" And my answer is this. I am far from being one of those "new women" you despise, who take their experiences as females with lightness. I am far from being one whose feelings and mental energies are directed at all other things in life but sentimental emotions.

Love – with its disappointments, its tragedies and its eternal demand for happiness – is at the centre of my being. But I cannot accept that this great belief of ours, this elevation of Love to our most favoured modern deity, means we should so mistreat women as to reduce them to incessant carriers of infants.'

She winked at the crowd, who thought, 'Love at the centre of her being, eh, and she at least fifty.'

'My point is that all women, married or not, have the right to enjoy *both* sexual pleasure *and* the bearing of children as it suits their well-being. Marriage should not be some conspiracy of men ruling over them, but a state that allows them the freedom to flourish.'

'Madam, I agree with you on free love.' A gasp went up at those racy words, and then all the heads shifted to examine the young man who had intervened. 'Even if love will never be free, because of jealousy, the arrogance of my sex and the irresponsibility that erupts in all of us, free love is surely how we should live. But contraception freely available? Sanction that and you can be sure the state will use it to curb the reproduction of the feeble-minded and sickly. No decent person can accept this. Rather the government must make the conditions of motherhood easier.'

'That's not what women want!' a woman about her own age shouted. 'They want to be in charge of their own bodies.'

'Hear, hear!' yelled Sophie.

'Mama, no!'

'I do take *his* point,' said the woman on the box. 'Governments will be only too pleased if we give them an excuse to shape a population they can manage. But that is only another task for us, to hold government to account for *all* its misdeeds.

'Besides, don't neglect the other aspect of my argument. Most married women in this country alive today will *never* be treated as equals. Most unmarried women today, who are still unmarried tomorrow, will for the rest of their lives be officially denied all *pleasure* in life, beyond the satisfaction of filial duty; they will waste lives that could have been just as happy and productive as those of their married brothers and sisters. It is in *pleasure* that we demand equality.

It is a terrible cruelty we practise, with our present conventions, that does not allow *all* women sexual happiness.'

'Please don't speak, Mama, I'd rather you didn't.'

But that night their digs became her rehearsal studio and she worked on her spoken voice by listening to the wireless. ' "This is the BBC Home Service." H–owe–me, Leksy, not Ho–oa–me, say it.' So much, so much did she want to speak that in search of her content she went daily to read in Penge Library, while Leksy drew pictures beside her, until she was ready.

It was a dull grey Sunday morning, when the horse-chestnut leaves, three-pronged and the size of teaplates, were already turning yellow and falling. Leksy held them up to find the biggest. Having mentioned that she would like to speak, she took up a position in the crowd to get in the mood.

The young man who had raised the worry that birth control would encourage governments to tailor their populations was back again. The desire to contradict him excited her. She pushed her way through the crowd to stand at the front.

He had a soft mouth. She watched it enunciate from the midst of a full beard. He wore a white shirt and a short red tie. His long hair brushed back from his face made his forehead seem even more prominent than it was designed to be by nature. His bright, clear eyes, filled with intense longing, surveyed the crowd from time to time, willing them to cease their mindless petty hostilities and agree with him that a better world was possible. He rested his eyes on Sophie for a moment before he began again. How he deplored the waste of 'women and others' who could not find their niche in present-day society –

In fact she agreed with him in everything except the contraception issue, but mainly the crowd was hostile.

'What "others", you bloody pansy?'

Laughter rippled through the crowd.

'Any man or woman in our time who wants ease of soul struggles with the absurdities of convention. I can tell you my own story. A life of ease and high honours lay before me. But, ladies and gentlemen, my soul was stifled. I longed to run out into the open air and pick up a hammer and an axe and craft my own existence in nature.'

The crowd clicked sarcastically. *Ts–ts–ts*.

'So I left the university. I gave my fine clothes away. I went to live in the countryside as a labourer, and my restlessness and bitterness ceased.'

'He'll be saying he's Jesus Christ next.'

'I could see that respectable society was sick with its own lies.'

'Pansy!' Some aggressive males refused to give up their taunting.

'But I promise you the gloomy and depressing wage-slavery of today will one day give way to productive work with the character of spontaneity and gladness. And with these feelings inside you, ladies and gentlemen, you too will rediscover Art and Beauty and the Joy of Living.'

Then, even while she was a little mesmerised by that speaker's glistening idealism, he finished and her turn arrived.

'She had a vision of her own salvation. The world must change to accommodate her.'

'You could say that, Leksy. But . . . she would become more than that. Give her time.'

She felt nervous. And she had no pamphlets to sell. And no bonnet to wear.

'Ladies and gentlemen, my topic today is . . . .' There was a hush.

She wanted to repeat what she felt about contraception. That was her intention. She was ready incidentally to join her voice to the British suffragettes. But what actually came out surprised her most of all.

'I stand here today to explain to you the prison of unwanted motherhood.'

What had come out of her? All she could hear was the crowd booing.

35

'Leksy!' She couldn't see him. 'Leks, where are you, don't hide from Mama.'

'What's the matter, lady?'

'I can't find my boy.'

'You who were just decrying motherhood! You don't deserve a child.'

Others thought they must have misunderstood.

She pushed through the crowd to its edge.

'He can't be far. Anyone here seen a little boy? How old?'

'Five. Dark-haired. Quite tall. Like his father.'

Not finding him she ran in the direction of the boating lake. 'Sir, madam, excuse me, I had a child with me, my son, my Leksy, Leksy is his name, did you see where he went?'

Concerned strangers shook their heads.

'He must have wandered off and that's a worry because he doesn't know his way in London. He's so young. He couldn't find his way home to Pyenzh. What am I saying? I mean Penge. Yes, my son Leksy. Alexander, that's right, it's a Russian name, but we call him Leksy.'

'*Llyekseee. Llyek–sea!*' Her piercing Russian cry pitched through the air. They couldn't have imitated it had they tried.

People looked at her. She was flushed and agitated. Her unusual clothes, now she had lost her poise, seemed eccentric, although clearly she could run in them, as now.

'Sometimes he calls himself Alex.' That they could follow.

'Aaah–lex! L–e–ksy! *Llyek–sea! Ne skrysh'sya!* Don't hide. Mama can't find you in the big park.

'I can't find my boy. HIM. NOT FIND. LOST. LOST BOY. NOT HIDING. LOST. YOU UNDERSTAND ME, SIR?' As she dodged from side to side the stranger thought she was trying to make a fool of him.

Someone said she was a Russian ballerina, that it was all a performance, because she looked like that, in that strange Futurist outfit like a pair of triangles stitched together. When she stopped to catch her breath she brushed the hair back from her face, or she screened her eyes in the hope of seeing better. But if you came close to her you could see the terror on her face, a flicker waiting to burst into full flame. 'My darling, *kuda ty delsya*? Where have you got to? Come on now, it's Mama, listen to Mama, come to Mama, we have to go home and – '

'Easy there, ducks, we'll find him. There's a few of us will help you look.'

'Hyde Park is not exactly someone's back garden,' said another. 'It's a big place.'

'That's not an excuse. This lady needs help. She's lost her son. Come on there, lend a hand.'

'I should find a policeman in your position, madam,' said a man in a beige raincoat and when their eyes briefly met she knew he was talking sense. His whole being exuded calm citizenship and faith in the law. But that meant a loss of time and she and her three help-mates were already off again combing the green expanse of trees and meadow. Lake, yes, the boats, he liked the boats. Let's try it again. But the boy will fall in, he can't swim.

'Everyone loves kids. If anyone finds him they'll take him to a police station.'

'Oh yes, everyone loves kids? You could have fooled me. You hear stories of what they do to kids – '

'Don't talk like that.'

'There are types like that who should be locked up.'

'Don't frighten the woman! Most people are the decent sort.'

Now the sober-minded man in the raincoat, who had recommended fetching a policeman, a soft, jowly, avuncular-looking man whom anyone who didn't know him would be hard put to remember, returned with one. The helpful man had brown glasses and he was wearing a collar and tie beneath the open raincoat. And a trilby hat, she remembered, as she struggled to recall him afterwards.

It was the policeman she needed now. She flung herself on his uniformed breast. 'Help me find my son, please!' Still some of the people around thought she was play-acting and this self-dramatisation was all part of being a Russian refugee. She hurt her cheek on the row of metal buttons and there was a tiny gash under her left eye.

'Calm yourself, madam,' said the policeman, his head bathed in the sweated cream on her face and the smell of her fear. When he unpicked her arms from his uniform it was as if he were clearing his garden of sticky weed. She was trembling like a frightened dog. He knew dogs better than women. The dogs they sometimes picked up from the streets had been beaten, and they would take them, poor whimpering sick wretches, to the Dogs' Home. God knows what became of them. You couldn't keep alive every stray in London.

'How can I calm myself when I've lost my son?'

Out of nowhere he slapped her. 'Pull yourself together, woman! The sooner you give me some details the sooner I can get a search party out.' He took out his notebook and pencil. 'Name?'

'Asmus, I mean McFadden.'

'Which?'

'McFadden.'

She was shivering. Beside her was this figure in navy blue, in uniform, wearing a helmet.

'Where's my son?' But then suddenly she laughed. For a few seconds she refused to look at her assailant, this protector of the law who, instead of helping her, had treated her as one who had to be subdued. The buttons her cheek had collided with reminded her of something. Of shining buttons on military uniforms and of the power that her husband, in uniform, and his 'Commander', when they first met.

'Ah, I see . . . doesn't matter . . . '

'God Almighty! We've got a right lunatic here.'

'It doesn't matter, doesn't matter. *Nichego*.' She laughed.

'What do you mean, it doesn't matter? You've lost your son.'

'Sorry to trouble you, officer. I have to go now.'

'Madam, if a child is missing I must take details.' The policeman's voice trailed after her. She ran. He began to run. Not that he could catch her.

'Will you be all right, ducks?' someone called.

'Yes, yes, my Leksy is safe. I go now. Is all right. You very kind. Thank you, kind people everywhere.'

She took herself to Piccadilly Circus and sat down on a bench and wept until the bell of St James's Church chimed 2 a.m. Then she took an all-night bus home and slept.

164

36

'I'll be going away for a few days, Mrs Foster.'

'And Leksy, Mrs McFadden?'

'He's gone to visit his aunt.'

'I'll miss him.' Bunty Foster let the complicated sides of her lodgers' lives be. She was a practical woman. All she needed was good behaviour on the surface. It helped the days pass well.

Sophie took the bus to avoid the clanging bridge which hurt her ears. At King's Cross she stepped into a joyless compartment, with the travel bag Duncan had bought her over her shoulder. She had a third-class ticket, and stood in the corridor and smoked. She knew why people drew smoke out of a burning stump; why they inhaled, why they stared out of the window. Because, whatever hurt, they wanted to live and by smoking they marked the last little place available to them in nature where they could stand and freely breathe. To smoke she stood in the corridor and let the spare smoke vanish into the damp autumn air outside. The leaves had turned to brown-gold, in the parks and gardens. Cattle grazed in marshy, puddled fields under a massy grey sky edged with silver. The pressure of the uncomfortable bench on her lean backside eased until she had to sit down again.

Primitive man lit a fire outside his cave, to ward off the wild animals who would carry him and his family away. And now a modern woman alone was like a man defending his cave, defending herself, warding off the predators and the darkness. She went out again and lit another cigarette and leaned with her back to the window, wary of hostile strangers. Then she turned again and looked out on fields that had once delighted her. Black and white cows stood beside shallow beds of water. Less happily, the chimneys of strung-out grimy towns stained the blue sky. The train passed small groups of houses with façades in patterned brick and inwardly-turned villages. As the steaming express demanded its right to pass ahead of all else that breathed and moved, she inspected a small group of pedestrians and a horse and cart stalled at a closed level-crossing. Her smoke tailed away in fierce, long draughts that had an aggressive edge to them. A certain carelessness and energy always lay just beyond the bounds of what it was polite for her, as a woman, to reveal in public. Grief even accentuated it. Rejecting any reason for restraint, she smoked now to ward off the bad odours and the diseases that experience brought.

The stump burned between her fingers. The fire that blazed in hearth and home allowed primitive man to ward off his predators. So now a modern woman carries a little fire with her too.

There was a danger in so arming herself. Because it looked like an invitation, as she stood there alone making those sensual gestures of enjoyment and relief. To smoke showed she was modern and could be approached with the offer of a light by a decent sort, or someone less decent, but who scented that careless, energetic readiness to abandon herself. Now she didn't want even what the decent sort offered, when males passed she simply gave a sign that this was where she was encamped, in this little space that was her temporary home, on a moving train, holding a thin white paper taper stuffed with exotic weed and glowing red at its tip, and they should manoeuvre around her as they could.

'Tickets please.'

She did have a ticket, courtesy of Tamara Nikolaevna, courtesy of Sir Peter Salomé.

'Thank you, madam. Change at Crewe and Inverness.'

Crewe. Carlisle. Glasgow, Inverness and over the precipice into the cold sea.

'What time do we arrive, sir?'

'Only five minutes late,' the second of the journey's three conductors replied.

Her heart pounded as she walked through the station building at Crombietown and down the path to the High Street. Smart women in Crombietown, on the arms of their husbands, making their way to some social engagement, looked as their counterparts in London had done five years earlier.

'Sophie! Good heavens!' Sophie with her travelling bag had walked from the station to the Fergusons.

She had not been inside such a house, in England, since she visited the Davenports with Leksy. She had the very train Teddy Davenport had given Leksy in her bag. Everything was so comfortable and decorative at the Fergusons. They sat in the drawing-room, 'Good heavens, Sophie! How wonderful to see you.' Peggy forbore to tell her she looked well. In fact she looked strained and thin. They studied each other closely while pretending just to gaze in fascination.

'Now tell me, are you back for good? Claude will be delighted.'

'Claude Garon!' Was there anyone anywhere who did not remember fondly the name of that kind and subtle man?

'To tell the truth, Peggy – ' which of course announced a lie, 'I was so–oah homesick for England. For Scotland. I feel a great relief in coming back.' The last part was half-true, at least.

Sophie, as she drew one Players No 1 after another out of the packet, made Peggy feel that Alan was quite a moderate smoker. Peggy obliged with a flick of the heavy lighter that stood on the coffee table, alongside copies of *Country Life* and *Punch* and two jacketless library books in red and green boards.

'You got to like it here. Isn't that funny? You got homesick for this little part of the world where we catch fish and murky things happen in submarines which the government refuses to talk about. '

'That's right.'

'I don't mind saying I love Crombietown. When the sky clears we have this wonderful light.'

'I remember it. I loved it too.'

'If I had to leave Crombietown I wouldn't manage. With Alan somewhere else, no really it's unthinkable.'

'Truly, I was homesick for Scotland. I always remember when my husband first brought me here – '

Duncan McFadden! Why, Peggy saw him at council meetings. He was as active on behalf of municipal Knockie these days as Peggy was in Crombietown. He had an even temper and was conscientious and he got things done. She saw him more often than when he and Sophie were married but she couldn't say she knew him.

'Should I call him my ex? But we're not divorced, Peggy, you know, nothing like that.'

*

167

'She was deceiving herself.'

'I suspect they hadn't been able to serve the papers on her. Your father didn't know where she lived. Or he hadn't until now.'

Peggy changed the subject. 'You'll stay to dinner, Sophie? If you'd given me a bit of notice I would have invited some people. Claude for instance. He flatters me by telling me he likes my cooking.'

Sophie shook her head. 'Just to see you and Alan, Peggy, is very nice for me.'

Clearly Peggy would have preferred to plan a party.

'Peggy, if I could stay the night? I'll get my bearings tomorrow. It's too late now.'

No one, not even she, knew what her intentions were for the next day. Good and bad, open and closed, safe and not safe, joyful and wretched, try not to distinguish. Just live. Bits of language flowing out of her painted themselves on the empty air.

'Alan, darling? Alan, it's Sophie, you remember Sophie McFadden, she's come to see us, isn't that delightful?'

'Sophie!' Returning from work, still in his pinstriped suit and heavy black leather brogues, that successful and prudent Scottish lawyer came forewarned into the drawing-room with his arms wide. Sophie got up from the springy chintz sofa to greet him.

'Let me look at you again, Sophie, you look gorgeously exotic in that grey costume. Gin and tonic?' Alan would remain formally dressed in Sophie's company, though he took off his jacket. He mixed the drinks. Peggy opened a box of cocktail biscuits, in which the different flavours were divided by crinkly paper. 'How's Leksy?' Alan brought the glasses over, the women's first, and then his own; and lit first Sophie's cigarette with the heavy lighter that sat on the drinks table, and then one for himself. 'Smoke, darling?'

Peggy declined.

'He's fine.'

The Fergusons' drawing-room was a lovely comfortable place to be, with a view ahead vaguely in the direction of the sea and at the side on to the high-sided garden, with its lawn, and rhododendron bushes, which completely enclosed the house, and all of which

168

Sophie praised; though it was almost dark now, and Peggy drew the curtains.

'He's spending some time with his father.' Alan's occasionally pinched expression told her that some of her English words weren't clear. She didn't apologise. She didn't feel like trying too hard at anything.

Alan was 'absolutely staggered' by Sophie's powers as a linguist, he said. 'Not to undermine you, darling' – he turned to his wife – 'but this woman is a phenomenon.'

'She's an international woman!' declared Peggy, as she leaned forward. 'You know, Sophie, when you joined the circle it was such a boost for us. People still remember your talk on the Bolsheviks.'

'People here had much more to say about it than I did.'

They were skirting round the knowledge that Sophie, had, in fact, run away from her husband, with the Fergusons' unspoken connivance. That escape couldn't be mentioned because the letter in which Sophie formulated her plans and asked her father for money had never been intended for their eyes.

'So,' said Peggy. 'Have you come back to settle, Sophie, or is this just a social visit?' It was the second time she had asked the question.

Sophie tapped the ash stylishly off the end of her cigarette and spread her arms somehow to suggest the vast range of possibility that lay open to her. 'London, or Scotland. But I have to think of my career.'

'Your career! Do tell!'

'I went back to studying in Moscow. It's only unfortunate that the political situation – '

'One hears so many contradictory things. I've read Wells's book. I don't think even he knows. And anyway that was six years ago now. But if you say – '

'I'd say that everything is still very uncertain.'

'An extraordinary business, revolution. People talk about revolution here, of course. You remember that fellow Angus Nove at your lecture? Devil of a chap, always writing in to local papers and campaigning. But I have the impression no one really has the feeling for what it's actually like to overturn the past from one day to the next and build something new. You say that the minds of people in Russia are prepared and all that's needed are the appropriate institutions. But surely there is a personnel problem when so many people have been driven out.'

'Of course a revolution does create personal problems too,' she said, in the hope of making a joke but it fell flat because they thought she had simply misunderstood.

'Sophie can I tempt you to some of this claret?'

Peggy had 'rustled up' a meal so fine it took Sophie an effort of will to cope with it, mouthful by mouthful. Her insistently closed stomach, and an appetite dulled by an excess of nicotine, silently resisted the normality of appetite. She had eaten nothing like this good, vaguely French style of cooking since before they left Moscow the first time. 'It's delicious, Peggy, I don't know how you manage it.'

'I have a little man in the kitchen to help me. Sshsh! Don't tell Alan! His name is Escoffier.'

'Do you know it, Sophie?' queried the husband. 'Wonderful book.' His baritone voice was pleasant on the ear.

Peggy brought Escoffier's *Guide culinaire* in with the cheese course and Sophie pretended to have a look.

Ten miles away Duncan and Fanny and Leksy were eating bacon sandwiches. Alison was out. Leksy had his first experience of the impulse he would be taught to label greed.

'Alex, don't talk with your mouth full!' warned his father.

'But, Daddy – '

'Chew each mouthful twenty times!' That was Auntie Fanny.

'When's Mama coming?'

'In a while.'

Fanny thought the boy must miss his mother.

'Does he keep asking after her?'

'He only asked me why the man stole him from Mama. I said he was a friend of Daddy's and that it was a game.'

The cloak-and-dagger escapade, out of the blue, had made Fanny uneasy and she thought Duncan must have it on his conscience.

'Where's Mama?'

'He does ask of course. I always say she'll be here soon.'

Fanny disliked lying but there was nothing else she could say.

Duncan's solicitor told him he would have no difficulty obtaining sole custody of his son. The boy had been rescued from a mother who couldn't look after him. His mother was also a foreigner, who had never fitted in Knockie.

'Have you been to Penge, Auntie Fanny?'

'I was in London once,' said Fanny. 'I didn't really like it.'

'Did you see the glass castle? And the box where the people stand and shout?'

In fact he didn't take long to adjust to Knockie and the sea. Every day, if he wanted, they could go down to the shore and throw stones in the water. Soon he would be trusted to go alone.

Alison was fun, she bought him sweets and already let him run far away on his own and hide, and play with mud. But Fanny was better to watch trains with, because she could name things and didn't get bored. Together they imagined the engine-driver, and what his cabin looked like inside, and the stoker shovelling coal in from the tender, and they listened together to the stationmaster's thrilling whistle which made the train move, carrying with it all the passengers whom they also imagined, and whose faces Alex McFadden painted at the windows of his imagined carriages. Such was his passion that Fanny wondered if he remembered how it was when his mother snatched him away.

'Did you remember leaving, and being kidnapped, and being taken back?'

'No.'

But I wanted Leksy to love her. I wanted him to remember and have pity. That seemed to be my task.

I said: 'She wrote that, once she'd left, she felt sorry for your father.'

'She could have spared him that.' He volunteered, going back to an earlier question: 'Probably Arthur suggested how to get me back.'

'But Arthur Gillard loved your mother.'

'He lusted after her.'

'That's unkind to both of them.'

'I mean it. He had no respect for her lawlessness. She represented some kind of limit for him, as she did . . . does . . . surely . . . for us all.'

'So Arthur thought he could get you back.'

'They worked in Intelligence. They had colleagues. It was just a question of watching out for her return. The Service always kept an eye on Russian passports anyway.'

'*They* sent a man to the park?'

'Two. One took me while the other advised my troubled mother to find a policeman.'

'My poor Sophie,' I thought. 'You poor darling, defeated by the mighty British State in the name of your husband.'

But then as I retraced her own journey back to Scotland I found that she did not regard herself as pitiful. Simply that she had arrived at a new stage of her life.

From Crombietown she took the bus that ran parallel with but just out of sight of the sea. Peter Bruce was not driving it. He had died suddenly a year ago. 'I'm so sorry, I used to know him.'

She got off two stops before Knockie, in open countryside. The driver warned her that this was the stop for Bannock Farm, otherwise – 'That suits me fine, good day to you.' She took a path down to the coast, through that farmland. She walked along the old path from where – but, no, the sea was her friend. She thought it a living being only unable to account for what happened on its shores, but no less beautiful and mysterious for that, because it was in itself the condition of every human life. Every given life, if it is not to collapse in denial, has to be lived on its own harsh and repetitive terms.

Round the headland her eye traced the three sides of the harbour. A man was walking his collie dog.

She felt her son's hand still in hers. She heard his voice. She saw him asleep. She saw him chuckling as Pa amused him and his delight on a red-lino floor in Penge as one marble given to him by Mrs Foster ricocheted off another, and his engrossed face as he examined the model engine from Teddy and showed it to Alan, the boy in the park, one day, to make up for not having a boat to sail. She was glad she hadn't seen his face when whoever it was dragged him away. They must have put a hand over his mouth otherwise he would have cried out. But he wasn't dead, wasn't hurt.

'I'd like to see Dr O'Neill. I'm afraid I haven't got an appointment.' The receptionist was new. 'Please, it's urgent. Sophie McFadden is the name. You'll have my records there.'

The young woman was surprised at the name she recognised and nodded. 'We can squeeze you in but it may be a wait.'

'I thought I recognised you.' It was Mrs Forbes from the Buchan Arms. She looked well. She had remarried. 'It's Mrs Riddell now.'

'Congratulations.' Sophie felt in Mrs Riddell some sympathy that went way back to the day when she had found a lame excuse for buying herself a bottle of whisky and taking it to drink on the headland, and now she returned that sympathy, unforced. Besides which, u.cre was always something comic-embarrassing about changing names, whatever the occasion, so it seemed.

'Sophie!' O'Neill shut the door to his consulting room and after a moment's hesitation took her in his arms.

'You got my letter?'

'That's not why I came back.'

They sat down in their respective places, he as doctor, she as patient.

'No, no.' He seemed to consult his blotter.

'I was . . . sorry to hear about . . . Micky.' She had repressed it for a long time.

He shook his head. He had written to her about it and indeed she had received the letter.

'Did you always know, John?'

'It was common knowledge before you left.'

'You said he was to marry Alison.'

'Even while you were still here Micky began courting Alison. But that was to be near you. He lost interest after you left.'

'Poor Micky. I loved him.'

John O'Neill expostulated. It was a pretty shallow love on his understanding. They sat in silence. Only the sound of footsteps crossing the waiting-room was audible through the closed door.

She turned to herself, with the same weakness as had overcome her in Hyde Park. 'John, I didn't want a child. I was too young. I hadn't made the right marriage. Duncan forced a child upon me. There, I've said it now.' There were tears in her eyes. 'Then it was Leksy and I loved him. But that didn't mean I could turn into the woman I was not.'

O'Neill said, at length: 'As you know, Sophie, Knockie is a small place. People teased Micky for that business with you, and I could see why. As for you, my dear, I've asked myself many questions in my work as a doctor, but I never found an answer to how a pregnant woman could behave like that with another man. Is your body not sacred to you? I presume only God and poets and Mrs Sophie McFadden know the answer to that question.'

'You can't know.' She wept.

'He killed himself.'

'So you wrote to me.' She paused. 'John, what can I do or say? There's nothing I can do. Micky and I found and lost each other. I was with him and then I couldn't go on. I thought he'd understand. In a place like Knockie we couldn't go on like that. We might have managed in a freer place like Moscow but he would have needed to come with me, and how could we have arranged that? Now I'm back here because my husband had Leksy kidnapped from me while we were living in London. I can't just leave it at that.'

'Duncan kidnapped Leksy, as you say, just as you stole away with him to Moscow.'

'I didn't steal him. He was, he is, my son. He came with me because I could no longer live here, in that house, with that man and his sisters.'

'Sophie! Fanny and Alison will care for Leksy and Duncan will be an excellent father. I can assure you of that. In any case, under Scottish law Duncan has the right . . . '

'Don't tell me, John. I'm quite sure no Scottish law is going to be friendly to me. Besides, what can I offer? I don't have a home. Except in a place where I can't live.'

John O'Neill sympathised with her, not with what she said but with who she was. Perhaps on that definition he was a touch in love with her, despite his disapproval, just as was true of Arthur

Gillard. Certainly John O'Neill thought less of his friend Duncan for losing her.

'I've brought this. Leksy left it behind.'

'Won't you keep it, Sophie? It will remind him freshly of you just as he is settling down.'

Without too much reluctance she put the wrapped train back in her bag. She kissed O'Neill and left.

She walked to a place on the far headland where she could stare at Seaview, at a distance, opposite, across the little valley which brought the dependent village face to face with the unthinking sea. Then she reversed her walk, and her bus journey back to Crombietown, by which time she was heartily tired and hungry.

On the train back to London, down the east coast, via Aberdeen, she ate a buck rarebit of poached eggs on top of cheese on toast, and drank a pot of tea. Then she drew a translation out of her bag. In the midst of this crisis she had found work.

37

In Knockie, Duncan's action made O'Neill almost as uneasy as Sophie's affair with Micky. He and Duncan were friends and he waited for him to defend the kidnap.

They finished their putt at the second and, replacing the flag, strolled with their trolleys in tow to the next hole.

'I learned that I couldn't trust my wife,' the man who had been promoted and was now Captain McFadden confessed, as the ball landed well short. 'After that it seemed to me I could use any means at my disposal, of an equal kind, to get my son back.'

'You were angry at your own mistake.'

'It's true, I should never have trusted her in the beginning.'

'And so you punished her for your own gullibility, man. Isn't that the case?'

'I'm in a better position to bring up my son than that woman will ever be.'

'But you loved her.'

'Of course.'

'It doesn't seem obvious to me.' O'Neill won the hole. 'I knew you both and I have a personal interest in your welfare. Your wife's too.' He was trying to find in Duncan some tiny willingness to admit fault; but Duncan resisted.

'My ex-wife,' came the retort.

The doctor persisted, in the silence. 'Doesn't the boy ask after his mother?'

'Every day.' Even his father winced at that. 'Fanny tells him she'll come to visit when she has time.'

'That puts the blame on her.' The doctor let that reproach sink in. Then he began again: 'Fanny ought to make her own family, not persuade you to steal Sophie's child.'

'That's outrageous, John. You should consider what you say if you want us to remain friends.'

'You have your point of view. I'll take the risk. You see there are many sides to the nature of a woman, Duncan; we men need to know women better. Even as they too would benefit from more self-knowledge. Maybe together as new men and women we will get there and all be happier.'

'A new woman! What kind of new woman was Sophie? She was mad. Unstable. Either that or catastrophically selfish. Take your pick.'

Duncan was suddenly afraid that O'Neill, his own best friend, even O'Neill, had been in love with her. Every man who met her was in love with Sophie Asmus and disposed to justify her and hold her husband in contempt; just as every woman was ready to have her suspicions. Who was this woman who would go with a labourer on a clifftop and then abandon him to his fate. Was she a whore? She left even Peggy Ferguson uneasy.

'She's not a whore, and even if she were . . . you really shouldn't speak of your wife and yourself like that. That she was so desperate and you didn't notice, or were not able to do anything about it, my friend, where does that leave you?'

'She shamed this whole community.'

'And gave it something to talk about. Nothing so interesting has

176

happened here for decades. Come to think of it, not since your own drunken father left your mother. People talked about that too. You blamed your father for that. But you don't know anything about what your mother was like as a woman, I'll bet. What I'm trying to say, Duncan, is that patterns repeat themselves in a way that defeats us all. I'm not sure you should blame Sophie so much. As for that lover of hers, that was tragic. She abandoned him too. He was in the same position as you.'

'Nature doesn't have a place for a man who tups another man's pregnant wife.'

'Obviously it does. Or perhaps we're talking about something more than nature. Love for instance.' O'Neill was in the end prepared to learn from what Sophie had told him.

'The world my wife creates around her is no world in which to bring up a child.'

'I might just about agree with you there but I'm sorry it's true. She's been back, by the way. But your spies have probably told you that.'

'All right, John, so you won't forgive me!' shouted Duncan, driving a ball deliberately wide. 'It wasn't the most honourable thing to do, I admit. But she has everything against her as a mother: her politics, her character, her immorality – '

'Her beauty,' added O'Neill.

Somehow they got through the game. John O'Neill thought the whole business cowardly and sad and no way for a boy to start out. There were experiences he would remember and might one day trace back.

'Don't you remember what you told me after the war, that ever since you saw men who hadn't the slightest motivation to do so, unless there was something wrong with them, killing each other, you felt equal sympathy for winners and losers. It was humanity that mattered, and the chance to survive. You said it was wrong to fix your gaze on someone less civilised than you, less well off than you, less able; wrong to feel you were superior, British, chosen by God, entitled to win. Can't you see now that you've gone and done exactly the same thing with your wife? You've fought a war to prove that you're better than she is, more entitled to win – '

'I can't forgive her, John. She was my wife and she no longer is. She left me.'

Over lunch the conversation took a neutral direction, turning over the facts for the last time. Duncan had spoken to Arthur Gillard on the phone to thank him.

'How did they find her?'

'The name came up on the list of arrivals at the ports.'

'And then?'

'Where do Russians go when they arrive in this country without a home and without a job? They go to find other Russians. She got in with some ballet dancers. She was living in Penge. Penge, can you imagine!'

O'Neill walked over to the bar to order their coffees, and while he was there he paid the bill.

In fact Gillard's role puzzled Duncan though he could never ask him about it. Yet another man in love with her? He suspected it, the way Gillard behaved in Conny and then at the christening. But twice he had put it out of his mind.

Duncan asked Gillard down the line to London: 'Did Leksy make it easy for them? I've been trying to picture it. Of course he won't talk about it.'

'You've got your son back, Duncan. Isn't that enough?'

'I wondered how she took it.'

'You'll be saying you're still in love with her next. Of course, we're all a bit in love with her, aren't we, a woman like that?'

Duncan felt himself sinking into a quagmire no quiet reflection nor even forgiveness was ever going to dig him out of.

'Our man recommended she call a policeman. When she just ran round in circles he went and found a bobby for her. She was rather making a fool of herself. There was quite a carry-on.'

'I'm grateful to you, Arthur.'

'All part of the service, old boy.' Although, to be truthful, as an operation it was a bit of a mess.

No normal person can bear it when an emotional phone call ends. Duncan went out and walked round the port of Knockie, old harbour and new, in the rain, and felt his troubled lungs.

Fanny hoped the boy would in time forget his Moscow interlude and his mother who took him there and perhaps belonged there herself, but not here, unlike her son. She asked Alex what he liked for breakfast. Bread, he said, but not this bread. She offered him porridge but in the first days he spat it out. Poor little thing. But then he settled. He reawakened her heart, with his love of trains to which she could so easily respond. Every Saturday they trainspotted on the line that went east to Aberdeen and west to Inverness. She bought him a ruled notebook and in it, leaning on a post of the picket fence so well maintained by Jim, and now by Malcolm, Bruce, he noted the engine numbers and watched the signals rise and drop with a clatter and smiled when the locomotive whistled.

Leksy began a project to teach all the McFaddens Russian. 'I'm too old and silly,' said Fanny. 'But Auntie Alison's good at learning things.' Which was a nice reversal of roles which the sisters enjoyed. Alison pulled herself together to oblige and everyone agreed on the goodness of bacon sandwiches twice a week.

'I wonder how Mama is in Penge.'

'She'll be fine.'

'Not without me. I think she might like it better in Russia.'

Alison had started helping in the Children's Home in Crombie-town in her spare time. Like her sister, she rediscovered joy in children when Alex came back and both of them owed that to the heedless Sophie whom men slavishly followed and who had borne a child to their brother in Scotland.

Alison and Alex played castles and soldiers and war and peace.

'*Krasny*. That means red. *Pop* is priest. Say it, Auntie Fanny. P–oa–p. *Pravilno*. *Okno* is window. I'll teach you Russian, Auntie Alison, but you have to call me Aleksandr Dunkanovich. Go on, try!' He laughed. 'Then say *zhenshchina*. You are a *zhenshchina* and so is Fanny and so is my Mama. Guess what it is.'

Alex began by vaguely missing his grandfather above all, as if the interlude in London had slipped his mind, but after six months he wasn't sure what he missed any more. He could hardly place the sunny Moscow flat which had the thick door and which smelt of coffee; nor that city, the trams and the smell of kerosene, where every day Mama collected him from the kindergarten where Nikita taught him bad words and Comrade Bitova held sway.

Fanny bought Alex new clothes: short trousers and a grey pullover, and kept his hair much shorter than Sophie did. She taught him to say his prayers. At six, satisfied as to his intelligence, the local infants' school welcomed him belatedly.

Sophie sat in the Penge Public Library, where the heat was free, and looked at the newspapers and tried to calculate how fast she needed to work, and how many translation assignments an agency called Universal Aunts had to send her for her life to continue in bearable fashion. She had to admit that the fact she no longer had to buy food for Leksy and was freer in her search for work helped.

When she got home one evening a handwritten envelope had been slipped under her door.

'All right, dear? There was a letter for you.' Bunty Foster struggled to set her natural desire to pry into the lives of her boarders against what was only fair, to reward their good behaviour with a measure of security and privacy. 'Rather fine handwriting.'

'Isn't it?' But not Russian.

It was from Claude Garon who had also got her SE21 address, but from Peggy Ferguson.

Ma chère Sophie . . .

He would like to have claimed he'd read about her in the newspapers, for she was a natural starlet. But he'd heard it from Peggy. He was so delighted she was back in England and wished her to know that he was *à votre service*.

Now Claude Garon, a gentle soul in his early sixties, not made to marry, knew enough about his place in life to scent a situation in which he could be helpful and in which it would give him unearthly pleasure to help such a person in need. Not many people knew about that kind of pleasure any more. Probably the fault of the newspapers, but it seemed to him that public opinion had become violently literal; violent because it insisted on imposing its vulgar simplicities on those like Claude who lived in a subtler realm.

Every first Friday of the month he now treated himself to a visit to the British Museum. Perhaps some time she would care to join him and they could have lunch. He knew a French restaurant in Soho which while it did not reach the heights of Escoffier had an excellent way with '*les désserts*', which, he understood, pleased the ladies.

She would not cling to Claude as a man. But she would come to see him as he would most like her to see him, as another human being who wished her well and detested injustice and was aware of evil, who was no *naïf*, and all too conscious of what it was like to be a foreigner, more comic than subversive in his case, but the net result of being an outsider was the same. For her to sense the dignity that could be drawn from his willingness to serve her would help them both live well.

'I've changed my name back, Claude. Meet Miss Sophie Asmus.'

'*Bonne idée!*' he said, as they tarried over an *île flottante*.

At Universal Aunts they had high esteem for the half-dozen Russian women on their books who managed to transform themselves from members of one country's ruling class to another country's domestic servants without a word of complaint. They had such dignity and at the same time were so practical. It was, the Russians themselves knew, only another manifestation of Russian all-humanity, which other cultures lacked.

Sophie Asmus did a variety of jobs which brought her back into normal social contact and thawed out her self-belief.

One day Bunty Foster said to her: 'Swings and roundabouts, that's the nature of it, Sophie. Or should that be snakes and ladders?'

She should have written to her son but she didn't, persuading herself in the beginning that he had not yet learned to read English properly, and then fearing, or perhaps making the excuse, that her letters would not reach him, or would not be read out to him, out of spite.

She found herself now translating a whole learned paper for one Professor Orlov at Cambridge. On the pretext of clarifying certain points, she travelled to meet him. She relied on her beauty and charm to make a lasting impression.

Not six months later Sophie moved into the Orlovs' large house on Hervey Road, in the centre of Cambridge, to act as general assistant to the household. This was an innocent, slightly comic arrangement. Orlov was devoted to his wife and she, Masha, admired Sophie.

'Darrlink, your beautiful suit!'

The Orlovs had natural Russian hospitality. What was more, Eugene Orlov claimed to have met Pa. I'll write and tell him, said Sophie, to which Orlov replied that Pa's life couldn't be easy these days and perhaps it was better not to make the connection in writing.

So she went and lived on a new island called Cambridge and began again.

38

Sophie wrapped herself naked in a full-length blue flannel dressing gown, found her slippers and walked a flight down to the bathroom. In the bathroom mirror, where her breath condensed and she had to wipe it with a corner of the towel, her skin was fine again, because she had stopped smoking and slept more. Her nose was a little red because the house was always cold. But her eyes were clear and so serene that even she was captivated by their answering presence. It was as if, looking at her own face, she had a glimpse of classical modelled beauty. She quite forgot she was its bearer.

Zhenia Orlov – they called him Zhenia in the family, in their Slav way of sharply distinguishing between public and private – Zhenia had this huge house in Hervey Road at his disposal, according to the terms of the Fellowship to which he had been elected in 1919. Intrigues surrounded that election: the fact that he was a Russian forced to flee from the Bolsheviks played its part in generating a pressure in government circles that the Master of the College, Kenneth Trench, was powerless to resist. All he could do was reassure himself he had his own reason for the unusual choice, which was to widen the college's collective experience and thus to give it new strength in a new century. When, over the eight years since, glimpses of these hidden manoeuvrings entered Zhenia's own sights, in conversations in the senior common room, he was not greatly disturbed. He reproached himself for having trusted in appearances – something we are all inclined to do when decisions go in our favour – and accepted naivety as a small price to pay for the gift of a home.

The redundant size of that cold grey villa was why Sophie ended up living there, coupled with a feeling on the Orlovs' part that Russians should help each other. Had she been privy to that, she might have remembered the beggars in a Moscow street, demanding their share of any available charity. At the very least it ought to have struck her that, being socialistically inclined, as only the rare educated Russian was not, Zhenia and Masha would abhor the wasted space in such a substantial house. But she too, like the Orlovs, was simply relieved to have found a resting-place.

Zhenia, alone among all those who had helped her since her return to England, saw to it that she had work. He furnished her with a typewriter, on which to produce English versions of papers he wrote in Russian. These could be shown to interested colleagues who expressed puzzlement when the college's Fellow in Economics, admittedly a new science, explained his contribution to the subject as 'somewhere between Adam Smith and Tolstoy'. Where on earth was that?

'In the vision of Robert Owen actually.'

'I see. Ingenious.'

'We appreciate it because in Russia many of us were in favour of retaining the peasant commune over the capitalist system. Adapting communal and cooperative ideas.'

Professor Reginald Stairpath was so shocked it seemed his upper and lower jaws no longer met. Mrs Stairpath would need to make him an appointment forthwith.

'Shall I go on?'

'Just tell me, Orlov, why this wilful backwardness, pray?'

'Happiness, Stairpath, is it not obvious?'

It wasn't.

'You might, my dear Sophie, help me make myself understood.'

'I'll do my best.'

She read various titles for him and made summaries in English; and she clipped newspaper articles. Not that his reading in English wasn't fluent, but there was so much of it.

Then there was Zhenia's wife Masha, for whom Sophie was

an English-speaking companion. All in all hers was the vaguest of job descriptions, though work seemed to begin every morning at breakfast-time, when Sophie and Masha drank tea without milk, Russian-style, at the plain wooden table and cut doorsteps of white bread to eat with butter and jam. The kitchen was the only warm room in the house.

'Good-morning.'

'Good-mornink, darlink.'

Masha lapsed into Russian, the cat Khoroshenka brushed her ankles, and in that quarter no progress was made. She was in fact more of a companion to gossip to in their native tongue.

'How's your life?' Masha invariably paused to ask. Which drove Sophie out of the kitchen and out of Masha's faintly depressed company and got serious work underway.

Ten minutes later she sat down in a room that, on the same third floor as her bedroom, contained a single bed on which she laid out papers and the cool, alert and worldly Remington, which was perched on a bare table. The typewriter waited for her to begin, and she waited for her nose to redden in the cold.

Evenings were more relaxed. The three of them ate their meal in the kitchen and afterwards there were games and talk. The games revolved around a dictionary and a thesaurus that the college had tactlessly given Zhenia upon his election.

None of the Russians could do the cryptic *Times* crossword, but they all tried. 'Fetch the dictionary, prove me wrong!' Masha would cry, trying to slot a five-letter word into four spaces. Sophie would fetch the heavy volumes from Zhenia's study to resolve disputes.

'And don't forget the magnifying glass!'

Masha said her eyesight was lengthening as quickly as a shadow at sunset, a joke that didn't disguise her dissatisfaction with her age.

Or they would philosophise lazily, about Fate and Fairness, and History and Injustice, and a peculiar theory Zhenia held, in common with the poet Khlebovsky, that *Gesamtkunst* was the answer to Russian politics. One day all parties would combine, like leitmotifs in a great score, and rise up and play together, and full collective consciousness would happen on a yet to be invented chord.

Sophie would make them all a last cup of tea, not caring to think about the future at all.

'Evelyn! I was just running a few Saturday-morning errands for the Orlovs.'

Evelyn was the college's first woman Fellow. In Cambridge they were two of a kind on a desert island, and happily they recognised each other.

If anything Evelyn Glancy was even taller and thinner than Sophie, and wore a chunky olive coat and heavy hat to bulk out her shadow. She rode straight-backed and stately on the bicycle from which she had just dismounted.

'Shall we walk for a while?'

The contraption encumbered her, otherwise she would have taken Sophie's arm.

'Isn't it lovely here?' It was a particularly fine winter morning, when the sunshine seemed to coax the ancient honeyed-stone buildings out of hibernation. You felt better about the subdued parts of your own life in moments like that, Sophie Asmus noted. Half an hour stretched to three quarters as they walked round the green.

'When I first saw Cambridge it felt like a village because I walked the wrong way from the station. Then I asked someone and suddenly out of the fields appeared these extraordinary ancient buildings all in a cluster, and a civilisation built around them, by men, and it was mostly men, walking and talking and bicycling, still inhabiting them. It was like landing on an island. But at least geography prepares you for an island. Cambridge is such a surprise. The land is flat, flat, flat and then suddenly this great creation of men. Still populated mainly by men, of course. I mean look – '

Evelyn beamed. 'I'd like to show you my rooms. Have you got time?' It was after all Saturday morning.

'I'd love that.'

The bicycle parked, they were free to link arms.

'Come on, I'll give you my own special tour of the college. It was founded in 1542 expressly to promote knowledge in young gentlemen.'

'How one's heart aches for all the young ladies who missed their chance.'

'The only good thing is it gives a yardstick. We are here today.'

They crossed the court and entered the chapel through the cloister. 'There, every inch of the college is a treasury of the Christian faith.'

'It is beautiful. I only wish – I mean, I'm not a believer.'

'These days we tend to think beauty overrides its religious origins.'

'And becomes a carrier of history and a record of wealth, yes.' Although that didn't seem to her, as she spoke, to exhaust the definition of beauty.

Their voices resounded in the cold and ample, gracefully arched, finely embellished, space of the privileged past.

'Sophie, are you *very* radical in your views? I know that Dr Orlov – '

'Not really. It's just we come from a different country – '

She couldn't repeat the Russian's feeling that Cambridge was also a tomb, all this stone having no place in the life of the humble people whose pasts were constantly washed and burned and swept away, and who were actually Orlov's concern, as a socialist, now more than ever. As for herself, she always felt she was passing through – architecture and governance were not her concern. She might benefit from them or flee from them, but, in any case, her own politics were, as they had been since her original flight, suffused with her personal need to survive.

'The men of Cambridge would go mad without their "past",' said Evelyn, laughing like the almost confident initiate of this high and ancient form of academic life that she was.

The vision of madmen in academic gowns, pulling faces and dancing a jig at the threat of the removal of their collective past, made the enduring child in Sophie laugh. Her new friend joined in. It was an attitude that wouldn't do of course, but she had not long arrived.

'Come and have coffee.'

Evelyn had an upstairs room, to which the windows either end and the white paint gave a cool, elegant feel. There was a green sofa, a table with a vase full of catkins, a modern tiled fireplace, and, beside this recreational space, a small kitchen. 'The bedroom is across the staircase.'

'It's lovely. What more could a woman want?'

'Doctors free of the belief that study makes a woman infertile.'

'Isn't it crazy? Isn't it wicked? You wonder what those who still propagate that idea think science is.'

Evelyn referred to the recent pronouncement of a judge in some divorce case in the papers.

She produced, having set down the tray with a coffee pot and boiling milk and two pale-green cups and saucers, some printed papers with university crests. 'I'm recruiting you to attend university lectures, Sophie. It's our right, you know, to participate, and, if I know how the male mind works, we'd better damn well show we're grateful for it, or we'll be dismissed as ineducable children unworthy of what we are being offered.'

'But I'm not studying anything here.'

'I see no difficulty with that. Besides – '

Sophie talked more easily to Evelyn than to Masha because of the quality of her new friend's attentiveness. Unlike the turbulent Masha, who, in Sophie's view, was a little diseased by boredom, and had the need to trespass on her privacy, Evelyn never gave the impression of making sport with her confidences, or passing judgement, nor did she offer advice. She reviewed what Sophie told her as a contribution to human knowledge, and that was a fine qualification for becoming a true friend.

'You're right. Whatever I intend to do I must broaden my mind. Of course I'll come to lectures. It's time I took my life in hand.'

She had been shocked by the loss of her child. Shocked too that the question of 'home' – and of a home country where one could not, was even forbidden, to live – caused so much difficulty, so it was with extreme consternation she insisted: 'In a rational world we are all at home everywhere.'

'But you've had so much experience!'

People in Cambridge kept saying that to her.

'Perhaps I'll find a way of putting my experience to good use.' It struck her that Zhenia had done just that. He had relived the entire uprooting of the nineteenth-century industrial worker through what had happened to him and Masha.

Evelyn listened politely as Sophie extolled 'an internationality in which men and women live rationally'.

'By rational what do you mean, Sophie?'

'I made this discovery, when I was designing my own clothes – you know, there was nothing to buy over there, you had to sew what you wanted – I discovered how beautifully it is possible to live with self-knowledge. Trying to acquire it, despite the limitations. Moscow was like a great bazaar in those days, with every artist and every philosopher and every academic convinced he had found the truth . . . and this is what I took out of it. The importance of self-knowledge.'

In return for these confidences Sophie learnt that Evelyn came from an intellectual family and that her father believed in women's education. She had ridden to hounds as a child and studied biology.

'*Tu parles francais?*'

'*Oui, un peu.*' Evelyn spoke French with a strong English accent that was endearing.

'So you really will come to one or two lectures?' Evelyn insisted, as Sophie left with her overdue shopping.

'Of course.' Sophie was gone with a wave.

'I can't bear it,' said Masha. 'You're a beautiful, eligible young woman. You really must get married again.'

The cat jumped on to Masha's lap. 'Khoroshenka knows what she wants but our Sophie does not.'

'Please, Masha, it is my private life.' Sophie preferred to immerse herself in a translation and then, from time to time, in mid-afternoon, visit the cinema, rather than encounter and re-encounter Masha at a loose end. When she emerged again into the delicious muteness of those Cambridge streets she was all the happier for her brief estrangement from daylight and immediate human company. She felt a little in love with Cambridge the place, suffused as it was with the click of bicycle chains and the hum of subdued conversation. Who knew what purposes moved so many men, and the occasional woman, along the pavement? Who knew what life, and in particular her life, was meant to be? The mystical sensation took her away from her conscious rational campaigning and gave her a faintly neurotic comfort.

*

'That's you saying that,' observed Leksy.

'It was something else that divided her down the middle: her rationality, with the century, and her new-style mysticism, with the poets.'

'But she wanted this thing called self-knowledge.'

'Impossible, of course.'

When Masha insisted on putting her on show at the next College Guest Night. Sophie acquiesced. She'd had time enough to get a little used to Cambridge, and it was nice to do something a bit unusual.

The Orlov party gathered in the dark hall at Hervey Road to give each other a last grooming. It was a vain attempt, under a dim bulb and with a soft brush, to free their clothes of cat hair.

'We look smart, don't we?' Zhenia wasn't tall but he had an immense and noble forehead, set off by thick upstanding grey hair, which left him looking quite distinguished in a dinner jacket and bow tie. Tiny Masha beside him was at once slim by nature and rounded with the passing of the years. Sophie was too elegant for extra comment.

'We look first-rate.' As they closed the door behind them Masha took Zhenia's left arm, and he offered his right to Sophie.

'Your gown, Zhenia!'

They laughed at themselves. He released himself from both women and went back. Now with his wife on one arm, his gown wedged under the other and his protégée alongside, Orlov took his party on the short walk across town.

In the senior common room, where sherry was served, a very tall young man, wearing a similarly crumpled black soutane, came over. He took Zhenia aside, just as he was enjoying a conversation with a visiting Oxford philosopher, and with his huge paw gestured at the assembled company. 'You must find all this nonsense, my dear Orlov.'

'Oh, I – '

'Cambridge colleges are sumps of mysticism and perversion, full of men engaged in queer pursuits.'

'I – '

'Now the war is behind us we need to concentrate all our efforts on building a modern world, don't you find?'

'With that I agree,' said Zhenia finally. It was true Cambridge had bewildered him at first but he had since made adjustments and, besides, he didn't want to give offence. Colleagues found his work rebarbative anyway.

Percy Nair had no such desire to consider the establishment. He saw it as his duty to be at war with convention.

'Look here, Orlov, what I would like is to be introduced to the young woman in blue talking to your wife.' Nair had spotted Sophie, over all the heads.

'Of course you would. Let me take you over.'

Sophie and Masha watched them approach.

'Sophie, I'd like you to meet – '

'Percy Nair, Research Fellow in English.' He stuck out his huge hand, from which there seemed to be no retreat once she agreed to place her own in its grasp.

'Professor Nair,' she replied.

'Not the case, my dear. I neither occupy a university chair nor wish to.'

'Nor wish to?'

Masha Orlov intervened. 'Percy, Sophie is my husband's amanuensis.'

'An amanuehhnsees! I'm delighted.'

Though mocked, Masha bravely continued, 'Percy is also a novelist, I believe.'

That finally stopped him in his tracks. Percy Nair hadn't actually published a novel. He hadn't even finished writing one. He began to sweat. 'I'm afraid that's a very difficult reputation to live up to, Mrs Orlov.'

'All reputations are difficult to live up to,' Sophie interposed. 'Even the sex we are, and where we come from, may not be true and get in our way.'

He peered at her for saying something extraordinary. With what could he follow? He pressed his sherry glass against his lips, as if to create a physical cause for his silence.

'The Master not here yet?' Masha asked him, and Nair turned to ask the Dean, Michael Sprocket, the same question as their circle widened. The query gave Sophie and Nair breathing space while all around them it stoked the delicious anticipation on which every Guest Night thrived. Somewhere between a game and real anxiety lay this habit of speculating whether some misfortune had befallen the head of the college. A disaster preventing his arrival might threaten the survival of the intellectual community on which they all depended.

'The emperor still looking for his clothes?' mouthed, in Nair's direction, Reginald Stairpath, over the heads.

This preoccupation with the One who would lead them into dinner pained Nair. He disliked it because he found it queerly erotic. On the other hand, it was far better to seek immunity from the arcane project by standing next to a beautiful woman than it was to be nasty.

Then the Master did appear, and every member of the senior common room stole a glance at the pale, moustachioed face of a man in his mid-sixties.

He swivelled his eyes barely perceptibly. You wouldn't notice the split second of hesitation when he saw Sophie, a new face, if you were not watching him closely. With the evening's chief guest beside him, the well-liked Master made his way through the crowd.

'*Benedictus benedicet.*' *Eye–ket*, he said, which was not how Sophie had been taught to pronounce Latin. The grace was followed by the squeaking of chairs, the clash of knives and forks and plates and glasses, and the deep ventricular rumble of conversation released from the brief obligation of silence.

She was seated opposite Dean Sprocket, with a dark-haired man on her right, whose place-card she read. Dr David Jones, it said. She thought his hair long and noticed that from under his jacket no shirt sleeves protruded. The cuffs must be folded back. He found her expensively dressed and didn't smile.

Nair's position at the table made him furious, although it didn't surprise him. The Master had never warmed to him, if that frigid old parson ever warmed to anyone. His one advantage was that he had a good view of Sophie, like a bird of vibrant plumage in this gathering of men robed like crows.

Sophie exchanged whispered remarks with Evelyn, seated on David Jones's far side, behind his chair. 'It's crêpe de Chine.'

'It's gorgeous.'

Since he didn't know Jones, Nair took his envy out on Sprocket. The Dean was the kind of man, he thought, who must struggle daily not to become his own caricature, and yet there he was rewarded with a seat opposite a womanly apparition. The universe was unjust, but whoever suspected otherwise. He plunged his thumb into the soft bread roll on the plate beside him.

Across from Jones, between Sprocket and the Master, sat the Master's gownless visitor with his red bow tie. Everyone knew the wealth and power of Lord Maplethorpe. Maplethorpe owned newspapers that claimed to express the will of the people. No one here would have dreamt of reading his rags. But he was rich, and close to politicians.

'In my country all the newspapers have been nationalised,' Sophie told the chief guest, as wine was poured into glasses from behind their shoulders. Maplethorpe undoubtedly knew it already, but was gruffly gracious.

He looked fit and gave the impression that if offered a fight he would happily retaliate. David Jones felt like punching him before they had exchanged a word.

Maplethorpe said the young lady must be relieved to have arrived in a free country.

'If the revolution were only about nationalisation, Lord Maplethorpe, I would have stayed in Russia.'

The mathematician smiled at the rebuff. Magnus Maplethorpe, who liked contentiousness in either sex, and who took nothing personally, also smiled. Since he'd made his money people were so obsequious.

'Go on, Miss Asmus.'

'You should give the new Russia a chance. Everything is an experiment. We need your forbearance.'

Her native country was not her chosen topic of conversation but over and over she was forced into it. Besides, when she was here, and Russia was there, wherever here was seemed to need a dose of that other place.

'I should give the *Bolsheviks* a chance? Ho, ho.'

The businessman-lord shook his head. 'Their brutality is on a par with the Roman Empire. They kept Emmanuel Nobel in one of their stinking prisons for three months. Such lawlessness is too much for civilised people to pay for in the name of change.'

'But sometimes in a difficult situation a violent break-out is the only way.'

Beside her David Jones seemed to boil up. 'State ownership will mean a fairer society,' he declared, with rising tension in his voice

'A society to which all its members are proud to belong would be a better aim, Dr Jones.'

'And you think we have that in England?'

'I do.'

'Baah. Boo, booo!'

Somehow the stream of syllables was all the more shocking here. Sophie shivered and glanced up at the portraits of the intellectual ancestors on the peach-coloured walls.

'Proud of the past, aren't they?' said Maplethorpe, following her gaze.

'It must be frustrating to look down. Presumably they know better than us and yet they can't help. They're like fortune-tellers whose tongues have been cut out.'

Maplethorpe asked her what she did, or was, that the fortune-tellers could enlighten, and, disinclined to confide in him, she told him about her work for Orlov, translating and researching. Then the Master turned to Maplethorpe and she was momentarily alone.

She reached for her glass in a transparent forest of glasses, some empty, some half-full, mostly of a honey-coloured wine, though some determined souls had requested to start and remain with red.

Jones said: 'Hmmph! I think that's mine.'

'I'm so sorry.'

'I'm not sorry.' Observing the faint outline of her lips on his glass, Jones took a deep draught of the delicious white burgundy, through the lipstick. 'There, now, the communal cup. It's because I'm left-handed. I always put it back in the wrong place.'

Sophie, her heart banging, not knowing what to say apart from 'sorry' looked across to Sprocket. The side-plates with remains of bread were cleared, and they were served with roast beef.

'You make college life sound very dear, Dr Sprocket. Just like the England Lord Maplethorpe was talking about. Full of pride and affection for itself.'

All of a sudden the memory of Vera, and Pavel Abramovich, and Khlebovsky, and Dima, surfaced and brought tears to her eyes.

'Miss Asmus?' Sprocket was not at his best fathoming the mysteries of womankind, but he hated causing offence.

'I was remembering old friends in Moscow. As I was telling Lord Maplethorpe – ' she said his name loudly and he nodded to her from another conversation – 'the world needs to give the new Russia, my friends, a chance.'

'Did she really defend Russia after the time she had there?'

'It wasn't Russia she was defending. She was lonely. It was like defending subdued, unexplored parts of herself that had surfaced over there and been buried again when she came back to England.'

'*Gesamtkunst* would have made them all compatible.'

'That's what all of us dream of. We're all divided at heart.'

The silent advisers, no women among them, looked down on Sophie Asmus.

'What I think is, now we've lost the Tsar, our relationship with England must change. Our leaders are no longer related to each other by blood. We'll have to work much harder to bridge the gaps in understanding,' said the woman who had been reading *The Times* since her arrival in Scotland eight years ago.

Sprocket was touched. 'What would the diplomats make of your fascinating thesis, Miss Asmus?'

'I hope they'd assent to it.'

'One moment, Miss Asmus, forgive me – ' The Master wanted some fact from the Dean, but he returned to her.

She said: 'I met a Russian a couple of years ago who was perhaps the last beneficiary of the traditional Anglo-Russian friendship. The King made him a knight.'

194

'Not Peter Salomé by any chance?'

'Exactly him. How did you – '

'He's famous as a financial wizard. '

'And you've met him?' she queried with surprise.

'I have.' Peter Salomé had dealt with Sprocket's investments. Still the topic wasn't right for the table, and drove the conversation into a blind alley. It also reminded her of the moments in London when, seeking help from charitable strangers, she had been obliged to accept his banknotes.

Then finally David Jones spoke. 'I'd love to go to Russia.'

She shook her head, glancing up at the tongueless old augurs above. 'Really?'

'My dearest wish.'

Nair kept his eye on the end of the table that most concerned him. Idly he exchanged a few words with the philosophers beside him.

Sprocket told the story of a man who tried to buy his railway ticket in Latin, *per viam ferram*. And succeeded. Ha, ha.

Sophie livened up. 'Now it's my turn!' (Which was, she realised, not a very Cambridge way of speaking.) 'A professor of agronomy during the Civil War was entitled to a meal at the House of Scholars, which he knew would be cabbage soup. He knew that soup well. He'd eaten it many times and could calculate roughly how many calories it contained. Then he calculated how much energy it would take him to walk from his room to the House of Scholars. He decided not to bother because he would be dead before he got there.'

'Mmm,' said Sprocket.

'What a sad tale,' someone remarked.

Only Maplethorpe laughed, for which she rewarded him with a smile. 'Our Russian jokes are often a bit sad but I think they explain why we are not . . . materialistic . . . and why we have . . . great humour.'

'Miss Asmus, things will surely get better in Russia, won't they? One has a duty not to be too gloomy,' said David Jones in the biggest voice he'd mustered so far.

'We have a duty to hope for reason and equality, Dr Jones. I'm sure of that.'

'So that's what the Bolsheviks are after,' said Maplethorpe.

'She didn't believe it.'
'But now she'd left she wanted to.'

As fragments of the conversation got passed on down the long table, Professor Green, the visitor from Oxford, said hope, a vague word but a strong feeling, like love, was one of the Augustinian virtues.

'Remind me of the others,' said Orlov.

'Faith, charity – '

'Temperance.'

The little party within a party at the far end of High Table laughed contentedly at the indirect hint at all their vices, on a still clear evening in February 1927, when Sophie Asmus conjured with being several people.

As Maplethorpe prodded the hard caramel of his crème brûlée, she watched it crack like thin ice on a winter pond in her childhood. She could hardly keep her emotions in check.

'So you have a special interest in Russia, Dr Jones?'

'It follows since my politics are progressive.'

The St Emilion, which went surprisingly well with the rich pudding, made Sophie light-headed.

'My father used to say the only person in the world who understood our country was Pushkin.'

'The poet?'

'Not literally, of course. I mean my father – '

But she couldn't convey what she wanted to convey, and leaned behind David Jones to talk once again to Evelyn.

39

'Miss Asmus, the sophistication of London wafts about you, if I may say so.'

She raised an eyebrow, wondering what Nair meant.

'I love London. Sometimes, stuck here in Cambridge – '

He persuaded her to walk with her coffee to the far corner of the common room where they could stand with their backs to the wall and not be overheard.

'You see, university destroys the poetry in a man's heart. You know, Sophie – may I call you Sophie? – they call them places of privilege. But Cambridge colleges are just stuffy little temples of celibacy and spitefulness. Imagine, in the twentieth century, a place where only a qualification in Latin opens the door! You'd better know Greek too. I find myself locked up in a home for celibate classicists and certified hebephrenics.'

She wasn't going to ask him what that word meant. She could look it up later.

Finding she didn't react, he insisted: 'I'm a writer. I'm stifling here.'

'So move somewhere else!'

'But that's just it. I can't. I have my Fellowship.'

Her voice sharpened a fraction. 'You shouldn't feel too sorry for yourself, Percy. You're alive and well, in a country that allows you to choose how to live.' He invited personal comment.

Was that a reproach? He felt it might be. 'Perhaps you're right.' He wanted to tell her he was emotionally all stored up. He whispered: 'The problem here in Cambridge is celibacy. It makes me hate them.'

'What's that?'

He leaned back and gave her a long look. Wasn't she trying to make a fool of him.

But no, she said. She really didn't know the word.

'I do not wish to live and work in a playground of overgrown hebephrenics,' he repeated.

'No wonder they hate you if you call them names like that.'

'Very well. I'll say it plainly . . . I'm not queer.'

'That's all it is?'

'It seems like a great deal to me.'

'So you'll write about it then. How it comes to be so important to you.'

He squinted at her. He wanted her and had not the least idea how to go about it.

'And are *you* a feminist, Percy?' she filled the silence by picking up on his earlier curiosity about her.

'A suffragist in the direction of my political hopes, Sophie, while not supporting the violent manner of the protest of the actual ladies in question.'

'It's not so easy to get what we want peacefully. It will take years and years to change men's attitudes because men are so stubborn and recalcitrant and refuse to look about them . . . '

He blushed. He knew he would have been a candidate for the suffragettes to tear apart, though Lord knows he was trying to reform himself.

The Orlovs were together, talking to Maplethorpe who was telling them about the articles on Russia in his newspaper written by Mr Wells, 'some time ago but still relevant'. 'He went there, you know.'

'Very brave, I must say,' said Masha.

Dr Shilling, whose three Christian names Geoffrey Ironside Make-piece led intimates to call him 'Jim', listened in, until he found a moment to suggest the White defeat had been a tragedy. In life Jim Shilling often found himself listening in, when he would have wished to lead the conversation.

'It's difficult for us to see it that way,' said Orlov. 'Even where we have little sympathy with the Bolsheviks who evicted us.'

'The Whites are dominated by the Church,' explained his wife.

'Power returned to the Church would be a step back into feudalism.'

'But Orlov, it's well known that you do recommend "a step back-wards" in the, er, economic sphere, as you say, "in the interests of human happiness".'

'Into the communal ways of living, and of mutual support, yes, Stairpath, which is quite different from subordinating human dignity to the crassness of power.'

Shilling pressed his coffee cup to his lips and eyed the strange Russian, who continued: 'My enemy is capitalism and I think you will find there are a number of theories these days which align the rise of capitalism exactly with the Christian Church in its ready complicity with the political establishment and lack of concern for individual souls. Your Professor Tawney, for example.'

'With Protestantism.'

'That's a detail. Our Russian Church is not exempt.'

'Our Russian Church was thoroughly immoral,' said Masha, but noticing the rise in her husband's colour, changed the subject. 'But you, Dr Shilling, in your work . . .'

Shilling, an archaeologist, was an expert on Armenian stone crosses. When he named places Masha knew, the conversation took a merciful new turn, releasing Zhenia to find his way back to Professor Green and the joys of a mind he could agree with. It was Green, and his Cambridge host, Graham Savery, whose wit Zhenia had enjoyed at the beginning of the evening.

Maplethorpe, listening in here and there, decided the whole college was barmy and he wasn't going to give it a penny.

'Economics *is* a discipline, of course. I only have doubts about how Mr Keynes approaches it.'

'Would those be moral doubts, Orlov?' asked Green.

Zhenia's high brow gleamed, and his cheeks were flushed from the wine and the coffee. 'The trouble with Mr Keynes is that he is one of a long line of English philosophers who see pleasure as the key to life.'

'Too true!' Green shook his head. 'As to Keynes, I mean, and as to my countrymen, alas, but I hope you won't mislabel us all.'

'I knew you two would see eye to eye,' said Savery. 'You're two moral idealists at heart.'

He was fond of them both, in the loving but often bemused way a man is fond of his grandfather. He found that as academics they spoke far too personally, and that they failed to recognise that their disciplines were now sciences independent of the subjective point of view.

Sprocket watched Nair who seemed to have boxed Miss Asmus into a corner. He whispered to Miss Glancy of Nair's 'comminatory tendency' which he, Sprocket, didn't understand at all. He said: 'A prodigious intellect held back by a certain personality is the general view of Percy Nair.'

Evelyn was inclined to support the outsider, if only she could like him. 'I'd heard academic institutions were asylums for bad characters with good heads. Still, Dr Sprocket, surely it's intellectual achievement we're concerned with in Cambridge, not men's characters.'

'Asylums indeed.' Sprocket dodged the purist challenge from the new arrival. Women, when they did appear on the scene, tended to be literal-minded, he felt. Jones was another one who belonged in the asylum. Genius, apparently, but not a man to talk to.

'Do excuse me a moment,' said Nair, which at last left Sophie free to gravitate towards Evelyn's laughter and Sprocket's offer of a glass of port.

The portraits of the ancestors also lining the walls of the senior common room swivelled their eyes as she went.

'Men in the sky, men all around! You wouldn't think Nair would *need* to ask whether we were feminists in an environment like this.'

'He told me he calls himself "a suffragist in the general tendency".'

They giggled.

The biologist complained: 'I was trying to get Savery to concede that our women's problem is almost entirely a problem of language; that we're something other than the labels they stick on us. But he said that wasn't his branch. A word like mammiferous, for instance. Try looking up the synonyms for "womanly" in the thesaurus, Sophie. I'd like to see *them* characterised by their appendages.'

'We've got a thesaurus. I'll do that.' As their laughter made them approachable, the men surged back in their direction.

'Cambridge offers an education, but not through teaching. Oh, dear me, no. We rather suppose that schools have done their work before our undergraduates arrive.'

'What Dr Sprocket means, Miss Asmus, is we don't like to cast pearls before swine,' said Jim Shilling.

'It's true, Dean, that standards are falling, even in Oxford. But then they have been falling in the West since Plato.'

Idly Sophie thought she might like Green, but couldn't imagine a world in which he would become her friend.

'You appreciate our wine, Miss Asmus. Our excellent domestic bursar . . . ' Sprocket was fascinated by her capacity to drink.

Green and Evelyn went on discussing standards and how the arrival of women at the university must improve them. The arrival of women in academe would turn out to be a watershed in the history of Western thought.

I'll have trouble being anyone's watershed, thought Sophie. What do you think of that, Pushkin?

Masha glided up to her. 'For heaven's sake, we've given the Master long enough. It's almost time to say good-night. Why doesn't he come over?'

Finally he did, a gentle man, his personality almost entirely hidden behind his moustache, and old to Sophie's eyes. She listened to his prepared topic. 'Russian music! Now there's the sign of the genius of your people, Miss Asmus. Tamara Nikolaevna dances an extraordinary *Swan Lake*.'

It didn't seem appropriate to disclose her social encounter with the Russian dancers in London.

'The ba*llet*.' The Master stressed the second syllable, as if the word had only recently arrived from France.

She rather liked the shy Master, even though he had avoided her all evening.

Maplethorpe mentioned Stravinsky. 'Now there's a composer who epitomises the twentieth century.'

Whereupon the Master pronounced, like a judge, and everyone listened respectfully, though there had been no tapping of the gavel. He said the door to the twentieth century was one through which no man should pass lightly, and that he, given the choice, would refrain and stay with Tchaikovsky, though he hoped the college would flourish in future – 'should that be Futuristic?' – times.

It was as if he had acquired a magic aura. Everyone around him stepped back a little.

When normality resumed, Green replied, 'Seriously what worries me is Stravinsky's penchant for the sacrificial. It is at once Futuristic, as you say Master, and primitive. That and his complete rejection of *Durchkomponierung*.'

'So you're a Wagnerite, Green!' ventured Sprocket.

Maplethorpe, who had acquired a taste for opera too late for him ever to take the serious thing seriously, said: 'My God, those Germanic singers! One has to prefer *The Rite of Spring* to that.'

'Excellent evening, Master,' Zhenia Orlov stepped in.

'It has been a most wonderful evening, Master,' echoed Sophie, her eye scanning the room for David Jones and finding only Nair heading back towards them. 'I can't thank you enough for introducing me to the most delightful people.'

'It's been a success,' reflected Orlov. 'I'm so glad.' He took his wife's hand.

'Good-night, Dean,' voices called. 'Good-night, Master. Good-night.'

' "Pavv–lova", Master, not "Pav–LOW–va," ' But Sophie kept it to herself. As she and the Orlovs made their way into the chilly outdoors of the court, however, she briefly lost her equilibrium. Perhaps it was the effect of the wine wearing off, but her head roamed every place, every *place*, every *Platz*, every *ploshchad* she had ever been. Which way?

'Sophie!' Nair towered over her, his gorilla-like stature casting a gigantic shadow against the ancient wall. 'It has been a pleasure.'

40

'Good-afternoon!' It had to happen that they would meet again.

She was crossing the court having fetched some books from the college library for Zhenia.

'Er, Sophie?'

Jones had lain awake thinking about Guest Night, which had been quite an event for him. He had actually talked.

'I'm glad we met. I er – '

'So am I.' They stood for a while at a loss, until she took the initiative. 'Let's go for a cup of tea.'

'Right.'

'Do you know a café?'

'Mm.' It was a short walk. He didn't talk until, 'In here,' was appropriate, and he stood back to let her go up the stairs first.

At their table, before the waitress came over, he sat partitioning the sugar in the bowl like some Archimedes in search of a new discovery. He's self-conscious, she thought. Keen to assert who he is, in this non-verbal way.

He asked, still separating out matter and spaces: 'What does your father do?'

'He's a doctor.'

'In Moscow?'

'That's right.'

'I'd love to go and see what's happening out there. I mean, fancy actually achieving a revolution in favour of the working man.'

'It's not so easy . . . '

The spoon clattered to the table, scattering white grains across the tablecloth. 'You're bloody pessimists, all of you Russians over here. Orlov gave me an earful on "how difficult it was". I don't want to hear that.' David Jones pulled a face. It was a large, brooding face, with a long nose, piercing eyes and a blue chin he rubbed nervously, all perched on a thin body that seemed to be of no concern to him.

'It's important to be honest – '

'Oh yes, between the two of you you want to destroy me.' Jones examined the spoon.

The waitress arrived. 'Just a pot of tea for two,' Sophie said. She liked the expression.

They sat in a large light upstairs room with windows all round and a cottagey style of décor. It looked like a private drawing-room but with a lot of tables at which strangers sat.

'So your father's a doctor. And is he a Bolshevik?'

'He's become a member of the Party, yes. And your father?' She asked it as if it were the same kind of question.

'He's a teacher.'

'Go on.'

'No! I can't bear him.'

The tea arrived. Sophie waited a while, then poured in the milk, and lifted the teapot.

'My wife says the reason why I don't talk is I'm holding back anything that would please my bloody father.'

'That's interesting.' But she was quite aware he was riven with tension. It was the other fact that was new to her. 'So you've got a wife.'

'I've got two daughters too.'

'I have a son.'

As their mutual non-virginity sank in, it threw them both into silence.

He recovered first, suddenly exclaiming: 'How did you come to be married to a bloody Scot, for heaven's sake?'

'Why not a Scot? Have you got something against Scots?'

'Well, maybe. I'm a Welshman. Forget I said it.'

He'd managed to slop his tea, picking it up while talking, so that the cup stood in a puddle in its saucer.

'Tell me about your work.' She had looked him up in the university calendar. He was a physical mathematician, but that description hadn't helped her.

'I can't.'

'Is it a secret?'

'You wouldn't understand it.'

'Try me.'

'No! Where's your son now?'

'With his father.'

'No, no, get him away! He'll bugger him up.'

But already she couldn't imagine bringing up Leksy herself, alone. 'He'll be all right. My ex-husband is a good man.'

'Why'd you leave him then?'

'Because.'

He was like a boy, contorting himself in the chair, having these misadventures with objects all around.

Whereas she was smooth as silk. He found her so.

'If we can't talk about your work, how about telling me where you went to school.'

'I was at school in Bristol and then I came up to Cambridge. Why did I get married? I don't bloody know.'

She looked at her watch. 'I'd better go now. Zhenia will need his books.'

'Come here again, Sophie, let's.'

'I'll look forward to it.'

With no more to say they made their way back downstairs and out, separately, into the town.

41

'I thought we'd go out. I can't stand the prospect of all those gossipy old maids keeping an eye on us.' Percy had in mind Sprocket and the Master and others members of the college.

'Stairpath?' she asked.

'No not Stairpath. He's got a wife. But most of the rest.'

'Savery?'

'Not Savery. He's a decent chap. The others. They blight one's existence.'

His 'they' seemed exaggerated then, she told him; but, as to going out, 'Fine by me. I love the town.'

The weather had reverted to a breezy blue-grey, fresh as a harried North Sea. Sophie walked with her raincoat unbelted along the broad pavement, quite aware of how much he was enjoying her physical presence alongside him.

He had lain in wait for her, soon after Guest Night, as she was coming out of the door in Hervey Road. 'Oh, Sophie, what a co-incidence! I say, you wouldn't do me the honour of having lunch with me on Tuesday?'

Now she had.

'I must say you're looking lovely.' In a shop window he saw himself and his guest reflected like Beauty and the Beast. At least that proved he wasn't showing off, for her gorgeousness did make him stand out so.

'All well with you, my dear?'

'I've been going to lectures with Evelyn Glancy, and Zhenia's been keeping me busy. He's writing a paper that will define his anti-Keynesian position.'

'Cambridge keeps you out of mischief then.' He just wanted Sophie for himself. He made a vague gesture with his hand. 'I can't help it, I love King's Parade.'

'It is a lovely street.'

'When did you first see Cambridge?'

'It was August. The students were away.'

'Undergraduates, dear. You have to say that or they will mark you down.'

'I'm told ' – Evelyn had told her – 'that "students" is fine. One shouldn't make unnecessary fuss.'

'Students is a word used by people who've never been here. All I mean, Sophie, is that Cambridge colleges are not humanitarian organisations. If they can keep out hoi polloi they will. And if that means you and me, too bad for us.'

She didn't know what any of that meant.

'People not like themselves,' he added.

'But, Percy, we don't mind making our own way in life, do we? And as for using the right words, surely it's poets who are in the business of finding the right word. I mean even Flaubert searched for the right word, but not because some *social institution* expected it of him, but because he was a writer.'

'So you're an expert on Flaubert?' He pulled the two edges of his lower lip together.

'Hardly. I did a French class in Scotland. They stopped me studying anything in Moscow and I haven't gone back.'

'That's a pity.'

'Possibly.' She paused. 'Percy, didn't you want to show off this lovely place called Cambridge to me? We're talking too much and not looking about us.'

With an involuntary smile he took her arm.

'It's amazing that Evelyn Glancy is the first woman on the university teaching staff.'

'The terrifying Miss Glancy!'

Sophie disengaged her arm. 'Percy, no, that's not fair, you don't know anything about her.'

A look of pain shot over his face. He stopped and sighed. 'Guilty as charged. On the other hand, Sophie dear, men vis-à-vis women are known to be somewhat biased, often depending on looks alone. Should you get so het up about it?'

'I should. You're so full of prejudice against everything that is not you or yours! Did you really want me to come to lunch with you? You could have walked along King's Parade, had lunch with yourself and enjoyed the universe just as you like it, no questions asked. But what kind of attitude is that for a novelist? Evelyn and I are trying to build a rational world in which everyone has an equal place. And that's only going to work if we exchange our prejudices for real understanding. You should try to understand us.'

'Lord yes, if you say so. Forgive me. I don't mean to sound negative.' He offered his arm again and she took it.

If only he could tell her how prolonged and convoluted were his social and artistic sufferings! As it was she found him comic.

'It's just one does get *so* tired of the university. I'd love to get away from Cambridge and have a flat in London.'

'As you said, you must get "out from these four walls".'

'Did I say anything so banal?'

She nodded. He ushered her into the café.

'What does your father do?'

'He's a doctor. And yours?'

'He makes sunblinds.'

'Sunblinds! Is there a lot of call for those in England?'

Scarecrow-like, he waved both arms in horror. 'It's not the North Pole here, Sophie. The golden chariot has been known to rise over the Thames and even over the Cam.'

He blushed for his humble social position and she laughed at all this orotundity and excessive gesturing.

'You always use too many words when you get worried.'

'Oh, I do, do I?' Nair's enormous mouth, the most attractive thing about him, with its thick, generous lips, opened and closed on that limp string of monosyllables.

'Really, you didn't want an alcoholic drink, did you?' He recovered his role as her host.

She shook her head.

'Isn't vodka the Russian tipple?'

'On special occasions.'

'I don't know much about Russia.'

'It's quite different from here. Especially now.'

'Presumably that's why you're here in England.'

'Presumably.'

His eye roamed to catch the waitress.

'I didn't tell you, Percy. I have a son.'

'I thought you must have a past, if you don't mind my saying. Are you divorced?'

'His name is Leksy.'

'Are you divorced?' he repeated.

'Indeed.'

'When we were discussing suffragism you said something quite shocking about the inevitability of violence in bringing about change between the sexes. Too many words, sorry.'

'That's OK,' she conceded.

'Undoing repression does seem to involve violence, yes.' She had in mind her own desertion of Duncan, which she thought of as a violent act but one she had to forgive herself. 'If you're in chains you have to break out of them. The iron hold is not going to weaken with sweet talk.'

'That's nicely put.'

The waitress, having cleared their savoury plates, finally obliged him by bringing assorted cakes which he pulled towards him and ate one by one.

'Which is why you should be less disapproving of Evelyn. She's given herself a task which is terrifyingly difficult. Who knows whether she doesn't have to do violence to her own nature and needs in order to be a woman in today's society. I *ran away* from my husband, Percy. That's a kind of violence, isn't it? But as I say, it's not sweetness of conduct that is going to relax the iron grip of convention.'

'Reason maybe? A change in social understanding?'

'It would be nice to think so.'

'So you, ah, forced the issue.'

'Because I was leading an unnatural life. Because I didn't want to be a salted herring in a box. That's how I used to think of it. I saw those fishes boxed up on the quay every day and I felt afraid. Because I don't want to be boxed up is why I sympathise with your desire to leave Cambridge, if that's what you really want.'

'Good of you.' He meant it.

She studied his vast form. He resembled an unfinished sculpture, the block of granite from which he was cut still visible. He wanted to engulf her and crush her, now with his great body, now with his words. He wanted to make her an unprotesting part of himself, filling some gap he felt. She found herself shifting her chair just a little backwards, and sitting up straight, where he couldn't reach her. Yet in his grown-up male company she discovered her own needs openly, and the strength with which those needs gripped her took her all the more by surprise.

'Have you ever been attracted to your own sex?'

'No! Absolutely not. I can honestly say I have never felt the slightest homosexual twinge; never.'

'You make an awful fuss about it for one who denies it.'

'Since I attended a grammar school, no doubt that has made it easier. But no, never have I been the slightest tempted,' he insisted. He struck the table. *Dixit*. The man has spoken.

'It's just that that's the thing you always mention when you say you want to get out of Cambridge. The men who are converging on you. Sprocket and the Master especially.'

'I don't need psychoanalysing,' he shouted. 'I know who I am.' She kept looking for the chink of light in his character. And for the feminine streak in him.

'In Moscow I met a woman I desired. It was just a passing thing. She helped me see what kind of a woman I was. I believe in free love, you see.'

He was faintly nervous of this conversation in a café. Cambridge was provincial.

'I think we're all, ideally, a little bit woman and a little bit man. Shall I go on?'

He who had been observing that the tablecloth was primrose yellow nodded.

'I take it for granted that everyone has an erotic course, like a line of fate. Our eroticism is what takes us out of ourselves. It's what makes us act, it's what becomes our character. The problem comes when we can't behave naturally. Some people say the obstacle race civilises us. But I'm really not sure. Women have so few erotic possibilities in a bourgeois society.'

He struggled to say something. To object, to interrogate. Had she been an undergraduate of his he would have called an abrupt halt to the proceedings and demanded definition after definition. On the other hand it was rather exciting to listen to her.

'As things stand, if passion does not naturally come our way, we can indulge in a little pornographic play-acting with our husbands or we can abstain. What we real women must do is reinvent ourselves on every level and in every way.'

As what he couldn't imagine.

'And your child?'

'Leksy's with his father.'

'And now you're divorced men throw themselves at you round every corner. Isn't that so? Men like me, I dare say. And you have to decide whether to say yes or no.'

'All I know about you, Percy, is that the way you treat me as a specimen of desirable womanhood makes me uncomfortable. Why do you do it? From the first moment you saw me you looked at me in a way . . . that was almost rude.'

'But women fascinate me!' he wanted to shout in self-justification. Instead he hammered the yellow tablecloth. His lips were tight with self-hatred. 'There, you see, I can't even be discreet, which is the first requirement of a . . . *gentleman*.'

'A *gentleman*!'

'It's what I'd like to be.'

'That's like my saying I'd like to be an *ingénue*. You have to have some self-knowledge, Percy. It's part of being grown up.'

'Sophie, look. The truth is, I haven't lived enough. I was at school in Bournemouth, and then I came up to Cambridge. My awareness of the world is such that I know about men seeking prizes but not much else. Whereas, the surprising thing about you is that, on top of all your other assets, you have lived a great deal.'

'You praise me too much.'

'You're getting sick of it. It wouldn't be the first time a woman found my praise nauseating.'

'Percy, stop it! Stop worrying. Stop plotting!' She looked at her watch. 'I have to go now.'

'But we'll meet again, won't we?'

'Why not?'

He watched her. Her unbelted raincoat was like a dark sail that allowed her to glide through the city. He hoped she would put about, at length, and come back to him.

'She played them off one against the other.'

'She wouldn't be the first woman to do that. Her situation was really very difficult.'

42

Masha was not making progress with her English, even after so long, and she was unsettled. Sewing on Zhenia's buttons wasn't what she ought to be doing with the years left to her. It was like being stranded on a flat island when your unique talent was for climbing; like being a swimmer confined to a waterless realm. Zhenia was keeping long hours working on his 'answer' to Mr Keynes. Sophie pursued her own interests. Masha in her boredom took to grooming the cat.

'Masha, your arms! At least wear gloves.'

She had scratches like red laces criss-crossed over the veins of her wrists. 'I don't mind. It's a sign of love.'

'Not in any land where I'd like to live.'

Sophie began again: 'You remember the Master's guest Lord Maplethorpe?'

'The kapital*eest*!' Masha exclaimed.

It was true he had resembled his caricature, with the red bow tie and the after-dinner cigar. 'If you must. I liked him,' Sophie said. 'For his self-knowledge I admired him. He said to me that his one regret was that he knew no foreign languages.'

But Masha was unforgiving. 'He has surely to regret the crimes of a kapital*eest*.' She was removing crumbs from the table with a wet finger and popping them into her mouth, and then having to fish out a cat hair.

'The Master wanted Maplethorpe to give a bequest to the college but we spoilt it. He thought "the Russians were barmy".' Sophie got her information from Evelyn. Masha replied she didn't care a hoot how the college was funded.

Sophie took a breath.

'Masha, what do you think of David Jones?'

'He's crazy.'

'How can that be? How can he be crazy? He's a university lecturer in physical mathematics.'

'He's awkward. He'll get his life wrong if he's not careful.'

'I must like awkward people then.'

'Someone has to.'

'But Maplethorpe found us all barmy. Isn't it all relative?'

'Not really. Maplethorpe said what he did because he's a kapita*leest*. Sophie, you're not in love with that impossible mathematician? Married, isn't he, to boot?'

Sophie ran out.

Professor Eddington was gazetted to lecture on the internal constitution of stars one Wednesday morning. She entered at the appointed time and sat at the side, keeping her coat on. She listened with her eyes closed. Massive and to Sophie immeasurable timescales and unknown, never directly experienced substances loomed like mountains in the dark, over which shot comet-like questions about the speed of light and the origin of the universe. She listened long enough to realise that the great impersonal scheme of things, while it might prove an anchor to men and women of a sober investigative temperament, would never upstage her interest in the human utterance. She wanted to know about the universe, but even more passionately was she keen to be among men and women, and to join in their comments, and occasional howling, at their fate, utterances conjoined with the common origins of art and history and self-understanding; and the human encounter, and love.

Sophie asked Zhenia what he knew of physics. He was working in his downstairs study, and when she took him a cup of tea, together they stared out into the garden, where, despite their total neglect of it, daffodils had appeared with fat yellow buds protected by spears of grey-green.

'I'm glad I moved down here.' The stairs had been getting too much for him.

'You moved when I came,' she said. 'So, contemporary physics – '

'It's a tall order to summarise, but here goes. Think of it this way. Everything we think of as solid is actually on the move. We are ourselves on the move. The whole physical universe is dancing.'

'But that's extraordinary. That's what the poets in Moscow were performing. You remember Khlebovsky, Zhenia?'

'Alas, Khlebovsky.'

'But now we know he didn't live for nothing. He demonstrated a truth that people are only realising is true now because the scientists tell them so. I always think the artists get there first.'

'Certainly we know it's all one big dance of the atoms that make up the molecules that make up the objects we are. Although what difference that makes to us as human beings – '

'It ought to make us live *freely*.' She twirled a little, in what space there was in the room.

What a beautiful woman-child she was, he thought. He left her time in which to read newspapers and books and find passages of interest to him, all the while hoping, as if she were his own daughter, that she would deepen her self-awareness. She was now surely finding her way.

In her room she sketched outfits she would never make. Gorgeous suits and dresses took shape in terms of triangles and cylinders under her pen. They propelled themselves off the page on the slipstream of the age. She thought how lucky she was.

And yes, with her intelligent self she longed to grasp where Truth had arrived in 1927, and how she belonged to it, for there, in the pattern of Truth, we all have a place.

A. A. Levitan, Furriers. But that was before they took Leksy away. She had been walking along Oxford Street, a twentieth-century woman in search of 'an opening' in a still nineteenth-century society. She was a woman who had a child and no husband; a child and no money; no place to live; and a foreign accent she could never quite obliterate. Did Mr Levitan need a shop assistant? Still sticking to proprietory names that struck her as Russian, she had once again plucked up her courage and lifted her head to face a new challenge. She pushed open the door and a bell rang.

'Beautiful coats. This must be rabbit.' She was determined to keep her voice bright and not apologise for herself. It was warm weather in which to be contemplating buying a fur coat and she had the proprietor to herself.

'Too fluffy for madam. I would recommend sable for madam's strength of character.'

'How can you know my character? I've only this minute walked in from the street.'

Avoiding an answer, he darted away on tiny feet. 'A mink stole perhaps.'

'Actually I've come to see if – ' She told him, without perfect composure, that she could handle correspondence in English and Russ – other languages, German even – and take shorthand dictation, if perhaps he needed a secretary. Or an assistant.

Ignoring what she said, he released a fox fur from its hanger and held it behind her back. 'Please, please, try it on!'

Well! It was only a game. She found the sleeves and, in that lovely movement in which civilised men and women are so finely co-ordinated, he slipped it over her shoulders. Her long neck and oval face were framed in a soft animal mist of mink and grey.

'As I said, I can . . . '

'Stop, my dear, please stop! Why on earth did you choose me to ask for help? I've . . . I'm . . . '

'Just the name, Levitan,' she said. 'I'm sorry.'

He sighed. 'That fox would suit you down to the ground if only you had the money to buy it.'

'I'm sorry.'

'I am too.' He struck himself as a ridiculous figure. 'Well, hard luck, Alex. The only shiksa who comes into your shop has no money to spend. In addition she'd like you to give her a job.'

He pulled himself together. 'What did you think? That I was

214

Russian? I'm Jewish. We Jews don't come from anywhere except the desert.'

He put a closed sign on the shop-door and invited her to sit down. 'During the war they put me in prison. In case I was a German spy. When they locked up Alex Levitan it almost killed his business.'

'They may call it a victory but it was a terrible start to the century.'

'You're right there. I've been back nine years now but sales are nothing like before the war.'

'In the newspapers they say people are spending as never before.'

'Not in my shop they're not.' He looked on her kindly. 'So what are you going to do?'

'I don't know.'

'You're like my sister. Clever, beautiful and out of a job!'

'Do tell me about your sister.'

Alex Levitan's sister had signed on at an agency called Universal Aunts. 'They place women as personal assistants and translators and whatever.'

'Whatever?'

'Don't get me wrong! It's all above board. Sis works for some actor and his wife. Does their letters, fetches the shopping, has a ripe old time. Now you'll meet a man, Ruth, I told her, but she said I quite misunderstood. What she wanted was to be independent.' He paused. He felt almost cheerful. 'Well, Miss Asmus, you'll have your own views about all that. And when you've signed on with the Aunts and sorted yourself out, remember Alex Levitan has just the coat for you. You'll look a thousand dollars in it.'

'Thank you, Mr Levitan, I've really enjoyed our talk.'

As she left Alex Levitan could not resist making her a present of a fur collar. He liked guts. Besides, everyone aspires to beauty. Everyone wants to be caught up in beauty's embrace, all other things being equal, which they never are.

These days she wore the fur collar over her black belted pullover, with her wool trousers – in Cambridge, for instance, once again to join David Jones for tea.

'But, David, don't you have to teach?'

'My brain is too exceptional to be wasted on teaching.'

'I told Masha you were a genius.'

'And she didn't believe you, eh?'

'She got quite cross.'

He laughed. 'She's ignorant.'

'No, really, she's not, not at all.'

'She is. Tell her to shut up.'

'I can't do that, David. Besides, I like her. I live in her house.' Sophie flushed. 'Tell me about your work. Please.'

'Since the atom is divisible – '

'It brings new energy and freedom to everything we do.'

'That's a stupid thing to say.'

Her eyes filled with tears. She understood some things and not others. She knew there was something the poets and the scientists and even she and Evelyn in their work of liberation had in common.

'I think we are just tiny insignificant specks in the universe.'

'Nonsense. We have social duties. We *must* take ourselves seriously.'

He knocked down everything she proposed.

'Do you know French?'

'Not a word. I leave that to the Frogs.'

'But you said your father taught French.'

'Exactly.'

'I wanted to tell you how much I love French. That's all.'

They sat in silence in the old teashop.

'Look at this lovely floor.'

'It's original from the time of Milton. Milton's good. Republican. Feminist too.'

'When was Milton?'

'Seventeenth century.'

'The time of Peter the Great?'

'Earlier.'

'At Seaview we had these awful carpets.'

'Seaview?'

'The house where I lived with my husband. There *wasn't* even a sea view.'

He rubbed his chin, 'Must get back now.'

*

The heavy library book on Zhenia's knee thwarted Khoroshenka's efforts to find a comfortable position for the evening. The family pet drew all their attention when she leapt on to Masha and butted *The Times* from the underside.

'Make way, I am the most important creature around here. Imagine, Zhenia, Masha, if human beings were to live like that! I was trying to tell David Jones how important it is to me, to us, that human beings shouldn't be self-important, in the universe.'

'How are you getting on with your David Jones?'

'I had a talk with him the other day,' Zhenia intervened to stop Masha picking on Sophie. 'About the need for morality in economics. He fully agrees with me.'

His wife looked up from her crossword.

'Morality has to be in the political system itself, I said. Even Mr Keynes would allow that. Where we part company is over his insistence that morality amounts to giving everyone enough money to make their own choices. I simply ask: how are those choices to be informed? And Jones replied: "My point entirely. There have to be organisers and they have to be moral for the system to work." '

Masha persisted. 'Khoroshenka knows what she wants but our Sophie does not.'

'I do, I do.'

'What, fall in love with a man whose dearest wish is to go over there? You'd be better off with your free love than this torment.'

'Stop it, Masha! Stop it!'

'Is that supper I can smell?' The tension had been growing between the women over the last couple of weeks. Zhenia hoped the meal would restore their good humour.

'I'll have the soup,' he said.

'Me too then.'

'What's in it?'

'It's brown. I've no idea. So you talked to Orlov?'

'I want him to tell me more about Russia.'

'It's quite different from here. Especially now.'

He banged his fist on the tea-table. 'This country has to change too. We had one little chink of light and then the Tories came back.'

'My husband used to say things like that. He minded about occupying Turkey. It's the Empire that bothers you, isn't it? Although it was the war upset my husband.'

'The one leads to the other. Your Duncan was bloody lucky to come out of the war alive.'

'Alive but not unscathed.' She began: 'You weren't called up?'

'I was two months too young. That's the one thing the world has to thank my bloody parents for. That they produced a mathematician, and not a product designed for the mincing machine.'

'David,' she looked at him intently, 'why are we talking about all this and not about ourselves?'

'There's nothing to talk about. You and I are in this century up to our necks. You can't get out. I can't get out. We *owe* it to our times.'

'There are lots of young men *like* him in the Labour Party, Sophie. You should come along.'

Sophie stacked the empty plates with a clatter. 'I don't want someone *like* him, Masha. I want him.'

43

Before Sophie and Evelyn came for tea, Percy worked hard on the rooms he had furnished mostly with antiques, notwithstanding the odd modern touch. He set out the sherry glasses which he'd bought in an antique shop as a fine and pretty English advancement in which to offer a less rudimentary *copita*. On a side table he allowed a few leather-bound books to form a haphazard staircase.

'What a fireplace! You can almost walk into it!' was her first remark. She ranged about, testing the space, and seemed to sit down reluctantly, as did he, for he would willingly have danced with her, forgetting the very existence of her chaperone (for as a chaperone was how he saw Evelyn).

As he made tea – tea was what they wanted – the two of them

got up to examine 'the modern touch'. It was an oil painting by Wyndham Lewis. The constricted pattern of rectangles and grids in blue and pink and lilac and brown was difficult to like but it never failed to startle his visitors into speech.

'It strikes me as a kind of manifesto,' said Evelyn. 'A kind of "in case you haven't noticed, you bourgeois folk out there, human experience is not as nicely cushioned as you imagined". The angles are like shards of glass, prodding at complacency.'

Sophie thought Nair used it as a mirror, but she couldn't say anything so unkind. 'When I was in Moscow all the young artists painted like that. But their work wasn't so cold.'

'The coldness does rather negate the experiment.'

'What's your view, Percy?'

'Well, look, something has to change,' he began.

As Sophie decided, now viewing his room and his possessions, anyone watching him could see that Percy Nair wished to be modern but didn't yet have the full courage.

'Something has changed. A great deal of what used to be art has passed into life.'

'What does that *mean*?' he protested.

'Dancing in the street,' she reminisced. 'Not just hanging pictures on walls.'

For his part Percy would have liked to ask Miss Glancy, evidently an expert, why the biological instinct didn't choose human beings suitable partners and have done with it. That would save a lot of trouble for men like him who were not, otherwise, *puellis idoneus*. Instead he congratulated her on her arrival on the university teaching staff, courtesy of the new statute – some six months ago now, but still worthy of celebration. He raised his teacup and waved it. 'Look, ladies, are you sure you won't have a sherry to toast the occasion?'

They relented, a proper toast was drunk, and all agreed to be on Christian-name terms.

The afternoon gathering went surprisingly well. He got over his fear of the college's first female Fellow (though the word caused him to chuckle – 'Fellowess' should that be?). However, since it took him no further with Sophie, who afforded him no special glance, only quarrelled with him over what art was, when they had gone he fell into a slough of despond.

'Why don't you attract women, Percy? As a novelist you *have* to ask yourself why.'

He hurled his huge head against the sofa back with repercussions for the whole wooden frame. He stretched out his long legs on the red rug. He lit a cigarette and blew smoke at the Wyndham Lewis.

Back then to WORK!

Making her way back to Hervey Road, with Evelyn pushing her bicycle alongside, Sophie found herself analysing the thirty-year-old doctor of philosophy, who according to his own pronouncement would never be a Cambridge professor of English and didn't want to be and really desired to leave the university altogether to save his soul, because he was going to be a great writer. She asked Evelyn her opinion.

'Interesting man and very ambitious. But massively self-centred. Also he's crazy about you.'

'That's just embarrassing.'

His two women visitors had sat on the battered sofa where he was still stuck ruminating at midnight, calling it WORK.

'Erotic unworthiness is my subject, and here I do think I am a pioneer – asking the purely, or nearly pure, psychological question about why men – and women – succeed and fail. In their professional and in their private lives. It's almost never fair.

'Confess you've got problems.'

He closed his eyes and pinched the skin between them; then he took another swig of Scotch.

'Dear spirit of the writer's night, you do bully me.'

It relented then because he promised to try to tell the truth in his work.

I'll say it for her. 'Women who are waiting for a certain man don't sit in chairs nursing a whisky disputing with the midnight spirit. They stare at their body in a full-length mirror. They ask after their body's charm. Or in a cold English bedroom they consider their flesh stretched horizontal under a cage of bedclothes. How long will he make her wait?'

She wrote her diary while the Remington sat becalmed next door.

Jones lay awake, listening to owls and regretting his ignorance of astronomy. Everything made him angry except numbers.

'Which gives me an idea,' said Masha. 'There should be more Russian teaching in Cambridge. It's a scandal.'

Neither her husband nor Sophie responded.

'And I'd like to know of English writers who come close to our Russians. Percy Nair's a novelist, isn't he, Sophie? You could ask him.'

'He won't know. He's entirely caught up in his own work.'

'You spend a long time talking to him.'

'He's very ambitious. Even if he doesn't quite know what he wants.'

'He wants you, as you want David. We're all clear about that.'

But then it was time Masha worked on herself. She had to bridge the gap between where her life had flowered twenty years ago and where she was planted now.

44

She organised a raffle.

'Is he a good writer, Mrs Orlov?' Jim Shilling asked, with intellectual doubt substituting for his reluctance to spend money, when the Russian woman appeared in the senior common room. It wasn't actually her prerogative to be there.

Dr Shilling was being asked to buy raffle tickets to help Russian orphans. It was Mr Gorky's appeal, she explained. He had lent his great name to it, to raise money for the homeless children of Russia.

'Maxim Ivanovich did a very great deal to keep good men alive in the worst days, Dr Shilling. He is now himself condemned to exile.'

'Yours *is* a divided country, Mrs Orlov.'

'But, Dr Shilling, the children! Let us hold the dear children above politics.'

Why couldn't the Russian state look after its own needy? But in the end he bought a book of six.

'Did she sting you for her blasted raffle?' he asked Savery.

'Oh yes, but who can begrudge orphans, Shilling?' Savery who had more concern for his image, and a small private income, had not hesitated to buy half a dozen books. Sprocket was equally willing. But otherwise Masha made little headway.

'Why not try your luck, Reverend Montgomery?' urged Masha. 'It's in a good cause.'

The chaplain excused himself on the grounds that the purchase of raffle tickets was gambling, even if the cause was undoubtedly good.

Downhearted, she was turning to leave when she heard: 'Ah, Mrs Orlov, don't leave me out!'

It was the Master himself.

Stairpath and Shilling watched the old Edwardian and the tiny Russian woman swathed in her shapeless garments cross the court; he had invited her to The Lodge.

'Mrs Steel, would you be so kind as to bring us some tea?'

Masha met the eyes of a woman about her own age, who flashed back a look of disapproval. Masha thought, we women never get over each other, no matter what age we are.

'One has to wonder whether the Reverend Montgomery hasn't rather lost touch with his Maker these days. He makes me sick.'

'Doesn't matter, Master. We can manage without him.'

'I'm so glad we were able to have you and your husband join us here, Mrs Orlov.'

'I'm not sure what we would have done otherwise.'

He hesitated. 'Are you, ah ah, a believer, Mrs Orlov?'

She shook her head.

Since his own upbringing had been in the parsonage, Kenneth Trench said he had never really had a choice.

'I mean I have this vivid sense of God saying to twentieth-century man, "Look, I can speed up too. See how you cope with that." ' Trench clapped his hands. 'Bang. The century turned and there we had it. War and destruction. And women changed utterly. Savery says it couldn't be God's work, that that just proves there isn't a

God, but I'm really not sure. God's much cleverer than we think.

' "Chaplain," I said to Montgomery, "in 1914 the ruthless Old Testament God took over our lives. We were surprised because for decades we had basked in the charity of his Son."

'And do you know what he replied, Mrs Orlov? He came over all weary and superior on me. He insisted God was superior to anything he or I could conceive of so there was absolutely no point in speculating one way or another.

' "That puts you out of a job then, chaplain," I said. "I thought speculation justified your existence." '

'And what was his reply?'

'Oh, you know, that God's ways are mysterious and we should just put up with them and sing His praises on Sundays.'

Masha liked Kenneth Trench, as Sophie did. He was thoughtful and bashful and needed to talk.

'And would you like to learn Russian, Master?' Masha alluded to the one prize offered in her raffle. 'In six months I can teach you to read the Russian Evangelium.'

'Mrs Orlov! I would very much like to learn your beautiful language. I believe it to be a little like Greek, no? So I should have some advantage, at the start?'

'You would be admirably prepared, Master.'

So the Master won the first and only prize in Masha's raffle, and both were made happy by the result, which was a series of Wednesday-morning meetings in Hervey Road, beginning immediately.

'I'll have to announce the result *somewhere*,' said Zhenia, embarrassed, for he too had been pressed into selling tickets. He thought better of an oral announcement and pinned a notice on the SCR noticeboard instead.

In teaching Kenneth Trench Russian, Masha blossomed.

'The alphabet comes from the Greek, but not the lexicon, Master. To find Russian derivations from the Greek one has to go a long, long way back into the history of Byzantine Church ritual.'

Not a long time for him at all, he said, with his enthusiasm for Church history.

'The names of articles of priestly clothing and regalia are Greek. But then there are a few exceptional borrowings which continue to this day. I give you one of them, Master. It is *parus*. It means "a sail". *"Belyeet parus odinokiy,"* as the Russian poet says.'

He turned the line she gave him into: "So a lonely sail sails its whiteness to me." Which sounded fine to her ears.

'Won't you call me Kenneth, Mrs Orlov?'

'With pleasure, Kennet.' She could never manage the 'th'. Just as he had trouble with the Russian 'u'.

They worked together in the kitchen because it was warm and cosy and they could drink tea during their lesson. Masha had never realised the extent to which her language was her own story. Pleased for Masha, Sophie wiped the breakfast crumbs from the bare table and tidied the newspapers into a pile before every session.

The impression, nevertheless, of a careless domestic environment suited Kenneth Trench admirably. It even left him with the worry that he, personally, in the cramped Lodge, simply had too much stuff and should give it away to the poor.

'Of course, Masha, we don't know how ancient Greek was spoken. But it could not have been as slushy and whispery with sibilants, nor half so accented, as your Russian language. The way the syllables stretch here and shrink there, why, I think you are teaching me a new music.'

'The stressed syllable is approximately one and a half times as long as the unstressed, Master, our scientists have calculated.'

But Kenneth knew the first thing he had to do was forget about measurements and imitate his teacher like a child. Which he did happily.

'U–'

' "Oo".'

'U menya est' kniga i karandash.'

'Excellent.'

She had to break off to answer the door.

Sophie's friend Percy Nair stood there complaining: 'But don't you people have a telephone?' Thus huge dishevelled man called Percy Nair, College Fellow in English, just stood there and bellowed at

Masha. Having achieved the threshold the effort of knocking and not being answered exasperated him.

'Is he her . . . er, friend?'

'Very hard to say, Kennet.'

A big X of irritation had cancelled anything fair about Nair's facial features. She had been glad to close the door.

Now back to work!

'The old Slav for book plus a loan word from a Swiss commercial brand.'

'*Caran d'Ache*. Quite remarkable.'

'And an impersonal construction using essentially the Greek verb "to be" . . . '

When Kenneth was not at Hervey Road he spent hours, under the consoling yellow light of a fringed standard lamp in the cramped drawing room of The Lodge, practising his Cyrillic alphabet. It was history almost as fresh as memory conjoined him to the ancient past he was now following east. As once two Greek brothers carried the New Testament from Macedonia to the Scythian lands, so now Kenneth Trench joined them on their dusty journey. Had only the consonants d and f and g and l and p, and vowels o and a sufficed, Plato might have communicated with Dostoevsky. It was after all Cambridge, and learning proceeded everywhere.

Sophie disliked the university lecture theatre where, behind the charmless institutional façade, the tiers rose steeply in imitation of the original Greek tragic theatre. 'Imagine it's Athens,' insisted Evelyn. 'In a building like this the men of Athens met to share their agonies. And now we women are among them, involved in the debate.'

Professor Hitchens, a grey-haired American who, in a brief prelude, declared he had spent much of his life in India, began to expound on 'The Hindu Understanding of Women'. They hoped to learn something.

'The Hindu system wishes to avoid atomisation. It puts diverse responsibilities on each individual and the system functions well if each individual performs his or her functions.'

Beside Sophie, Evelyn raised her eyes to the distant ceiling. All the traditional religions found women difficult to accommodate as individuals with equal rights. 'They did then and they still do now.'

'These functions will be defined according to the natural tendencies of persons . . . there will always be exceptions . . . '

Sophie nudged her friend. 'That's us.'

' . . . but a society will not be designed for exceptions. And saying that design should not be there because of exceptions defeats the entire purpose of society. However, exceptions should have a way out of the system. They always have.'

'Can he not make it more attractive for us?' Evelyn whispered.

'Society is not designed for us. I find that view totally depressing.' Sophie poured in the milk.

'We're not Hindus, of course.'

'I'm determined not to be anything.'

When they came out from the teashop it was still just light, approaching six o'clock. They linked arms and walked to where Evelyn had left her bicycle.

Through the French doors a fox sped across the garden, startled at midnight as Sophie switched on Zhenia's desk lamp and sat down to read Percy's typescript there. He'd begged her to read it, and 'criticise' it, with his characters Edward, who was the successful version of himself, and Rufus, the failed version, and Peter, the faker and bluffer who could charm anyone and was what any self-respecting man must guard against becoming.

The fox with the tail, so long and thick, held out like a rudder behind him, had vanished on his way he knew where.

Was it more than eight years since she had first left Russia? Almost a year since she had arrived in Cambridge? She exchanged an occasional letter with her father. A postcard arrived from Claude Garon, who must have got her address from Peggy. Peggy and Alan replied to one she sent them.

Then it was Easter, and Hervey Road was transformed by the

Master's gentle insistence that something be done about the Orlovs' garden. Not one to shirk hard work, he arrived with a fork and spade strapped to his bicycle, and he, Sophie and Masha set to. It wasn't something for Zhenia, who had to avoid even a flight of stairs. He had to keep himself from strain.

The sight of their industry gladdened the heart of Harry Birkett, the Orlovs' neighbour, who all winter had struggled hard not to complain about the fence that had fallen down even before Christmas and was the legal responsibility of No 24. He joined them, and brought along his son John as an extra pair of hands.

On Easter Sunday Harry Birkett cut the lawn that had not seen a mower in years and Masha cooked lunch for seven. Zhenia opened the doors from his study to the garden and the smell of freshly mown grass flooded in. The new planting was excessively admired for a garden so modest but the whole occasion was an immense success. Sophie took pleasure in inviting Evelyn to the 'new growth' festivities.

Easter! Kenneth Trench confided in Masha. 'You Russians, you're all atheists, you can't know. But some of us come out of different times. Do you know what it is to have been brought up a Christian? I can tell you that on a certain date on the calendar a man who is a Christian feels personally guilty for the death of Jesus. The emotion grips him like a paralysing illness. He spends the day in solitary misery and then mercifully the calendar moves on and he is free to rejoice.

'Sometimes I feel most angry with a God in whom I no longer believe but who so created my humanity when I was a boy that I can't survive as a thinking, sentient creature without Him. I live in as much uncertainty as the next man.

'Only, when all else is uncertain, what is the harm in remembering, on one Friday a year, that it was absolutely wrong to torture and murder our Lord? Which is to say it's wrong to torture and murder people anywhere. And wrong to leave men without hope in their deepest hearts.'

45

'Madam Chair, one hundred fifty-six years ago – '

Zhenia looked well on the podium, despite the suit that had grown tight for him under the arms. Sophie only wished he'd mastered the numbers in English.

' – Row–bert Oa–wen was born. This son of a village craftsman had a business sense.'

He makes them that concession, Masha insisted. They must listen to him if he talks about business.

'When he was fifteen, Owen and a partner began making spinning machines.'

David Jones was there. Sophie had seen him as soon as they entered, as a party, with Masha and Kenneth. She crossed over to meet him.

'I missed you.'

She had opened her bag to look for a cigarette. She hadn't smoked for months.

All he said was: 'I'd better go in. I mustn't miss the talk.'

She nearly shrieked.

'At twenty-one Owen was a factory manager employing five hundred people. Later he employed fifteen hundred people, five hundred of them children. They were pauper children, and their parents thieves and drunks.

'Now, what year do we write now? 1927? Already more than a century ago Owen saw the horror of *inequality*. And the callousness of the factory owner who cared more for his machines than for his workers.'

Young men in the audience, familiar with cartoons in the *Daily Worker*, pictured obese entrepreneurs in chequered trousers and top hats, dehumanising the workforce for profit. Already they were ready to stand up and urge Orlov on.

Jones was the first to do so. 'Go on, say it, Orlov! We abuse the working class on a massive scale. Only a revolution will do away with such injustice.'

'Dr Jones, please!' Evelyn was chairing a college event that had been advertised across the university. 'There will be a time for questions.'

Sophie feasted her eyes on the back of David's head.

'Owen educated the children, and housed and clothed and fed the adults. Such was the response of the workforce that after sixteen years, in the village where he had his factory, they had helped him create a modern Utopia.

'News of this Utopia spread as far as Russia.'

'Ah!' Stairpath knew something had gone astray with that country's history.

'Revolution!' chanted a chorus of undergraduates. 'What do we want? We want revolution.'

'Ladies and gentlemen, it always happens that those of us on the Left are asked for numbers. Let me say that in Owen's factories, profit returned to investors was capped at five per cent, and the remainder redistributed to the workforce. The factory owner reinvested in the work environment, after paying his employees a living wage. He found that happy workers were more productive.'

Masha stirred in her seat, proud of her husband. She heard him say: 'Within the factory community, if the sale of goods exceeded the value of the labour that made them, the surplus was returned to the buyer, on grounds of honesty to all concerned.'

Stairpath shook his head. Glancing at Dean Sprocket he fancied Orlov was a lunatic.

'Small working communities – of no more than fifteen hundred people – can be economically self-sufficient. All we ask is that government allow the economy to be restructured.'

The Master was dreaming of Lincolnshire village life in his boyhood, when they never saw a motorised vehicle and no one had a telephone or a wireless.

Someone less partial to Orlov got up and left.

Zhenia concluded: 'Let's not confuse happiness with the pleasure Mr Keynes considers the focus of the economist's social work. I personally do not believe human beings can flourish without community. I also disagree with Mr Keynes as to the nature of our subject. Whatever human beings are, their lives cannot be ruled by the so-called economic cycle. This to my mind is a pure intellectual fabrication. First you have God, then you have Smith's Invisible Hand and now you have Mr Keynes's market cycles, and they are all vacuous pieties. We economists must consider what actually might make the world a better place. The real subject of our enquiry must be the ethical life men make for themselves, out of a pure intuition of human potential.'

As a handful more listeners dipped their heads and rounded their shoulders and left without comment, among those remaining there was a bemused hush in the room. Then people got to their feet and started applauding. The undergraduates, who had been calling for revolution switched to chanting: 'Capitalism must capitulate. Down with capitalism!'

'Bravo!' Jones shouted. 'Bravo, Orlov. If Keynes's inhuman view of economic cycles is allowed to prevail we will all be turned into impersonal machines in their likeness. Humanity will be sacrificed to the untouchable power of the economic cycle.'

The bulk of the audience cheered. But then someone shouted, 'Marxists like you want to tell people how to live, Orlov, and how to spend their money. Such crazy ideas may be welcome in your native country, but not here.'

At which Stairpath clapped slowly and deliberately, like a man scaring birds.

'Stairpath, you should be ashamed of yourself!' shouted Jones.

'On the contrary!' the other shouted back. 'I have every right to defend my country against this intellectualist meddling.'

'Madam chair, bring this meeting to order!'

'Excuse me, I need air,' said Zhenia who got up and went out.

Sophie could feel the heat coming off David as if he were ablaze. In place of Orlov David was mobbed by enthusiasts.

'Keynes stands for petty-bourgeois pleasure. Every last Englishman in his little house with its pocket-handkerchief garden can look to Keynes as his saviour.'

'Better a little house with a pocket-handkerchief garden than a collective flat with one lavatory for four families, Jones. I'm sure Miss Asmus could oblige us with the facts,' said Sprocket.

The Master handed Masha a cup of tea with a custard cream.

David Jones insisted: 'Where I differ from Orlov is only in his voluntarism. The working class can't achieve this revolution alone. It will take the Communist Party to make Dr Orlov's cooperative economics a reality,'

'Is Dr Jones a Communist?' the Master asked Miss Glancy.

'A Bolshie, Master, and no mistake.'

'And you evidently admire that.'

'I do.'

'And does Miss Asmus admire it?'

'I think – you would have to ask her, Master. She holds Dr Jones in high regard.'

Jones shouted: 'Indeed I am a Bolshevik and I expect Russia to show the whole world the way forward to a more just future.'

'Master,' began Stairpath, 'I'm shocked. How did we elect men like this?'

'Because they are brilliant in their field, Stairpath. I can't confine them to it.'

Stairpath nodded. The Master could not be blamed.

Sophie continued to hover beside David. Then they saw Zhenia, having taken the air, making his way over to them. Suddenly he stopped. People caught him as he fell.

46

Sophie studied Sprocket and Stairpath, as she listened to the Master's rolling periods. She would not see their like again.

'The passing of Dr Eugene Orlov puts us in mind of Tacitus' *Annals*, of that moving and timeless account of political extremism and depravity under the rule of Sejanus, who murdered, otherwise caused the deaths of and at the very least exiled from their homelands so many. Sejanus banished men to islands where there was no water. By contrast I think we can say that upon his banishment to our island, Eugene Orlov found conditions under which his brilliant mind could drink its fill . . . '

To be banished to an island where there is no water! she mouthed.

'. . . Eugene Orlov witnessed, as he said, "an apocalypse *sui generis*" in 1917 and after. He always behaved as if his exile were voluntary. That was the mark of his distinction as a free man.'

Masha in unflattering black twisted her hands and the tears flowed freely down her face.

'We hoped to offer him a safe harbour for a lifetime. We tried our best, while never expecting that lifetime to be cut short so cruelly.'

Evelyn caught Sophie's eye as they were leaving the chapel.

'Sophie, there's something – '

'Evelyn – '

'I just wanted to tell you . . . how wonderful John Birkett is. You remember, I met him at your Easter lunch.'

'That's marvellous news.' They hugged as Evelyn announced her engagement.

At the wake the Master brought his guest over to Sophie.

'Miss Asmus, Sir Bernard spent an eventful few years in your country.'

It was time to switch to that intelligent woman who read *The Times* again. 'Sir Bernard, the scandal this year was unfortunate for relations between our two governments.'

'Politics, Miss Asmus! It's natural for rivals to try to discredit each other.'

'Even so, Sir Bernard, relations between England and Russia really are so complicated. Interrelated royalty, two empires, and now the Revolution which frankly obsesses people here. A whole new academic subject might be based upon the complication.' She hoped not to be stuck with Sir Bernard for too long.

He pressed the sherry glass to his chin.

'They all do it,' Masha had observed. 'With the sherry glass, the port glass, the wine glass, even the coffee cup. In Cambridge the receptacle pressed against the lips expresses a craving to be left in private.'

'But they're in public life!'

'They try to live with their contradictions.' Masha shrugged.

As Sir Bernard weighed up Sophie's suggestion positively, she ventured further: 'Sir Peter Salomé is a man who's given some thought to Soviet Studies, I believe, and I know Dr Sprocket is in contact with Sir Peter.' Sophie watched David across the room.

'That's an excellent idea, my dear. Leave it with me.'

Sir Bernard could see his name attached to the new chair in future, the Bernard Langham Chair in Anglo-Soviet Understanding, while Kenneth, as soon as it was explained to him, imagined Lord Maple-thorpe reconsidering his support for the college.

But then David vanished from sight and Sophie joined Masha.

'The Master made a good speech.'

'Ah, Sophie, life doesn't make men like Zhenia, or Kennet, any more.'

As they packed Zhenia's papers for safe delivery to the college archive – Masha didn't think they were qualified to sort them – she talked and talked.

'I loved Zhenia. Even that side of things – '

'I'm happy to hear it.'

'Of course with Kennet it wasn't that sort of thing at all.'

'No, I didn't suspect – '

'We were friends, like children are friends. He is a child, in some ways.'

She needed to talk, not about her late husband, it seemed, because that was a closed and perfected business, but about this recent friend, this child, this dear man who had never become aware of himself as a sexual being, but who, in fear, had vanished from her side, now that she was a widow.

At the end of that tumultuous week Sophie for the first time went to the college chapel alone, to listen to evensong.

The Master, safe in that haven, approached her afterwards. 'Ah, Miss Asmus, how pleasing to see you here.'

'I'm sorry I've taken so long to savour what is best about the college, Master.'

'The choir has in common with our Lord that the very idea of its possible existence is beautiful and the reality even more so. It's really the best we can do, Miss Asmus, to see that the finest aesthetic emotions known to Western man should be stirred, and nurtured. It's hard to see how civilisation can do without that.'

Kenneth Trench had stepped back into the nineteenth century, after barely poking a whisker beyond it.

47

Percy Nair invited Sophie out to a country pub for lunch. Term had ended and he had, if not time on his hands, the feeling that a point had been reached. Wrapping up his work, incorporating her comments into his typescript, he proposed now to tidy up his neglected life. He offered her an expedition to the Three Horseshoes in Hardwicke and when she said yes he arranged to borrow Savery's Hillman.

'There must be a woman behind this enterprise.' Savery, small and neat, was wearing a patterned sleeveless pullover over a shirt with the sleeves rolled up to reveal hairy forearms. '*Bon courage, mon ami.*'

Percy took the encouragement kindly. 'I'm grateful, Savery. I do most awfully need to impress her.'

She wore cotton trousers and a shirt of her own design. Percy, who at heart shared Harry Birkett's dazzled assessment of her as a film star, began: 'Have I seen that blouse before? It's very charming.'

'Thank you, Percy.'

He opened the passenger door.

'I'll drive,' she said, tucking herself into the available space, and Percy accommodated himself to that, though he had to add: 'So long as you know what you're doing.'

Harry Birkett, like a dog who just loved to be part of things, arrived with cuttings of thyme and sage just as they were leaving.

'Just ring the bell, Harry!' she called out.

'He wants to civilise us wild Russians,' she said, now they were alone.

'Perhaps he likes Masha.'

'She's impressive the way she has so many admirers.'

Sophie was competent at the wheel. Cupped in her left hand the gears changed without a glitch of protest and the whole engine sighed willingly.

'Where did you learn to drive?'

'In Constantinople.'

'They call it Istanbul now.'

'Now what does that chap think he's doing? No signal. He just stops.' She hooted loudly.

But then the noise of the open road forced them into silence, as the fresh air streamed benevolently through the open windows.

'He didn't deserve you, that husband of yours. Otherwise he would never have let you go.'

'I left him, I told you. I ran away.'

'You know I'm in love with you.'

'I do. I . . . I'm touched by it.'

He burst into tears. 'Sophie! I'm so afraid of failure.'

They were still sitting in the car, though they had come to a halt.

'You won't fail.' And when he'd recovered himself, she knew he loved to talk about it. It was the best she could do for him.

At the Three Horseshoes the door was left open so that the sun intruded a walkway of light on to the brown polished tiles of the lounge bar. The pub smelt of leather and sawdust, and the horse-brasses on the wall had been newly polished.

'You didn't want to sit outside, did you?'

'Inside is fine by me. Are your characters still thinking about success?' she asked him. 'No, what's the word, are they *ruminating* on it? I heard Mr Eliot give that marvellous lecture, just after you and I first met. That was when I first heard the word "ruminating". Evelyn Glancy said I couldn't miss that occasion, with Mr Eliot such a famous poet. I had to go along. I thought you might be there.'

'It's my subject too, you know. I can't just sit there and take what Mr Eliot says.'

'So you *ruminate* alone.'

'I know, I know, it's not the best way to be in life. One needs to experience fully what's on offer, take on all challenges and then sleep soundly at night. I just can't manage it that way.'

'None of what you're talking about is simple.'

Now they had found seats that suited them beside the cold fireplace he was ready to get up and go to the bar.

'What can I get you?' He seemed to have forgotten that he didn't drink alcohol at lunchtime.

She tried a Scotch egg, with a glass of shandy.

He liked to talk about his own enthusiasms. 'I love open fires. It's my one regret about summer. The summer does not give the same rapturous sense of comfort as an open hearth in winter.'

'You do have that fabulous fireplace in your rooms. As you say, you could walk into it if you were the size of Jim Shilling.'

'You remember everything. I can be quite a nasty man, it's true.'

'Nastier than Stairpath?'

'Oh no.'

'We called him Starepast. Zhenia said he was always looking past you, over your shoulder, to see if there was someone better to talk to.'

'That's Cambridge for you. I told you I wanted to get out.'

'I don't think that's the reason you don't feel quite comfortable here.'

'It's the ambition, Sophie. That can make one disliked. I'm seen as ruthless and selfish. But I don't intend to do anything about it.'

'You like having all manner of modern anxieties, and having them tolerated.'

'Modern man is my subject.' He grinned and raised his empty glass. 'Can I get you another?'

She watched him at the bar.

'We women feel success differently. It's not the same.'

'I can't argue with that.'

'But you want to.' She let him drink.

'Not at all.'

'You told me your characters' lives were entirely in their own hands.'

'Rational, I call it.'

'It doesn't seem to be like that.'

He proposed a walk down the lane as far as the church, or farther, if she cared.

Occasionally he dared to guide her elbow, or propel the small of her back with the lightest of touches. They made for the churchyard, but the graves interested neither of them, so they passed into a meadow. He took off his jacket and laid it down. 'You don't want grass stains over those lovely pale slacks.'

She settled herself. 'Is your novel to be a matter of conformity, Percy, in the end, or real self-discovery? Whichever it is, discerning readers can always tell the difference.'

Conformity by a circuitous route, or self-discovery: it was a momentous question he ignored and his future critics would hold that against him.

He seized her hand and lay next to her. 'Please, just for a minute.'

'But *your* shirt. *It* will have grass stains all over it.'

'Damn my shirt, I'd take it off if it wouldn't get me arrested. Should you mind, by the way, if I did?'

He lay on his back with his shirt open, and holding her hand ᴀꜱ she sat. She preferred him clothed. The pallor of his skin was repulsive. But then she lay back so she was beside him, looking up at the sky.

'Oh, Sophie.' Percy Nair turned and buried his head in her breast. He had a quotation from *Hamlet* ready to authorise his plunge. He wanted success, and a wife, but just now he wanted to be inside a woman most of all.

'So are *you* ambitious?' he asked. Finally that faint possibility had occurred to him.

'Of course I am.' The unspoken question: 'What would you do with my life?' hung in the air

The tension dipped.

'I'm getting cramp. Let's go back. Help me up. You drive.'

They reinstalled themselves in the stuffy Hillman which had been standing in the sun. With the windows wound down it was hard to hear each other but they had to be able to breathe.

'So now you've read three-quarters what do you think? Overall, now you've been able to put it together?'

'As I said, not bad at all. You really need to finish it, and then for it to be a success.'

He slowed for a T-junction, together they glanced at the three-way signpost and then he drove on.

48

'So she moved back to London?'

'She had no choice when Orlov died.'

'She could have found a job in Cambridge. Evelyn was her friend.'

'Unable to make her life with either David or Percy Nair? It had to be a new start.'

'Always a new start,' I offered as criticism.

But Leksy defended his mother. 'There's nothing wrong with a new start. She ran her own life. She had taken a job with Orlov and now she chose to go back to London. You'll see, it was the happiest time of her life. Besides – '

'Go on,' I said, somewhat fearfully.

'Her life had hardly yet reached its pinnacle. And that's what you're interested in.'

Already I wondered if that was the right metaphor. My strongest impression was of a woman riding on a choppy sea, *une mer agitée*, the waves slapping against her, and she trying to harness them, or ride them out.

'Strange to London, are you, madam,' a policeman who had been watching her asked.

'I'm looking for a room.' She still had an accent.

The glazed board outside the newsagents was full of rooms to let. Prospective landlords and landladies advertised on plain postcards and envelope backs, some in wild, dislocated script, like the slanting hand in orange crayon which seemed to offer not a home but a trial by fire. While the flames leapt at her ankles –

' – and how that *grosse mer* chopped and flowed beneath
                                                    her feet –

' – and how the elements we love conspire against us!'

'You love her more than I do.'

'I'll change your mind.'

*

She thought the policeman seemed ready to accuse her of loitering, so she walked on.

There was a pub on the corner of the road where men were rolling barrels of beer down into the cellar. Above were rooms hung with grey net curtains. 'Nice quiet room suit professional lady. All mod. cons.' With relief she walked farther along the terrace, and then past number 58 Royston Avenue all the way to where the road ended in a green space. She sat there for a while and let the sun fall on her face, before choreographing her return.

'I've come about the room.' The corridor was a dark rectangle behind the woman's shoulder, as they stood in the angle of the door. The door had two leaded lights, the decorative effect of which recalled the tassels on Fanny's chairs. All London houses at a certain level smelt of smoke and cooking. But you knew in a trice whether you could adjust.

'Thank you for showing me round.'

'I don't appreciate having my time wasted.'

'I can assure you that wasn't my intention.'

But the woman despised Sophie Asmus for not making her life easier. Wordlessly she slammed the front door with the two coloured glass panels framing the dark mass of her back in retreat.

Address number two was a large detached house standing tall and sturdy in a half-derelict garden. Set back from the road, it had trees on either side. The three storeys of the façade, four if you included the basement, with a nice pattern of ornamental brickwork and a red front door, peaked in a pretty gable. She didn't knock. Instead she watched from a distance, on the far side of the road, where there was a low terrace of small shops.

A woman in a cloche hat and a long skirt and cardigan, rather elegant, urged two children out of the door. The boy wore grey knee-socks and short trousers. He jumped from the third step to the level path and challenged the girl to copy him.

'Wait, John!'

The woman fumbled the lock and had to pull the heavy door to her with a hand in the letter box.

John was calling his sister a coward for not jumping. The mother seized both children's hands and whisked them off.

A while later, calm and young, the children smiling, she returned with a basket of shopping. Just as she opened the door a young woman, wearing red and in a fashionable hat, carrying a leather music-case, emerged.

'Morning, Molly.'

'No breakfast for you today, Joanna? I hope you're not under the weather.'

The children stretched and shrank her name fondly. Djwanna, Jo–annaaaaah.

'Under the weather, eh?' Joanna shook her head. She hoped Molly wasn't suggesting she was pregnant. She did feel rough.

'I like your skirt, Clare.' It was easier to talk to the children. The little girl, all of three, in tiny shoes and white ankle socks, pirouetted.

'Look after your sister, John. 'Bye, Molly. I must dash.' Joanna was always 'dashing', Molly thought, as she shepherded the children inside.

Sophie followed Joanna up on to the High Street and watched her enter a café beside the market. She watched her order a cup of tea and toast and light a cigarette.

Sophie also bought a cup of tea, in the café where the door stood open to let in the sunshine.

Back at the house she let fall the heavy brass knocker and when the door opened looked straight into the eyes of this rather young and spirited Molly, a good twenty years younger than Mrs Foster in Penge. Molly had high cheekbones and short blonde hair and a large mouth that bordered on the grotesque when her face was in motion. 'I've come about the room. Do say it hasn't already gone!'

Covertly sizing each other up, they seemed to feel some affinity, and Sophie felt no need to track down the third advertisement.

In her new room she threw open the sash window and leaned out. The road far below led under the railway line, which was close enough for cinders to drift in. She liked the regularity and reliability of trains, and welcomed them as neighbours, along with, perhaps, the likeable Joanna.

She was twenty-nine-years-old when she took Molly Shearer's top-floor room. After two weeks in the women's hostel in Kensington, where there was a frenzied scramble to find friendship and support, she toyed with calling herself Mrs Sophie McFadden again, to ward off unwanted advances. She longed for a room of her own.

Molly provided breakfast but Joanna sometimes ran away to the café to start the day alone. I may do the same, Sophie reflected, or perhaps I'll manage.

In the High Street all the canopies with their giant lettering were unfurled, sheltering hams and fancy goods from the sun. 'Frequent Trains South' speeded up the pace of life while a poster for The Cornish Riviera delivered a sudden storm of glamour.

Touched by the sheer variety of life, she strode out gaily.

'Nice to see a woman laughing. Like to share the joke, love? ' The men didn't lower their prices, didn't throw in an extra tomato or two, but they were grateful for a momentary lift in their mood when she passed. Mostly the sellers were women because men had heavier work.

'Rag–boa, rag–boa,' cried the rag-and-bone man and the children called after him and his mare.

A gang of men had dug up the surface of the street. Misery if a child were to fall into that abyss of rubble and stinking, gleaming wet clay. 'Careful there!' she just stopped herself calling out.

Clip, clop, clip. Rag, clop, boa. The sound pleased the children most, and there were always older children standing around in the street. Leksy's age, he must be, that boy, long-legged in short trousers. That too was London, children alone, wandering in search of diversion, along with the constant exchange of money and goods. Dlip dlop dlip dlop. The meek good grey mare, with the decorative horsebrasses at her temples, and a shoe loose.

Sophie bought biscuits from the grocer's, and a couple of bread rolls from the baker, and from the market beetroot and tomatoes and lettuce, as well as a pound of apples and a few plums, and took them back in brown paper bags. The fruit and the tomatoes she arranged in some raffia bowls she had from Cambridge. She made herself a salad sandwich for lunch and put the biscuits away. The monastic life led in one room, with time spent reading and writing, may have occasioned Greek love in Cambridge men, and the need to resist it and be happy living monastically; but it made this woman eat biscuits.

In the afternoon she caught, from the platform opposite the sign signifying 'Frequent Trains South', the electric train north to Waterloo. She walked out beyond the canopy to wait for her first sight of the approaching engine, and stood where the sun could fall on her half-bare arms, in the grey suit, with a short black woollen top beneath. At her destination she stood on a clanging railway bridge over the lines. Beneath her as many as a dozen rails ran parallel. Others curved as if with a mind of their own. Lives diverge. Each has its destination. The world is full of meaning.

'I had some luggage sent from Cambridge.'

The wooden shelves in the dark goods hall were so broad that in Moscow homeless men would have slept on them. While she reminisced, a railwayman in a peaked cap, white shirt and black waistcoat took her receipt and went to search.

'Here it is, miss. Mind how you go.' The box containing the Remington was so heavy he insisted on winding string around it to make a handle she could grip.

'You're very kind.' People were, on the whole, kind in England. They answered the doorbell when you rang and they didn't spit in the street.

'Happy to be of assistance, miss.' He watched her go, glad to his marrow that two sexes existed.

In fact it was easier to carry the box with both hands just as it was, but she waited till she was out of sight to heave it up in front of her. The package made it difficult to go and check the mood of the river. She should have done that first, for she counted herself a lover of the Thames, and it was still warm enough for the children to paddle. But the sight of all those rails leading in so many directions had distracted her.

Back home and up three flights of stairs, greeted by the tomatoes in their bowl, and the apples and plums in theirs, on top of the white-painted sideboard with the barley-twist legs, she set the box on the bed and unpacked it. She laid a hand on the cool iron frame containing a suspended alphabet. Masha had bequeathed it. Masha didn't herself want the memento. The typewriter properly belonged to a Miss Sophie Asmus who had once used it to type up work for Zhenia Orlov, an émigré Russian professor of economics. Sophie patted the beast. The machine would never disclose its inner life – how *it* saw its purpose.

Now stop that!

But no! Assembled in rows behind a fence of inked ribbon, the keys stuck up like closely arranged coat-hooks, each with a letter of the alphabet on its flattened tip, each letter like a new beginning for someone. She set the Remington on the table and there it stood ready for her possible use.

So her time in Hervey Road faded. Not like a dream. More like a receding tune, when, once the singers on their winding, piping procession towards the horizon are out of sight, the music stops.

The table now stood under the gable, in front of the window. After she had taken the room she had pulled back the curtains and found the arched window so church-like that she had removed the curtains altogether. She liked her new Gothic window so much she learned to sleep without curtains to admire it, and to keep the typewriter pushed to one side not to obscure the view.

The trains chuntered into town and back, criss-crossing the city north-south, regularly. She liked the company of trains: the way each was an individual travelling along its own track.

When she boarded the arrowed train it conveyed her efficiently back and forth, now to her favourite iron-canopied Waterloo Station, now also, with a change, to Victoria, and she walked from there.

All English life was divided, as the very towns and cities were, into a time and place for commerce and a time and place for privacy. But surely there was no plan. Bits and pieces accrued. Sophie Asmus was one of those pieces. No one had planned for her to be here, in London, and to flourish.

The brass nameplate in Kensington was freshly polished, the way brass more commonly was north of the river. When she pressed the ceramic white nipple someone came down to let her in. She followed a long straight back up the steep staircase to the upstairs office. Nothing had changed. Universal Aunts was a small, inconspicuous business in a tall building of other offices. You had to know to look out for the brass plaque. A staff of two worked in separate offices both leading to a reception desk visible through the large glass pane of the main door.

'Have you been on our books before, Miss Asmus?'

'I was a translator for Professor Orlov. I went to work for him privately in Cambridge. He died.'

'He's still listed here.'

'I can assure you he's dead.'

The woman behind the counter pursed her lips. 'We disapprove strongly of people making private agreements with our clients, Miss Asmus. How are we supposed to maintain our business?'

'I know; it's not good enough.' She and the Orlovs had taken things into their own hands.

'On the other hand I'm not here to be your personal conscience. Our clients were always very happy with your work.'

Women these days had a special way of being businesslike. To remain professional they distanced themselves from other women and adopted a brisk tone.

'How are you on politics?'

'Excellent.'

'We also have an encyclopedia of art with articles by Russian scholars.'

'I can manage those too. I've studied for a degree.'

'When did pride cease to be a sin?' I answered my own question. 'When women became self-reliant.'

Leksy stirred his coffee.

'Thanks,' she called in parting, 'I'll have them back well within the deadline.'

If visiting the agency was generally satisfying, and the work itself nicely varied, on alternate days she went out anyway to have a change of scenery. Because she enjoyed the journey, and liked London, she took the train north and worked in the Westminster Library, which had moved around the corner since she'd visited it last. The fine new building was made to look several centuries older than it was.

'Why on earth?'

'It's a kind of apology for not believing in God, to be so respectful of the past,' Percy Nair had explained to her, when they had gone about Cambridge comparing the truly old with the modern replica. 'The problem is one can never move on,' he had added. 'The whole country is awash in nostalgia.'

It was comfortable to sit in, all the same, with tall windows to the street and more light streaming in from the roof.

She caught the Underground to Leicester Square or occasionally she walked a brisk, envigorating forty minutes from Waterloo. Another footnote from Percy Nair which she took to heart as she strode out: 'We English are good at the past and you Russians are good at the future.'

Funny that. Maybe it was true. She herself was determined to be good at the present.

She'd learnt quite a bit from Percy – Percy somewhat frustratingly married to celibate Cambridge, ever poised to get divorced – and was grateful.

For distraction at home she had Proust, in English, and Mrs Woolf's new book was next on her list, alongside the as yet untouched Joseph Conrad. Her reading reminded her of Maud Arrowsmith and she regretted they weren't in touch. Often when the sound of Joanna playing the piano filled the room from below, when the lime trees stirred through the open window and the late summer sky darkened to a twinkling mauve canopy, Sophie's happiness overflowed. She had a room of her own, and a profession of sorts, as a translator.

'What were you playing last night?'

'Chopin.'

'It's music that makes one glad to be alive.'

'In such a sad way. As if he would soon have to leave and never come back.'

'That's how one appreciates things, when there's a risk of losing them. *Tu parles francais?*'

'*Sûrement.*'

'*Bon. On se tuttoye?*'

'*Avec plaisir.*'

The next morning Jo and Sophie walked together to the station pleased at having formally agreed, after ten days or so, to be friends.

Molly wanted a lodger who made no emotional demands. She had her children to look after and otherwise her task to make ends meet. She didn't eat with her lodgers and avoided conversation at mealtimes. Because of Joanna's need to set each working day on course with tea and a cigarette in the company of strangers, Sophie usually breakfasted alone, except now in the school holidays, when the children joined her.

John a thoughtful, ponderous boy, was content to show her his scholarly efforts while his quiet sister hugged a large teddy. 'Has he got a name?'

'Peter.'

'Peter suits him.'

Molly owned this big bare house, unusually painted white throughout and hung with paintings.

'Is she a widow?'

'He upped and left. But she doesn't like to talk about it. Forgive me, Sophie, I ought to protect her privacy, as much as yours and mine.' Sophie thought this commune respectful of privacy was just what she had always wanted.

She would be either working or thinking how happy she was when John made it an adventure to climb to the top of the house and carry out an investigation through her closed door. It sounded like the scratching of a mouse as he put his ear to the panel and his eye to the keyhole, and whispered far too loud: 'Tshshsh, Clare! Don't make a sound!'

'John, is that you come to see me?' Sophie sprang the door open. 'Heh, found you!' He laughed and they hugged. Invited in the boy looked round and his heart seemed to skip a beat with the thrill of all that was different about Sophie's room.

'What's that?'

'A typewriter. We can try it if you like.'

The Remington stood there, summoning her to work as an

originator, but all she ever did, quite contentedly, was translate, and copy, and otherwise make occasional notes in the red exercise book, about men, women, children, and the curiosities she spied in London streets.

Men need women, women need men.

We are all a little bit man and a little bit woman.

But this Proust's mind is *too* feminine. It must take a certain kind of man to love reading Proust.

John sat on her knee and pressed a few keys. 'Clare,' she said, 'why not put Peter on the chair. He can watch us. Do you want to do some drawing?'

John learnt to type his name. Jay–oww–aitch–enn. The little girl finally overcame her hesitancy and scribbled on some paper on the floor, leaving Sophie to write a letter.

Dear Pa – I'm very lucky. Life gets more interesting here day by day. I wrote to you about what London is like. It's absolutely cut-throat if you're not one of the rich people. Also it never helps being Russian. You don't realise until you go abroad what the world thinks of you. I spoke to people in London about that before. I met a Jew who was always being 'accused' of being Russian, or German, or something. It's dreadful to be accused of one's existence. But I've found this terrific household to live in . . . and I'm so happy living freely like this that I wonder if one really needs a country . . . just the right kind of people who leave you to be what you are . . .
Your loving daughter, Sophie.

The sound of Joanna playing the piano filtered through the ceiling, or was it up the stairs or through the window. Feeling that her glass was overflowing, Sophie stubbed out her cigarette, brushed her hair and went down.

Joanna's long slender gifted fingers climbed the ladder of notes then flew back like white birds to begin again. Unlike Chopin, whose *Ballades* Joanna often played, Schumann hadn't *lost* anything. Joanna's room lower down the house had a proper high ceiling and a large rectangular window, and she had filled the room with knick-knacks and gorgeous fabrics draped over Molly Shearer's second-hand, white-painted furniture.

She stopped playing and they sat together. 'You've done it beautifully.' The room was softly lit and atmospheric in a faintly Eastern way.

'I've been here three years now. I was twenty-eight when I came and now I'm thirty. I really ought to be married. Do you expect a woman of my age to be married? You do, don't you?'

'Society expects it.'

'I don't care a jot for society. *Je m'en fou.*'

'You have a lover, Jo. That's enough for any woman. That, and her own thoughts.'

'Aha!' Joanna swept herself towards the window. 'You've been watching me.'

'Nonsense. I live in the same house.'

When she was at home she could hardly miss Jo's lover. He called on weekday afternoons, twice, sometimes three times a week, and always rang the doorbell three times.

'Dring, dreeeeng, dreeeng!'

Sophie got to recognise the burr of his voice on the front doorstep, three flights down from her window. 'Yeee–sss, Anne, it's me.' She didn't like the sound of him and didn't know why he called her friend 'Anne'. From the heavy tramp of his feet on the staircase she thought he must be a big man. He certainly wasn't light-footed. Or Sophie had got used to a staircase only ever trodden by women and small children.

Joanna and Jimmy spent a couple of hours together and then he left.

'I don't know the accent – '

'It's Irish. Molly and I have an agreement – '

'Why would you and I need an agreement? I'm . . . happy for you.'

But Joanna was mindful that there were sometimes hectic exchanges on the stairs which disturbed the household.

Jimmy would say, of some longer than usual absence: 'Anne, I just couldn't get away.'

'Oh, sweetheart, don't go! It's surely not time!' From two ends of the house Sophie and Molly could hear Jo wailing loudly, 'Oh, oh, I can't bear it.'

248

'I *will* be back,' he insisted.

'You're always leaving, taking a part of me with you.'

'Be brave, my little one!'

Jo had a nice way of sweeping across the room as if she were in a play. 'I've got some whisky left. Let's drink to something good for both of us!'

'*À l'amour!*' Sophie was still sorting her thoughts about this lover who called her friend by another name.

The children meanwhile had turned Jimmy's visits into their own game. Whenever they heard 'Dring, dreeeeng, dreeeng!' John cried, in a great hurry, ' 'Bye, Sophie, 'bye! We have to "make ourselves scarce".'

' "Make ourselves scarce",' imitated the little girl, and found it funny to scamper off, and then came back for her doll, after which she had to take the stairs at speed with her tiny legs. In fact this way they were bound to collide with Jimmy on his way up, and John knew that.

'Ah, children!' Sophie heard the visitor say.

Joanna told them to go down to Mummy now.

Sophie and Jo clinked glasses. The glasses were red with a sparkling cut border.

'Do you like the glasses? I bought them in Venice.'

'You like nice things.'

'It's a weakness.'

'I love your taste. When I was married our house was full of the ugliest objects. It quite put me off making a home. His sisters insisted on keeping it just as it was.'

'I don't like the sound of being married.'

'But, Jo, don't you want to marry your Jimmy?'

Having poured the whisky, Jo had settled on a pile of cushions from where she looked up at Sophie, who was sitting on the bed. 'Sophie, you must know I haven't got the option. He's *marrieeeed*! In any case, it might spoil it. Something would go.'

'I had something like that once.'

'Do tell.'

'I was the married one. I thought I could switch him on and off at will. I was wrong.'

'It's not like that for us.'

249

'I'm sure not.'

'Why's Joanna crying, Mummy? Why are you crying, Joanna?'

'Children, I told you! Get back inside!'

'I suppose everyone heard that business the other day.'

'It wasn't important. What can you do when you all live together?'

Molly had come into the breakfast room and lifted the tea-cosy and insisted on making Sophie a fresh pot. 'It's not the best arrangement, I know, Sophie, but the ways of the heart . . . '

'Joanna is my friend and I love living here, Molly.'

Sophie went back upstairs. Pa wrote to her whenever he found some colleague in a third country he could trust. Now he must have found one in Germany.

My dear girl – How are you? London must be wonderful. Your mother and I have been rushed off our feet this whole summer, but we are well and things are improving. The hospital has been given additional resources. There are to be more Communist doctors, and all new medical students are Communists, it goes without saying. They are taught to care for the health of the whole of society, as well as their patients', and their favourite remedy is purgation. In my view purgation is crude medicine by contemporary standards and I don't mind telling them so. So we proceed.

Your mother gives classes in literacy in her free time.

She doesn't have a lot of free time but we all want to improve our country.

The other day I saw your friend Kolya. Apparently it's fashion to wear an army jacket and boots. He's not actually enlisted but he wants to renew the Revolution because he thinks we're slipping back. 'You're a bourgeois intellectual, Dr Asmus,' he told me.

I thanked him for the advice, of course.

Most recently, and this might interest you, the mining engineers have been shown to be the enemies of progress.

Keep well, Sofka, and let us know how your life is proceeding,

Your loving Ma and Pa

She peeled off the German stamps to give to John, then she reread the letter, lingering over 'jacket' and 'boots' and 'purgation' and 'slipping back' and 'enemies of progress'. Sometimes when Sophie felt that nowhere in the world could she escape the politicians and the generals she turned off all sense of any action around her and watched the world happen as on a screen, thrilling but quite separate from herself. As if she had been given a preview of heaven or hell, and could only watch the officials organising themselves against any true revolution, of course, and meanwhile policing the world.

Now David Jones . . . but she left it.

She sipped her whisky.

'But, Jo, you would marry Jimmy if you could, wouldn't you? It's normal to want to join one's life to that of another person.'

'I never see it like that with Jimmy.'

'And Molly, doesn't she want to marry again?'

'We never talk about that.'

The whisky bottle was empty.

'I'll get another one.'

'Don't worry. It needed finishing.'

'There's commitment. And then there's sex.' '

'You're telling me!' Jo was stirred by the very topic. 'But what about a man for you then, Sophie? Do you keep saying no, or what?'

'Well!' Sophie counted on her fingers. 'First I avoid the drab men, and then I avoid the jealous ones, and there has to be a certain way about them physically and they have to have a certain ambition . . . '

They laughed.

'But you, Jo, you still haven't told me: why a married man?'

'I chose the man I love. I knew we might never be together.'

'I know, *you* want to make the love choice. Even if it's absurd.'

'Like Tosca I'm ready to leap over the cliff.'

They fell silent.

'And Molly? And this beautiful house?'

'He left it to her.'

'It's the first time I've seen anything really modern in England.'

'She used to sleep up here but when Hallam left she moved herself and the children into one room downstairs.'

'To pretend she was somewhere else.'

'To have everything she was close around her. She's better now.'

'Now there's a woman who could attract men! Her looks are astonishing.'

'It was *really* hard for her, Sophie. I can't – '

'We three are modern, like this house, don't you find?'

'I think everything will change when more women start to live like us.'

'When I was in Cambridge the men often used to talk about what modern society should be, and how to be fair to the industrial worker, and how to stop machines destroying the community. But they never really asked themselves what would happen if women no longer put men at the centre of their lives. For myself I don't think that need get in the way of marriage, but for men it has to be quite an adjustment. The different ways in which women can now live, and the kind of objects men and women wish to live among, and create: all that is what it means to be modern and what we're caught up in.'

'I'll drink to being caught up in *that*. You should write it down, Sophie.'

'No, no, I'm far too lazy.'

Instead of words Sophie had taped two *Vogue* covers to the white wall of her room, and they looked marvellous.

The children came up to 'play' the piano after school. That was a charming condition of Joanna's tenancy that the children should have music lessons. 'Do what Joanna tells you. Mum will get angry.' Clare's tiny supple fingers were soon producing tunes in common time, so it was a pity John, who had learned politeness and respect towards grown-ups, wouldn't himself settle. When his turn came he irritated Joanna by banging the keys. The event travelled upstairs.

Through the whole autumn and winter she so enjoyed her room. But then, equally, as the sunshine returned in March, it was a pleasure to take her reading and contemplating out into the sunshine.

'Free-flowing experience brought under a certain degree of control by language.' As the words pieced themselves together from memory, Pavel Abramovich's definition of the novel seemed to her even now 'the only satisfactory classification of what has happened to us'. That way we can grasp our experience without its turning into something else. We experienced revolution as art. A kiss in the air. A lasso on the surface of the ocean. But then we were very young.

God speed, Pavel Abramovich. She sat on a bench on a patch of London green and let the sun fall on her closed, skywardly-turned eyes.

Later she smoked alone, with the gabled window half-open. Spring couldn't be ignored. It mingled with the smell of coke from the trains and the comforting sound as they rattled past. She turned and looked up the street at the grander houses towards the open space of the Common. The trees would soon obscure them.

The long light evenings were such a strong invitation to live a full life that just before Easter 1929 she told the Aunts she could also give Russian lessons, translation being on the whole dry work.

49

Dick Charteris said: 'I hope I'm not too early.' He looked at Sophie directly, with the same open curiosity as the children spying on a new face in the hall. He was young and a little heavy-set in the jaw. He was less than her own height.

'Not at all. Come on up. It's right at the top of the house.'

He followed Sophie up the staircase. He was used to living in the middle of a large London house, not under the eaves.

Something else was different. The walls beside him were white and there were paintings. His parents couldn't have managed anything so simple.

'Isn't that a – yes, look, it's a William Roberts.'

'My landlady has good taste.'

'I'll say.' He felt satisfied that he had decided to take these lessons, for they carried him into an utterly unfamiliar environment, even with these children who wanted his attention. 'Heh, are you coming with us?'

'My landlady's children . . . John and Clare.'

Molly Shearer, ironing with the door open, raised her voice.

'John, come down here! Leave Sophie alone!'

'Go on then, children,' said Sophie, and to her new pupil, 'We don't bother too much. We're not at all formal.'

'Oh, I like it.'

Once she saw him standing in her own room he appeared stocky and strong-looking. Under the coat he took off and wondered where to hang he wore a dark jacket and a collar and tie. She took the coat from him and laid it on the bed.

Her room fascinated him. He hadn't expected domestic circumstances. 'This is where you live? And you're Russian? Fantastic!'

Anyone else might have sounded mocking but she instantly believed him and joined in his appreciation.

When they had sat down she turned to face him and spoke a stream of her language at him, guessing he would be too polite to interrupt or protest. Indeed, intelligent creature that he was, he liked the sound of that other language he didn't understand, and let it lap around him, finding its music so different from what he was used to.

She spoke to him as if he already understood it because, she said, she wanted him to hear Russian whole and living, not broken up and laid on the slab, and it was, of course, as if she were delivering herself.

Everyone knows how language lessons begin. 'My name is Sophie Asmus and I'm your teacher . . . .'

But then every lesson continues in its own way. 'I was born in Moscow into a professional family in fortunate circumstances. We had enough money to hire an English nanny who stayed with us for seventeen years, and to pay a governess to teach me French.'

His keen, soft eyes tried to find some meaning in the stream of syllables.

'What you can hear is the music. Feel the music and then when you become a master of actual words your speech will sound quite natural.'

She went to move the typewriter.

'Heh, let me carry that!'

'On the floor will do.'

Now they had room to sit side by side. Beneath the uncovered Gothic window in the strong April light he looked to her barely over sixteen.

'A, B, V . . . '

A week later he could already read the alphabet. 'I didn't want to waste your time, Miss Asmus.'

He told his name. '*Menya zovut Dick.*'

'Perfect. But tell me, why Russian, Dick?'

'That's a big question, Miss Asmus. Possibly our whole future lies in the Russian way.'

'*Bozhe moi.*'

'Don't you think?'

'I'm saying I'm surprised and faintly horrified,' she laughed.

'But why? The biggest, most important things in the world are happening in your country right now. Don't you miss being there? I hope I'm not rude asking.'

They sat for a moment. She had no answer to the question, except, after a while, 'I think it's something men want, to be "with world events".'

Then the second Wednesday lesson passed and several more weeks passed, and each week the Aunts paid her the appropriate fee.

'Don't they teach Russian at your school?'

'Heavens no.'

'Let's practise then. Have you got brothers and sisters?'

'One brother, one sister.'

'Younger or older?'

'My sister is older, my brother is younger.'

'Now, Dick, the important thing with a language is to learn sentences straight off. Otherwise the language has no muscle. So, "I live in London." "I live in a big house." "I live in the country." '

'*Ya zhivu v samom velikom imperii v mire.*'

'Oh, come on!'

'No, absolutely. I'm ashamed of it.'

'You're saying you're ashamed off living in the greatest empire in the world. You'll be standing on a soapbox next, trying to persuade people in Hyde Park to feel the same.'

'I'm sure they already do.'

'Come on now, pay attention! "I live in London." '

'*Ya zhivu v gorode London.*'

'You're too good. Everything's easy for you.'

'My school,' he replied apologetically. 'I love this house by the way. How do I say that?'

'I love it, too. I was lucky to find it.'

'The William Roberts looks Russian, doesn't it?'

'Let's look at it on the way down.'

'Dick, hello, Dick!' Clare giggled and vanished.

'Why, hello, Clare! Where have you been hiding?'

The figures in the painting were realistically painted except that they were exaggeratedly angular. What the painter had done was forge them deliberately as if they were parts of a machine. Yet he didn't press his vision very far. The scene was a crowded London park, with scores of middle-class people enjoying their free time. If he had Russia in mind it was difficult for him to leave his native tradition behind.

'In Russia it would be a village scene, romantic and modern at the same time.'

'Why do you say that?'

'Because we don't have a class like that. People are either rich or nobody; either idle or enslaved. Lately it's only been the nobodys who've given us a vision.'

He was dazzled by the house, and the circumstances in which she lived, and what she told him about her country. 'Maybe because we don't have classes like you do we don't compartmentalise so much. We are all working together to make the future. Read the poets – listen to me! – but then you must also listen to the teachers, and read the economists, and the journalists, and sympathise with the priests, and know that we will all find common ground one day . . . and that will be art . . . that's what we used to believe, when I was young.'

'You're still young.'

Her room was radiant, with the coloured raffia bowls and the *Vogue* covers and the bright counterpane and bold cushions she had recently bought. The white walls picked out the vivid reds and magenta and gave him a kick of aesthetic satisfaction.

'It's good that you notice beautiful things, Dick. Not everyone does.'

'Not everyone is able . . . to . . . ' He wanted to say 'embody' but he settled for, 'create them, either.'

'I think to create objects of beauty is our human duty, Dick. How else can we encourage each other not to lose heart? But, Dick, about you, is your love of art something you might make a career of?'

'I'd be an art historian, happily, Sophie, if I didn't feel I should do more for society.'

'To me you'd be doing enough.'

'Not in these times.' He shook his head.

He took off his jacket, with her permission, for it was a warm afternoon, and after he moved the Remington and they took their places alongside each other she could smell the faint tang of his sweat.

Dick's voice entered her head. Alone, out walking, or late at night, she replayed the least important things they said.

In a fit of uncertainty she suggested: 'I'm like your mother.'

'Not at all. Except that she's beautiful. You're like her in that.' At the end of their sixth lesson it was her turn to blush.

During the seventh she said language was a matter of impersonation. 'You want to pass as a Russian, don't you? You have to impersonate a sort of generic person who doesn't actually exist, but who you might be.'

Intonation and pronunciation were essential to get that person right, to make him sound true. 'But then you learn so easily.'

'I think I said. It's my school. I can't fault it. It just embarrasses me.'

'But that's good to be able to learn, isn't it? I'm grateful for the good habits my school gave me. I'd be a complete wastrel without that.'

'I don't know.' It was something that troubled him and his friends, how to account for their privileges.

'Sophie, how exciting you make language! I'd like to meet a school-teacher who could do that.'

'Because it's communication and communication is a feeling between people. You have to create that feeling. Then you can add the details.'

Now, as they closed their books, she made him a cup of tea on the calor gas and offered him a cigarette. The little stove also came out of her newly boosted wages.

She dared ask him why he had specified the lessons must be on Wednesdays at four o'clock. Because it was the only hour at which his school would not miss him, he said. Also they wouldn't ask where he had been at home. On Wednesdays, Dulwich boys played sports.

'So you're here in secret!'

'My political mission.'

Political! She thought she hated that word. 'Are you crazy, Deek? What is this "Dullitch"?'

She sounded Russian when she was worried, and something Zhenia had once said about David Jones flashed through her head: 'Now that this dear nation called England has lost faith in making the rest of the world part of its own great empire it has a whole stock of perfectly educated young men who need another cause to serve. They're leaders. They're teachers of civilisation. They are made to be great men. And they need an outlet. They think Russia is now the country they should serve. Communist Russia is the future.'

'Tell me, what is this "Dullitch"?'

'So you've never heard of it? Good for you. Dulwich College is a bastion of the ruling class, Miss Asmus.'

Her faint shake of the head, a sense that she might be trying to tease him out of his zeal, made him stick all the more firmly to his guns. 'It's a place where you go if your parents are rich. As soon as I've finished at Oxford I intend to work for a better society. My parents expect me to join a bank in the City. I'm afraid they're in for a shock.'

'But you will go to Oxford first? I spent some time in Cambridge. You have to experience it.'

'I go up to Balliol in October. Unless I flunk my exams.' It was a concession, but how else was he to get inside the ruling class, to make the changes he wished to see. Now she wasn't going to ask him what this Bailey–Ol was. She didn't want to appear so ignorant. Instead they lit up silently. Smoking they communed most pleasurably with nature, side by side. Nothing in their use of the ritual smoke was about warding off predatory beasts. It only showed what each could enjoy, in a certain way, and in what measure.

She stood forward to the window and watched the passers-by below returning home. She was wearing indigo cotton trousers and a black sweater belted over them.

'I met a Russian banker here in London once. He was very grand. The King had just given him a knighthood.'

'That's typical of how power works in this country. Money, education and royal patronage all shelter each other and that's how you get a ruling class.'

'But you're free in this country. You can opt out of the class system.'

'Only an outsider could say that, Sophie! It's true it's different here from how it used to be Russia, but it affects everything. It *has* to be abolished.'

'I admire you, Dick, for making choices of your own.'

'You must have made your own choices, Sophie.'

Perhaps. But it never felt like that. She was just the person she was.

He blushed. She looked at her feet. Then all the more joyfully they met in that room which Sophie had made entirely her own, with the raffia bowls of fruit, and the *Vogue* covers on the wall, and the bright bedspread and cushions, to which she added small objects bought out of her new earnings. In the summer, in the evenings with the window open, south London lost the more pungent aromas of the working day and smelt and felt like the countryside.

He told her about all the fabulous Dutch paintings he had seen at the Royal Academy earlier in the year. 'It's not on now but we could go. There must be something else.' The Rembrandts he especially loved, and that whole room devoted to the 'unhappy genius' of van Gogh.

Hard to describe, but it mattered to her so, where the art that was a purely human creation met nature round about, like the moment they were living through now, talking about Rembrandt, with the evening air drifting in fresh through the window, and their smoke vanishing outwards.

She and Micky had found each other like she and Dick did. They had invented and protected some mystery that mattered to them.

What they made together blessed them and no one could say they were guilty or belonged somewhere else or were fated to suffer this or that. They were free. Some other person can do that for you. Set you free. It's a pity to define love by how it ends up and who is to blame.

So they set each other free, and smoked and talked.

'But you were pregnant, Sophie, with your husband's child.'

'We meant well. We drank a lot of this too.' She swirled the amber-coloured liquid in the glass. 'You want to be free, too, Dick, I know you want to be free, and that's why you're here with me.' Nothing had yet hurt him, this sweetest of dear creatures.

She had a surprising number of questions for him, it being almost a year now since she had lost the conversational opportunities of Cambridge.

'Are we all part of a machine? Is that how life is?'

'For the working class.'

'You have to admit – ' she painted the outline of his eyes and nose and mouth with her finger, 'no one looks particularly miserable in that painting.'

He bit the finger and kissed it, and kissed her and stroked her, but she insisted he answer. 'That's because it's stylised. Not directly representational. But what am I saying? Almost no art is, of course, just representational.' He loved questions like that.

They went out together on a Saturday afternoon to the National Gallery, after which they went for a meal. In the Strand they passed a couple of his friends and he felt so proud and she was so proud of him. When Dick wasn't there, for he still had exams to sit, Sophie walked for miles alone. It was Dick who in the end made London live for her and gave her the courage to be loyal to the several people she had been there, since way back.

The main roads of Pimlico were lined with the smart stuccoed houses of the well-to-do. They were tall thin houses with many windows, and had she been able to put down roots in Pimlico, and not worry about money, everything might have taken a different course. Though they would still have swooped on her to take Leksy and what would she have done, a childless mother? Arthur Gillard, now there was a character! He had always seemed somehow fond of her, somehow willing to help her. He too taught her to be alert to the politicians and the generals, even if he had signed his life over to them. Worse, his professional loyalty to Duncan had made that cruellest blow to her possible.

How naïve she had been to imagine even for a few hours living with Leksy in Pimlico. The letting agent, with the card index, had given her the practical advice she needed. Valerie Davenport had done her best too, matching her to the Bermans. She imagined a woman like herself arriving now from Russia for the first time and didn't envy her.

Almost nothing of London looked like Moscow, because of London's million private houses. It was only in areas like Maida Vale, and St John's Wood, and parts of Hampstead, where the smart residential streets were lined with modern mansion blocks of flats, that a Russian with a sense of home could imagine living.

Most exciting about London though, as she found, was what people did with their private houses. In a million cases you could only begin to guess.

You could see the eccentricity on the outside. London had acquired whole colonies of vast and whimsical brick villas, with turrets and towers and ramparts, all in the last fifty years or so. That was why the Bermans had rented such a house in Hampstead, next to the Davenports, because that was where the new rich lived. Merchant-class Moscow had immediately sniffed out an appropriate London home in a suburb that wound itself round hills still as green as when Constable painted them. The air was good in the hilly suburbs.

On the other hand the Bermans' life in London had been so obviously impermanent. They had been just sheltering in the cocoon of their wealth, and in some tacit connection with 'the politicians and the generals' back home, until they were sent back, in that embarrassing clash between the two governments that had come to light before she left Cambridge.

'Molly, I'd love to take John to Hyde Park,'

He objected: 'We haven't got a boat.'

'We'll make one with paper.'

'Can you make one out of paper? Really, Sophie?'

They went one Thursday afternoon.

Everyone loved that fusion of open countryside and formal town garden in the heart of the city. She bought the fattest newspaper she could see and from a double spread folded a boat, or was it a hat.

'Will it float?'

'I don't see why not.'

'Let me try!'

'Don't fall in!'

He needed a stick to coax and govern it with. She found one under a spreading oak and stripped it of leaves.

In what remained of the newspaper she chanced on a review of Percy Nair's first novel. 'Wait, John, wait a moment!' Having lost the paper boat to water out of reach the boy was picking up stones from the path and aiming them at the swans and the coots who were deceived by the prospect of bread. 'John, don't be cruel. You mustn't be cruel.' A swan arched his neck and hissed at the boy. Sophie tore out the half-page to keep it for later. Her aim must be not to lose another boy in Hyde Park.

' "Well constructed and engagingly told".' Well I never! Good for Percy!

John launched another boat, which might otherwise have been a hat, and let it sail away. 'Got another one, Sophie? It won't come back.' It was a good way to keep her attention, to keep losing them to the high seas. But their boats were also threatening to fill the lake with soggy litter. Of that, where it came back to them, she knelt and fished out what she could with the stick. John found that the best game of the afternoon, fishing out the debris from so many ship-wrecks. He lay flat and she held him by the ankles as he leant forward. He dipped his face in the water. She had to stop him drinking it.

'Can we come again?'

'Only if you don't throw stones at the birds.'

They went home by a chain of buses and for parts of the journey hand in hand.

'When Clare's a bit bigger we can all go together.'

'That too.'

She had of course also to come back to Hyde Park alone, on a Sunday, out of sheer curiosity, to see where opinion had arrived. No talk of women, nor of contraception, but speaker after speaker denounced capitalism. She thought the socialists had more and more supporters now.

Molly had shown rare animation when she broke off listening to the wireless to announce to whoever was listening in her white-walled modern house: 'That's it, we've got a Labour government, at last!'

Zhenia had said: 'These young rationalists who love Russia may be this country's only moral beings. Cambridge is full of them. I take my hat off to them.'

Now among their number was Dick. In the National Gallery she revisited all the great Italian paintings Dick had insisted she experience. Her parents applauded but from on high Khlebovsky laughed and call her a *burzhui*.

Michael Sprocket, so busily in dialogue with himself that he had no time for general reflection, passed her coming up the steps to the British Museum, one of the many fine temples built by the British philhellenes in their land, centuries after Greek civilisation had vanished. Sprocket was consulting sources. To have woken him from that inward turn would have caused embarrassment to both.

London was Sophie's lover when Dick was not beside her. What with him having to go up to Bailey–Ol, there were longish times when he was absent.

'Heh, stranger!'

Jo greeted her on the stairs, as she was putting her key back in her bag.

'Jo, come up to me, for a change!' Sophie went ahead to her own room and threw open her door. She turned with flushed cheeks. 'Jo, I – '

'Don't I know it! It's made the whole house sing.'

'It's difficult to be discreet when we share a house.'

'So you took a leaf out of our book and just didn't hide it.'

'I didn't feel like hiding it. But Molly – '

'Molly doesn't mind. She just doesn't want another man in *her* life.'

'But she's beautiful.'

'None of us are how we look. We're great big bundles of needs and impressions besides.'

'I can't disagree with that. How's Clare's piano coming along?'

'She could be really good. John just fools about, but Clare really applies herself.'

'John misses his father.' They sat down.

'Molly *ought* to mind our men coming. It is her house.' Yet as Dick had said: Fascinating house! Bloody marvellous women!

'It's all the same to her. And you know why? She tried to kill herself when Hallam left.'

'Oh Lord. And that's where you come in – '

'I was her lodger and I found her – '

'You saved her life. That's why it's special between you – '

'Sophie, I wanted to tell you sooner. It was just, for her sake – '

'The children would have been orphans. That's unimaginable. Unless their father could have taken care of them.'

'She just couldn't exist with Hallam's empty space beside her. Then after she recovered she couldn't bear what she'd done to the children.'

'And you? Does she hold it against you that you know all this? That you made her face it?'

Jo shook her head. 'She's just happy to be here for them, as their mother. By the way, she's almost normal since you came.'

'The rent money makes things easier for her.'

'You can say that again! Sophie, I don't know about you, but I only just about manage. One pupil fewer and I'd have to walk everywhere.'

Sophie, who these days allowed herself a coffee out, and a copy of *Vogue*, and a bottle of whisky, still readily recalled her leanest times with Leksy at Mrs Foster's. 'We used to go out with a packet of marmite sandwiches and an apple.'

'Keeps you slim. Mmm, is that a new *Vogue*?' They pored over it together. They looked at a suit Sophie had picked out to sew. The conversation meandered from talent to talent until Sophie all but accused Joanna of under-representing herself in life, only playing the piano in private, when she could be a star in her own right.

'Why don't you go on stage? You're a fabulous pianist.'

'I have tried to find an agent, Sophie. It's not easy.'

'How are things with Jimmy?'

'Bliss.'

'Bliss.'

'There's so much sex in me I sometimes wonder whether I should feel guilty.'

'Why on earth? I think you should celebrate it! I was just telling my father how good life was here.'

'Do you manage to write? It must be nice to feel so close to your father.'

'It's difficult but, one way or another, a few times a year.'

'Is all well?'

'As much as can be expected in Russia.'

'Sophie, I know I sound silly. You know I don't read the papers.'

'Things are always changing there. People changing games and changing sides. They remind me of John. I think we Russians must be a nation of political children.'

'He cheats, it's true.' Both Sophie and Jo had insisted, a number of times, when they played some game, 'John, John, be fair!' To which he responded with a mysterious smile to himself.

'Everyone cheats over there, that's about it. Now and again it comes to fighting, or getting rid of members of the other side. Or stirring the soup, as my father used to say.'

Jo lit another cigarette. Sophie said she was trying to cut down.

'I'm glad it's good with Jimmy.'

'Just because men don't understand how we are doesn't stop us falling in love with them.'

'Right. There'd be something wrong with nature's design if it did.'

She just couldn't give him up, she conceded.

'But you know, once you let them close there are some that start telling you what you are and what you're not and what you should be – '

'Don't I know it. In the end they make it so you can't even be with yourself. Your head is full of their words telling you – '

*

Her memory was of Duncan here, surely.

'Telling you there's something wrong with you. But surely not Jimmy.'

'No, not Jimmy. That's what's good about him. He doesn't want me to be someone else.'

Sophie passed over her observation that Jimmy made Joanna someone else when he called her 'Anne'. Perhaps all lovers have to live with love's impersonations.

She tucked up her legs beneath her dress on that warm summer evening: 'It's good to be a woman. Our sexuality is our voice, it's for *us*, not for them. It – ' She laughed. 'Sex just happens to be best for us with men. For me at least. Don't you think?'

Jo wept a while. 'You're so brave about it, Sophie.'

This long melancholy conversation cemented a friendship in which there had been only one breach, the day the electricity supply was cut off. Jimmy was there and Jo had put a record on the gramophone he had bought her. He usually bought her a present after one of his long absences. Molly's iron went cold. Sophie who was sitting reading in broad daylight wouldn't have noticed the supply going off had not Molly and Jo erupted into the hall at the same time. Both had the same instinct, to flick the light switch as a test. Nothing happened. Sophie came out and stared down.

'Heh, Molly, the electricity's gone off!' Jo first called down, and then went in person, which wasn't quite seemly, because she was wearing only a dressing-gown. Jimmy followed, in trousers and a shirt, but barefoot. It was the first time Sophie got a proper look at him. He had a large face, and the way he grinned made him seem like a priest who found the world infinitely jolly. His rather long, thin, curly hair was pushed behind his ears.

'Hello, Sophie, this is Jimmy.'

'My dear.'

Molly showed him where the fuse-box was, under the stairs.

Sophie's disapproval, despite herself, must have showed through, because Joanna had cried, hurt: 'And where's your schoolboy today?'

'At school, as you say.'

Sophie had retreated upstairs. 'Don't, Jo, don't! We mustn't do this to each other!'

Now it was months later. 'We must avoid telling each other off, Jo. Even you and I fell into that for a bit.'

They were on their third whisky.

'Love's a drug.'

'The drug we need to survive life alone.' As Sophie had read, in *Vogue*, ' "We're all hedonists now, after the war." '

That long summer of 1929, as Joanna mastered Liszt's *Années de pèlerinages* and Sophie really believed her friend was good enough to perform it on the world stage, Molly Shearer's house, with its translator and its piano teacher in residence, and its wild use of men, was a scandal no one noticed. Here lived three women, essentially *without* men, who didn't want to be reprimanded or dissuaded from their course.

50

Robert Wilson began his Russian lessons in the same month Dick went up to Oxford. He came twice a week, on Tuesdays and Thursdays, at 7 p.m. He couldn't have been more than a few years older than Sophie, and she thought him attractive in a desiccated way, with clear eyes and skin that betokened wise living. He reminded her at first of John O'Neill, even-tempered and unerring, but as to whether he was also a compassionate man, he gave no clue. He was very fit. He had the sort of fitness she could feel, in his presence, not just see.

She tidied her room and repositioned the Remington. Robert Wilson followed her upstairs without comment and inside her room with the door closed they sat side by side. The textbook she had used with Dick gave the structure of the lesson.

Ya zhivu v gorode London. He listened to her and faultlessly reproduced what she said. She could explain the most perverse rule and he would nod and take it in and wait for more. Her task felt less like explaining and more like feeding crumbs into a bottomless maw. He wasn't like John O'Neill. She would have to assess him differently.

Wilson said he worked in the region of Trafalgar Square . . . *okolo ploshchadi Trafalgara* . . . *Trafalgarplatz. La place du Trafalgar.*

'I know. Near the National Gallery and the Westminster Library,' she echoed. 'It's an area of London I like.'

In reply to her questions he had to talk about himself. 'I was born in Exeter. My mother still lives there.'

'I have never been to Exeter. Is it like Cambridge?'

'No. Not all.'

She wouldn't have known had he been lying, and, frankly, with a faceless pupil like this, only the grammar mattered. But he took the initiative and turned the questions in her direction.

She answered, unthinkingly. 'My mother lives in Moscow.'

'And your father?'

'My father too.'

Conversation practice needs personal input. It's easiest, in the beginning, to talk about oneself. He volunteered, about himself: 'My father died in the war.'

'War is a terrible thing.'

'But sometimes necessary.'

'The devil it is. I don't agree.'

Duncan and Dick had teased her. *'Ya – patsifist.'*

Wilson was circumspect.

'Have you been known to change your mind, Miss Asmus?' He asked, in English, as he was leaving. 'There are sometimes causes that must be defended.'

'I'll bear it in mind.'

The civil servant and his teacher sat side by side at the table in front of the uncurtained, prettily gabled window high above the quiet street, as the late autumn darkness encroached as early as mid-afternoon. He practised everything in his own time and his answers were perfect and he forgot nothing.

She asked him what his actual job was.

'As I said, I'm a civil servant.'

'We call it a *chinovnik*. A man who takes his place in a hierarchy of ranks.'

'There's certainly a hierarchy,' he said, finding the thought amusing. He wished her good-evening until the next time. From the window she watched him cross the road in his overcoat and hat and walk briskly towards the station where the electric trains ran frequently to north and south.

'The civil service in my country is one of its horrors. When you know Russian better, you will read how it is, Mr Wilson. The ways of our nineteenth-century state bred a mean, passive, submissive class of minions. It's just like that now. Except now they've added jackets and boots to the ranks.'

'Jackets and boots?'

'I have it on the authority of my father, who still lives there, that our new society has taken a militaristic turn. Because some people think the Revolution is losing ground. They must have had the wrong idea of revolution in the first place. We, when we were young, were much more inspired. We wanted to keep alive the souls of our cities and of our words, and the souls inside us.'

At night, when she reviewed her father's news, she heard 'Jackets and boots, jackets and boots' and the words became the things and the things became people and suddenly whole armies were on the march again.

Robert Wilson encouraged her to talk. She swallowed. She shouldn't let her personal preoccupations reveal themselves. But then, how can we know what preoccupies us, except when it suddenly announces itself in a slip of the tongue?

'Much now disturbs you, Miss Asmus, about your country.'

'In my country what is good is unpredictable and what is bad repeats itself. I worry for my parents.' She felt him intruding. But you can't teach language without holding conversations.

'What does your father do?'

'He's a doctor.'

'A very necessary and respectable profession.'

'In Russia all the new doctors are Communists now. They have to be Communists to study.'

'How do you get your news? Does your father write to you?'

'He does. When he can.'

'He must be an ingenious man.'

'We like to keep in touch.'

' Good-night then, Miss Asmus.'

Now, whenever he left, she felt she had talked too much.

It was a wet November evening, eight-fifteen, and Jo came home in some difficulty having lost the heel of her shoe. She ran a deep bath and recuperated in the warm embrace of hard London water, softened with a sandlewood-scented bath cube. She heard the footsteps of Sophie's pupil descending the stairs, the footsteps of a man aware of what those very footsteps sounded like, she always thought, for she didn't like him. After she heard the front door close behind 'Robert Wilson', she let out the water and got dressed again.

'Sophie? Can I come in? I've had such a day.' In a loose pair of slacks and a sweater, she looked more interesting than elegant.

'Come in, darling.' Sophie set them both a knife and plate, and brought the raffia fruit bowl within reach, with apples and late plums and ginger biscuits. She ate her meal at six these days, before Robert Wilson arrived, and was hungry again after he had gone.

'How's your civil servant?'

'Rowboat Wilson? He pays the bills.' Of that fact Sophie was unusually aware, because it made all the difference that Wilson had lessons now three times a week, up from the original two. She had never been financially so comfortable.

Jo was troubled how deep an imprint Robert Wilson was leaving on Sophie's life when he was nothing to her.

'Why does he trek all the way out here?'

'It suits him, I suppose.'

'Where's he coming from?'

'Trafalgar Square is where he works.'

'So he gets a bus down to Waterloo and then the train.'

'I'll ask him,' Sophie's voice turned sarcastic.

'Trekking here, there and everywhere to catch a train, to catch a bus to reach some destination, and then to have to go all the way back home again! He certainly can't be short of time if he doesn't mind travelling forty minutes each way for a single Russian lesson.'

Sophie was irritated. She wanted Jo to drop the subject of Robert Wilson, but her friend pressed her.

'For God's sake! Perhaps it clears his head to learn Russian. Perhaps he isn't married. What do you want me to say? I can imagine regular train journeys are excellent opportunities for learning vocabulary. Maybe the kids are all over him at home and he needs to get his work done on the train.'

Silence. They would have needed the presence in the room of Jo's gramophone, or Molly's wireless, or Jo at the piano, to soothe them.

'He does have a home, then.'

'What a question! Everyone normal has a home. Even you and me.'

'I mean, why not teach him there? Or at his office.'

'He's hardly going to ask me to teach him at home, a professional man like him.'

'Different from us then.'

'Entirely. One hundred per cent. You and I do what we can, whereas he works for a hierarchical administration. He draws a salary. If we had an employer like that we'd have more . . . anonymity too.'

'Exactly. As it is, if someone wanted to find out about our private lives we're easy pickings. You are especially, Sophie. Teaching at home, in your only room, like this. Teaching people to speak a language by using the examples of speech that come into your head. Anyone with the ready cash can arrange to be your "pupil" and come in here and know so much about you.'

Sophie tried to make it sound like an absolute choice on her part. 'You go to the houses of strangers to teach. I wouldn't want that, Jo. At least my pupils come to me.'

'I teach children. It's different. Their parents don't know anything about me except that I know how to play the piano.'

'You might get murdered.'

'Or seduced. That's how I met Jimmy. He was the father of a pupil.'

'Oh.'

'I don't teach his daughter any more. How else is a piano teacher likely to meet someone?'

'Agreed. Look how I met Dick.'

'Is Robert Wilson perverted? "Learn Russian in a Lady's Boudoir"? Does he yearn to see your smalls drying in the bathroom?'

'That's not how the Aunts work. They're professional.'

'Doesn't stop him having those ideas in his head.'

'Jo! Where is all this fantastic stuff leading? All because you lost the heel of your shoe!'

They hugged, but the hug didn't last.

'Sophie, I'm worried for you. Ask him what he's up to. Robert Wilson doesn't sound like a real name to me.'

'Not his real name? What are you on about? We've passed the chapter where we learn to say our names. *Menya zovut Robert Vilson.*'

'Oh, very good!' Jo banged the arm of the chair. 'Ask him what the hell he's up to, Sophie!'

'And Jimmy? What's Jimmy up to, then, with his "Anne"?'

'Damn you, that's quite different.'

They almost had a row but instead of fanning the flames it helped that they were both tired.

'No hard feelings, Jo. Can you get your shoe fixed?'

'It'll cost me, but yes. Good-night, darling, sleep well.'

51

Sophie went to bed early and read over the latest letter from Dick. He wrote every week, and sometimes several times a week. Dear Dick. She was still traversing London, and looking at paintings, in his honour. Although recently, when she strolled through the gallery on Millbank, she found herself staring at the Gainsborough and the Hogarth and the Constable actually as if her greatest gain might be to see into the heart that beat inside Robert Wilson. It was true, she had no idea who he was. Was he lying when he said he had two children? Or was it true, and did he sail expensive boats, with varnished wooden hulls and white canvas sails, with his son and daughter in Hyde Park? Generally, when he caught the train at Waterloo, and instead of travelling to Surrey, got off after a mere ten minutes and walked through the engrimed streets of south London, breathing in the smell of the brewery, what did he think to himself, a man of his social standing?

She remembered what she had advised Dick, that language was a matter of impersonation. 'You want to pass as a Russian, don't you? You have to impersonate a sort of generic person who doesn't actually exist, but who you might be, and I can show you how to do that very well.' The question was: why did Robert Wilson want to pass as a middle-aged student of Russian.

When she crossed Trafalgar Square on her way to the Westminster Library, she found herself looking out for Robert Wilson who worked 'nearby'. Generally she was apprehensive, and when traffic threatened her she raised a fist.

Joanna now had other things on her mind. She hand-painted twenty invitation cards which were charming creations and showed her talent as a painter too. Sophie recalled a pregnant stage-designer she had liked ages back. Nadya, wasn't it? She'd never caught Nadya's second name. Nadya whose husband was determined to recover his lost fortune, and could, as he fled one country for another, and ended up living in a bedsit in Bayswater, only countenance moving among the rich.

Jo's design for Christmas 1929 turned The Three Kings into a jazz trio. Balthazar played piano, Melchior was on the fiddle and Caspar plucked at a man-sized double-bass. Curtains the colour of burnt umber parted to reveal them merrily performing on stage, each wearing a yellow crown.

'I'd like to send one to Dick.'

'I'd like him to have one. They're gorgeous.'

'It would be fun if he came, wouldn't it?'

'His term finishes on the fourth.'

'Will you put the address on and send it then?'

Jo had toyed with keeping the invitation to Sophie's lover a secret, but some better instinct won over and she left Sophie to decide.

Jo said: 'I'd like to ask "Robert Wilson" too. Perhaps he'll reveal his true identity over mince pies and mulled wine.'

'Let's try him.'

'Speaking of which – '

'Of the true identity of Robert Wilson?'

'Of mince pies. Can you help me make them?'

Sophie rubbed the fat into the flour, added water and then rolled the pastry to something like a rectangle.

'Tell me again how you came to leave Russia. You make it sound as if you just wandered off.'

'It felt like the right thing to do.'

'And again when you left Scotland?'

'Exactly.'

Sophie had a teaspoon and was spooning mincemeat from a jar into the circles she'd cut with the rim of a cup.

'Does Jimmy . . . have a job?'

'Why do you ask like that?' Sophie must suddenly have sounded like Jo's parents. But then the subject of Jimmy always made her touchy, like 'Robert Wilson' did Sophie. 'Why shouldn't he have a job?'

'He seems bohemian. Difficult to place.'

'He's a journalist.'

'That's glamorous. Which paper? Does he work for Lord Maplethorpe?'

'Who's Lord Maplethorpe?'

Jo didn't read his newspapers or anyone else's. 'No it's some news agency. He doesn't have to be at work when other people are. Then he's working when other people are asleep.'

'I met Lord Maplethorpe in Cambridge. Apparently he owns most of the newspapers in this country.'

'Maybe he does own Jimmy then.'

'Don't you want to know?'

She shook her head.

The pies, once the pastry was rolled and the rounds cut, were easy to assemble. They crimped the edges with a fork and pricked the tops to allow air to escape while the gas oven heated up. Molly had given them the run of the kitchen.

Other invitations for the December tea-party went to Molly and her children, all of them invited individually, with John acting as postman. The envelopes containing the gorgeous hand-painted cards were handed out at their next scheduled lesson to each of Joanna's half-dozen pupils, with the option to bring parents, who might get a taste of the artistic life on the threshold of which their children were poised. After all the cards were delivered eight unused invitations remained. 'Please send me one. I'd like to keep it,' Sophie insisted. Which made seven.

Every year Jo created an occasion like this for her pupils to perform in front of a small audience. Her own teachers had done the same. It was part of their duty. Pianists, just like singers and actors, must get used to facing an audience. Christmas was a good excuse. The shy ones and the slow learners and those who would never be more than stolidly competent, and knew it, could persuade themselves they were just going to a party.

In the market where Sophie went to buy a Christmas tree all the talk was of the world slump, though individual moods had not yet been quite trimmed to fit the bad news, and the fruit and vegetable sellers were in good spirits. 'It's not here, it's up north, in the factories, where the jobs are going.' The miners' families, whom Masha Orlov had helped, before Sophie even met the Orlovs, were poised to suffer the new crisis too, on everyone else's behalf.

Sophie carried the tree home bound with string and John was entreated to dig soil from the garden and carry it in bags *carefully* upstairs until they had enough to fill a large bucket. The galvanised bucket looked ugly, so they covered it with red crepe paper, on which Jo stuck a pattern of stars. Now the tree grew out of a wizard's shoulders and looked very fetching. They decorated the self-mythologising tree with a string of fairy lights, and placed on it little parcels and tinsel. In Sophie's bowls they heaped up clementines in one and walnuts in the other. The plan was to serve tea until the performances were over, and then offer mulled wine warmed on Sophie's calor gas to any adults who wanted to stay on.

John ran about and banged the piano keys until subdued by the arrival of the men. Molly Shearer, tall, thin, and with her blonde hair pinned up away from her face, looked rather fragile and fine, except for her large and powerfully expressive mouth. In Clare's arms a few sheets of music had replaced her teddy bear.

That Eastern atmosphere which Joanna knew how to create round the central presence of the piano contributed to everyone's greater ease. The curtains were drawn against the already dark late afternoon and the room bathed in a soft glow as the recitals began. When Clare played 'Claire de lune' Molly had to steel herself not to cry. It was some sort of private epiphany. Even John managed a few bars of Czerny, after which Sophie clapped enthusiastically. The parents of the young performers mostly remained standing, as if they weren't sure where and what it meant that they had been invited, and, with a mince pie on a plate, they made polite conversation with others in the same awkward situation.

Dick and Robert Wilson hogged the space to the side of the window, which effectively gave them a corner to themselves. Dick threw entreating glances at Sophie but, when she didn't reciprocate, or when she pulled a comic face and indicated all the tasks she was juggling with, food and drink and children, was content to fall back into the manly conversation that felt most natural, in a room otherwise full of women and children. Dick was at Balliol, Wilson had been at Wadham. They discussed tutors, and courses, and the usefulness of Greek. 'And now you're learning Russian from Sophie?'

'She's quite a find.'

'Are you learning Russian for anything special?'

'These days . . . ' Wilson began.

Dick absolutely agreed. Russia was the country one had to know about.

'Spengler!' said Wilson. 'Didn't he predict the rise of Russia and the downfall of the West?'

'I don't know Spengler,' said the Balliol fresher. 'Should I?'

Wilson demurred. 'He's just another fortune-teller. They're always around in times of confusion, when the rest of us decent people must take care to remember who we are.' His face was white, despite the heat in the room, and he stood there impassive.

Dick didn't know whether he was talking to a friend or not. Moreover, if both he and Wilson were learning Russian, perhaps the fortune-teller was right.

'So you think we live in a time of confusion?'

'Chaos.' Robert Wilson pressed his teacup against his cheek.

Dick said it was true people were worried about the rise of the National Socialist Party in Germany. Germany had been fomenting unrest since her great defeat and it was always a threat when a big country was unstable. 'The money we demanded from the Germans can't have helped. As Keynes said, it was very poor psychology and extremely poor statesmanship.'

Wilson said: 'It's socialism I worry about.'

'I see.' Dick hesitated. 'Some people think socialism is our only decent option.'

'They might, apparently. But that's not my view.'

The last Czerny sonata was played by a smug girl in a pale blue party dress. As she closed her music and returned it to her mother's care, Jo set a Christmas cake on the top of the piano and cut it into slices that Sophie began to hand round.

'Three cheers for the galley-slaves!' called Dick. 'Hip hip!'

'John, I've got a job for you. Be a waiter!'

'Yes, Sophie!' he beamed. That freed Sophie to make another round with the teapot and milk jug, but two of the three mothers declined a second cup and said they must be going.

Wilson, who was socially lazy and only talked to Dick, insisted tea has been his favourite meal at school. Sophie mused, could I spend the rest of my life making cakes for Dick? I do love him so. Glimpsed from across the room, her nineteen-year-old lover had a special emotional intelligence which set him among drowning people like a great broad raft.

'I went to public school too,' he was telling Wilson, as if the fact might be in any doubt. 'Schools like that get us young and make us the way the establishment wants us to be.'

'But surely you and I both benefited from our schools, Charteris.'

'But at whose cost? This country really needs to become a fairer place. The school system is frankly class-biased.'

Wilson was busy with his teacup pressed to his lips. 'Is that what they teach you at Oxford these days, that this country is unfair?'

'I make my own observations. Wilson, where do you think these two children, living here with a mother who has no money, will get their education? For the girl it will be all over at fourteen, if she's lucky.'

'And your point is more state provision.'

'Universal provision on merit. With a special helping hand for girls.'

All the while he was talking to Wilson, Dick, who found it was mainly men who wanted to bed him at Oxford, longed to see Sophie alone. 'Excuse me.' He followed her out as she went to fetch the punch she had set to warm in her room.

'Sophie, you must answer me.' He shut the door behind them.

'Hold me.'

They stood clinched, but not kissing, as the alcohol began to bubble in the pan and evaporate, bathing the room in a fragrance of cinnamon and cloves.

'I can't, Dick. I can't say yes. When you look back in a year or so you'll see I was right.'

'We're equals, right? We take our lives in our hands. We give each other freedom . . . Sophie, come on, we have so much . . . there's so much we can achieve together . . . and this . . . ' he began by kissing her neck and would happily have continued.

She stroked his hair. 'Of course, my darling, of course. Everything you say is true.'

Back at the party, Joanna held the glasses as she poured out the wine from the hot pan.

'Wilson had to leave, Sophie. He said to thank Mrs McFadden profusely. Why did he call you that? That hasn't been your name for ages.'

'Oh!' she cried. 'It's just not fair.'

52

Sophie retreated to her bed and wondered what to do. Cancel Wilson's lessons of course. But what then?

Meanwhile, with Christmas so close, there were outings with Jo because, Jo said, it was a time of year she liked.

They went up to Oxford Street to enjoy the Christmas shop windows. Each was a pageant, portraying the excitement of other lives and stoking envy and fantasy. Selfridges prevailed like a vast cathedral, richly decorated in pseudo-Oriental excess, in a blaze of light. Sophie, nearing thirty, and Joanna now thirty-two, walked through electrified twentieth-century London as if through a fairground. Festooned across Regent Street scores of thin blue neon lines wove themselves into significant shapes, as if the night itself were the artist's canvas.

Electricity had happened. Perhaps that was where the very idea of revolution had been born. After all, that a dark street could become light at the touch of a switch obviously suggested a country could be transformed overnight. In Moscow, in London, in Paris and Berlin and Rome and New York, lights criss-crossed the skies and lifted human aspiration into a new dimension. Yet as Sophie looked up now into London's portion of that sky, the rows of lights seemed to burn into the skin of her face like hot nails.

'Sophie, watch out!' cried Joanna. They were crossing one of those narrow roads which led behind the main thoroughfare into the murky hinterland linking Regent Street to Soho. No one expected a car to be turning in that direction. Sophie stepped regardless off the pavement. The car honked. A man pulled her back, but then fell himself, as the car's nearside tyre ran over his foot. A small crowd gathered. The irate driver got out and saw Dick on the ground. 'Serves you right, you young beggar. Look where you're going.'

'Dick!' both women cried, at a slight interval.

'Scrooge!' yelled someone, not entirely appropriately. 'It's Christmas and all you can do is run people over.'

The driver handed Dick his card, got back in his car and drove off.

Looking up at her from the ground, Dick asked the woman who refused to marry him: 'Go on, Sophie, ask me what I'm doing here. No, wait,' he sought for a phrase they had used in class, 'Ask me what the matter is.'

'*Deek, chto s toboi?*' she asked, with tears streaming down her cheeks.

'I've hurt my foot,' he said in Russian and grinned. 'I think I can manage.'

'*Deek –* '

He limped off.

'It was your fault, young lady. You want to be more careful.'

'He's right, didn't you see that motor?'

'My mind was elsewhere.'

'Just like a woman.'

' – !'

Joanna slipped her arm through Sophie's. They found a pub with leather bench seats and mirrors that made the light sparkle. It was a nice place to be. They ordered two glasses of ginger wine, and drank them with their gaze entirely focused on each other, to avoid the eyes of men who misread their reason for being there.

'Molly had this terrible crisis when Hallam left her. Just imagine, they painted the whole house white to mark Clare's birth, and the furniture too, and it meant for them a new world in which everything was a clean sheet . . . They thought they belonged to a world that finally knew how to create happiness. And all it did was make it easy for Hal to leave . . . '

'And now?'

'Now she's beginning to think that when Clare goes to school she can start something fresh . . . '

'But that's great.'

'*On y va?*'

Sophie felt better, and they went out into the not at all cold but rather damp night air and continued to make their way down Regent Street.

A pickpocket threaded through the crowd and stole the wallet out of Dick's coat pocket as he rested against a wall before limping the rest of the way to the tube station at Piccadilly. In the back of his mind he hoped desperately Sophie was not in some kind of trouble.

Keeping a night vigil through the gabled window, Sophie saw a man walk naked down the street with his arms wide open, as if inviting the brotherhood of man to join him. Oh, Dick, she laughed, but you wouldn't do that, would you? God bless.

53

Jimmy had turned his non-appearance at the Christmas party into a longer unannounced absence. He sometimes vanished for a month, sometimes six weeks, pleading commitments. The festive season suspended the satisfactory everdayness of life and rendered it cruel. Children stopped their piano lessons for as long as a month. The Aunts told Sophie business would resume in mid-January.

The two friends with so much time on their hands attended a performance of Massenet's *Manon Lescaut*. Both looked forward to the singing in French, which always added an extra degree of enchantment. From the pavement they climbed six flights of cold stone stairs which finally debouched into a gilded theatre. The auditorium was old-fashioned, and with its chandeliers and gold paint and red plush, it made Sophie think of a style of women's make-up long gone by. In their bench seats they craned their necks forward and waited for the magic moment when the lights went down.

Fleetingly Sophie thought: the Revolution was theatre too. How we loved being part of that!

It was a good story, well sung. A man and a woman of different situations meet by chance.

'She's a courtesan, he's the son of a duke.' Jo treated them to a programme. 'Manon is a mixture of demureness and vivacity, of serious affection and meretricious self-seeking.'

'What do they say about him?'

'I can't find it.'

'I bet there's nothing about his character.'

'Shshsh!'

Nous vivrons à Paris! Tous les deux! Tous les deux! Et nos coeurs amoureux à Paris.

'It is terribly beautiful, *quand même.*'

'Shshsh!'

'She longs for the high life and leaves him for a richer lover. De Grieux replies that he will become a monk if he cannot have his Manon. Neither of them can bear it and fall back into each other's arms. She spends all his money. He gambles to get it back. While he's in prison she gets arrested as a prostitute. He gets released, she gets sick. It's all a terrible mess. After which she dies in his arms.'

'I suppose we're allowed to weep at the unfairness of it.'

'That's what it's for.'

Shuffling downstairs with the gratified audience, they wiped their eyes and made for the nearest source of ginger wine.

The tavern was smoky. The weather was wet.

'When I first came to London I met these Russian dancers. I thought what they were dancing gave their audiences a taste of some exciting future I was part of. I still feel that. You and I, Jo, we're part of a world quite different from the one that made that opera, when women were stuck in poverty and dependence.'

'Even so I feel properly worked over by that bloody opera.'

'What it reminds us of is this: in the bourgeois order of things only a woman outside society can be a prostitute or a nun or disguise herself as a man. Hell, my friend Evelyn and I used to talk about that in Cambridge. It belongs to past times. We're free now.'

Jo sat preoccupied.

'Sophie, I've left this very late. But, would you come with me to stay with my parents? I can't bear to go alone.'

'What about leaving Molly?'

'She'll be fine. Besides, I'm being selfish. I want you with me. We'll be in the country. Sheep outside the window! Do say yes!'

Her eyes were still red from the tears that 'bloody opera' had forced her to shed.

'Sheep from the window, eh? I haven't been in the country since – '

Since she and Percy went for a final lunch to the Three Horseshoes.

54

They left London on Christmas Eve. They were met at the station by a large man, wearing a country jacket and wellingtons. Joanna said: 'Sophie, this is my brother.'

There was something vulpine about Clive Manning. He stowed their bags in the boot of the car while saying he was always pleased to meet a friend of Jo's. Really? Would he like to meet Jimmy?

But some curious contentment settled on Jo.

They must have driven for about fifteen minutes, enough for silent curiosity to replace the initial polite conversation. 'That's us. Through the trees. You can always see it in winter.'

It was a rather grand house at the bottom of a steep hill. The tyres swished as they forded a stream. Clive swept them into the drive, guided by a light over the front door. The light showed the holly wreath that presaged more decorations inside.

How strange, after life in a room, to know that for some a home was soil beneath the feet. As they got out of the car, an owl hooted.

'Darling!' Jo's father Philip Manning who embraced her was the same build as his son; a second wolf in tweed. His eye rested on Sophie a fraction too long before they shook hands.

The visitors clumped up carpeted stairs. Clive put Sophie's bag in her room. 'What is it you do then?'

'I teach Russian.'

'Oh my.'

'It's my native tongue.'

'You must miss your home country, Miss er – '

'Sophie. Not particularly.'

'I would miss my country.'

'Thanks, Clive. I'll be down in a while.'

The bedroom was painted white and pale green, and papered in a floral pattern which combined those colours with touches of cream and plum.

Jo's mother Patricia had more poise than her daughter. Altogether she seemed physically perfect. She wore a black v-necked dress to mid-calf and her ash-blonde hair fell in natural waves. Her husband looked more relaxed now in corduroy trousers and a sweater. On the tall Christmas tree beside the window, red and silver tinsel twinkled in the light, and the air was fragrant with the smell of hyacinths.

'But you've gone to so much trouble!' said Sophie. 'It's charming.'

Reaching for their heavy coats to combat the cold outside they went to church, with Philip and Patricia, Clive and Maisy, for the midnight service. Maisy, Jo whispered, was Clive's second wife. Sophie kept her eyes open during the prayers and puzzled over Maisy, who was young, younger than she was, and seemed, as her small, immature face emerged from the fur collar of her coat, happiest when she was singing. Maisy risked a smile in her direction and Sophie returned it.

'Not a believer, Miss Asmus?'

'Do call me Sophie, Mr Manning. No I'm not, as it happens. But I thought it was a splendid service.'

All the paintings of the Virgin Mary Dick had taught her to look at, and then that great step taken by Vermeer to show women as they were, full of memory and longing and private emotion, made her feel that to be a believer she would have needed to live a long time ago. Even then.

In the morning the view was of green fields overlaid with frost and indeed, of sheep grazing. The silence was perfect. At breakfast how easy life seemed, compared with London. The family gathered around the tree to exchange presents. Sophie received some bath salts and some chocolates from the Mannings and another book by Mrs Woolf from Jo. She gave them a bottle of Jerez sherry and Jo a novel by Rosamund Lehmann.

'I haven't even read the Conrad yet,' thought Sophie

Clive gave Maisy nylons and perfume. She gave him cigars.

There was a traditional lunch.

'Mrs Mansell always does us proud. She insists on cooking the lunch at least, and then we can fend for ourselves.'

Digesting his plum pudding, Clive remarked that there wasn't much sign of the world economic crisis round here. It's mainly up north, said his father. They pulled crackers.

Sophie observed that general disasters tended in her view to hit certain people more than others. In this environment she was most effectively that intelligent young woman who read *The Times* and had progressive views. 'The people who work in mines and factories, for instance, their jobs are always vulnerable.'

'They've elected a Labour Government. Let a Labour Government deal with it,' said Clive. Maisy risked a glance at Sophie.

Philip Manning said the crisis was not even of Britain's making. 'If our American friends had not indulged in their speculative orgy . . . '

'It's difficult for people at Christmas, even so, darling,' said Patricia. 'It can't be easy to lose your job.'

Her husband shrugged. 'When there's prosperity no one complains about their share in that.'

Maisy helped Patricia clear.

'But it's never much of a share, is it?' Sophie persisted. 'You have to have capital to make capital. When I lived in Scotland the unemployment was terrible. It quite wrecked people's lives. I saw in *The Times* recently that it was difficult for young men to find even manual jobs.'

Philip and Clive developed a theme of their own.

'All and sundry undercapitalise their businesses for years and then, bam, they change the rules and you happen to get hit. That's the game.'

'Completely let down by the bank,' said Clive.

Maisy was fashioning something out of the tin foil that had wrapped a chocolate. It took the shape of a dagger. One of the dogs was enjoying been pummelled by her stockinged foot.

'Two of my pupils have already given notice,' Joanna suddenly interposed. 'It's the first thing that goes in a crisis: any concern for artistic things.'

'Luxuries are the first things people must cut down on, and when things get better again . . . ' said Clive.

'Art's not a luxury.'

'Whatever it is those children will have missed their chance.'

Sophie sat thinking how much she would not now earn, since she had stopped teaching Robert Wilson. The Aunts objected: 'But Miss

Asmus, we've so little work on our books – ' 'I'll manage,' she told them.

They walked the dogs in the drizzle. Phizz, who was an adorable liver and white setter, had bounded ahead when a mud-splashed long-distance runner suddenly confronted them at a crossing between the trees. The crossing was one huge puddle. Sophie let the runner go first, noticing his sinewy white legs and arms since he was in just a singlet and shorts.

'And a Happy Christmas to you too, you heathen,' hissed Philip, seconded by Clive.

Maisy laughed. 'He's having fun. Let him have fun!' But it seemed she was probably talking about Phizz.

Later Jo said she could live any life with Jimmy, because he would transform it and she would feel it to be right, whereas she just didn't want to live like her parents.

'I really think you'd be better without Jimmy.'

'But, Sophie, without Jimmy what would I do? Who would I be?'

What kind of a man must Philip Manning be to have allowed his daughter to plunge into such anguish? Fully aware of the blight on his daughter's life, Philip Manning thought this Sophie woman could only encourage it. His son agreed.

A card game called 'Fleet Street' set these considerations briefly aside. From the moment Patricia dealt, her expertise lifted the evening.

'You have to collect sets: titles owned by the same firm,' Jo explained.

The cards had headlines like 'Deadlock in Coal Conference', 'The Peril in India' and 'League of Nations meets in Geneva'. They did what games must, and persuaded the players they were not abandoning contact with the serious world; but perhaps even preparing for it. So it all appeared to have a point, or, if you were Sophie, you could find that point in how others played, coupled with the joy of trivia.

Philip and Clive played against each other in earnest. There were bright cards which instead of words had pictures of elegant women, advertising clothes and soap, and apparently those titles brought in a substantial income for their owners. The literary pages were represented by a half-naked woman in flight from aggressive hordes in a faraway, uncivilised place, like Turkey . . . or Russia, Sophie mused.

Patricia won. Sophie raised what was left in her port glass to that. Jo's mother's victory gave her the courage to say what all along she had felt. 'Now your social duty is done, girls,' she whispered, as she carried glasses into the kitchen. 'It's been lovely having you.' Truly she was grateful for the company of these volunteers who couldn't afford Christmas.

Sophie and Jo sat talking through midnight in Sophie's sweet and comfortable room, Sophie on the soft bed, Joanna at its foot, with a plate of mince pies and a bowl of mandarin oranges. Peeling off the threads of pith, Sophie divided people they knew into those who had some secret ambition to be themselves, and those who didn't. Dick Charteris and Molly Shearer were both candidates for a tick.

'I don't know what to say about Jimmy. It's a difficult question to answer.'

Only Sophie wasn't interested in Jimmy.

'Robert Wilson?'

'Why should we bother about him? He's not a friend whatever his ambition is. Jo, let's talk about you. Where's your life headed?'

'I live for the next time I can see Jimmy. Oh God, Sophie, my life is a disaster.'

'The music you play isn't a disaster. It's magnificent.'

'I didn't write it, did I?' They sat in silence.

On Boxing Day morning Joanna's parents, and Jo herself, went hunting.

'But you haven't ridden for years,' protested Clive, a protestation Sophie remembered, because it made her realise that what followed happened on the spur of the moment and she had no right to fear a conspiracy.

'The exercise will do me good.'

'Let me see you in your gear! You look great. I want to hear all about it when you get back.'

'I'll bring you a bit of fox.'

Maisy went to visit their neighbours who had children, which left Sophie and Clive to prepare lunch in Mrs Mansell's absence. They were in the kitchen. Sophie put on an apron. Clive stripped the bird of its meat, while she peeled potatoes and washed the salad.

'Did you ever study for a university degree, Sophie?'

'The war intervened and then I left Russia. I don't know how much a degree would be useful to me now.'

'The other day Cambridge University gave the Soviet Ambassador an honorary degree. Cambridge will live to regret its generosity, don't you think?'

Sophie pictured the flowing opaque gowns, the sea of black and red, and heard the speeches in Latin. Some pressure must have been applied behind the scenes of the kind Kenneth Trench had felt when Zhenia Orlov was up for a Fellowship.

'I don't follow politics.'

'You could have fooled me, the way you were going on yesterday.'

'I feel sympathetic towards people who lose their jobs, that's all.' It was that aspect of her heart that she had left for ever with Micky Dewar that spoke. 'It's a tough life out there.'

'Jo told me you're in touch with your father in Russia.'

'One is normally in touch with one's father.'

'It's bad in Russia, so I hear.'

'I guess it is. My father can't get letters through.'

She had peeled three potatoes each. Did he think that would be enough? The menu was for mash, with cold turkey and beetroot and pickles.

'Put in a couple more. They'll have a whale of an appetite when they come back from all that galloping.'

'Jo's amazing. Fancy just going off like that.'

'If you learn it as a child you don't forget. Rather like your native language.' Clive put the carving knife and fork in the sink and was washing his hands free of turkey grease.

'I find it so hard to believe you're not homesick, Sophie. I mean, it must be difficult for you to make your life here. Just like my sister; you're a couple of odd women, aren't you, no place to live, no place to go. Or is it that you've grown attached to this country?'

'I like where I live. I like my life. Can you say the same? I think you're terribly rude.'

'I don't know what kind of influence you are on my sister, but let me just say this, in your place, I'd be bloody grateful to this country for rescuing me.'

'I've never felt rescued. I'm a free person.'

He moved around her to dry his hands on the roller towel fixed to the door. 'Some people would say that was ungrateful.'

'I'm not sure what you mean.'

'I mean they might feel that you ought to want to pay something back.'

She undid her pinafore and put it back on the hook on the back of the door. Suddenly Clive was behind her, kicking the door shut. He behaved as if she had in front of her not a solid wooden door but a sack of gold coins for his greedy hands to sift through.

'Oh, you oaf! You beast! Get off!'

He was breathing down her neck.

'Get *off* me!' She tried kicking backwards but he was leaning against her with his legs spread, so all she struck with the back of her heels was air. She wanted to elbow him, but his bulk squeezed her flat. She had to twist her head not to be skewered by the coat hook.

Afterwards she went up to her room and sobbed face down on the floor.

Clive set the potatoes to cook on a low gas, so that when the hunting party returned, and also Maisy, everyone could sit down to lunch together.

Maisy longed for Sophie and Jo not to leave, while for them the hour of the train could not come soon enough. Sophie toyed with Clive's gamble that she wouldn't say a word. Who would believe her? What would they do, even if it were true?

'I'll drive you to the station,' said Philip Manning. He felt something in the air.

Sophie kissed Patricia and Maisie, avoided Clive, and wanted to whisper to Maisie: 'Your husband's a bastard,' but what would that have served either, when Maisie already knew it?

She shook Philip Manning's hand in the station forecourt, and both of them watched him drive away.

'I wish – ' said Jo.

'I know it's difficult,' said Sophie, taking her arm.

They settled in the train. It set the seal on their escape and they felt able to talk again.

'How did your parents meet? Your mother is kindness itself.'

'He wouldn't stand for anything less. There's some sort of deal between them, which is why she puts up with him.'

That house, Sophie thought. That way of life. She liked Patricia. Who wouldn't like her? She was kind and hospitable. And she had given in completely to her own timidity.

'What does Clive do?'

'He's a stockbroker, whatever that is.'

'His Maisy is very young.'

'Maisy is a complete idiot.'

'I felt sorry for her. Did you say Clive studied at Cambridge?'

'Some minor college.'

'And it didn't civilise him. What a pity, with all those good new ideas in the air.'

Joanna bristled slightly. 'You didn't like him. I'm sorry.'

'Jo, the way he treated his wife!'

But they didn't quarrel, because soon enough they returned together to their old lives.

'I've offered to teach Katie for nothing, provided she *practises*. You remember Katie?'

Sophie didn't but was sympathetic. 'Even so, how are we going to manage, Jo? Might you ask your parents for help?'

'I won't if I can avoid it. Jimmy sometimes helps me . . . He can't bear to see me struggle so much.'

55

Since no new pupils waited she walked old routes and visited familiar pictures.

'Mrs McFadden!' He hailed her where she was watching the pavement artists outside St Martin-in-the-Fields. 'I'm so sorry you don't have time for me.'

She saw him as Clive Manning, and had to steady herself not to run away.

'Mr Wilson!'

His lips parted in a faint smile. 'I'd so like to go on with the Russian.'

'But, Mr Wilson. I've already taught you everything I can.'

He made as if to join her in looking at the impromptu chalk sketches. 'I always wonder how anyone can be flattered by these trivial versions of themselves.'

She nodded.

'Why not come to Bayswater? I'll pay your fare, of course. I mean, wouldn't it help in the present situation?'

'Whatever it is I'm not interested. Good-day to you.'

He slipped a card with a W2 address into her coat pocket. 'Get off me, you bastard,' she muttered.

As the politicians and the generals closed in, Sophie tried not to be afraid. She wasn't going to give in. It helped her to think of a marvellous woman, Vera Nikolaevna, who surely survived the pressures, and a priest called Dima.

Staying at home, she read a lot. Joanna lent her an illicit edition of *Fanny Hill*, her first taste of pornography, which she tossed aside, finally, in favour of Conrad's novel about a man who failed himself. Sitting on the floor, leaning against the edges of the chairs, letting the sweetish spirit burn a course down inside them, the two friends listened every evening to the gramophone which had been one of the still absent Jimmy's first presents, before Sophie's time.

Over breakfast, which Sophie prolonged and enlarged, to minimise the cost of lunch, and in the evening over supper, when she ate everything Molly provided, she listened to the BBC on the wireless that had found a communal home in the breakfast room. During the day she went out to the library, catching the headlines on the newspaper placards on her way because newspapers were too expensive to buy. Good Lord, they've discovered a new planet! She walked from Waterloo to save on the tube fare.

'You should consider serving the country that rescued you, Mrs McFadden. We'd like that.'

'Get off me, you bastard.'

Then came the day Jo could hardly speak. She threw herself on Sophie's breast, sobbing. 'Jimmy came back, Sophie.'

Two giggling, growing children spied on 'Anne's lover' as he climbed the staircase behind Joanna. He was thinner and quieter. Either he was acting the reason for his absence, or one truly existed which would make both lovers weep all afternoon.

Sophie took out of a drawer a letter she had received some months earlier.

'That one looks as if it's been round the houses,' Molly had said.

The letter sent to her previous address in Penge had been forwarded to Masha Orlov in Cambridge and sent on c/o Shearer, London SW. If Molly was aware of how long it had been in Sophie's possession, unread, she didn't say. She watched her for a second reading intently that morning, and went back into the scullery to fetch the toast. The envelope was a messy weave of good intentions, with one address deleted after another.

She assembled the coins in her purse and rang him from a call box.

'*Sophie, mon ange. Quel plaisir, enfin.*'

'Claude, I need your help. How soon can you come down? Where shall we meet?'

Claude Garon was now seventy-two years old. Age had inclined him recently to review his life. He used to go back to France several times a year, and for the purpose he retained a flat in Paris. But he didn't feel like travelling any more. They met outside the Houses of Parliament, he clutching a bouquet of white roses. In embarrassment she took his free hand and they beamed at each other. 'Ever more beautiful, my dear.' She took the flowers and kissed him on his smooth cheek. '*Mon cher Claude*, the kindest man I ever met.' Not counting Pa, but as good as.

They walked arm in arm along the Thames Embankment. Beyond the to-ing and fro-ing of small boats and the elegant glide of a barge downstream the factory chimneys of the south of the city pumped out dark clouds of smoke.

With her arm slipped through his, she said she had come to think of herself as a spectator, while knowing it was not enough, and others were critical of her for that. Still others wanted to take advantage of her freedom. He didn't interrupt. She asked him why he left France, so long ago.

'My father wanted me to be a businessman and that didn't suit me. So I became a schoolmaster in Edinburgh, which was my vocation.'

'You could have stayed in France.'

'My father was the kind of man . . . to put it bluntly we needed a sea between us.'

'Claude, I have to leave London.'

'Come back to Scotland! Are you ever in touch with Peggy? She is a fine woman. And how is your son?'

'It has to be farther away. You understand that. What is all the water around this island for, if not to give some of us a chance to escape? As you say, sometimes there needs to be a sea between one person and another for each to have a chance to survive.'

'We're not going to discuss this in the street.'

He took her arm and steered her towards Bentley's of Piccadilly, where they had oysters and champagne.

'So you will go to Paris. You will live in my flat. The flat would enjoy your company. You could eat better and Paris is a good place to be Russian.'

'I don't need to be Russian, Claude. No more than you need to be French or English. I just need to be who I am.'

After Claude left she went to the cinema alone. It was a startling film, a bourgeois tragedy projected for the first time on celluloid. In it a young woman befriended by a policeman was forced to become the policeman's wife because, on the one occasion she took advantage of her freedom and went home with a strange man, the man attacked her and she accidentally killed him. The policeman knew she was guilty and forced marriage on her in exchange for his silence.

'What film was it?'
'Hitchcock's first.'
'My mother certainly had a knack . . . '

As she emerged from the darkened auditorium, the bright light of an early evening in summer flashed its message before her eyes. 'Because of the way I live, which they disapprove of, they want me. Because I am my own world. Because no one notices me, because I refuse to take sides in the big games that rule our days, they want my services. Pa, you know how to deal with them, you just laugh at them as if you were laughing with them, and they accept it, but I can only run where I hope they won't follow me, because they treat me like a criminal.'

When Sophie got home Joanna had spent a longer than usual afternoon in bed with Jimmy. The house swayed and swaggered with its intravenous dose of immorality, as Sophie arranged Claude's white roses in a vase.

'Molly, I know this will come hard but I have to leave. I can pay to the end of the month.'

Molly Shearer was sitting over her sketchpad in the breakfast-room. Now it turned out that Sophie's departure was just what Molly Shearer needed, finally to draw a line under the past.

'I was so afraid you would take it badly.'

They kissed on the cheek.

'Not all. You're an example to me. Good luck, Sophie.'

As the driver put her trunk into his taxi, a necessity on which she spent the last of her English money, John, now seven, dived away from the ground-floor window. A school-age Clare was crying. Molly took her hand and kept it waving. John ran upstairs to verify the typewriter had gone. He wished Sophie had left it behind, so he could become a journalist.

'Come and stay!' Sophie mimed to Joanna. Rain kept the well-wishers inside, behind the glass.

'I'll come for a weekend with Jimmy, when you're settled.'

She shouted back unheard. 'You've got the address.'

And then she was checking she had her passport and tickets. The rain darkened the streets and set windscreen wipers in jerky motion, so that, for every person staring through a windscreen into the future, every thirty seconds the future was flattened into oblivion.

56

Dover was a place of porters and grey skies. Hectic activity, goods in chaos, the wind blowing inhospitably through the half-covered railway terminus. An hour later the agitated sea was its natural extension, grey and inescapable.

She was travelling with an imagined armful of white roses from Claude Garon. Their perfume mingled with the smell of oil from the ship's engine, and with the vomity fug that rushed out of the saloon. Something fishy and marine clung to the ropes that bound the lifeboats close to where she stationed herself. *Ma . . . po . . . et . . . ark . . . po . . . ver . . . ol . . . ic . . . ri . . .* she hurled down to the passing depths.

The wind howled on deck. It froze her cheeks, and the hands with which she held the rail, but she couldn't bear to go inside. At last land appeared as a thin grey strip.

The journey from Calais passed quickly. Having handed her trunk over to be delivered next day, she stepped lightly into the cold train, which quickly filled. A final jolt, a short queue of eager passengers in the corridor, doors prematurely opened, and she was in Paris and Paris was all around. She inhaled the smell of coal, closely followed by vanilla, chestnuts and coffee. Outside the Gare du Nord, when she descended into the métro in the light evening, the ornate iron entrance symbolised to her a pair of balletic arms upstretched. Passing beneath the interlocked hands, she fell into step with the scores of Parisians who carried handbags and briefcases and caramel-coloured batons of bread and folded newspapers, as, in her ears, the long, gangling strides of the English gave way to a pretty language of mincingly even steps.

The underground train whined into the station. In London, train carriages were made to look like comfortable sitting-rooms on the move, as if Londoners couldn't bear to be away from home, but here people allowed themselves to be conveyed like items in despatch. Yet it was just as efficient, and less crowded.

A feline woman with a snub nose and small eyes carried a hat box on her lap with the name Galeries Lafayette. A man with a white moustache was reading the financial newspaper *La Bourse*. Sophie checked the time on her own wristwatch against his, reading it upside down, and counted the stops to St-Paul.

It was night now and definitely Paris was more glamorous than London. A half-moon appeared and reappeared amid unruly dark clouds that showed silver-edged against the fading blue sky. She looked up to the tall buildings distinguished by so many fine windows set into ornamental facades. The street was full of electric light, moulding the evening space. She walked towards the Bastille, but before she arrived turned into a side street to find Claude Garon's *garçonnière* in the eighth arrondissement.

The whole side street was bounded by an immense wall, like a fortress, with a frill of chimneys high above. Chimneys always seemed like late, unwanted children: not really part of the design. So high up, so close to God, and yet so often deformed.

Had she perhaps come to the unmarked rear of a great residential building set in a city wall? Her key reassured her this was the entrance and admitted her to an immense baroque space, an *hôtel* spanned by a horseshoe staircase which created a gallery on the first floor. It left her puzzled. All around the gallery were doors to apartments. The glazed roof let in plenty of light, but where more apartments were recessed around the edge of the space on the ground floor they were dark and seemed more like safe-deposit boxes than places to live.

She fished in her bag for Claude's instructions; a couple came down arm in arm and wished her good-evening. The stone staircase was as wide and elegant as if the ground floor of the *hôtel* had once been a ballroom. Under the chandelier at the head of the stairs turn right, wrote Claude. *Aller jusqu'au bout*. Go right to the far side and you will find 3 *bis*. Through a scuffed white door she let herself in.

A large window provided ample light but a single bed filled most of the narrow space and only left just enough room for a small table and chair alongside. She set her coat and bag on the bed, and found what she expected behind the partition beside the chair. The unpleasant smell might dissipate, now that she used it and flushed it. The bad smell came up from the drains. Opposite the screened-off WC, from just where the bed ended and on its far side, almost touching the wall beside the door, was a washbasin. The walls and paintwork of this ensemble were painted a flat, soothing pale grey, the best feature of the room so far. She kicked off her shoes and, moving the bags to the table, with the keys, lay on the bed. A brown water stain turned the ceiling into the map of South America. A sulphurous brown mass tapered away towards Tierra del Fuego. She turned out the light by a switch that dangled on a wire. The bed was of the kind where instead of springs there are chains which have worn slack. She covered herself with her coat and slept.

That week the weather recovered from its late-summer brutality and turned into a warm moist autumn, the streets punctuated by wet brown leaves swept into neat piles. She began exploring out of her own window, where, down in the narrow street, far beneath the chimney-pot house demons, morning and evening, people passed, invariably with a baguette for the next meal. Some men carried briefcases while others rode bicycles, for, as was always clear, these were details that defined their different kinds of work. The politicians and the generals, and those who did their bidding, carried briefcases.

A delivery cart was taking ice up the main road, to keep the oysters and the lobsters outside the brasserie fresh. In the brasserie, painted red, she went for a coffee. At the baker's, where the shop-bell rang every time a customer crossed the threshold, she wondered how the baker could live with the constant signal to remain alert.

When her trunk arrived she hung up her clothes behind the door and upended the empty trunk between the table and the windowsill. The second chair, tucked as far underneath as it would go, now directly bordered the bed and she had to walk on the bed to move from the window to the door. She wanted to use the space under the bed to store the Remington, but she'd need to clean first. A concierge on the ground floor lent her a broom and a mop.

In their first conversation Sophie watched the woman search for a ring on her finger before addressing her as '*Mademoiselle*'.

'I'm Russian,' Sophie told Madame Fillon. 'And a friend of Monsieur Garon. I've come to stay.'

'Russian,' repeated La Fillon, and told her to be sure to lock the door to the street at night.

Yes, yes, that's what she was. Russian.

In the *quartier* the narrow streets were packed with tiny shops and workshops. Grinders and mincers and saws and hammers made quite a music. On every square, some of them as tiny and cobbled as someone's back garden, but always with trees, were cafés. A café could be a table or two in the sun behind a private house. Or it could cover a huge area on the corner, with the main street full of seductive metal-rimmed tables for two, overspilling on to the pavement, and with all Paris to watch pass by.

The *garconnière* known as 3 *bis* must once have belonged to a maid or manservant. It was itself no larger than a storage cupboard. She let herself in with a childish thrill and unpacked the oil and sardines and dried haricot beans she had bought from an excellent grocer's. There was a street market near the métro, and a small formal park at the centre of the *ancien-régime* place des Vosges.

The great sights of Paris seemed to have been laid on for her entertainment. She strolled up and down, across bridges, along embankments. In Monparnasse she bought herself a cup of tea and beside the window watched undisturbed the endless parade of pedestrians and traffic – horses, cars, trolleybuses and gendarmes with white traffic batons.

She read every notice – it was already a habit from London – and the name of Beate Wischnitz claimed her attention on a poster advertising a photographic exhibition. The gallery was in rue Cardinal Lemoine, a small lane on the Left Bank, close to the river and the Île St-Louis. She found she could walk to it straight from the Bastille, over the long bridge that took in the tip of the Île and opened up a view of the unfinished cathedral of Notre Dame. The sight was good enough for a life to close its eyes on. She rested there awhile.

As she approached the gallery a waiter in black with a white apron was leaving with an empty tray under his arm. Sophie looked into the display window.

Mon Dieu! Bozhe moi! COMMUNISM IS SOCIALISM PLUS THE ELECTRIFICATION OF THE WHOLE COUNTRY: the city in the picture was plastered over with modernising slogans. In a second picture, out of an ornate building from the previous century emerged an anonymous young woman, beautiful and oblivious, in a grey costume that could be an artist's vision of what an athlete or an engineer might wear. She carried a briefcase and a jacket over her arm.

Sophie felt wet under the arms and her heart hammered. Yes, yes! It was like that. We had so much gaiety and poetry and hope. Poetry was how I felt it.

It was 1923, she the same age as the century. On Tverskaya the awnings were extended and women in below-the-knee dresses and cloche hats were shopping. In the next shot the beggars with their chopped-off limbs were staring straight into the camera as if the lens were the conscience of God. How had He let such things happen? Surely what connected these photographs was the answer to a mystery. The viewer of the exhibition just had to look hard enough to spot it; had to imagine a *Gesamtkunst* to pull it all together.

Her head whirling, Sophie took a private moment to commune with her father, who said: 'You know the joke about the peasant who comes to Moscow for the first time to visit the zoo? When he comes to the giraffes he exclaims, "*Bozhe moi*, look what the Bolsheviks have done to our horses! They really can change things." '

With a slight smile on her lips, she entered the gallery and examined the rest of the exhibition.

With the Kremlin wall as an unrelenting dark backdrop, useful to the photographer, a number of giant caricature figures were entertaining a circle of bystanders. The spectators kept their distance, as if these were dancing bears, but bears all the same. You could just make out, from the Cyrillic letters painted on their costumes, the names of Lloyd George and Clemenceau, the Western politicians who had been unsympathetic to the new Russia. Everyone knew the names then, and she had been no exception.

On the empty reception desk she rang a bell. Out of sight she had heard a man and a woman talking. They must be drinking their coffee. Now a woman emerged, dark and elegant, with a long yellow scarf around her neck and a close-fitting black sweater nipped in at the waist with a thin leather belt. Her black trousers were full and mannish, and she was smoking a cigarette in a long holder that accentuated her fingers.

'*Bonjour*, Beate. *Je suis Sophie.*'

'Sophie, I don't believe it. What joy!' Beate put down the cigarette on the edge of the desk and they embraced.

Sophie waved a hand. 'All this! It was us!'

Beate looked a little sheepish.

'No, no, you kept a record. People will remember you for it.'

'*Toi, tu étais toujours si belle.* And now you are still more beautiful.'

Perhaps, but she knew she had changed. There was more character in her face, and more strain, accentuated by her short hair.

'It's a strange thing for me to see my past on someone else's wall.'

'Russia will have changed by now.'

'Oh, certainly, from what I hear.'

'You haven't been back?'

Sophie shook her head, as they laughed and hugged, searching for an ease between them.

'I suppose you've had a lot of interest?'

'Russia's a hot topic here.'

'So people come here and say, ah, yes, that's revolution. They see that revolution is only a few degrees away from ordinary life and doesn't at all look like a catastrophe. The changes, as I remember them, were in the little details. I mean, what happened if you didn't want to march in the parade, or you sided with the politicians who were publicly ridiculed.'

But Beate wasn't listening to her. No one convinced ever listened to her.

'I've had a lot of visitors but also some nasty letters pushed through the door.'

'What do the nasty ones say?'

'They are from fascists who believe France is about to become Bolshevik: they say that I'm destroying their country.'

300

'I see, well Russia does make people afraid. Who's this?'

It was a studio portrait of a writer, above a text endorsing the exhibition. 'You didn't take this.'

'It's publicity. What can one do?'

'Romain Rolland,' she read.

'He's a great novelist, if you haven't read him, Sophie.'

But the disapproval must have shown on the new arrival's face. 'I can't be bothered with writers like that.'

She picked up the printed list on the desk. That her own image was far, far more than she could afford made her smile. What was more, with the red dot in the corner, it had been sold.

She pedalled fast, but the past receded from her inexorably. Between her and the past now stood people who knew. They knew what it was and never considered that experience, once it had flown by, was impossible to recapture.

'Sophie, won't you come round and meet my husband?'

'Beate, dear, I'd love to.' Sophie went to peer round the screen behind which Beate and her male companion had been drinking coffee.

'Ah, no. This is Pierre, my assistant.'

Laughing at her mistake, Sophie shook hands with a thin-lipped, epicene creature with tightly curled hair; a perfect candidate for Greek love in Cambridge.

'My husband is Serge.'

'I remember you mentioned a Serge.'

'The same one!' The photographer leafed through a red pocket diary. 'Can you do the seventeenth?'

Sophie nodded.

57

'*Salut!*'

The name on the bell was Lavergne, and the flat was new and quite far from the centre, near the Bois de Vincennes. The air was unusually fresh, with a smell of lime blossom, when Sophie got off the bus and followed the map. Serge and Beate Lavergne lived on the fifth floor of a mansion block in a chic suburb.

'It's wonderful.'

Once you had entered from the hall, it was one large room, facing south. At one end were soft furnishings and books, at the other a large glass dining-table in the Bauhaus style, with metal and leather chairs that created a quite unexpected impression of lightness. Serge, quite the opposite of Beate's assistant, was tall and broad-shouldered, with thick upstanding brown hair and brooding brown eyes.

She leaned this way and that. In the flat the images were of Berlin. 'Do you ever go back?'

'It's a fascist country now,' said Serge. He was wearing a beige pullover, which had a zip from the chest to the collar, over a black shirt.

'But you must have family there, Beate.'

Serge handed Sophie a filled glass as if the shared wine was the only answer to some vast new problem on which each of them had to base a decision, presently.

Sophie stared out of the black expanse of glass. From the balcony beyond the dining-table, which was laid for dinner, you could follow the lines of street lights back into the heart of the city. Only the great *bois* lay in absolute darkness.

Seeing her turn from the window and take in the living space, Beate spoke for her. '*Oui, on est bien.*' There was no virtue in the Lavergnes denying they were comfortable.

'So, Sophie, what brings you to Paris?'

'A friend offered me his flat and I thought, "Why not?" '

'England hasn't changed you. You were always, well, just what you are, entirely yourself. And how is . . . '

'My son?'

'Leo – '

'Leksy.'

'What was the name of that horrible – '

'Nikita.' Sophie set down her drink. 'You can't trust the Revolution to encourage the right types. I used to quarrel with my father over that.'

Serge pursed his lips. 'In principle it will lead to a higher level of social consciousness.'

Sophie struggled to reply.

'Don't do it, *chéri*, you're always interrupting conversations and making them difficult for people. I can tell you, Sophie, Serge's great problem is that he's a philosopher.'

He did smile then, and Sophie saw the possibility of liking him.

Beate passed Sophie a plate containing wafer-thin slices of smoked duck. Serge topped up all their glasses, and then held his own up to the light.

'*À la nôtre.*'

'*Na zdorovie!*'

'*À Margaux '26!*'

'But, Serge, all I meant was that Nikita was a criminal and a danger to others. Why should any society encourage people like that? He was the one who – '

'Took my camera and smashed it.' Beate finally said it.

'He didn't want you taking photographs of his country in distress.'

'On the contrary. Her foreignness was just an excuse for aggression.'

There was a silence.

Serge began afresh. 'I envy you coming from Russia. It's such a place of achievement, and hope.'

'The poet Khlebovsky wrote a line about Sophie and me. We were "two butterflies in a coal-hole".'

'I remember fluttering about.'

'They read Khlebovsky's poetry now at the Sorbonne, Sophie – '

'So we pass into history, as butterflies.'

Serge wondered how to talk to her. 'So you were in London after you left Moscow?'

303

'Then in Cambridge for, how long was it, nearly two years, and then back to London. '

'And Pavel Abramovich? And Vera Nikolaevna? Where are they now?'

Sophie, made aware of the pattern of the butterfly's flight, smiled opaquely.

'But the Revolution is absolutely scientific. Dialectical materialism is its basis.'

'Ah, Serge, that's too much philosophy for us. Let's eat.'

Beate served an entrée of Jerusalem-artichoke soup.

'Scientific, Serge? My father used to say he could never remember which came first, the politics or the philosophy. The pretention to science was the worst part about it – '

The soup was followed by a rich and delicate rabbit casserole, of which surely Pushkin would have approved. More than that, Pushkin would have favoured cooking rather than the philosophical pigswill of the politicians and the generals. Sophie felt she hadn't eaten such a meal for years, although, in fact, she and Claude had lunched very well. 'It's delicious. I don't know what more I can say.'

With Sophie finally relaxed, Beate raised her glass and said: 'Welcome to Paris!'

Serge commented from time to time, as he isolated a few vegetable fibres on the side of his bowl and fished for tiny rabbit bones, 'C'est bon,' and reached for yet another piece of bread.

After the salad, which picked up the last traces of sauce from the rabbit, Beate brought in a runny Vacherin cheese, to be spooned out with a teaspoon. The bread was replenished and a second bottle of the Château Margaux '26 came into its own.

Serge explained his passion for the films of Eisenstein. 'Always that teasing element of the symbolic in what appears to be a realistic universe.'

The memories seized Beate. 'Sophie, what was the priest's name?'

'Dima.'

'One of my friends is married to a Russian. Elsa Berman,' the husband said.

'I did once meet Elsa Berman, with her sister.'

'She's a leading figure now in the PCF.'

'A Communist,' said Beate.

'A Communist now, is she?'

'Elsa's husband is the driving force behind the Party. He's French, she's Russian. It's a real marriage between Paris and Moscow.'

'One has to commit oneself, Sophie, that's what I've learnt.'

'The times we live in,' confirmed Serge.

Commit yourself, don't commit yourself, they get you anyway, because, you know, if you're free, and for yourself, they think they can use you for anything they need. You're a quantity without a name, and nothing attracts them more than what they think is an empty space they can impose their name on. You see, when everything is political, as it seems to be now, no one is free, except I can say I have tried.

'Sophie, how about this: you teach me Russian and I'll teach you dialectical materialism.'

'Serge,' warned his young wife, not perhaps without a tinge of competitiveness, 'you've forgotten how much work you have to get through between now and March.'

'I'll teach you Russian with pleasure but I never had a head for philosophy.'

Sophie went to the bathroom, where the walls were tiled and had lights above the mirrors. She smiled at herself there for holding up so well, but shed a few tears on the way to the métro.

58

In the flat the light was good. She bought chrysanthemums for the table. The street she looked down was historic, but what did that turn out to mean? Historians write it, photographers record it, whereas the past itself remains a silent and irretrievably empty space. You lavish your loving glance on the past and all for an emptiness. There lies the truth. Swallowed up.

An occasional pigeon perched on the windowsill.

She went out and, having asked in the Russian bookshop in a street near the university, she found an agency that might take translations into Russian. The staff were not welcoming. There are one million Russians in Paris, *mademoiselle*. Writers, journalists, painters, clerics, all of them, and their wives, in search of income. And now their children too. What are you offering that is different?

In her tiny room she put the bright cloth from London on the table, and the counterpane and cushions on the bed, and fruit in one of the raffia bowls.

She climbed up to the *butte* of Montmartre, taking a flight of railed stone steps, green at the edges, and watched the artists sketching. Tourists gathered round who wanted their portrait made as a record of their visit. '*I was there.*' Crazy fools.

She had stopped and watched other human subjects clamouring to be portrayed by these pavement artists for hire on the east side of Trafalgar Square, when Robert Wilson had materialised beside her with his impossible, 'Mrs McFadden! Won't you serve the country that rescued you?'

Get off me, you bully!

She made the gently winding descent along the rue Caulincourt. Taking long loose strides down, and down again, towards the river, under the gaze of the white basilica, she felt as if she were slowly drifting in to land, in the centre of Paris, on the back of a great bird, not yet shot down.

> Souvent, pour s'amuser, les hommes d'équipage
> Prennent des albatros, vastes oiseaux des mers,
> Qui suivent, indolents compagnons de voyages,
> Le navire glissant sur les gouffres amers.

Like the albatross she overflew Pigalle, with its garish posters on the theatre fronts, and its mixture of soldiers and sailors and workers and painted women, and the sailors allowed her another day of life.

Far away on the other side of the river, warm under the thick wool cape she had brought from Scotland, she liked to sit and read in the Jardins du Luxembourg. The serenity of the grass and the trees was a comfort, and the nannies with their prams a comedy. She fell to thinking it might be possible to find a *poste* as a governess, teaching the children of some elevated family English. Another kind of agency would have such jobs on its books, and surely welcome her.

An intense solitude came over her, as she, *indolent travelling companion of the ship that glides over bitter depths*, lay staring at the water stain one rainy afternoon. She was for a few whole days immobilised, and after that, although she exchanged daily greetings with Madame Fillon (always behind her internal window) and the baker and the flower-seller and although she kept walking out of habit, she remained inwardly stilled. Christmas and New Year passed. The flat was centrally heated but not warm.

When she ventured outside again the weather was dry underfoot but there was an icy wind. She made the effort to install herself in one of the large cafés to watch the passers-by. 'La Coupole,' said Serge. 'You must go there. Everyone goes there.'

Go to a place where I am expected? You've no idea, young Serge. Sophie Asmus needs the city of Paris to dissolve in. To live just under its surface is her aim. To dwell just beneath the level of intelligibility and obligation that the politicians and the generals have set for her. All officialdom insists she endorse their view of how things are, but there is a way out: with a few francs to live on, she can live below the surface.

'One has to forgive the English their disgusting food because they are so kind.

'One has to forgive them their grey and dreary island because the men are so courteous.

'In London art is a mostly rather expensive embellishment of life. Whereas, in France, yes, one lives the great unfinished novel from inside . . . '

Oh, oh, the people I have been and the subjects I have pronounced upon!

She toyed with a title she liked in French, *Le grand roman inachevé de l'art et de la liberté*. If someone would write it she would read it. But how could anyone write what never stopped happening? The last page could only be turned when every human life simultaneously became meaningful.

'We Russians feel too sorry for ourselves. Everyone suffers. Everyone risks a hard time in life.

'When I arrived in London, I was so young, I tried on ideas like I tried on new outfits, for the fun of it, and then again in Cambridge, to see who I could be.

'Cambridge was such a sober and masculine place. But I learnt things about myself there. What I might have been with a proper education. Like Evelyn Glancy, perhaps. I liked her. I hope she's happy with John Birkett.'

Sophie Asmus went back to the Russian bookshop and browsed. In rue Daru she mingled with the Russian church-going crowd, and it felt like playing a bit part in someone else's film.

Why should I chose a role? I am myself to myself.

What is the great fear, Sophie?

Of being trapped, of course. Animals know that. But whereas animals are trapped in cages, and with wires, it's talk that does for us. Silence too, because that is also a kind of talking. They won't let you be free, so, of course, you play with their words.

'Just one question, Mrs McFadden. Have you ever thought of serving the country that rescued you?'

They give you *that* role, of the infiltrator and the informer and the dishonest friend and the false witness, and think of it as a gift to fill your emptiness.

She replied she didn't ever feel she had been rescued and she had no intention of *serving* anyone.

'But with the present political situation, Mrs McFadden, your expertise – '

'No.'

'But you know the truth.'

'I do.'

'We would say your only, your last illusion, in this life you've made for yourself, is that you are free.'

No doubt it's the wrong word; no doubt.

The little street with the enormous wall and the dubious chimney-pot gods was called rue Jacques Coeur. Now lying on the bed in the flat at 3 *bis*, she imagined that though the building was itself like a great cathedral, she herself was living in a strange and secret space carved out from within a gargoyle. She inhabited a flying buttress suspended over humanity and beneath the gods. What was beautiful to her looked ugly and menacing from outside, perhaps. She'd never imagined it that way before. As she lived on the outer edge of that huge and elegant space called 'an acceptable way of life', creatures like Robert Wilson pounced on her.

In the uncomfortable bed, with the Remington, shipped from England, gathering dust beneath, it was as if hordes of strangers over thousands of nights had slept here before. As a physical being she was a stranger to herself, lodged in a room where she couldn't freely walk between the window and the door and had to cook in the same place as she washed.

Imagination revived the past, as it held her captive in that no man's land. Lying under the sign of the water stain, she was sailing again from Sochi. She was lying full length on the bench under a blanket and listening to Pyotr Nikolaevich, captain of the *Chaika*, chat with his sailors.

She went nevertheless to replenish her chrysanthemums, for she had to have colour beside her, and it was then that the flower-seller in the rue St-Antoine told her an extraordinary story.

'It was a Russian.'

'I can't believe it.'

'He shot the President of the Republic point blank.'

'But how could that be?'

The woman shrugged. 'People say he was sick. But maybe that's just an excuse.'

There was a library close to the Hôtel de Ville, a pleasant walk along the rue St-Antoine, and there she looked it up in the newspapers. The event was history now, but, for all that, not long past. She couldn't talk to the man himself, but she could read what they said.

'You might say the beginning of the story was the Great War,' she began, when she reviewed her notes in the evenings. The Remington bowed its keys and pinged its bell, and words appeared on the sheets of paper she rolled in.

Writers remembered the butchery and the absurdity and the miserable pathos of lives terminated in a flash. What could you do but howl and stumble over words and push the words aside and howl again? It was writers then who saw themselves as witnesses. Apollinaire (but he died himself), Blaise Cendrars, Jean Cocteau, Pierre Jouve . . .

The names were a blank to her, but she wrote them down. 'Blaise Cendrars, *ancien Dadaiste*', said a café poster that caught her eye and gave her an inkling of the work she might do, to tell her tale.

Ten years after the war ended the President honoured these survivors of the Great War who, through their writing, turned it into what the President was due to call, in his speech, 'our heritage'. A library just like this one organised a book fair dedicated to 'our heritage', bloody but just.

Monsieur le Président arrived with members of the cabinet and representatives of the press. And some of the writers themselves. Not Apollinaire, as I said. He died in the trenches. But his books too were laid out on a series of tables.

And there suddenly appeared *un pauvre type,* a human dead loss, with a gun. He stepped out and fired three, four, five times.

A woman screamed. [It's always women who scream, how I dislike that.] The Minister of the Interior got to his knees and tried to staunch the blood with his handkerchief. Witnesses remembered its impeccable whiteness.

That human dead loss had shot a good man five times in the head.

He started to run. No, no, he wasn't going to get away, and surely he didn't try too hard. He didn't get out of the exhibition room before a cameraman smashed him over the head with his flash bulb. The sheer weight of the thing brought him down, and there he lay, blood trickling from his forehead where the smashed bulb caught him.

'*Mais non! Laissez-moi*. Let me live, I beg you.'

The men took off their belts. They tied several belts around the assassin (for the President was already dead). Someone wanted to string him up with one, and had that happened the exhibition-goers would truly have been back on the battlefield of the Great War, in the company of some traitor who didn't want to fight and was about to be dispatched. As it was visitors to the exhibition had anyway been treated to an act of violence that truly brought alive the crack-cracks in the poetry on which their gaze reverently fell. But then the ambulance arrived and the police; and perpetrator and victim were taken away to that strange marriage ceremony of criminal and victim.

She had asked, 'So it was a Russian who shot the President?'

'So my husband says. He read it in the newspaper.'

Now she read it too, and everything else she could find, and wrote down the sad life of Gorgulov, or Gorgouloff, as his name was spelt in France. Same sounds, just different letters.

Gorgulov left Russia in 1921. Some people say he was a White, some say he was a Red, a situation many of us can imagine.

He was a doctor who fully intended to make a new life in France. Only in France they wouldn't allow him to work as a doctor, because the French professions had to be protected. He could have worked in a factory, or as a waiter, or a taxi-driver. He probably should have acquiesced. But these options seemed impossible to him. He had his pride and his skills. He insisted he would work as a doctor. And he ended up making his living carrying out illegal abortions.

No one doubts the horror of that act. Yet, was it a sin? Think of the women he rescued; among them women who were pregnant not of their own choosing; women who had been raped in the street, violated by their own husbands, or, simply, it happened, and they could not contemplate bringing into the world another life. Poor women, for instance; older women, already too tired; women with nowhere to live.

Our doctor helped women whom France could not bring itself to acknowledge existed.

Gorgulov, *mon semblable, mon frère,* when they discovered your crimes – and who was it betrayed you to the authorities but an angry husband – when they found you ministering to those women who were needy in this unspeakable way, they took away your permission to live in France, and that wasn't fair at all.

Even you, with your tricks, and your capacity to survive, couldn't live without that. Sooner or later, the police would pick you up, without papers. So you 'emigrated again' – absurd term that, implying it was your choice – no, my brother, my likeness, you fled over the border into Belgium where, equally, you had no legality.

You felt it was the end of the road. You weren't a patriot, but the world was so organised that a man had to have a country. You were born, by some great misfortune, in Russia, which ceased to exist as you knew it. You fled to France, and France threw you out. And now you cower just across its border, waiting for the chance in the darkness to slip back, because all your choices are futile.

' "Father, they know not what they do," ' you said, for a long time ago you had a Christian education at school.

'They don't realise that they cannot deny my existence, not with their papers, not with their words, not with their policemen, they can't say I don't exist, because I do, and with that they must reckon, as surely as with all the little children I stopped coming into this miserable world, where half of them would have ended up wretches like me.

'I exist, and I can prove it, by demonstrating the laws of causality. If I cut the cord in the womb the baby will die. If I plug a man's head with lead he too will cease to exist, leaving me, for just a short time, to exist in his place. Nothing they can do about that. *C'est moi. Je suis là.*'

'*Eto ya,*' she echoed.

They said this Gorgulov was mad. When he pulled the trigger he shouted, '*Vive la France! Vive la Russie! C'est bien mourir pour la patrie.*'

He needed *a* country to die for. Anyone's country. Well, you can believe that, if you will. Or you can accept that he was simply a cornered human animal, who had run out of options who to be.

Gorgulov was executed. He went to the guillotine. Even though people protested that he was sick and sad and should be spared.

The politicians and the generals were afraid that if they spared him France would look soft on Bolsheviks. Or Fascists. Whichever, whatever, he was.

We'll never know. The past takes the truth with it.

*

'If the story had ended there . . . '

'As you know, it couldn't have.'

'But let's imagine it. My mother as the author of a single book, in French, with the title *Vie de Gorgouloff*.'

I had a copy of the 1993 reprint and laid it on the table between us. It had buff paper covers and just a stencilled frame to enclose the author's name and title, and its very flimsiness made me wrap it in plastic, so it wouldn't get dog-eared in my backpack on my way to our meeting in South Kensington.

'Why on earth did they dig it up over there?'

'Immigrants. High-profile assassinations. In '93 it had become topical. But no one bothered to find out who she was. It was just a text which cost no one any money.'

Leksy said: 'It's quite something to stare your life in the face. Finally, to discover who you are.'

'Quite another to decide what you will die for,' I had to add.

59

In the old *hôtel* the refined clientele came and went with minimal fuss. There were no children. No wooden stairs creaked. But also no fabulous paintings hung on the walls, except perhaps behind closed doors.

The scale of the building, nothing less than the Café de Paris without the dancing, was grand enough to swallow voices but not the routine clatter of keys grinding in locks. She could hear doors opening on un-oiled hinges and closing like thunderclaps. The cavernous spaces accentuated every sound.

Now and again the Célines arrived from the country to occupy Flat 3. The footfall was effortfully light, as if *madame* wished to make a sophisticated impression in the city. Her slight, trim husband seemed so kindly disposed towards life and so ineffectual that Sophie could find no words in which to speak to this man whom she certainly liked. She felt she knew the Célines by the habits of their postbox. Alphonse et Françoise Céline (one could read the names on items too large for the slotted box, which Madame Fillon kept in her own box-for-living) had a magazine subscription, whose product grew ever thicker, and included bonus material. Sometimes Françoise had parcels delivered to save her carrying her purchases back from the shops. The Célines visited Paris together at the weekend, for he had a passion for contemporary music. Or Monsieur Alphonse came for a night alone midweek, on which occasions, after a recital of Schoenberg or Webern, he was a model of marital fidelity, so far as his neighbour in 3 *bis* was aware.

Sometimes Madame Françoise came midweek to shop. Sophie liked these honest people whom she was content to keep at a distance. Many people who have other faults are honest. The majority do not cheat and lie and deceive. The routine of the Célines, split between town and country, was one of the clocks of longer duration by which Sophie measured the passage of those days through December 1933 and onwards into January 1934, when she lent her own heartbeat to the defunct and forgotten Gorgulov.

The bell from the street rang. In principle Madame Fillon existed in her ground-floor box-for-living to answer the doorbell and vet strangers and provide retrospective evidence for the police; but, even then, sometimes she failed to answer. She had to show that she was not a machine, and that, for better, for worse, she could never be mechanically replaced.

The ringing was insistent one Thursday morning. Can you hear it? asked Françoise Céline, who was looking for company while drinking her coffee. She stood in her doorway and watched Sophie remove the furniture from 3 *bis*, all except the bed, to sweep and mop the floor. Sophie did the room once a week, after which she sent a postcard to Claude, saying something like: 'Paris is a Marvellous City!' or 'Happiness is to live in France. *Mille mercis.*' Françoise Céline, in silk stockings and slippers, rocked too and fro on the threshold of her own flat, sipping from her little cup and asking God's forgiveness in advance for all the unnecessary purchases she would make that day to escape boredom.

'Where do you recommend for a new suit?' Sophie convincingly enquired.

'Galeries Lafayette, without a doubt!' For the general range of goods, and a guarantee of quality, that department store was unbeatable.

Madame Céline paused. 'Although, obviously, if one had the time one would visit the rue St-Honoré.'

Dreeeng, dreeeeeeeng.

'Madame Fillon must have gone out,' said Sophie.

'I don't like to say it but it is entirely possible Blanche is getting lazy.'

'Is that her name? She doesn't like strangers.'

'Just the right attitude for a concierge.'

'Our stranger is persistent.'

'He's not used to taking no for an answer.'

' "He"?'

'Surely. A delivery boy.'

'Poor soul, she should let him in!'

'My impression, Mademoiselle Asmus, is that you are a charitable soul.'

'Supposing it's for one of us?'

Then it stopped.

'*Enfin!* I feared he was composing new music with his drrrdrrrr.'

'Madame Céline, you are a woman of imagination.'

'Not a bit of it. With Alphonse I hear it all the time. Dreeng, dreeeing. Baaaah.' They laughed themselves silly at the expense of Alphonse Céline and Schoenberg.

Sophie spluttered: 'Our lazy Blanche must finally have opened the door.'

'Or he went away. Well, good-morning to you . . . *on se tutoye*, Sophie?'

'*Avec plaisir*, Françoise.'

A slight breeze reached up the staircase and chilled Madame Céline's ankles, waiting to be eased into short leather boots with a neat heel and a lavish collar for her day on the town.

Sophie finished replacing her furniture in the cleaned flat and closed the door. Leather soles descended the stone staircase. There was no echo and the sound wouldn't wake you at night, unless you were apprehensive, or a very light sleeper. But you knew if someone approached up your side of the staircase. The tread, which got louder and louder, was too firm and brisk for Alphonse Céline. Then *dut*, *dut*, *dut*. Someone rapped on the door of 3 *bis*.

'*Oui. J'arrive.*' Sitting cross-legged at the typewriter, on the made bed, with the sentences having just begun to form in her mind, she asked: Give me a moment! *Une petite seconde*, Madame Fillon. In any case I would prefer . . . .'

But it was a man's face, and from the blue shadow on the chin she could see that he'd had no chance to shave that morning.

Something moved in her throat.

'Aren't you going to ask me in?'

She was listening to the sound not of his voice but of her own breathing. 'As you see it's not – ' But no evidence supported her, other than that it was a tiny, crowded space.

Like a caravan, he thought. But caravans were rationally planned. He noticed the upended trunk extending the windowsill so that from window to table was a continuous surface. Even so, this was a cupboard improvised as living space.

'Sophie, I couldn't wait any longer – '

She watched him. A figure of middling height, solid, not tall, carrying a suitcase.

'I just kept thinking about you – '

As he stood beside the washbasin, she felt behind her back the hard outline of the chair tucked under the table. She was pressing her back against it to create some distance.

'Speak to me, Sophie.'

'David. *J'aurais voulu que tu viennes beaucoup plus tôt . . .* '

'I don't understand French. Speak English!'

'I've been here a while now. How easily one forgets.'

'I saw your neighbour.'

'Madame Céline.'

'That was it.'

'Has it started to rain? She doesn't like going out in the rain.'

'It's me. Remember?'

He stepped forward.

'Stop it! Get off me! You can't just walk in here.'

'If I walk in here you can't walk out, that's true.'

316

He'd changed somehow. His manner was easier.

'You can't stay here. Not . . . just like that.' Her head was turning and she felt cold. 'On the rue St-Antoine there's a hotel.'

'And which, pray, is the rue St-Antoine?'

'David, it's been six, nearly seven years!'

He shrugged. It seemed to him he was offering himself entirely; she prevaricated for no good reason at all.

'You could have said something sooner. You could have come to find me in London. Masha knew where I was. Wasn't it Masha who helped you find me now?'

'Masha and then someone in London.'

'Joanna. The rue St-Antoine is the main road you walked along from the métro,' she added, unrelenting, but what irked him was métro, pronounced in a foreign way.

'What's the bloody hotel called? And don't give me any more French.'

She shook her head. 'You ignorant monoglot. You pathetic xeno-phobe.' Relenting, she wrote it down for him.

'So we'll have dinner tonight? I'll call for you at seven.'

He took the suitcase and backed out of the door. 'You might ask your warder downstairs to listen out for me so I don't have to ring for ten minutes.'

'Madame Céline congratulated you on composing the opening bars of a modern symphony.'

He shook his head. 'Discussing my interests, eh?'

Sophie, still pressed against the chair back, watched him leave.

The January weather had turned again and was now rather mild. A bout of rain had stopped and far below the street was drying out. Over the river there were long low luminous breaks in the cloud. She opened the window wide and sat on the trunk. Her thoughts were given over to the coming of a spring that on the calendar was still far away. She remembered how in London, in the early evening, the warmth of an occasional exceptional winter's day had lingered and walking out she had bathed in alternate layers of warm and cold air. The patterns of day and night, and the seasons, and love and hatred, are only a very rough guide. Her whole being seemed suspended; absorbed, like ink in blotting paper.

Three raps on the door. She replayed the scene. In any French theatre that's how the performance starts, with three equal taps. The herald stands at the door and then the action begins. In this case the messenger arrived to announce . . . himself.

They dined in a restaurant on the same rue St-Antoine. Who knew what they ate?

'*Bon fin de soirée, monsieur-dame!*' The maître d' took his leave of them with a gleam in his eye which she had trouble in forgiving for its indiscretion.

It was an impossible idea that anyone might know who she and David were, or that anyone might be watching them in Paris.

'I take you out for dinner in Paris and you hardly eat a thing.'

'It's not a time for eating.'

'Don't I know that blue dress?'

'Did I wear it then?'

'In Cambridge the night we met.'

'It's crêpe de Chine,' she announced with perfect redundancy.

'And here you are now, as slim and beautiful as ever.'

'David, you haven't come all this way just to flatter me.'

'I suffered for you. I was sick the whole way.'

'When I came over there was a man on deck reading to take his mind off the rough sea.'

'Did you get talking to him?'

'He didn't want to talk. I decided he was a type from Cambridge.'

He fixed her with his eyes. 'Thank God I've left.'

'But you can go back, surely?'

'No.'

'You'll explain that to me. David, what's changed you?'

'My father died.'

'Is that all?'

'You wouldn't say that if you had one like mine.'

'No, I love my father. I hope he's still alive.'

'Any reason why he shouldn't be?'

She looked at him harshly across the table. 'He lives in Moscow, remember?'

He squeezed her hand as if it were his job to console her for any recent unpleasantness. 'Come, let's walk round that square I saw out there.'

They made a slow turn, arm in arm, under the cloisters of the place des Vosges. 'It's terribly old and crumbling and beautiful,' she said. 'I didn't know you had the patience for things like this. I think of you as a complete philistine.'

And then they were back in rue Jacques Coeur, upstairs in 3 *bis*.

'Doesn't that mean "heart"?' he enquired.

'Yes but it's just someone's name.'

Once they had manoeuvred themselves into the space beside the washbasin, so that they could close the door, their mouths met and their hands stroked warm skin. The warmth and the strangeness of what she felt silenced her.

She stood on the bed to close the shutters. He clasped her legs.

She reached up and put the light out from where it dangled above the bed.

'We've got a broken street light outside.'

'Is that why it's so dark?'

'It's always so much darker with shutters than curtains.'

In the common space the little room gave them to meet in she cried out with shock. Whoops of joy sounded which had no other place. She cried. He didn't say anything, being the kind of man he was.

He got up and used the WC and washed.

'At least it's handy.'

The tiny room, enjoyed *à deux*, smelt foetid.

'What's the time? My watch has stopped.'

'Listen. You can sometimes hear the St-Paul church clock from here. It depends which way the wind is blowing.'

The thought of the world outside blowing by gave her heart.

'It's very quiet.'

'Madame Fillon is lazy and Madame Céline has . . . gone back to the country, I suppose, despite the fascination of you.'

'Don't let's get up.'

They slept again and the bells sounded twelve noon.

'It feels earlier.'

'It's an hour later here.'

'I'll get used to being abroad.'

'Have you really never been out of England?'

'I'm a mathematician, Sophie, not an explorer in ordinary dimensions.'

She raised her eyebrows. 'What an excuse! Monoglot! Xenophobe!' She rubbed her cheek against that long flat warm other country they now shared, and which ran from his neck to his groin.

When they dressed and went out it was time for lunch. The power of habit ruled Paris, and they gave in gracefully and once more faced each other across a table, with wine in their glasses, and for her a vast appetite.

'You must be hungry. You hardly ate a thing last night.'

'I'll take it slowly. The soup and then the chicken for me.'

'Delicious bread!'

He reminded her of Dick, and also of Serge. Bread seemed to be a man's thing. She said: 'Everyone loves the bread here. The best in the world.'

'Remember the glass? I always wondered whether you did it deliberately.'

'The answer is I don't know. It happened. And then, of course, I was pleased that it happened. I liked you, so tongue-tied and so angry and so determined to be someone else.'

'You asked me why I left Cambridge. The whole place is too full of people in search of a reputation, and power, and success, with no one in search of truth.'

'Yes, that was what you wanted, I felt it. You remember Percy Nair – ?'

'For God's sake, I hope you didn't go to bed with *him*.'

'No, no. But he interested me for the same reason.'

'His truth couldn't have been the same as mine. All he ever wanted to do was fit in.'

'On his own terms. Agreed. But who would stay out on a limb for the sake of it?'

Fragments of conversation returned.

' "I'm afraid," you said to Maplethorpe, "that people like you

320

always find it convenient to imagine the moral life is not their responsibility." '

'Did I say that to him?'

'You did. I liked you for it.'

'You were blunt, and rude, but I suspected you were moral.'

'My rudeness is what Lissie got fed up with. That and not talking.'

'Lissie?'

'My wife.'

'I see.'

'She's better off without me, I think.'

'And the girls?'

'Hell, Sophie, you know how it is.'

'In Cambridge I ached for you and you took no notice.'

'I couldn't – '

'What changed your mind?'

But there was no way back, whatever he said.

'Really, Sophie, that bastard my father just couldn't let loose. Can you imagine, maths is your subject and your bloody father is so proud he won't ask you to explain it. He has to go and sign up for a degree so he can try to follow what you're doing on the sly. Advanced mathematics became his passion, my mother said. And then he pegged out.'

'David – '

'What! What? Back then we met, didn't we? We had tea, and another tea, and a lunch. But we were like different people, not saying what we meant.'

'You were. You wouldn't talk. I didn't know whether you felt any-thing for me.'

'And then there was another Guest Night without you and I was drinking my wine and not wanting to talk to my neighbour and then I remembered our shared glass and I burst out laughing and I thought, they'll say Jones is going mad, that's what happens to the very clever ones.'

'*Tu es un peu fou quand même.*'

Mad anyway. Best if he didn't understand.

They walked after lunch. She took him on the long circuit which took in the Île St-Louis and the rue Cardinal Lemoine and as they passed she told him about Beate and Serge. The next day they did St-Germain-des-Prés and the Odéon and the university, and pondered the little bronze plaque, now the colour of a much used Victorian penny, to James II of Scotland, who took refuge in Paris so long ago.

'They study Khlebovsky here now as a world-class poet.'

'I don't know who Khlebovsky is.'

'I knew him in Moscow. Even that seems a long time ago now.'

'Did you have a lot of affairs in London?'

'Just one.' She took his arm. 'I read that Percy Nair published his novel. Bravo, eh? And that the Master died. Who took over?'

'Some political appointee. Sir Bernard Langham.'

'Oh Lord.' She paused. 'David, I still don't know what made you suddenly decide after so long. You must be a little bit mad – '

He sighed. He stopped stock still on the pavement, so people had to make the effort to pass them on their way home. It was suddenly dark, with people streaming like motor traffic down into the métro at St Germain des Prés.

'All I can say is it happened. My life. Cambridge. The world situation – '

'Even so, to resign your Fellowship was a huge decision.'

'One has to take chances for what one believes in.'

'Surely you knew before what you wanted to do with your life. I mean, why did you ever begin in Cambridge?'

'Sophie, how can I say it! I was so bloody brilliant at what I did. All I knew was, certain things I didn't want. I didn't know what I wanted until I met you.'

It was too much for her to believe. How can anyone believe they can make so much difference to another person just by existing?

Returning, they climbed the broad and elegant staircase of the *hôtel* together. They took a few turns dancing on the balcony, before repairing to 3 *bis*. '*Trois bis*,' she said. 'In case you get lost.'

'Why is it called an *hôtel*?'

'Large private buildings for graceful living. The English turned the word into what it means today.'

'Cunning, these languages. You never quite know where you are.'

'It's not a bad thing. I like it.'

He shook his head. Just as she thought him a little bit mad he thought her the same, as if her too disparate life had gone to her head and weakened it, like a constant leaking of champagne into the bloodstream.

60

In the mornings David went out, to allow Sophie 'to get up'. He would have his *café au lait* near by and return mid-morning. Today she dressed, in the wool trousers and the black sweater that were comfortable indoors, and went down for the post. Although larger packages were kept by Madame Fillon, the postman, once admitted to the building (reluctantly, for Madame Fillon found him low-class), delivered letters straight into a row of letter-boxes. When she was alone Sophie had checked her box far too often. Claude didn't communicate nearly as often as she would have liked. Joanna had written once that she had a part-time teaching job at one of the London music colleges, no mention of Jimmy; Molly Shearer had let Sophie's old room to Dick Charteris through summer and autumn after Sophie left.

Dick, Dick, be strong. It couldn't have been.

Clare Shearer had taken her first music exam.

Madame Fillon's eye rested on Sophie as she examined the airmail envelope that had arrived that morning. Blanche Fillon was neither old nor unattractive. She had this snobbish streak, but that amounted to an offer of solidarity with the right class of person.

'Not bad news I hope.'

Sophie looked up. 'No, no, it's – it's always good to get a letter.'

But then our Russian lady, as Blanche Fillon referred to her, dashed up the ballroom staircase to fetch her coat and umbrella. Even though the flat was empty, she had to go out. She walked up to the café on the corner with rue St-Antoine. As she settled, the aproned waiter recognised her. A woman with an interesting accent. Not Parisian. Not Belgian.

'Are you Swiss, *madame*?'

'*Je suis russe.*'

323

'Russian. You don't say!' He excused his curiosity, but the rain meant fewer customers. Above all, no tables to wait on outside. She ordered a *café crème*, thinking while she waited for it that the rain shaped everyone's fate that morning. Everyone was subject to its inconvenience.

The letter from Pa was posted from Warsaw. The blue stamp bore the cover denomination of thirty groschen. Dear Pa had trained her to notice. He collected stamps from all around the world, though he never had time to stick them in.

She was afraid to read.

Pa and his Polish colleague would each speak their own language, slowly, for the other one to understand. If you knew Russian you could make out simple Polish, and vice versa. They would talk about children. About those innocent creatures who deserve our total love and devotion.

She was terribly afraid.

What's a human life for if not to create some object of beauty and nurture the young? The Polish word for love, *miłosc*, had mutated into the Russian word for kindness, but apparently if you went back in the history of the liturgy they were the same. Love and kindness, all she had ever received from her parents. And now this.

She read it three times.

They've arrested Ma. But it must be a misunderstanding and I'm sure by the time you read this, my dear Sofka . . .

Pa, you must insist on who you are. She panicked. You remember, you wrote to me you were furious at those incompetent boys who didn't know who you were, when it happened to you. Yes, he'd insisted that he was a great doctor, needed by society. But afterwards he had been ashamed at singling himself out.

Nonsense! It was necessary then, and you must do it again now. Boast of who you are. Save Ma's life! Make the same fuss again! Say it, Pa: 'My wife is a decent woman and a fine doctor! We need doctors. You political illiterates have no idea how to build a good life.' My dear father, I read that the red of our age is darkening; changing its colour from red to brown like blood turning old.

In any case, Sophie, I want you to know that your mother and I love you dearly and I hope that when I write next this madness will have passed. They seem to be stirring the soup again.

Your loving Father

The coffee tasted bitter. It had gone cold. She pushed it aside.

She went back to the *hôtel*.

David came back with bread and milk.

'Good-morning!'

He tried out the bed in the cold light of day. 'I swear that's the last night I'm putting up with this torture hammock.'

His lips rested on the nape of her neck, their embrace perilously close to the water he'd set to boil in the open pan for his second coffee.

'*Non, non, non!* Be careful!'

He warmed the enamel pot with some of the water and flooded two large spoonfuls of grits with the rest.

'What's the French for mattress? Where does one go to buy one?' David was admiring Claude's ancient crimson enamel pot, tall and with a long handle and a deep spout.

'David – ' But she couldn't. '*Un matelas*. You'd better measure it. Blanche Fillon will lend us a tape measure.'

He opened half the baguette and spread it with butter and jam. 'I'm starving. Aren't you hungry?' The mattress was duly measured.

'So, I'm off.' He traced his route on the map. 'Chausée d'Antin. Change at Les Halles. I'll be thinking of you.'

'And me of you. Don't get lost.'

She would tell him later.

Now that she had typed up three copies of *Vie de Gorgouloff* and despatched them to publishers, she had reverted to translation. Translating meant working in the library, with the requisite dictionaries. In that library close to the Hôtel de Ville, where the rue St-Antoine opened out into the rue de Rivoli, she worked well. The insight she developed that day into the labelling of aeroplane parts eventually paid for half the mattress.

Blanche Fillon and Françoise Céline watched it being delivered.

The couple laid it on top of the chainmail bed and covered it with a clean sheet to honour its arrival. The mattress transformed their nights, although David still had to contend with the cold wall against his back, when he lay on his side. There wasn't room for two to lie flat. He wedged a blanket there to reduce the freezing impact.

'It's a good shop, Galeries Lafayette. You can get everything there.'

'You were ages.'

'I walked all along the rue de Lafayette as far as the Gare du Nord. I sat in a couple of cafés and looked at newspapers I couldn't read.'

'You'll learn.'

Unexpectedly he sat up, picked up his shoes from the floor and hurled them one after the other across the room. 'That's for my father's life. And another. Old bastard.' One hit the door with a thud, like a bird crashing into a window pane, and the other hit the wash-basin. Both came to rest as twisted wreckage on the floor.

'You've got over him, haven't you? Well then. When we're settled I hope we have time to go to galleries together.' She added, when David said nothing: 'Look at the ceiling!'

'You want me to paint it?'

'I want you to see it as a map of the world. Shall we travel? I've never been to America. You've never been anywhere.'

'The woman pours scorn on me.'

'I do.'

He still had much to explore among the objects that were her life. The fur collar she wore over a black sweater to warm her shoulders. The two postcards tucked into the raffia bowl kept for odds and ends which showed the High Street and the Library in Crombietown and the harbour at Knockie.

In truth she thought of him as little more than a child, a child with a great mathematical brain.

'That's where we lived.'

'And this Claude doesn't want any money for the flat?'

'When he comes over we'll take him out to Boulestin's. Or Brasserie Lipp.'

Her tears dripped on to his chest.

'Heh!'

'David, there was a letter from Pa. I'm so afraid.'

326

She felt less anxious in the daylight. She lay there, with her pillow against the wall and the covers drawn up to her chin, watching her lover make them another coffee.

'Ma's probably back home now. Pa said it was probably a mistake – '

'I'm sure it *is* a mistake.'

'Even so – '

'Russia is vast, isn't it? Communications must sometimes get confused. It's like the Roman Empire. Your father will sort it out. I still hope to go there.'

'I just wish he would write again,' she replied, as if she hadn't heard him. 'Poor Ma. I can't believe she's not safe now.'

'She will be.'

'I have to put it out of my mind or I won't be able to work.'

When she returned he'd been to Galeries Lafayette again. He liked the walk, he said, right down to the bottom of rue Lafayette.

'I bought some glasses to celebrate our being together. Two to drink out of and two to try this with.' He snapped off a glass stalk as if it were a twig. The gesture shocked and oddly delighted her. She laughed as she hadn't laughed for years.

'Oh, new-born nest of light . . . ' He set the bowl with its broken stub on the table. 'Now I need lipstick.'

'Lipstick?! In my bag.'

He daubed the stub red. 'For you, my love. You have breasts like champagne glasses.'

'Ha, that's funny. I like it.'

Next day he glued the inverted glass bowls to a piece of white cardboard and hung the result on the wall. '*Homage à l'amour!*'

'*À l'amour!*'

They had a hundred francs left between them.

'I know. I have to get some kind of job to tide us over.'

61

The street market was close to the steps down into the métro and also on the way to the Hôtel de Ville. There she went and took the pulse of local life. Cheeses were prodded, tomatoes examined, the price of boletus mushrooms denounced, and she joined in and did the same.

'Everything's gone up since the Germans stopped paying.'

'*Les allemands sont des cons,*' a woman chimed in.

Someone else said the rise in prices was the fault of America. France was a victim of other nations' greed. The phrase 'a speculative orgy in America' came back to her.

'There'll come a day when you won't want to blame the Germans out loud,' said a young man to the woman who had been so out-spoken.

'As for you, you worm, you can shut up right now!' An older man grabbed him by the lapel.

'Leave him, Henri, he's a poor sod.'

His skin was red and shiny, as if he had some rash he was trying to scrub away in private. But he wasn't cowed.

'He's right. This country has gone to the dogs.'

'*Ah non! Les allemands sont des salauds.*'

'So you like Germans, *messieurs*? I think I've heard enough of this stupid talk for one morning. What will it be, *madame*?'

Sophie, gratified to be addressed as a married woman, took the second-quality tomatoes and the sharper onions and the slightly wilting salad, in order to have more change left over.

David had his back to her as she came in and was doing his best to read the newspaper at the chair normally tucked under the table. She put the shopping basket in the washbasin.

'Madame Fillon says her nephew has lost his job. It's not a very nice atmosphere out there.'

'I can believe it.'

She waited, casting a glance at herself in the mirror over the basin. 'You're not listening to me.'

'Trust me, Sophie, I know what I need to do.'

She pinned up Claude's postcards on the wall, alongside the champagne breasts.

Sunday had begun clear and frosty, after a week of leaden grey and rain, and ideally suited their plan to explore the boulevard St-Germain. From the métro stop Maubert Mutualité they walked up under a blue sky to the Odéon, and then turned to explore the historic streets between the boulevard and the river. The seller was standing on the corner of rue de Buci.

'*Lutte des ouvriers contre le socialisme bourgeois . . . Merci, monsieur.*'

They sat outside in the sun, over a headline which pitted workers against bourgeois socialists, and ordered two hot chocolates. Sophie watched the crowd out enjoying the crisp weather. It drifted by in both directions. Like that painting on Molly's staircase that had so pleased Dick.

She said: 'The newspaper-seller isn't a worker. He's an intellectual.'

'I didn't know you watched strangers so closely.'

'It was you who was so fascinated by him.'

David looked up and made as if to frown.

She asked him, redundantly, for the newspaper was *l'Humanité*: 'So you're still a Communist?'

He nodded.

'So – ' she ran her eyes over the cover story – 'you're against "the bourgeois socialists".'

He nodded again.

She sipped her *chocolat chaud*, already forming a skin in the fresh air. The parade of suits and fur coats, and the dogs and children, and the lovers hand in hand, was a delight to savour.

'*Moscou, Moscou, Moscou . . .* ' She read from the front page, irritatingly faster than him, though evidently his French had made progress. 'Don't these French Communists have any ideas of their own?'

'It's not the place called Moscow they're talking about. It's the politics and that's international.'

His reading in French took all his concentration. As she watched a woman in a fur coat tug a small dog away from the tree it was sniffing, she began again. 'In London they were saying it's Germany we have to worry about. Only the other day in the market people were arguing – '

'Exactly.' He mixed the dregs and the undissolved sugar and drained his cup. 'We Communists are the only political force in the world willing to fight Fascism. The bourgeois socialists will just cave in.'

'It's like when I was a girl. You had to choose. You had to be Red or White. I wanted to get away from that.'

'That's just selfish.'

'I believe you. Shall we go now?' She wanted to look at the booksellers on the quai St-Michel. David steered them back past the newspaper seller and gave him a wave.

The next Sunday he left Sophie to have a lie-in while he fetched l'*Humanité* alone. The seller with the emaciated face turned out to be a high-school teacher called Roger Duclos and he was bursting to talk.

'Are you English? I know English from the movies.'

'I wish I could learn French the same way.'

'To confess, *monsieur*, I'm a classical linguist by profession. I have an advantage.'

'My wife's a translator. She never lets me forget how hopeless I am at languages.'

Two customers were queuing for the latest bulletin on the French Party's view of the world. 'And you're living here?'

'I'm in your way.'

'Not at all.'

'So how . . . ' They talked so long David was barely back for lunch.

'We'll be doing our sightseeing in the dark.'

'Sorry, darling.' But she knew he wasn't. He was excited. He spoke faster.

Then it began to happen on the occasional weekday evening that he was out too.

'I'll be late for dinner this evening.'

It helped that Gallimard had accepted her *Vie de Gorgouloff*. They had a life together, two consciousnesses running their course side by side.

The Communist Party cell had the use of a back room in a café on the rue de Solferino, on the Left Bank. It was a room like a small classroom, but with adults in their outdoor coats filling the benches. Duclos beckoned David over. '*Bonsoir, mon ami.* I'll introduce you when the moment comes.' To an official who asked, the newspaper seller replied: 'He's with me.'

A few minutes into the meeting Duclos stood up, indicating the figure beside him. 'Comrade Jones is a mathematician who wants to serve the Party.'

Yoness, he pronounced it, to make it French, so that the meeting welcomed not David Jones but Comrade Jonah.

Now it was clear who was present, and a record had been made of it, the agenda could be tackled.

Duclos, the classics master from the lycée Henri IV, got to his feet again, welcoming the news that the Party leader had returned from Moscow. When he spoke it was as if his nervous volubility were consuming him from within.

'Comrade Duclos, what news does he bring? What are our instructions?'

'We are instructed to continue as normal.'

David could feel the discontent and impatience in the room.

'But the election results were disastrous. We have no support from the people of Paris.'

Duclos finished delivering his report to the cell with a gesture that could have meant, 'What can we do?' or, perhaps, 'That's irrelevant.'

The floor was given over to comments and questions from cell members either taking issue with, or commending, what Duclos's shrug meant to them.

'Whatever the people of Paris want or do not want, there can be only one official Communist policy,' said a man called Katz. 'We remain opposed to the Social Fascists.'

'Correct,' said a woman with thick black spectacles. David wasn't used to women in politics and smiled when his friend whispered: 'We call her Catherine the Great.'

'We stand shoulder to shoulder with Moscow,' said this Catherine, to applause.

When David put up his hand in subsequent meetings, Duclos encouraged him.

'Go on, Comrade Jonah. I'll translate for you.'

Catherine the Great welcomed a new ally and activist.

'The greatest threat we face at the moment is an anti-Communist war against Russia, waged in Europe. Our sources tell us it will be forged by an alliance of Germany, Italy and Great Britain, with whom the French Fascists will throw in their lot. This is why the Moscow Party is absolutely right in its directive.'

'So why does the electorate not support us?' someone asked.

Comrade 'Alice', who seemed to David barely out of her teens, got impatient. She said: 'I don't know why we can't be honest. I hear our Leader was so distressed by the election results here that he wept in Moscow. He begged them to see that Paris was not Moscow and must decide what to do in view of its own situation.'

'Nonsense,' shouted Duclos, who knew it was true.

The conversation reverted to the German threat.

'That's precisely what Moscow doesn't understand.'

'Moscow is too theoretical.'

'Moscow is absolutely right. There can be only one theory, if we are to pull together across the world.'

'Who's that?'

'His name is Katz.'

'I agree with him that deviation is unacceptable.'

'We cannot deviate,' said Jonah out loud, to the whole meeting. 'Comrade Katz is right.'

'The good thing is Roger Duclos likes me. I'd be stuck without him translating for me,' David told Sophie. 'He teaches classics at the lycée Henri IV. That's grand, that's like teaching at Eton. But then there's a tailor, Monsieur Katz, and Madame Catherine Forestier is a typist and the very young girl is a pastrycook.'

'How is it you know them all by what they do?'

'We're all workers, Sophie.'

'I thought you were a mathematician.'

'Leave that, will you? I told them my wife was Russian.'

'You did? Why on earth?'

'Boasting, I suppose.' He took her hand across the table.

'Do you know what happened? Someone shouted out: "Comrade, don't confuse love with politics! Just because your wife is Russian." '

'Someone with a sense of humour, evidently.'

He mostly didn't hear what she said. 'People are worried about what's happening in Germany. They want Moscow to tell us what to do about it. I think that too. We're all waiting.'

'I don't know about Germany. It's bad enough here. The Célines have laid off three workers in Compiègne. At the market there's a really bad atmosphere brewing. They blame the Germans. But look, David, after so long, can't we lead our life together? '

He promised 'to stop talking about politics', or, at least, 'not all the time', and they went out for a sauerkraut supper.

David said: 'You look wonderful.'

'You don't look so bad yourself,' she joked. Her most recent translation topic, English to French, had been ovens. The theory and practice of gas-powered baking had bought them several good dinners.

'*Bon fin de soirée, monsieur-dame.*'

As they prepared for bed she called out from the WC. 'Your meetings with the teacher and the tailor and the typist and the pastry-cook sound very jolly.'

He spat out a mouthful of toothpaste foam. 'It's actually terribly serious.'

'I can imagine.'

62

In the desirable and historic fourth arrondissement Comrade Jonah's task was to stand now in the rain, now in the snow. The cold bit into his cheeks and his toes froze in the leather brogues that used to suffice him in Cambridge. Constantly blowing on his hands, he resolved to buy gloves.

'*L'Humanité! L'Humanité. Merci, monsieur. Merci, madame. Bonne journée.*'

Otherwise he was always rushing out early on weekday evenings. 'You're not allowed to miss a meeting without a good reason.'

'Who's to be the judge of that?'

'All of them. They put you on trial for your absences. Comrade Jean protested his wife was sick. Comrade Katz told him he had to put the Party first.'

'Katz sounds like a brute.'

'He's doing it for the Party. The Party has to stand together.'

'What about you and me standing together?'

But he waved her joking aside.

'*Vous avez une tête tres théoretique, Comrade Jonah.*'

'That *is* a compliment from Katz,' said Duclos, who, himself, would never have praised a man for having a very theoretical brain; at least, not for that alone.

David asked: 'Is he really a tailor?'

'He's an autodidact.'

'But I mean, what does he do for a living?'

'You never can tell with people like that, Jonah.'

'See you next time, *mon ami!*'

'*À bientôt*, Jonah. *Bonne journée.* Regards to your wife.'

On the electric ring Sophie fried spicy sausages in a pan. She washed a lettuce, dried it in a towel and dressed it with olive oil and lemon juice and opened a bottle of red wine.

'Ah, *merguèzes!*' He rubbed his hands and broke off a wedge of bread. The little room was still thick with the smell of meat and spices when they tucked themselves in for the night.

'They still haven't repaired the street light outside.'

'They'll do it eventually, after someone gets murdered.'

'Katz has got more power than Duclos.'

When she said nothing he began again: 'I thought you might like to come to the cell meetings with me.'

'No thanks.'

David now sold the paper unsupervised. When he made his pitch for the attention of passers-by on Sunday mornings, she listened from the café behind to what sounded like humanity for sale. A couple pausing to have their shoes shined distracted her. She thumbed

through the lighter newspapers kept by the café. *Kiki Super Gonzesse!*
Kiki's Quite a Bird!

'Sophie! The world is in a state of emergency.' He joined her when
he'd sold all his copies.

'I know it really matters to you – '

'I'd like you to join us too and help the cause – '

'Do you know what I want, David? I've wanted it all my life. To be
free.'

'That's bourgeois.'

'*Tant pis.*'

'*Merde!* I say *merde* to your bourgeois freedom.'

The quarrel repeated itself at home. Françoise Céline heard the
door slam. Poor couple, what could you expect, cooped up in there?

63

David and Duclos grew close. A combination of French politics and
arcane learnedness cemented their friendship.

'*Ouf!*' He was adopting French mannerisms, a mark of that friendship. 'Be rational, Sophie! All that fuss you made about your mother
and as you see she's fine. It was just a mistake.'

Pa had managed to send word via Helsinki. She gazed at the blue
stamp which bore the value of two and a half maarka.

'I just have a feeling – '

'That's exactly the problem. You're fantasising.'

'We have stamps in Russia, of course. It's only that we can't send
and receive letters. I remember – '

'You were just a child then. You can't remember. No one can
properly remember what life was like when they were a child.'

'I wasn't a child.'

'In spirit you were.'

'*Tu m'agaces.*'

'Don't start chucking that French at me again!'

The poor things, thought Françoise Céline. If only they had more
space.

'*Foutes-moi le camp.*'

On the wings of a universal insult David stormed downstairs.

Duclos, who loved and wanted to understand Comrade Jonah, asked him about his father. He was a teacher of languages, so David found languages difficult. David's father embarked on a university degree in mathematics in his spare time because his son the mathematician would tell him nothing about his work. Too much love, murmured Duclos, all going in the wrong direction. 'Jonah, I bet he was madly jealous of your abilities.'

'He just wouldn't let loose.'

'I've got a pupil like that. When a parent is jealous of a child it can destroy that child. When the child streaks ahead to where the parent can never catch him up – I take it that's your case – it's torture for an ambitious but disappointed progenitor left behind. It also means the child has to run away in order to succeed. But then, perhaps, one day, he can also turn back, and understand, and forgive.'

They had a beer in the rue Buci café. Duclos said psychology was the other reason why he enjoyed teaching. Trying to nurture young lives. Sowing seeds. Transplanting young growth, if the parent had got the first sowing wrong. 'In short, I feel sorry for your father.'

'That idiot! That proud old fart! Did he think he could learn quantum physics at night school?' The son scoffed, though, thanks to Duclos's nurturing, more with relief than unkindness.

'You *can* be kind to his memory because you did get away, Jonah. You're a free man.'

'As you are, my friend.'

Duclos was affectionate, and David appreciated the affection. It was as if a whole new emotional life had happened for him in Paris. If Duclos was late or he was early, David even enjoyed running his eyes over the popular headlines of the bourgeois press.

Duclos urged him to go on talking about himself and his father.

'He was jealous of something I was master of and he was not. Of some place I had gone to where he couldn't follow. But he never asked me to explain to him!'

'You never offered.'

'He was a bourgeois old fart.'

336

'That's why you're a Communist?'

'No!' It really was outrageous for Duclos to say that.

'Tell *me* about physics then, Jonah.'

'About physics!'

'I have some capacity to understand.'

'It's complicated.'

'So is Greek grammar.'

He made a start. The teacher smiled and listened.

'And we don't know what will happen when we put it all together. Because putting it all together seems to mean . . . the opposite. We've found this great energy to tear the world apart.'

'You renounced it.'

'I can't say that. I just felt the world situation needed me to act.'

'Can I see your father's letter?'

She'd put it away. 'Of course, if you're interested.'

'Of course I'm bloody interested. I want your mother to be safe. I look forward to meeting both of them.'

She manoeuvred the trunk on to the bed and unclipped it front and sides. There were several smaller cardboard boxes inside. Only she knew which one to open. He would have searched blindly.

'Your trunk reminds me of those Russian dolls.'

'What else can one do in a room with no cupboards? Here.' These days she found the flat impossibly cramped, filled with more and more of their shared belongings and papers.

'It's in English!'

'I told you. Pa's letters get written down in Swedish or Finnish or whatever, to get them out of Russia, and then whoever's carrying the message gets it translated it into English and sends it on.'

One morning as she was setting out her work he asked: 'What's the paper?'

'It's a paper put out by the Russian émigrés here.'

'*No–vo–sti*,' he deciphered. 'News.'

'I didn't know you were learning Russian.'

He grabbed her by the shoulders. 'Can't you understand, Sophie? I must.'

'And why not from me?'

'You're so busy.'

'Foutes-moi le camp!'

In the market they said it was that young man with the shiny bad skin throwing stones who started it. The grocer fiercely denied it. 'It's us, normal people. Didn't we vote in a government to help us in these hard times? Where's the help I'm getting, eh? People are fed up with this soppy government.'

'Five cabinets in five months! France is a laughing stock,' said his wife.

'While over there in Germany they just get stronger and stronger.'

'Eh, ba, c'est ça.'

So the first anti-government protest came from those who felt France was humiliated by its weak government. The demonstrators massed in the place de la Concorde, a formal space bordered by the majestic Tuileries Gardens. They gathered opposite the parliament building, the Palais Bourbon. Parliament was the institution they had a grudge against. The police chief stationed a battery of his men on the bridge. But demonstrators are living beings, not chessmen. Five, ten, twenty, fifty of them quickly ran along the embankment and crossed by the Solferino, the next bridge along. They ran back along the opposite embankment towards the parliament across the end of rue Solferino. The fighting started when that breakaway group came up from behind and the police on the Concorde bridge had to face both ways.

The group that opposed them in the Tuileries Gardens, well, what was it? Had it ever intended to stage a peaceful protest? In which case it was the hour they spent restrained by the police, and the river, and the railings of the park, enraged them, for they took the police for their feeble and unpatriotic government. They were like wild beasts, yet with human arms, which made all the difference as they tore the railings apart and hurled the pointed stakes at those bourgeois officers of the law. In fact they threw the sharpened railings pretty much everywhere, because they weren't all good shots. It was like some medieval battle. Stones and outsize iron arrows sped through the night air. In the Middle Ages they didn't fight at night, but Paris in 1934 was quite different. The scene was lit with street lights and lights from passing traffic. A driver was pierced by one of those decorative javelins right through his own windscreen. The police had their own arc lights, which picked out the elegant façades of antique Paris and passing bats. But in the Gardens themselves were great pockets of darkness and blind hand-to-hand fighting.

Katz told an emergency meeting of the cell that a Fascist coup had taken place. Now the cells would have to respond. As meetings were held all across Paris, the situation was desperate. France was about to overthrow its elected representatives and install a Fascist government that would link up with its allies and launch an attack on Moscow, thus to destroy, in the company of France, Germany, Great Britain and Italy, the world headquarters of Communism.

'Comrades, we can't let this happen! We must do something!'

'Tell us what!' One hundred and fifty Communist cells of up to thirty members each, that meant four thousand five hundred souls in Paris alone, awaited instructions from Moscow how to resist the Fascist coup on their doorstep.

The Leader, who recalled his humiliation in December with pain and fear, took to his bed. He asked his young mistress what she would do.

'How can you even ask? Fight! We've been fighting all our lives, haven't we? Fighting to survive. Fighting to get a fair wage.'

So now the Communists took to the streets against the police and once more the javelins flew.

64

SIX DIE IN THE STRUGGLE AGAINST FASCISM was the *Humanité* headline.

'They kept charging. We put anything we could find in their way. Café tables, bicycles, a couple of vans, tree branches.' It had been, Comrade Jonah thought, a case of the police not wanting to be ridiculed a second time.

A tear ran down his face.

Sophie asked where it was Madame Duclos lived.

'It's near the German border. The bit the Germans just took back.'

Which to both of them somehow made it worse. As if the enemy had got the mother too.

'The school and the cell. They were his life.'

'And friendship with you.'

'We'd only known each other a few months.'

'So you went to the school to make yourself his executor – '

'I – yes, I thought, why not me. I wanted it to be me.'

' "Sit down, *monsieur* – " '

'Did they speak English?'

'At a lycée like that? Of course.'

' "My name is Dr David Jones from Cambridge and I was a friend of Maître Duclos. I'd like to do what I can." I went round to the flat. I had to overcome this awful sense of intruding. I'd never been there with him. He never invited me into his life to that degree. It seems there wasn't anyone or anything else. Just masses of newspapers and books.'

'You were his friend,' she said. 'When you visit his mother she'll be almost as happy as if he had come himself. His death will only hit her after you've gone.'

'There's not much I can take to Madame Duclos, just a few photographs they gave me at the school. I can tell her of his work for the Party, that he turned up for a meeting every week and always had ideas. I don't know what else I can say.'

'Her last memory of her son will wear your face. It'll be easier for her like that.'

He was sitting at the table with his head propped on his hands as she sat cross-legged on the bed.

'Sophie, I love you.'

Whatever reciprocal sound she made, she meant: 'I love you too, my dear David, even though I fear you more.'

65

'Did Duclos's mother speak English?'

'We managed with sign language.'

They went on Sunday to see who was selling the paper on the corner of rue Buci after Duclos. The comrade said, by way of small talk: 'We have to work *with* the Social Fascists now. We'll never defeat Fascism without the support of the middle classes. As our Leader has said, it may now become attractive to be a Communist in Paris. I can't say I regret the change of policy, Comrade Jonah. It's a relief no longer to be exiled from the people of Paris.'

Sophie took a copy for herself and unfolded it in the nearest café. ANTI-FASCIST ALLIANCE ACROSS EUROPE.

They went home for lunch, drank a bottle of wine and made love.

'I've found that after a while – '

'After a while what?'

'After a while life falls into a certain pattern.'

'It does?'

'Didn't Roger Duclos talk to you about life's patterns? I always felt he taught you something.'

'We talked about my father.'

They had a new passion for couscous and went out to satisfy it in a steamy salon where the *patron* was a genuine Tunisian.

'The good thing will be when we can begin a proper life together. I'd like something that can really be called a flat . . . a house even.'

'It's a good idea, but Sophie how on earth . . . ?'

That much was true. She paid the bill and they wandered home.

They went for a turn on Saturday afternoon around the place des Vosges. The beauty of the city always gratified them. She was talking about their future again, and it was quite clear to him she wanted to get married and live here in Paris and have children with him. He was thirty-three, she almost a year older.

'Surely you don't need a lot of French to teach maths. You could learn just a bit more.'

'They won't let foreigners teach here.'

'So it'll have to be manual work. You won't mind that.'

But David said he was going to write a book explaining what Communism really meant, and with that he took over the typewriter at rue Jacques Coeur.

66

'Hello, Ma.'

'*Est-ce que je te connais, jeune homme?*'

It was a young man, dark-haired, with attractive, deep-set, rather piercing dark eyes, his height approaching her own. He was lightly built but he looked strong.

'It's me.' The sound still had to break through some barrier in her ear. She was listening, not hearing.

Not a man but a boy. '*Ty kto? Lleksy, eto ty?*' Her words got lost in the collar of his jacket.

As they walked the couple of hundred yards back from the baker's shop from which he had spotted her emerging, her legs moved reluctantly and her head felt dizzy.

' "Rue Jacques Coeur",' he read aloud.

Blanche Fillon stared.

'Is this where you live, Ma?'

'Isn't it grand?'

His eyes roamed the huge and majestic space. They climbed the staircase and then she opened to door to 3 *bis*.

'Leksy, you should tell this part of the story yourself. Write it down as you remember it!' I had begged him

But he insisted. 'You tell it.'

'But it's *your* mother!'

He shook his head.

'Sit, sit. Tell me everything.' She patted the unmade bed. The window was open, airing the room. 'No, better here.' In Russian she indicated the chair but he didn't understand. '*Luche tuda.*'

'I tell you I don't speak it.' He raised his shoulders and opened his hands.

She laughed to herself. Oh happiness! What a lovely boy!

'So we'll speak English. Let me make the bed.'

She took off her shoes, stood on the bed and closed the window. 'Now there.' She smoothed the counterpane to give the room what she was sure was a nicely furnished look and went herself and sat on the upended trunk, with her stockinged feet on the pillow. Most of the light from the window disappeared into her body. She became for him this strangely looming figure he had to get to know.

'You look like your father.' He was really, she said, astonishingly tall for thirteen – was that all he was? – wearing grey woollen trousers and an informal jacket with capacious pockets either side, and two button-down breast pockets. 'You look quite the traveller.'

'Pa died.'

'Oh.' Her hands flew to her face.

'Dr O'Neill said he'd been prepared for years. He was injured in the war.'

'We used to talk about it. Did he talk about it with you, Leks?'

He nodded.

'He told me how much reading he did when he was . . . waiting to live again.'

'Do you read? That's good. And do you play an instrument? I have a friend in London and when she plays the piano you'd think you were in heaven.'

'The piano, badly,' he said. 'Auntie Fanny insisted. But Pa – '

'Yes. He was a good man.'

Her son paused. 'Ma, is this where you live? How can you manage?'

'Don't you like it?' She stirred against the window, for him a giant female creature spotlighted on the glass.

'I'm used to a house.'

'I remember the first time I saw Seaview. I mean, there are houses and houses. I wasn't used to a house like that at all – '

'Pa said you never liked living in Knockie. That was why you left.'

She saw that he might cry.

343

'I can make you a coffee. Do you drink coffee?'

He shook his head. So she made one for herself.

'And Auntie Fanny?' She turned from the sink.

'She's getting married.'

'My goodness! How can that be?'

'Ma! Because she's in love with a man, I suppose.' His face wrinkled into a half-smile.

'Did she find one at last?'

'My mother was always wretchedly unkind about my aunts. She arrived prejudiced and stayed that way.'

'Don't blame her, Leksy. The role they played in her life, not of their own choice, I know, but it was wretched.'

'She could have tried harder.'

'Fanny policed her. Even I can see that.'

'Who's my dear Fanny marrying?'

'A doctor in Crombietown. A widower.'

'But she's forty.'

'Thirty-eight.'

'Well I never. *Madame Fanny*. Not that she'll go in for any nonsense like that. And Alison?'

'She's going to live in Crombietown too. She's got a full-time job at the children's home. 'They want to sell Seaview.'

'Good riddance!'

But the tears came into Sophie's eyes too, tilting at old windmills.

'Auntie Fanny's future husband owns a big house in Crombietown so they can all live there.'

'In a commune. Knockie was so cold.'

'We used to say the wind blew from Siberia.'

'Everyone blames bad things on Russia.' She meant it as a joke but it came out of her in some other way.

She stood with the coffee she didn't want poured into a cup. 'Now you must be hungry.' She felt confused and fussed and neglected her son, offering him coffee but not the food he needed.

'Is that bread going spare?'

'*Manges!*' He ate with exaggerated politeness but she could see how hungry he was. 'Eat! *Kushai, kushai!*' She pushed everything she had to offer nearer his plate. 'These baguettes are only air.'

'I suppose you came on the boat-train and then from Calais. Lovely journey, isn't it, with the White Cliffs, and then the open sea. What will you drink? '

He accepted a glass of milk.

'How – how did you know where I was?'

'Through your old friends.'

'Peggy and Alan?'

'Is that Mr and Mrs Ferguson?'

'It is.'

'They've got this huge house.'

'Is that the kind you like?'

'Mrs Ferguson sends her regards. Mr Garon too.'

'You told them you were coming?'

He nodded, noticed the champagne glasses on the wall, with the red lipstick nipples, and blushed.

'Do you do French at school?'

'*Bonjour, je m'appelle Alex.*'

'*Mais voilà. C'est excellent.*'

'Don't exaggerate, Ma! It's babytalk.'

She wrapped her arms around his face and kissed the top of his ample hair, which reminded her of David's.

'The woman downstairs didn't exactly welcome me.'

'Madame Fillon. I'll introduce you.'

'Who did she think I was?' Then, realising the possible replies, he waved a hand.

'By the way the facilities are a bit primitive here,' she said. 'We usually go out while the other one performs. When you need to, just say.'

He nodded, half-smiled, looked like her when he did that.

'Do I look like her?'

'Yes.' I inflicted that guess on him.

*

David gave his usual single tap at the door. He could hear talking as he put his key in the lock. They normally never had a visitor. There was no space in which a visitor could stand, or sit. As he pushed the door open gingerly she looked at her watch. It was just after midday. 'Greetings.'

'This is Leksy, David. Darling, this is my friend David.'

'Can I come in? It's actually not easy to get in here. Greetings! *Salut. Zdrastvui*,' he said to the boy who was sitting on the bed. Leksy got up. He stood beside the basin in his socks and he and David shook hands. Sophie herself stood behind her son, or alongside, depending which way you looked at it, in any case pinned against the wall, between the door hinges and the water pipes. She reached out her hands and embraced them both. Happy moment for any woman: her lover and her son.

'I've heard a lot about you, Lex. Is that an English newspaper you've brought with you?' It was lying folded on the floor beside the bed, under the table.

'Of course, sir! Please take it.'

In spite of himself David liked that deference. 'You'll call me David though, won't you?' He raised an eyebrow. 'The way we live here we have to be the best of friends.'

'Cheek by jowl,' said Sophie, fond of the expression. 'Coffee, darling?'

He glanced at his watch and shook his head. 'No. We're going out to lunch.' She thought this was the David she'd always wanted.

It took some planning for the three of them to live together and one thing they did was keep the door ajar when they were all there, to make the space breathable. The other trick was, at night, to make enough space to lie down, to put some of the furniture outside. Before midnight David carried out the table and chairs and put them in the corridor beside the front door. The other residents might complain, but since *la femme russe* and her lover and now her son were tucked away in their own special wing, since they were so little part of the main body of the building, who really would want to protest.

For the first week Françoise Céline kept thinking they were moving out. As she told her husband, 'No one has said a word to Blanche about anything.'

'Leave them,' Alphonse told his wife. The music-lover defined himself additionally as one who did not interfere in the affairs of others. 'Myself I always found Madame Asmus charming. I can quite see why her husband would want to join her. And whoever else – '

'Alphonse – '

But his attention was elsewhere.

They became, effectively, Monsieur Asmus, Madame Asmus and the young Monsieur Asmus to those who encountered them daily. Each learned to open the front door with caution, to allow whoever was inside time to arrange themselves appropriately. The men dressed and went out to give Sophie her breathing space in the morning.

When David couldn't resist trying out his Russian on Leksy, at last establishing himself as something superior to the least competent linguist on the planet, Sophie noticed it had improved beyond measure.

'You've got a good accent. I'd never have expected.'

As he read her the odd paragraph from a source he wanted to include in his book, she wondered aloud, again, why it was not she who was teaching him.

'You know how it is, between couples, Sophie. I just couldn't face learning something else from you.'

'So who's your teacher?'

'Someone in the Party. Elsa Berman found her.'

'Elsa Berman!'

'She asked to be remembered to you. She said you'd had friends in common.'

Sophie was thrown into a state where she would have needed to pace the room and clutch at her hair and bemoan all the pasts that now flowed away from her into the darkness, without leaving her free of their grasp.

She shouted: 'In my country we divide into truth-seekers and rule-givers. The truth-seekers must first pull everything down because the foundations are rotten. The rule-givers are forever reorganising the rubble and rebuilding. These two kinds of people act together without ever being friends. That's our politics for you. Put that in your book about Communism!'

They took the rare moment of Leksy's absence on a shopping errand to have a row. Then he was back, and all of them looked to the future.

'Leksy, you have to go to school. You mustn't neglect your education.'

'Ma, I don't know French. How can I?'

'I won't hear such nonsense. Get out there and learn it.'

'You will learn,' David also stepped in, and there they were – they had become fully-fledged parents between one day and the next.

David took Leksy to the Hôtel de Ville, where there were free classes. 'It's not far. One stop on the métro.' He signed Leksy up, waited for him after his first class, and then they walked back along the busy pavement, talking.

'Your third father.'

'I was bowled over. He made more impact on me than my mother.'

To make sure Leksy went to his lessons David often accompanied him, had a beer meanwhile, and waited so they could walk back together. The early evening was light now, and people on their way home from work lingered in pavement cafés over a glass of wine or a demi. Soon Leksy learnt to order a demi, a small lager beer in a tall glass.

The half-hour they spent in a café together in the morning was another chance for Leksy to get to know his third father. He wanted his company, because his first two fathers were dead.

'Where are you going?'

'Back to see your mother while you stay here. So we can all continue to live.'

The boy slowly smiled.

'You became your mother's rival.'

'I had everything to learn from him. He inhabited a different universe.'

'It's a socialist government we have here. They're more inclined to help outsiders. That's why you can learn French free of charge.'

348

'But that's good, isn't it?'

'I'd say so. It's a poor sort of country that has no policy of integrating outsiders.'

On another occasion he told Leksy about the riots in which his friend Roger Duclos had died. Leksy listened intently. No one ever rioted in Crombietown, although Donald Bruce, who was unemployed, and a now rather elderly Angus Nove stirred them up.

'The French don't like their police. Once a government here is identified too strongly with the police it's not popular.'

'But that's good for France, isn't it?'

'I'd say so.'

'Trust him, Sophie, he's a good boy. He can go to school in September.'

'He has to read then. And you have to teach him maths in the meantime. Not just politics.'

'OK, OK, I didn't know you were such a dragon.'

'Nonsense. He's my son.'

She was sitting in the open window, smoking. David lay on the mattress on the bed.

'Agreed then. September it is. But David you must watch him. He's so much younger than he looks.'

Sophie offered her son a course in Virginia Woolf but the intensity of the prose was not to his taste. 'Conrad then – ' He shook his head.

'I remember that. She ruined my chances with Mrs Woolf for life. I always found her books so artificial, and the female consciousness tedious.'

David told Leksy to work on reading the newspaper in French.

Quite the linguist now, Sophie thought to herself, but she liked the role he took.

David's own sovereign time at the flat was mid-afternoon when he sat typing with regard to his book and Leksy did whatever came to mind. He walked the streets, or he went to a film.

In another part of Paris Sophie did a translation in a café or she walked too. Sometimes she stayed in the Jardins du Luxembourg right up until the park-keeper rang a handbell before he closed the gates for the day.

The city became their willing partner in life as a threesome.

In one of her diaries she imagined the question: 'Are you an expert on the Dada movement, Sophie?'

'Perfectly. I'm a Dada woman. Since I read Cendrars. *Je suis femme dadaiste.*'

And: 'I can tell you it's not a movement. It's an anti-movement. It's not a word, it's an anti-word. That suits me very well.

'I'm reading the men whose books President Paul Doumer was examining when Gorgulov shot him.'

'But that's sad!'

'It's of our era.'

'I've noticed there's a kind of art gallery that accompanies her life, as you've told it.'

'She noticed paintings. I've tried to bring that out. She travelled from one painting to the next: from the Fergussons John O'Neill had on his wall to the Kandinskys and Malevitches she saw in Moscow, and the agitprop trains that Beate photographed; from a print of the White Cliffs of Dover in a London property agency to the Wyndham Lewis in Percy Nair's Cambridge rooms; from the William Roberts on Molly's wall to the eclipsed Dadaists of the previous decade in Paris, of whom Cendrars was the closest living relative. When a person whose life you're writing notices paintings you have to take an interest, just as you would make a note of where she travelled or whom she met.

'Besides, she loved Dada for the unresolved gesture of fury and longing it was. Gorgulov's life was Dadaesque. Only had a dead soldier risen up from a war grave and shot the politician who was honouring him would that gesture have been more appropriate than Gorgulov's own. Dada was a refusal to forget the war in which generals released lethal gas because they were curious what would happen. Dada sounded forth with a raspberry on the terrible danger of forming political and artistic movements of any kind.'

*

Against which David and Leksy now sprinkled their evening maths classes, as well as their morning talks, with politics.

'There's one sort of politics that goes on at ballot boxes and in parliaments, and another sort which is more like warfare.'

'And which do you believe in?'

'The first, of course. But the two get mixed up. One glance behind the scenes and you understand that you can't separate them.'

'And you saw behind the scenes that night of the riots?'

'I'm a Communist, Leksy. For the time being, for us, everything happens behind the scenes. Then, eventually, the battle will be fought in the open and power will change hands.'

'You mean you're fighting a war by another name?'

'Politics today is desperate. It's like when you see a house on fire. You don't just stand there, do you? You get your hose and try to put the fire out.'

'And did you join in the riot?'

'I threw stones. If you're in front you can't do much else. Stand still and you're the target. All we wanted to show was that we were a . . . quantity . . . to be reckoned with.'

'And so you lost your friend.'

'The world lost yet another good man. I was devastated.'

Sophie needed David to talk to but he was half-asleep.

'Nothing makes sense. We have to accept it. Pushkin said that.'

'What are you talking about?'

It was now his non-availability, either working at his book or teaching Leksy, that caused her to write so much down.

Man and boy did their maths at David's favourite café in Montparnasse. Over a demi they sat with a supply of paper and pencils and worked at algebra.

'Will I ever need it?'

'That's not the point. You need to refine your mind. There are things out there you need to understand.'

'Did you have a best friend at school?'

'Yes. But as I see now, not so's I'd miss him.'

Leksy slept on the mattress on the floor and Sophie and David were back in the chainmail bed. That was how they arranged their nights.

'I'll just put the cat out,' David had taken to saying, about the table and chair that had to go into the corridor at night, in order for the mattress to lie on the floor.

'Bloody cat! Who decided to get a cat?' Occasionally he wanted Sophie to himself and not to talk and not to go through all these contortions.

'Did you ever have a cat?' Leksy asked David, seeking to ease the atmosphere. They were waiting for Sophie to emerge from the WC and turn out the light.

'My father was a bastard. The cat gave my mother something to love.'

'Soot's not a very original name.'

'My mother wasn't after originality. She wanted a living creature to love.'

Every night there was so much to think about that Leksy was reluctant to sleep. He spent time distinguishing the breathing of his mother, who snored, and her lover. He felt, every day in those weeks, the world growing larger; opening itself up to him, like a great nut cracking, whether he wanted it to or not.

'I do remember that.'

67

At a *bouquiniste* on the quai St-Michel she bought a creased map for a few sous. Leksy stacked the dirty dishes in a bowl outside the door so they could have the table free.

'Where shall we start?'

'Within a hundred kilometres.'

David had a compass.

'You really are a mathematician.'

David swore at Leksy. Leksy swore back. *Un con.* Everyone used it.

'The precious feminine opening which Ronsard called a tiny garden,' she said, in an attempt to shame them both.

'Fontainebleau. Rambouillet. Senlis.'

Her men were still making amused eye contact.

'Draw a wider circle. We can't afford to go to any of those.'

'Isn't that where the Sun King – '

'Exactly. Not for the likes of us.'

'Beauvais then. There's an aerodrome there.'

'How about Compiègne?'

'That's where the Célines live.'

'Where Alphonse listens to his Schoenberg.'

'Don't be ridiculous. He has to come to Paris for that. In any case, they're mostly here these days.'

'Who's Schoenberg?'

More smirks.

She smoothed the map. 'Come on you two, this is serious.'

The hour-long train journey was just far enough to feel like a real outing. The line from Paris Nord deposited them in the provinces then continued to Brussels.

David said he'd come this way when he went to visit Madame Duclos.

'I thought she lived in Saarbruck.'

'She does. Nice little terraced house. She keeps it very neat.'

'But Saarbruck is in the east.'

'Did I get it wrong then?'

'You must have.'

'Speaking for myself this is the first train I've ridden on since . . . well . . . since I came here,' she said.

Leksy asked his mother when exactly she had arrived.

'September 1932.'

'Nearly two years ago now. That's what makes your French so good.'

'I'll have you know I've been learning French since I was knee-high.'

'Your mother led a privileged life in Russia, Leks.'

'That's right, darling. I'm the enemy. I suppose David wants you to join him on his side, Leks. Don't! As they used to say, Dr Jones is quite mad.'

'Your mother's a feminist with a lot of determination.'

'And a writer.'

'Not forgetting her beauty and her knack with the frying pan.'

'Stop it, you two!' she protested. 'I don't want any of your labels. Just leave a woman to be what she is.'

The town of Compiègne had grown around a vast former royal palace, and struck David as a petrified beggar kneeling at the feet of a rich man. The palace, the rich man's vision, was vast, while, in its debt and shadow, the town was grey and ugly. As they walked the grid-plan of grey streets, David scoffed. 'Fancy leaving a legacy like that. I'm glad I'm not a French king.'

'You're obsessed, David, let other people live.'

'We're trying, aren't we?'

Leksy realised he didn't know the first thing about the French Revolution and kept quiet.

The letting agent gave them some details, which they discussed over lunch. 'How can it be so much?'

'But we're agreed we like the situation overall.' In fact, with its metallurgy plant and glass factory and sugar-beet plant, David was won over by the industrial fringe that crowned the ugly remnant of despotism. In addition, it really wasn't far from Paris.

'What's the name of the river?'

'Oise.'

'Waz?'

'O–i–s–e.'

'We'll look further afield. I don't want to live next to a factory.'

Arguing, ridiculing differences of language and ambition they couldn't overcome, they eventually found La Châtre, bowling along a lonely road in the letting agent Monsieur Prévert's Citroën.

That was fun too. She couldn't remember when she'd had so much fun, as they planned to spend the advance from her *Vie de Gorgouloff*.

'What a view! How long has it been empty?' The stone elevation to the road alone was impressive, and that was just the barn.

'Let's go in. We can't live in a view.'

The agent opened the windows and the shutters beyond to let in the afternoon light. It was like breathing life into a being, but one too long starved of the human touch. 'As you know, *monsieur*, *madame*, the war left so many families with no clear line of inheritance – '

'The war was ages ago.'

'Time moves slowly in the countryside.'

'And that's exactly why the young people leave,' she said.

'It's true they're not going to wait to inherit. They need jobs, *monsieur*.'

David Jones nodded, forced to accept that his understanding of French provincial life had gaps.

While the adults lingered in the big downstairs room with the open fireplace, Leksy went off to explore upstairs.

Sophie enquired after schools.

'In the village, in the town, there are schools, *madame*. It's possible to live a simpler life here than in Paris, I imagine.'

Relieved, she did a little twirl and imagined the meals she would cook on the kitchen range, a device incomparable with the electric ring at rue Jacques Coeur.

The facilities were simple. But, oh, the space! And there was running water, and, as Leksy reported back, two large rooms upstairs with bare floorboards. They could have a bedroom each. He could have his own.

They reassembled outside beside the woodpile half-covered by a tarpaulin. Beyond them lay an overgrown kitchen garden. 'It's wonderful.'

'Perfect.'

'Agreed then? We'll take it.' It rather astonished them that as one person they had suddenly wanted to move from Paris.

Picardy was in bloom between them and the horizon.

'Is this where Pa was?'

'No. He was in Loos, it's in Belgium. Same fate though. His general just had to try out his new plaything.' She held up a wetted finger to the wind.

'Only a *con* would release poisoned gas when the wind was blowing in the wrong direction,' Leksy said. 'It's like what you said about politics, David, it's either *connerie* or people are fools.'

'The imperialist war was both. Mostly politics is a bit of both.'

'Leave Leksy, David. He has to make his own mind up about things.'

But back in Paris David sat with Leksy after dinner and they enthused. 'If we can make Communism work right across the world that will mean an end to all war. All the feebleness of old-style politics will be swept away.'

'Is that true? *Formidable*.'

'That's enough, you two,' she said. But even when she said: 'There are dishes to do,' she couldn't stop them.

So they moved, whereupon David found himself in an ideal situation. He found work in a factory in the town and, by doing the early shift, could apply himself to his book in the afternoons. Having paid the rent six months in advance, Sophie used what was left to buy a bicycle which was kept in the barn. David cycled back and forth to work.

She sent Lesky to study with the monks at a distant school; he had to get up at six and take two buses to arrive on time in the morning. 'It'll be best for you there, you'll see.' He told her he liked it. Father Dominique was his favourite teacher and he found a friend in Alain Duclerc.

David opened a bottle of St Emilion on Leksy's fourteenth birthday.

'The wine that Arthur Gillard brought my father in hospital in Chelmsford. It became a legend in our family.'

They bought a second bicycle because David needed to cycle to the glass factory in Compiègne when she began teaching infants in the village.

David's happiness soared when he placed the introduction to his book on Communism in a left-leaning journal, with a pledge from the editorial staff to bring his still imperfect French up to scratch. Flushed with success, he arranged to continue his work at the Remington at a desk beneath the window to the long back garden at La Châtre, while outside Sophie planted carrots and potatoes for an early spring crop and harvested her first lettuces. An old apple tree yielded an abundant crop of fruit, only superficially blighted by a black fungus.

September 1934 marked the peak of their life together. While Sophie read, and gardened, in town David set his eye on the river flowing past, where the barges came to collect the sugar beet for processing. He was already encouraging the factory workers to make demands for better conditions and a fairer wage.

68

That autumn, however, the monks complained to Sophie of Leksy's increasing absences.

'But he goes off every morning. I see him leave.'

'He doesn't arrive, *madame*. We don't see him.'

'Leksy – ' But her son stormed out.

She turned to David. 'Did you talk to him? He listens to you.'

'He told them he was sixteen at the canning factory.'

'You put him up to it, didn't you? He wants to be like you.'

'I did nothing. I persuaded him to go back.'

Leksy in that growing-up period had learnt to lie and it hurt.

David was lying too, just as he had lied over whatever he did on his German trip, which, in that it lasted four days and he left from quite a different railway station than would have taken him directly east, could not have been purely devoted to visiting the bereaved Madame Duclos.

Sophie sat with her preparation for her school classes, just as her sister-in-law Fanny had once done. Leksy left for the abbey school with his working clothes stowed in his bag. He had three fathers and he emerged into adulthood as at least two people.

'I can't stop you writing that.'

'Would you want it any other way? In our lives we all become split. It's how much we become conscious of it, and what we do with the energy that sparks across the gap that matters.'

' "Create something of beauty," she said, "and nurture the young." '

'Surely she wasn't wrong?'

David and Sophie lit open fires in the evening, which they loved. The richly coloured wood from the stack was like tinder. It was dry and fragrant and soon the whole cottage was full of its smell and drew the family together; despite Leksy's efforts to stir up the workers at the canning factory and David's incendiary comments to the glass-workers; for she struggled to make the domestic arrangements work and both her lover and her son wanted a home, together.

'*Salut!*'

David waited for Leksy on the way home, ostensibly from school, in fact from the factory.

'*Merde.* What are you doing here, old man?'

'Your heart is in the right place, Leks. Only don't give up your education. That wouldn't be wise. The Party needs men who can think and organise, as well as those who can work.'

'I hate that school. *Je m'en fou.*'

'What about Father Dominique?'

'Everything is between him and God.'

'Alain then.'

'*C'est un bourgeois.*'

'Do it for the Party, Leks. Stay at school. I'll do the work in the factories for now.'

They walked along the river, when the weather was still mild, with David pushing the bicycle. It was hard to say whether the sound of the water or of the bicycle wheels spinning with a regular click or the balm of each other's company was most soothing to them. They got on so well.

'You really think they'll have me in the Party?'

'When you're eighteen, no doubt. The rest of the time you must prepare well.'

Communication between Sophie and Leksy suffered from his lying, however. She was hurt and he didn't want her constant reproach.

'Isn't Alain his friend any more?' she asked David.

'I think they've quarrelled.'

'That's a pity. Such a nice boy.'

'I can see there are things they don't have in common.'

'Such as?'

'This is a very conservative area. The boys he's at school with come from families with . . . all their interests are rooted in the land.'

She sighed and returned to her reading of *Jacob's Room*.

David worked the factories while Leksy, on the orders of his third father, returned to the abbey school.

It was one evening when she went to bed early, tired after a day's teaching and an evening working in the garden and preparing food for the next two days, that she overheard her lover and her son talking at home. She woke to the sound of their excited voices next door, in Leksy's bedroom.

'We have to resist Fascism. It will crush all our hopes.' David was explaining to Leksy 'the real basis' of his work in the factory.

'I want to work with you.'

'Soon, Leks. I have every confidence in you.'

'*Merci*, Comrade Jonah.'

She thought about it as she walked into the village, with the last of the berries shrivelling on the bare brambles and hawthorns. She mostly shied away from talking to Leksy about his Russian background.

'Do you remember *dyedushka*? You were three when we left.'

He shook his head.

'He loved you. He started teaching you Russian. *Krasny. Khorosho.*'

'*Krasny.* That's red isn't it?

'See, you do remember! He's a great man, your grandfather. He's a doctor.'

'And a Communist?'

'That's not important to him.'

'Why do you say that?' Leksy banged the table the way he had seen David bang it. He shouted: 'My grandfather is a cadre. David told me. We Communists have to show the way.'

'His job is to cure sick children.'

'And my grandmother?'

'They arrested her. I still don't know what happened. Except that Pa got her released.'

'The Party makes mistakes. But it will sort them out. Everyone makes mistakes.'

'Is that what the monks say?'

'It's what I say!' She made her son furious and he first truly felt like a man in his fury against his mother.

She knew it too. It was a man she saw silhouetted against the window that grey Sunday afternoon.

'Leksy, what is this Party you talk about? Did you get that from David? You say, "The Party makes mistakes." Personally I don't regard any Party in the same way as I regard a person.'

' "The Party exists to carry out rational scrutiny of the situation and take correct decisions." Ma, you have no idea about politics. Leave it to the men.'

She slapped him.

He swore at her, something about her little garden.

'*Mon Dieu!* The kind of French you speak now!'

'*Foutes-moi le camp!*'

'It's not only that I'm your mother, *Alexandre*. I know a great deal more about life than you do. You have no idea what I have seen, in my time. Please go to your room.'

He slammed the door. She reduced him to a child, just the opposite of what David was giving him the chance to be.

The second time she came to see the monks, alone, they told her: 'He has these political ideas, *madame* . . . '

That made her furious with David.

'You were supposed to teach him maths. You're using him like an experiment.'

'That's ludicrous. He fully supports the cause of the working class.'

'No, no! You fill him with revolutionary ideas. He's working for you. He's your agent.'

She paced the room that Saturday afternoon, with all the lights on and the fire blazing. The view over the garden and out beyond, to the west, where eventually the sea began, was beautiful whatever the season. She loved it best in the rain.

David and Leksy came back from a football match, where they also spread their political message. Alone she tackled David again.

'I'm just helping to educate the boy, Sophie. You forget, I'm a Cambridge don.'

'Not any more.' And she wanted that to hurt him. 'You're a purveyor of nonsense. You fill his head with nonsense. How is it that Communism can change every bad thing in life? What is this magic Bolshevik formula?'

'Maybe it can't. But it's our only hope. We're pretty close to another war. You must know that.'

'The world is *not* at war, David. I've had enough war. Let's be happy that we are living in peace.'

He shook his head.

Now the secret kept by two-thirds of the family was out in the open, now neither of them hid their commitment to the Party, Sophie tried just to put it out of her mind. But the result was only that mealtimes became a torture, as each of them hurried to finish his plate and leave.

David hammered away at his book on the Remington, and that blocked further conversation in the evenings. Leksy did his homework.

'I ask you not to corrupt my son, David. He has his whole life ahead of him.'

Leksy had a picture of Stalin in his room and a copy of the Communist Manifesto in French, urging *prolétaires de tous les pays, unissez-vous!*

The reply that Leksy's third father gave was sarcastic.

After a particularly fraught meal she had to pick up the overturned chairs before washing the dishes. In her notebook she wrote: Life is impossible. I spit on life. As for me, *je suis femme dadaiste*. As for my son, I am his mother.

David and Leksy were learning Russian together. They shared a manual. David wanted to pass on what he had learnt from that teacher of his who was a friend of Elsa Berman.

Sophie wailed, '*Vous êtes des cons, tous les deux. Je m'en fou.*' She slapped David and Leksy covered his eyes and ran away.

Next day, in place of his dinner, David found the champagne glasses with the red nipples smashed on his plate. They could hear Sophie weeping upstairs.

That night David slept on the couch.

69

The cottage was damp in winter. Mould speckled the white walls of the bedroom like an inside-out sky. Outside too the gaps in the roof grinned down into the barn. They ate late. As late as nine, the last possible hour at which he could expect a dinner to be cooked for him and eaten together, he threw himself on the sofa and poured a glass of wine, vaguely waving the bottle in her direction.

She sat with her marking. 'Did you bring bread?'

'Bugger. We'll manage tonight, won't we?'

The ate well: soups and casseroles, chicken and beef. But it was often biscuits for breakfast because he didn't bring the bread in the evening.

He sat at the typewriter until well past midnight.

'I thought we'd go and stay with Ma and Pa for a while. Maybe I'm a bit homesick. David, it will help what you're writing to go there.'

'Go to Moscow?'

'That's right. '

Something made him hesitate. 'It would be like rue Jacques Coeur again. Tripping over each other.'

'Rubbish, it's five times the size of that. You could finish your book and Leksy could learn Russian. What do you think, Leks?'

He shrugged. He was fourteen and a half.

'We've got the money for the tickets, with what we earn now.'

She fetched the wine bottle and poured a glass for her son, while refilling David's. When the fire was mature, in mid-evening, and the shutters were closed, the dark cottage held them in a pure embrace.

'So we'll go to Moscow then! *À la nôtre! Na zdorovie!*'

'To us in Moscow.'

She said they'd have to give up La Châtre.

'Why on earth?'

Sophie sat at the table, Leksy, anxious for his own company, stood by the stairs. David turned to ask his question in surprise.

'With this damp everything we have would be ruined in a couple of months.'

'But La Châtre might not be here for us when we get back.'

'David, how many newcomers has the village had in the last ten years?'

He softened. She had managed to turn an unexpectedly resistant key inside him.

'You two will need visas. I'll go to Paris at half-term.'

But her lover and her son weren't interested in the details.

The topic over the next few days was aerial warfare. The monks placed it on the history agenda and Leksy discussed it with David.

'So England got off lightly because it was an island?'

'Until they invented aerial bombing.'

'*Merde*.'

'No one expected the Bosch to destroy Swan and Edgar, but there, boom, it was gone.'

'What's Swan and Edgar?'

'Lord, don't you know?' David was momentarily abashed. 'It's a shop in Regent Street. My mother used to shop there.'

Leksy exclaimed: 'So you're a bourgeois too, you *con*. After all you've been telling me.'

'What I also told you was that one can leave one's origins behind.'

'What's that shop in Paris you like?'

'Galeries Layfayette.'

'Where we bought the mattress,' Sophie said, passing in earshot, and adding: 'If you were at all consistent, Comrade Jonah, you'd be prepared to bomb it.'

'I think I could do that.'

'You're mad.' She said as she left, 'Don't forget to wash up. I don't want to come down to a mess.'

She travelled back to Paris in the half-term of February 1935 and was immediately greeted by Blanche Fillon, who had changed her hairstyle for something short and elegant.

'Sophie! Françoise will be pleased to see you.'

'Likewise.' They were neighbours in Compiègne, but because of their different status in the countryside they only ever saw each other in Paris.

Sophie roughly sorted the post, which included two cards dated six months apart from Claude Garon and a letter from Joanna Manning. Then she got out the key for 3 *bis*. The broad old staircase had lost none of its grandeur. In the flat she opened the window and lay in the cold wind on the bed, happy to be alone.

It was only a métro journey across the river, not far from the Eiffel Tower. The Soviet Embassy was a grand building in secluded rue

Grenelle, with a high wall around it and a tall wrought-iron gate. But as she crossed the street suddenly her courage failed her. As if fearing the traffic she rushed back to the pavement she had just left, risking greater danger from her indecision. Only it was a quiet side street.

Happy, happy, happy, she shouted out. That's what I was. But there was no echo in that wide boulevard comprising a row of plane trees and august buildings of stone.

'There once was a man who said if he had all the power in the world for one day he would make sure things had their rightful names. But he was wrong. He was a criminal. The time when everything has its rightful name we will finally have lost the possibility of freedom for ever.'

The next day, at the post office, she applied for the visa forms by post. She mailed the application forms to David and Leksy for their signatures. Another three more days of waiting and she put the forms together with the passports and dispatched them registered to their destination, after which she revisited her favourite cafés, and the library beside the Hôtel de Ville, and the Jardins du Luxembourg, where she waited until dusk to be chased out by the park-keeper's handbell. Blanche Fillon noticed her check the postbox in the entrance several times a day.

She took a stroll down rue Cardinal Lemoine, past Beate's gallery, and out on to quai de Montebello, where she browsed idly through the books.

Back at La Châtre she proposed that she and David go ahead at the beginning of the week to sort out their belongings in Paris.

'Can't we just leave them there?'

'Claude wrote . . . that he might need the flat. It would be a courtesy to put our trunks in store.'

'Why not move everything here?'

'The damp! We really should let La Châtre go.'

'But Ma – '

'Why should we pay rent while we're away? Now,' and she rushed on. 'I've got the train tickets for the end of the week. But Leksy there's no reason why you should miss another week of school. So you come and join us on Thursday.'

364

'Your mother's right. A week here, a week there – '

He didn't mind. He'd come grudgingly to admire the monks and had found a way of enjoying Alain's company while concealing his political ambitions.

70

They got back to rue Jacques Coeur on Tuesday afternoon. It was a mild afternoon in January. Sophie said she had to clean the flat. 'You go out if you want. I'll manage it better alone.'

He sat outside a café on the rue de Rivoli and read *l'Humanité*. A figure glanced at him and was ready to look away again, but David felt his attention. 'Comrade Katz, how are you?'

'Comrade Jonah!'

'Garçon, deux cafés et deux whisky.'

'I heard you were working for the Party in the factories.'

'I have been. But now we're going over there.'

Katz's face was always a mask. 'So, you'll see how it is.'

'Indeed. My lover is Russian. She can organise it.'

'I salute you.'

And he did, literally, in a way that turned David into a hero.

Curious, the role Comrade Katz played in David's life, for it was he who inducted him into the Party proper, after he said, admiringly: *'Vous avez une tête tres théoretique, Comrade Jonah.'*

There had been, subsequently, the first visit to Party headquarters.

'Come, Jonah. *Venez.* What happens in the cell is not what happens at Party headquarters. It's time you were promoted.'

Their destination had been a tall, outwardly rather handsome building at the other end of the rue Lafayette. The thick wooden doors to the street belonged to an age in which the dividing line between fortification and normal residential privacy was blurred, and that suited the present situation too. Katz rang the bell and said something David didn't understand. The hall was narrow and the desk beside the lift made it impassable beyond that point, until a woman behind it handed him a paper pass.

'Don't lose it. They'll never let you out again,' Katz joked.

It was a huge building which could have served as a government ministry. Five floors and a basement.

'All these rooms with closed doors.'

'It's true, Comrade Jonah, you have to concentrate on not getting lost. But then, I am here to help you.'

Though it had windows, the building seemed turned in on itself, with corridors on every floor leading into uncharted spaces. But then they entered an auditorium flooded with light, filled with rows of chairs. On the wall were portraits of famous leaders.

'This is where the Central Committee meets.' It was, he could see, a kind of alternative parliament, and as he thought that the building both shrank and reshaped itself into a concentrated hub, as he contemplated a different world order.

'So,' said Katz, as they sat down to cups of strong black tea in an office one flight up again. This was obviously the office of a real person, who insisted on curtains and easy chairs, and wished to put newcomers at their ease. 'The Party has a task for you, Comrade Jonah, a man of your calibre.'

'David, we're meeting Leksy at the station. He can take the afternoon off and come and join us.'

'Huh, you found your vocation as a teacher, Sophie! You make him work right up to the hour of departure. You're like my father.'

'I don't want him hanging about here. We'll meet him on board.'

'Tell me again.'

'2200 hours, Gare de l'Est. Carriage F.'

With only a suitcase each they walked from rue Jacques Coeur to St-Paul, then took the métro to Châtelet. The red line, Line 4, carried them north. Smaller than the adjacent Gare du Nord, the ornate shed that was the East Station was another nineteenth-century creation of iron and glass, as, long ago in her memory now, the Crystal Palace had been. The Palace was that strange English hybrid creation so intent on cancelling out any 'message' it might have had; but the station belonged to an era when iron and glass were the materials of hope, the reverse of what iron was shortly to become, in the war that felled so many good men and was the beginning of her story, as it was of Gorgulov's.

'I've never been here before. Fancy that.'

'I have.' He knew it from his return from Saarbruck.

'When?'

'I can't remember.'

'I don't know why you have to lie to me.'

The carriage that would go as far as Moscow had a familiar smell, nothing to do with Paris. It smelt of some familiar disinfectant and she thought she could detect herring. Russia was now spreading its ways to every capital across the globe.

'Before Leksy comes, can I kiss you? My dearest, most beautiful Sophie, who drank from my glass and changed my life.'

That was it, he wanted her because she was Russian. Yet so much had grown up between them since.

'You're the bravest man I've ever known.'

'Did she mean it?'

'She wanted him to feel it. That's what he wanted to be. You remember, he was too young to fight in the war. She told him too of what Eugene Orlov used to say of all the beautifully educated young Englishmen of his generation who no longer had an Empire to serve because with their new politics they despised it. They needed a country to serve and they chose Russia.'

'He would have dismissed that as rubbish.'

'Which doesn't make it untrue.' I found, saying that, that it was the first time I felt warm towards Leksy's third father, who led them into an impasse, as a family.

At a quarter to ten David exclaimed: 'Heh, look at the time!'

She took his hand as if to pull him down and make love to him, but he resisted. 'Sophie, God, not now!' He slammed down the window and stared back along the covered platform.

'You'll get soot on your collar if you're not careful.'

Her lover wasn't listening. He called out into the electrically lit vaults where steam was rising from the fired engine: 'Where the hell is he? He's perfectly well organised when he wants to be.'

She sat, as if both looking here and now and gazing far away on another time. 'I'm proud of Lesky. I love him.'

David turned, as she again reached up to him to pull him down beside her. 'Stop it! You're drunk or something.'

'And you, darling, I'm proud of you and I love you too. The way you look these days you could be my son.'

'In her mind they were her one great love.'

'She wanted to be with her lover. I always thought that.'

There was a mechanism beneath the carriage which coupled one chassis to the next. Suddenly it clicked tight. It was like a horizontal door locking so now they could move forwards.

'Sophie, what are you not telling me?' He looked at his watch.

'David . . . Perhaps he doesn't want to come.'

'He does. He does. He's set his heart on it. Oh, hell! Sophie . . . he's your son. You can't leave him.'

'It was the obvious thing for him to think, I give you that, but not for you, Leksy. Not now.'

'She was selfish.'

'She was many people.'

The train jerked and the platform began receding with David still hanging out of the window. There, in the growing darkness, he saw as a mirage a lithe dark figure running and waving towards him; his own true son and heir.

'You can't abandon him.' David lent over and grabbed her by the shoulders. 'He's your son.'

'Leksy can follow us. I want to get things organised first.'

'But you've got his passport.'

'It will just mean a delay. It's difficult over there, David. We'll need time to establish ourselves. We must see how things go.'

The two lovers sat for a while in silence; he not looking at her, she serene.

'Now tell me what happened in Germany when you went to visit Duclos's mother.'

'I visited Duclos's mother.'

'What was so important it made you lie to me?'

'All the Party's old contacts had been arrested in Berlin. I had to find someone new. I did see Duclos's mother. She was happy I came.'

'You could have told me.' They sat in silence again. 'But you'll finish your book in Moscow.'

'Maybe.'

'You will.' She took his hand. 'Let's speak Russian. *Davai, pogovorim po russki.*' And she wanted him to believe, if ever he had a rational moment to reflect, that she had done it for him.

The train moved slowly through the white-lit outer suburbs, punctuated by the brighter colours of the café-bars. Silent factories stood in the shadows.

'What was Elsa Berman's friend like? Did she try to seduce you? I never liked Elsa.'

'What nonsense you talk! She was fifty and she needed the money. Elsa paid. Or her husband. It was a Party matter. Don't you see? '

'You know, David, what I worked out long ago is that when politics is everything no one is free anywhere on earth.'

'The final struggle lies at hand. After that no more politics. Just the good life.'

They ate a third of the sandwiches Sophie had packed. After they drank one of their several bottles of wine their mood lifted.

'Russia's changed since you left it. People say it's fabulous. I was talking to Katz. You remember, the tailor from the Solferino cell?'

'Ah yes.'

The conductress slid back the compartment door and handed in fresh linen for the night. David pulled out the bench seats either side of the compartment to make a bunk. They crawled over it on their knees, like children, to make up their bed. David wore the tracksuit he had bought for playing football at the factory. Sophie was in her

369

petticoat with a shawl around her shoulders. When the conductress brought glasses of tea and wafer biscuits Sophie thanked her in Russian.

'*Spokoinoi nochi, gospoda.*'

'Why did she refer to us as foreigners?'

'We'll get over that.'

She lay holding David's hand across the improvised bed. The wheels of the train turned rhythmically beneath her ear, and she had her eyes closed. Behind those eyelids – for how else can one picture the inner life except as the inside of the body – behind those veils of pink skin given to us all as shields against what corrupts and hurts us, she was consigning her son to England, so he might be safe.

To create something beautiful and to nurture the young and, above all, to save her son; in that moment all the people she had ever been, all the self-inventions she had ever offered to life *in extremis* shrank back into the one person she was, who could take this irrevocable decision, for she knew, as Pushkin knew, what lay ahead. All that she had tried in vain to tell David over the months.

But now, with Leksy safe, it was David who was her child and she would do what she could to be there to hold his hand, although –

'I told Lesky we'd be in touch when we'd sorted everything out.'

As the effect of the wine wore off he listened in silence.

'He'll be better off. I paid the rent of the cottage for three months. Alain's mother, and the monks, will help him. He can go to Paris any time. I wrote to Claude. And I've left him the name of my friend Beate. She'll help him.'

'What's he supposed to do for money?'

'I left him what we had.'

It was one Saturday in March 1935 when they arrived at the Belorussian Station. Comrade Jonah sniffed the Moscow air and took the arm of his Russian lover, and she laid her head against his shoulder.

'I was twenty-three when I was last here.'

CCCP! The blue neon letters which set his heart ablaze reminded her of Piccadilly Circus.

'What does your father look like?'

'He's . . . He'll send someone. He's an important man. Look, over there, that's the car for us.'

' "Adieu, Leksy," she wrote. "I did my best. À *Dieu*." You must be touched by that.'

'They didn't have to go.'

'How can you say that? She rescued you from Comrade Jonah. From what he was turning you into. You were her only son.'

'What was I turning into? I would have shaken it off after a few years.'

'She would have lost both of you. She couldn't bear it.'

I read from her notebook:

'You know how good a home-made soup can be? It doesn't need anything added. Well, our Russia is like that. A few foreigners love our soup. But they want to add their seasonings. They even want to leap into the soup. And a few do it. There they sit, our foreign admirers, on top. They're like the little green flakes that don't taste of anything, but look nice. And then Russia heaves and the spoon turns in the bowl, and all the little green flakes disappear into the brew. Everyone forgets they were ever there. Only they are in there somewhere, drowning. David, my dear David, would be such a fleck.'

Leksy cried.

I saw it as my job to make him cry for her but still I couldn't be sure that was the direction of his tears.

'So how did you manage?'

'I stayed with Alain and his mother until the end of the school year and then I moved back to Scotland to live with Fanny and Andrew. I finished my education in Scotland, where I began it.'

'Did you ever go to Russia?'

He shook his head. 'The Cold War was my excuse. And then I retired.'

Did I stage it right? I wanted to ask him. But then he didn't know Wagner so I took a chance when I imagined them happy, stepping into the Russian night, both of them finally enveloped in love, another beautiful creation of hers, and a son left elsewhere to grow.